I0831872

refuge

translated from Hebrew by
EDWARD GROSSMAN

The Jewish Publication Society
Philadelphia · *New York* · *Jerusalem*
5748 - 1988

refuge

Sami Michael

Refuge *was originally published in Hebrew under the title* Ḥasut.

First English edition
Manufactured in the United States of America

Library of Congress Cataloging in Publication Data

Michael, Sami.
Refuge.

Translation of: Ḥasut.
I. Title.
PJ5054.M44H3713 1988 892.4'36 87–31086
ISBN 0–8276–0308–8

Designed by Adrianne Onderdonk Dudden

1

Marduch was in the bathroom, and his voice was muffled behind a towel as he asked, "If Israel is wiped out, what will future generations remember about it?"

Shula, who was dressing obstinate, helpless Ido, mumbled something.

"Only two things." Her husband answered his own question. "Fantastic desert agriculture, and the royal screwing the Arabs got. And I've got nothing to do with either."

Shula and Marduch both belonged to the Party, and thus stood disgraced in Jewish society. But Shula balked silently at wearing the yoke of ideological discipline the Party imposed on its members, whereas Marduch questioned everything and everybody. Now, as she held out his shorts for him, Shula's son thrust his head forward. "Children your age can dress themselves," she scolded him. Ido stared at her stupidly with his beautiful eyes.

"What did you say?" Marduch asked from the bathroom.

"You can always change jobs. You're not married to the stationery company. You could sell tractors just as well."

"Right. I'm not married to anything."

Shula knew this trait, this mark of transience, impermanence. As if Marduch went about with a knapsack on his back, prepared at the first sign to set off again on his wanderings. Ido, the retarded child, was his only anchor. Her husband loved but did not trust her—trusted no one. Ten years they had been married, and it still seemed as if he were expecting her to make some important announcement. As a result, Shula felt, deep in her heart, that she was still in love with Rami.

She struggled with her son's rigid, twisting feet. "I can't fasten your sandals for you this way. Relax. Come on. Relax."

"What?" Marduch said.

"They won't wipe out Israel!" Shula called.

"How do you know?"

She gave Ido a pat on the knee and shrugged. How? Because Rami's a lieutenant colonel. Because he's standing up on the Golan Heights like the mast on a ship. Because the end of Israel would be the end of Rami. Because they won't get by him so easily. Aloud she said, "Because!"

Marduch laughed his flat, intellectual, jailhouse laugh. "Glorious empires have collapsed before," he said. And added, without connection, "When they hauled me off to the desert, I saw a buffalo run amuck and destroy an entire village. Left not a single mud hut standing. Killed ten Lords of the Creation. A dumb buffalo, who can't drive a car or row a boat, killed ten human beings like the ones who sent a rocket to the moon. Can you imagine?"

Shula pulled Ido to his feet and held his limbs, slack now, between her knees. She combed his hair, so like her own. "You just don't know these people," she said, but what she meant was, "You don't know Rami." She was thinking of Rami this morning because last month she'd heard that he was divorced and last night she had dreamt about him. In her dream it's spring, she wears a springtime dress and a smile on her lips, and they're on their way to a gallery to see an exhibition of paintings. They go from room to room, and there are flowers, nothing but flowers, and the walls shimmer like transparent screens projecting light, and they don't even look for the paintings, which aren't there anyway. The light speckles Rami's eyes, and he walks without touching her, striding along in his army boots, and he's big and strong and she's a little girl from Kiryat Haim. Twice she called him "Daddy," but he didn't hear.

Her own father had always been an old man.

Marduch, too, is a father of sorts. Maybe he has more of the qualities of a mother than of a father. He's dark-skinned, but he's not an Arab, and he had knocked Rami out of the running. Shula's mother, lying on her single bed, separated by a wide space from her husband's, had spent many sleepless nights. She and Haim the Technion student and Mahmoud the teacher had made a pact against Rami. Yet it was precisely when Shula's ties with Rami dissolved that her mother was seized with panic—she feared that Shula might take revenge on her by bringing an Arab home. She would sit in the company of some of the women comrades from the fifties, who had buried their husbands in the forties, airing her worries until the others got fed up and silenced her with the pious reproach: "You're a chauvinist!"

Most of these comrades didn't have children, and not a single one had a daughter. These blighted old women abhorred male flesh and for the objects of their Platonic love chose none other than the Arab leaders of the Party. In those crucial months when Shula and Rami were separating, Marduch seemed heaven sent. An airplane had brought him from Iraq, straight from jail after he had served a sentence of thirteen years' hard labor. The hearts of the women comrades went out to him. Only once in a great while would he straighten up to his full height. He seemed still to dread that cudgel raised to strike him in the back. He preferred *tête-à-tête* conversations—otherwise he listened passively. But he was all the rage. He'd been arrested at the age of seventeen, the women comrades said, taking pains to be precise—really just a child. He had been brought to Israel against his will. Released from prison in the desert, he was dispatched by registered air mail to the Jewish state. For a while, the Arab members of the Party had bided their time; but when they realized that he preferred not to speak of the atrocities that had taken place back there, they offered him their sincere friendship. His smile was as bashful as an adolescent boy's. He shunned loud noises and bright lights. He couldn't dance and he garbled foreign names. When Shula took up with him, her mother accepted it; she even resigned herself to people cracking pumpkin seeds in the living room and relieving themselves in the courtyard.

She kept a sharp eye on Shula's belly. "What, already?" she cried. That same month she withdrew her savings and bought a spacious apartment for them, up on the slopes of Mount Carmel. Four bedrooms for the flock to come. Mother tried to teach daughter the principles of prudent married life, but the only method that she knew was abstinence. Her talks with Shula veered off course and went in circles, leaving the mother blushing and the daughter bewildered.

To the mother's growing astonishment, the deluge of children failed to materialize. Two rooms stood empty and unused. Ido was the obstacle. Six years passed, and Tova, the mother, asked Shula, the daughter, "Well?"

Shula shook her head.

"It was just chance," said Tova. "It doesn't mean anything."

"It's an omen," Shula replied.

"You're giving up!" Tova cried, as she did during question time at Party meetings.

"He doesn't want to."

"What?" Tova could not understand. She herself had been obliged to employ some curious stratagems to wean her Zalman from his beastly habits. From time to time the English had helped by jailing him for considerable periods. And Zalman was a mild-mannered fellow, a bookworm. Marduch's a solid hunk of a man, and besides, he comes from there, from

Iraq, from an Arab country. "But how? How can it be?" Tova asked, her voice trembling noticeably. Secretly, she hoped that Shula would let her in on her clever little tricks. "Just like that, for no reason? He just doesn't want to . . . ?"

Shula exploded. "It's disgusting! Your generation finished sex off, but you're still nosey about it."

As far as Tova was concerned, her daughter might have been speaking in Sanskrit. She heard her out and then said, "So tell me . . . tell me about it." She blushed. "I don't have to teach you how."

"He's afraid, Mother."

Tova suppressed a smile. She'd never heard of fear holding a man back. "Afraid? Of you?"

"Of another Ido."

This she could understand, and it made her furious. It was a clear evasion of duty. Here is a man refusing to ram his head against a wall, just because he doesn't believe he can break through. "Listen, child." Tova adopted her Party-meeting tone. "Do you know how many brothers and sisters we were in our family? Seven." She raised seven fingers, stained yellow with nicotine. "The first was buried the same day he was born. The second came along and he was just fine." She folded two fingers and dropped one hand to her angular knee. "The third was so-so. We cried when he laughed and we laughed when he cried. He grew up but he stayed a baby. One day he went to have a look at the mob that was looting the shops in town, and we never saw him again." Her thumb pressed flat in the palm of her hand. "The rest of us? Look at us now. . . . No problems!"

Shula shook her head. Hatred flashed briefly in her gray eyes and then was snuffed out.

"Tell your husband he's making a mistake. He's from back

there in Iraq, and when it comes to complicated matters like this, he obviously doesn't know the first thing."

Now that she had dressed Ido, Shula was weak and irritable. Marduch was in the other room. "Have you invited them already?" she asked him.

"No. Anyhow, Shoshana's going to be here soon, and you can tell her."

"And you'll sit around the whole evening reciting Arabic poetry?"

She remembered that Rami detested poetry. When they were young, he had refused even to pretend for her sake. He said that poetry readings smelled like the slogans that she and her parents spouted. Only the simple-minded believed that human thought could be expressed in a couple of words, contained in rhyme and meter. By its very nature, poetry, like propaganda, negates doubt. And doubt is what sets man apart from the beasts. So go to the university and philosophize there, she challenged him; stop hiding in a tank. You can meditate in a tank, too, he answered. She told him that that sounded like a line of poetry, and he said that it was just a fact.

Haim the student and Mahmoud the teacher told her that after reprisal raids, Rami dismembered the Arab corpses, arranged the arms and legs like so many sausages, and then photographed them.

She confronted him with this and he said that if she believed that, she must be sick.

"Shula," Ido said, "I want to go to Daddy."

"So go. He's in the kitchen."

"Daddy! Daddy!" His shout was like that of a ten-year-old, his lurching walk a three-year-old's. "Shula says I can eat with you."

"OK. How about a kiss?" And a moment later, "I think the kid's running a temperature."

"I'll tell Shoshana not to take him out."

Another smacking kiss.

The sound drove her to the bathroom, where she stood facing her reflection in the mirror, thinking of Rami again. Her thoughts gravitated to him, though not out of desire. She got no erotic thrill thinking of him. She didn't consider him a missed opportunity. She loved Marduch—loved him as a woman loves her husband after eleven years of marriage. Yet her womb cried out for Rami. She tried to persuade herself, with her own special brand of logic, that with Rami she wouldn't have conceived Ido. And even if Ido had come along, Rami would have tried again: He's a soldier, and if the first assault fails, he doesn't give up.

Marduch is stamped with the caution, the excessive caution, of a man who's been in the underground.

Once and only once in his life he had blundered, and he paid for it back there with his whole youth. Once he had quoted a saying to her from the folk wisdom of another people: "A wise man doesn't fall into the same hole twice."

He keeps the contraceptives under a heap of towels in the closet. Eight months ago, while he was away, she climbed up on a chair and found the packets. She took a pin and poked. When she drew the pin out, she saw the fine rubber sealing over the hole she had made. Although she was alone in the house, she glanced over her shoulder; then she bit into the rubber, its taste vapid on the tip of her tongue.

For three weeks she concealed a sly smile behind her gray eyes. When she opened her mouth, laughter would roll out. She hugged the children at the kindergarten, embraced the jars of sugar and jam in the kitchen, and spread her arms around the azure bay visible through the windows of the apartment. She walked on tiptoe, as if dancing. Her whole being was focused on the sweet tick-tock of her body's inner clock.

Marduch suspected nothing, but her radiant face aroused his feelings. Within a week he had used up all the packets under the towels and bought more, and she welcomed him, giggling shyly, like an Eskimo girl.

This charade ended in a crimson nightmare. The clock was turned back and started ticking away again toward the next month, hopelessly.

From the bathroom she asked, "Do we have to invite Fatkhi, that poet of yours?"

Ido caught up the word *poet*. "Poet, doet, shoet, Shula's crazy!"

"Fatkhi's okay," Marduch said.

"That's what you think."

"When we're out working in Tel Aviv, all the girls devour him with their eyes. I have to pinch myself to prove that I'm there too."

"You're silly," she said with genuine affection.

"I'm not blind," he said.

"Are you jealous of him?"

"Sometimes."

"No kidding." She laughed. Suddenly the clouds inside her dispersed; her spirits glowed. A ray of light, a sudden surging moment of happiness. "You're more of a man than he is. My girlfriends . . ."

He gagged on his coffee—he wasn't used to compliments from a woman. "Well, then," he asked, "is it yes or no?"

"If that's what you want, it doesn't matter to me. But it'll be just too bad for both of you if you sit around reciting Arabic poetry all night."

"Okay, okay. I promise. Shalom, Shula. I have to run."

Ido panicked. "Daddy!" he cried.

"Son, tomorrow's a holiday, we'll spend the whole day together."

"What holiday?"

"Tomorrow's Yom Kippur. That's why you're not going to school today. Shalom, Ido."

He opened the door in that cautious way of his and, although he was late, he took the stairs down to the street slowly and deliberately. After all these years, he still had not rid himself of the habit of checking every corner along the way.

"Marduch," Shula called after him, giving voice to the happiness that was surging in her—but her husband was gone. With an urgency that she herself couldn't understand, she hurried out to the balcony, hoping to see him emerge from the staircase and get into the car. But he was already in the car. The exhaust pipe coughed transparent fumes, Marduch drove off, and she didn't see him. She leaned on the railing and gazed at the smoke of the refineries and tried to recall when she had last seen his face. She stood consoling herself: People who live together rarely look one another in the face. When she was depressed she didn't see people, and this morning she was very depressed. She hadn't caught a glimpse of that hard face, marked by the blind assurance of a man who can cross the desert alone, who learned from childhood to master loneliness. Suddenly she realized that she was sucking her finger, and she took it out of her mouth and turned this way and that to see if anyone had caught her red-handed, and blushed even though no one was there. You're crazy, she scolded herself. He went to work. He'll come back. This is his home. You are his wife.

Sometimes it seemed to her that Marduch wasn't as sure about this as he might be. On several occasions she had discovered him propped up on his elbows, gazing at her face in the uncertain, deceptive light of dawn. His dark eyes were keen and penetrating, and she imagined that his eyes alone had awakened her. The first time this happened, she snuggled up to him and murmured, "Can't you sleep?" And dozed off again without waiting for an answer. Once she started up out of her sleep and laughed to conceal what she felt. "What's the matter, Marduch?"

His smile then was odd, very odd. "You're still here." He paused, raised his arm and pointed east. "Back there, everything vanished with the dawn."

His face, she saw, was glistening with sweat. The tufts of hair trembled on his bare chest with every breath he took. "You're sick," she said. She wiped the sweat from his brow and kissed him on the temple.

He shook his head, frightened still. "How long?" There was a kind of wonder in his voice.

She hadn't understood, and tried to soothe him. "It'll pass, all this will pass away. It won't last long."

He shivered. "No, no," he cried. "It will pass, sure, but don't say so. That's terrible."

"Are you scared?" She couldn't believe it.

"When I was back there, I imagined what you'd be like. Gray eyes, a nose just like this . . ." Dreamily he started to unbutton her nightgown. "Two big dark crowns on your tits." He threw the blanket from her. "Legs . . . even all these different colors. Have you got any idea how many colors your body has? Black, gray, white, pink, brown . . ."

"Enough!"

His pupils were wide open. "Even your voice."

"My voice is as ordinary as can be."

He was hurt—she had struck a blow at his fantasy. "What are you saying? It's a voice that comes from deep in the garden. It carries the scent of water. It's a woman's voice."

"You see what that Arabic poetry does to you?" she said.

"And every morning you'd fly away, you'd escape from the coughing and the T.B. and the rattling of our chains. I never held that against you, Shula."

She put a finger out to his face, touching him. "Did they put you in chains?"

He drew back, laughed uneasily. "Oh, it was nothing, nothing . . ."

"Tell me. I'm your wife."

"You're spoiling the fantasy," he said and bent to kiss her. "What is there to tell?" he asked, evading the question like a child.

She moved away from him, angrily. "Tell me!"

He shook his head.

"You told me you got the scars on your wrists and ankles when you were a child. But it's not true. You lied to me."

Again he shook his head.

"Look!" she pulled at the blanket, wrestled with him and touched the pale, purplish, dried-up skin. "They took a little boy, chained him, and threw him into the desert."

"I wasn't a little boy then," he said defensively, as if guilty.

"And all his time you haven't said a word."

"It doesn't hurt any more."

Her eyes flashed. "You were afraid of embarrassing the comrades, weren't you?"

"Oh, come on! Really, you're ripping the fantasy to shreds."

She flopped down onto her back and said, in a dry voice that was unfamiliar to him, "What kind of fantasy could you have had back there?"

"You see? You're asking completely senseless questions. Fantasies flourish back there. Once we called a strike. They surrounded the prison with armored cars and cut off the water. We dug a hole with our fingers in the courtyard until we reached damp mud. The leaders of the secret Party cells were talking of manifestoes and petitions, but all I was thinking was that thanks to the strike, I could lie in bed longer in the morning, and you wouldn't run off."

She relented. "Baby."

"And then . . ."

"Tell me, go on. Why stop?"

"It's not important."

She embraced him, her nose touching his cheek. "And then?"

He pushed her away gently, and gazed at the ceiling. "Then . . ."

"Is it so hard for you?" she asked.

He nodded.

"Then don't tell me," she said, frightened, as if she were standing on the brink of some dark abyss.

"And then they took him away."

"Took who?"

"My brother. Next day, at dawn, they displayed his body in the square. He was as shy as a girl. Ours was a rough man's world. And he was so gentle. They had to pick him, his body, to show off to the women and children, hanging from a rope." Marduch rubbed his face in his powerful hands. He came back to his senses.

"Enough," he said. "Let's get up."

Shula stayed where she was. "And you're still afraid."

"Because of you."

"Because of me," she said modestly.

"You might slip away again."

"I'm here. I'll always be here."

He was on his feet now. "Everything slips away. The only thing that's sure is what's already been. As for tomorrow, I'm no prophet."

"If I leave," Shula said, "you'll find someone better than me."

He threw her a reproachful look. "That's not funny."

It never occurred to him that this same fear, multiplied and magnified, was settling into her own heart. She could never be certain that he had stopped wandering and really intended to settle down. He came from back there. She didn't know anyone from his family. He was tied up in knots that he had yet to reveal to her. She wanted to know about his past. About every day of his life. Only after reliving his life would she know whether he'd stopped roaming.

Ido had been quiet too long, so now Shula left the balcony and found him in the bathtub, rolling in soapy, milk-white water. His shirt and pants stuck to his skin and the dirty water spilled from the corners of his mouth like saliva. "Ido, what are you doing?"

Occasionally words meant nothing to him, tones of voice made no impression. But he was always sensitive to faces. He looked at Shula. He tried to get out at once but slipped. "I wanted to clean the tub," he wailed.

The doorbell rang, and Shula called, "It's open!"

Shoshana came in and pushed Shula to one side. She attended to the child, saying in a comforting voice, "They can really drive you up the wall."

Shula wept silently and didn't respond.

"It's no disaster," Shoshana added. "I'll dress him in a minute and take him for a walk."

"He's a bit feverish."

"Then we'll stay in."

"Shoshana."

"Don't cry," she scolded. "At least he's not unhappy."

"But what could be worse than this?"

"When your son's got an I.Q. of one hundred and forty and his father's an Arab and his mother's a Jewish whore, that's what."

"How's your back?"

"They took a beautiful X-ray. There are three screwed-up vertebrae."

"Don't you dare do any housework," her friend warned her. "Put the child to bed and rest a while."

Shoshana was Shula's age, but she looked like a horse that had been let out to pasture. Only her sense of humor remained from her carefree youth, and in the meantime even that had become embittered. "Your mother's paying me good kosher money."

"Is your conscience bothering you?"

"Conscience? What conscience?"

"Then rest a while."

"Spare me the rest. Rest is all I need to go crazy."

"Shoshana, I'm going to fire my helper at the kindergarten. You want the job?"

"Do you think that's more respectable than taking care of Ido?"

"You're awful."

"We need the money."

"Well?"

"Amir and Naim and Victor stuff themselves with *humus* and jam. Your mother's money is good money."

"It's not nice for me."

"You're crazy. Just think how many meals I turn this money into."

"Marduch wants to invite you and Fuad and that poet Fatkhi over for tomorrow night."

"Then he should get the American cigarettes ready for Fuad."

"Call up Fuad."

"Okay. So go already."

Shoshana got Ido dressed and played with him a while and then put him to bed. Then she swept the spacious apartment. She stood in her bra and panties facing the mirror and spat into it. Then she wiped it off with a newspaper, cursing it and her mother and her brother and the Arabs and the Chosen People. She poured a cup of coffee and sat herself down next to the telephone. The editor-in-chief's obscene, measured voice sounded in her ear. "Good morning, Shoshana. How are you?"

She sensed the restrained anger in his jovial voice.

"Let me speak to Fuad."

"He's in an editorial meeting. It's Friday."

"Editorial meeting! All you do there is screw each other."

"What do you expect us to do? There aren't any women here."

"Go get Fuad."

"Is it an emergency?"

"No. I just wanted to tell him that he forgot to comb his hair with brilliantine this morning."

"Fuad, the woman's on the line."

"What?" her husband shouted.

"Fuad . . ." And she stopped short, hearing two voices shouting at each other and the screams of a third rising above them. "Fuad, can you hear me?"

"In this madhouse? Comrades, a little quiet please. Hamdan, control yourself. Keep your antics for home. What we're telling you is that your writing is shit, so face it: It stinks. One of these days you'll land us all in the soup. . . . Yes, that's my opinion and I'm sticking to it. You're a member of the editorial board here, here in fucked-up Israel. You're not the P.L.O.'s foreign correspondent. If you want to write . . . No! Listen to me. If you want to write just to please them, then go do like Fakhri did and go to Beirut. Here you've got to consider public stinking opinion." Fuad remembered his wife. "So what do you want?" he said to her.

"Marduch and Shula have invited us over to their place tomorrow night. Pass the invitation on to Fatkhi."

"The females in Tel Aviv have turned his head. He took today off, and he's taking tomorrow, too. . . . Your Jewish Yom Kippur."

"So what should I say?"

"You want to go?"

"Only if we haven't got any other place to hang out."

"You know very well that I like Marduch. Hamdan! I piss on your innuendoes. I'm weak-kneed, am I?"

"I'm hanging up."

"Listen, woman. Hamdan, as far as I'm concerned, you're still a child. It's not fear, I tell you. You won't find a single Jew who'll swallow the P.L.O.'s program whole."

"I'm listening," his wife reminded him.

"There's no paycheck today."

"It's already the fifth of the month."

"The treasurer's broke."

"Get a loan from somebody else at the office, then."

"They're all *tafranim* [paupers]. The only reason we're winding up the meeting is we've run out of cigarettes."

"There's nothing at home, Fuad."

"What can I do, woman?" he burst out. "I can't carry the whole world on my shoulders. Didn't you get some cash from Shula?"

"She doesn't touch it. Her mother handles the money."

"So ask her."

"I won't go to Kiryat Haim to beg."

"Okay, so we'll drink air and chew water. So long, woman."

"So long, Fuad."

2

Shoshana was paid her salary for taking care of Ido and preparing lunch, nothing more. The money, which came out of Grandma Tova's pocket, wasn't enough to feed Shoshana's ravenous sons. On the other hand, it was linked to the cost-of-living index. Grandma was irascible and picky, yet generous in her way. And the work was easy. After Shula went off to the kindergarten, Shoshana would accompany Ido to school and come back and make lunch, and later she would take Ido over to her own house, so that Shula could get some rest in the afternoons. This was an important condition that Grandma Tova insisted on.

Because today was the eve of the holiday, with the schools closed and the child slightly feverish, Shoshana's job was simple. Four pots bubbled simultaneously on the American-made stove. Shoshana's heavy body darted over the kitchen floor with remarkable efficiency, and by nine-thirty she was sitting in the living room with a cigarette in her hand and a second cup of Turkish coffee beside her. The coffee made her nervous . . . that is, it made her nervous to take time out for it. Ever since her earliest childhood in Yesud Hama'alah, Shoshana had believed that leisure was only for those who were really sick. All she had was a backache. She went to the refrigerator to defrost it and to clean the shelves. This was supposed to be the job of the maid, who came three times a week. "*Elan rabah!*" Shoshana said when she opened the refrigerator door. She could imagine her three wolves at home falling upon all this abundance, most of which was destined to be thrown into the garbage can. In her own home she had to water the milk, and even at the height of the season, as her son Victor said, she would buy "apples the size of plums, plums the size of olives, and the olives—may Allah have mercy on them!" Her friend Shula was afraid that she would offend Shoshana if she filled her bag with leftovers. Now Shoshana piled the mottled fruits and vegetables, the abandoned sausage and dried-up yellow cheese in a big heap on the marble sideboard, and then made her escape from the kitchen. On second thought she returned, stuck everything into a mesh bag, and went downstairs to the garbage cans, hidden away discreetly among the bushes. Only when she lifted the lid and was struck by the stench did she understand why she had fetched the leftovers in a clean bag, rather than shoveling them straight into Shula's waste can. Here were soft pears, over-ripe tomatoes that were good enough for soup, three varieties of hard cheese, and almost half a turkey sausage, which she had seen in the refrigerator a month before. Shame, shame, she thought, and just couldn't bring herself to throw the food out. She went back upstairs with the bag and put it on the kitchen floor next to the refrigerator. "Food is food, hunger is hunger," she said.

Next she had a bright idea and went over to Marduch's bookshelf. "Bastard, bastard," she murmured affectionately upon discovering, in amongst the obligatory Party books, the abominations of Solzhenitsyn, Raymond Aron, and Eugène Ionesco. She cradled Ionesco in her bosom and went out to the balcony. A tiny tugboat was pulling a white mountain toward the port area. Gunboats speeding out to the high seas trailed white traces behind them, like dogs that had slipped their leashes. Shoshana sat in an easy chair and gazed north toward the Lebanese border, toward Rosh Hanikra, shrouded on the horizon. The gunboats were fanning out, shielding the port and the bay. Someone upstairs was beating a pillow or mattress. She heard someone say, "Shula?" It was Tuvia's voice, Tuvia the pensioner, and he sounded surprised.

Without lifting her head she said, "Shula's gone out."

"Morning, Shoshana. I didn't recognize you."

"That's strange—I didn't get dressed up today." Her gaze had come to rest on an intersection on the slope of Mount Carmel. From where she was sitting she couldn't tell if it was Independence Street or Herzl.

"How's your husband?"

"His Hebrew's improving, but he's still an Arab."

"No offense meant."

"Heaven forbid."

"You're a sharp one, all right."

"They told me that back in first grade in Yesud Hama'alah."

"You despise me, don't you?"

She had no choice but to turn her fair face toward him in astonishment. "Despise you? Don't take things so personally!"

"Hannah's sick."

Shoshana got to her feet. "You need help?"

"It's just the flu."

"Well, I'll go up anyway."

"No, thanks very much," he said, shaking his head. "It's a shame. A shame." And disappeared.

Shoshana sat down again, not knowing whether he was referring to her or to his wife. And she still couldn't decide whether it was Independence Street or Herzl. On the horizon, Rosh Hanikra and the mountains were lost in mist. Only the gunboats stood out clearly on the calm sea. Opening the book, Shoshana immersed herself in Ionesco's wit. How crazy he is about France, she told herself. Only an immigrant could love his foster country so. Marduch's an immigrant, too. What does he really feel?

The telephone rang. Shoshana lifted the receiver and, before she even heard who was speaking, said, "Good morning, Tova."

Her caller was not taken aback. "Good morning. How are you all?"

"Okay." It was the start of the usual daily report.

"There's no school today."

"That's right, Tova."

"Did you go out walking with him a bit?"

"No," Shula said. "He doesn't feel well. I put him to bed."

"How long has he been sick?"

"I really don't know."

"Isn't my girl there?"

"She went to the beauty parlor."

"And where is his father?"

"He left for work before I got here."

"He went off and left Ido just like that?"

"He's not sick, Comrade Tova. Maybe just a slight cold."

"How do you know?"

"I'll go wake him up," Shoshana threatened, "so he can say Shalom to you."

"No! Don't bother him while he's sleeping."

"He loves talking with you. Such a sweet child."

Grandma smacked her lips on the other end of the line. It sounded like boots treading in mud. "Terrific kid."

Shoshana stuck her tongue out at the receiver. "He's happy."

"It may seem that way to you," Comrade Tova said. "Pachtner," she added, "will be arriving there soon." Pachtner was her husband. She never called him by his first name. "I sent him over with a couple of chickens and some meat. That shlemiel is liable to dump everything at the door. Do me a favor and put the meat in the refrigerator."

"What?" Shoshana burst out.

"In the freezer, of course."

"There's no room," Shoshana said.

"These children don't eat a thing."

"They're on a diet, Comrade Tova. A diet."

"What won't they think of these days. . . . Will they be wanting to go out tomorrow night? I'm free. I can take care of Ido."

"They've invited some people over."

"That's going to mean lots of trouble for my girl. I know her. She'll get all nervous. The lord and master will sit with the guests while she collapses. Who'd they invite?"

"Us," Shoshana replied, valiantly. "And Fatkhi, the poet."

"Nu . . . so it's all right. You'll help her, of course."

"I won't let her down."

"She needs you, she really does."

"Anything else, Tova?" Shoshana hoped that she would mention her wages.

"Say hello to Shula and Marduch. I'll call them tonight."

"Shalom."

Shoshana retrieved the Ionesco and returned to the balcony. The mist had cleared and Rosh Hanikra could be seen like a scar on the sea. The gunboats brooded, motionless on the water. A strange lethargy spread through Shoshana's limbs. She yawned, and in her mind's eye tried to call up her mother's face. She had known, when she married Fuad, that the gates of Yesud Hama'alah would be slammed in her face. She yearned for the apple orchards and Huleh Lake. The lake was gone now—they had drained it. In the summertime she used to splash in the lukewarm water, where tractors now roared. She shook her blonde head and suddenly, as clearly as in a dream, her mother's face appeared before her. Right now she's probably plucking chickens for Yom Kippur, for herself and her two sons and their families. The cypress trees have kept right on growing, straight and upright in the strong wind, while Shoshana's brothers still walked hunched over from shame. About twenty years had passed, the new orchards had blossomed, the old ones had wasted away. The years weren't to blame. . . . It was Shoshana's fault that everybody had grown old. Even the disease that had spread through her father's liver was only a secondary cause of his death. The mark of disgrace that she had brought upon him had decided the matter. "And she was his own darling little girl," people said, mourning for her while they mourned for him. Upon learning of his death she had gone to Yesud Hama'alah, and they had thrown her out at once, before the neighbors could see. In the bus going up to Safed she had nursed her rage so as not to break down sobbing. Nevertheless, her eyes had filled with tears. She remembered how the world would expand, the horizon retreat, when her father lifted her onto his shoulders. He used to dance that way on Simhat Torah.

There was one thing she hated about her easy job at Shula's. Here she recalled the Jewish holidays. In her father's house, and later, when she got her teacher's certificate, the holidays had stood out from her daily life like glittering islands. In Wadi Ein Nesanas, on the other hand, every day was like the one before, as identical as beads strung on a cheap string. But back in the village, in Yesud Hama'alah, everyone quickened the pace of the day's work, hurrying home from the fields on the eve of holidays. She yearned to be there, if only for a tiny instant. The apples shining like drops of blood in the dark foliage, the warm earth beneath her bare feet, the fragrance of the meadow and the sounds of the tractors. Suddenly, just like that, death came into her thoughts. "If I croak, where will they lay my stinking body?" In the Haifa cemetery, no doubt, all moist and damp, near the sea. She longed to be there—at least then her bones would rest. You idiot, she sneered. Nevertheless she went over to the telephone. How much would a long-distance call to Yesud Hama'alah cost? A fortune, no doubt. And it would be plain robbery, an abuse of trust. Then Shoshana remembered how Tova pulled the water and electric and telephone bills down from over the refrigerator and stuck them into her purse, in spite of Shula's protests.

Shoshana's thick finger stroked the green belly of the telephone. All at once the years fell away from her. A mischievous spark of childhood leapt into her blue eyes. And then, in that house in the village, open to the fragrance of the apples and the meadows, the telephone rang, and the receiver almost fell from Shoshana's hand.

"Hello?" she heard.

Her throat felt clogged. She bit her lip, trying to calm herself. But she couldn't answer.

"Hello?"

That same serious voice—the voice of a boy who's never smoked, who'll marry the first girl to rise to his courting.

Shoshana put on an official tone of voice. "Mr. Whartman?" she asked.

"Speaking."

"This is Wurtzel's office calling. Wurtzel the attorney."

"Yes?"

"We wanted to know whether you received the letter that we sent you."

"We haven't gotten any letter."

"That's impossible. It was sent by registered mail."

"Listen, we haven't gotten any letter from Wurtzel-Shmurtzel, and that's that!"

"Perhaps you ought to check at the post office. This is an important letter, Mr. Whartman."

"My name is Avi," he said resentfully, as if shaking off the conversation that was being forced on him.

"Listen, Avi. There's a suit being brought by our office against you and your family."

His pealing laughter made the earpiece quiver. "I've got bad news for you on Yom Kippur eve," he said. "I've already arranged things with Kilbnov. It's all settled between me and him. You're not going to get one thin dime, not from me, not from him. It's just a waste of telephone calls and stamps. If I know Kilbnov, he's already playing deaf and dumb. You won't get so much as a flea out of his dog's tail."

"You're referring to another suit, Mr. Whartman."

"Avi."

"Avi, we are dealing with your father's estate."

"What estate?"

"A creditor has retained us to represent him."

"Would you mind telling me who is speaking?" He was silent for a moment, then he whispered, "Wait, wait a minute . . . " And then he roared, "Shoshana! Shoshi!" Next, suddenly, as if he had swallowed the receiver, his voice faltered, coming all broken from his belly. "Shosh, Shoshi!"

It took a while before she recognized this moaning sound as a man's sobbing. Then she, too, broke into tears. "Avi . . . "

Her brother sniffed back his tears and said in a booming voice, "Baby, where are you? We heard you were in Czechoslovakia."

"We've been back in Israel nine months now."

"Baby, baby."

"I'm not a baby any more, Avi."

"Yes, you're right. That was a long time ago."

"Nineteen years."

"Where are you speaking from?"

"From the house where I work."

"You're a maid?"

"That's not such a terrible thing to be, Avi."

"Give me the number at least. I'll go tell Mother. That loony still keeps your paintings and your toys."

This was too much for Shoshana. "No, Avi."

"Okay, okay," he said hastily, afraid she would hang up. "Just don't get excited, baby."

"Silly, I dye my hair. What's this baby stuff?"

"That's what we call you."

"Say hello to Mother and Nahum."

"Don't hang up, don't hang up."

She pictured him holding the cord of the telephone, pulling it toward him.

"I have to hang up. This call's costing the landlady a fortune."

"I'll pay for it. At least tell me where you're living."

"I've caused you enough grief, Avi. Really, there's no need."

"You're talking nonsense. Give me the address."

She couldn't refuse him. "Say hello to everybody," she said with finality. She didn't have the strength to go on with the conversation.

"Will I ever! Mother will have a heart attack. What a present, what a present for the holiday. You know she has . . ."

"What does she have?" Shoshana panicked.

"It's not important."

"Tell me!" But she knew he wouldn't.

"Some other time, baby. How happy she'll be!"

"Shalom, Avi."

"Shalom, Shoshi."

She felt like running out to the balcony to breathe deeply, but she was afraid that some stranger might see her. Even after she had gone into the bathroom and rinsed her face, she couldn't find the courage to look into the mirror. She went out on the balcony and gazed at the gunboats scattered over the water. After a while she began doubting her judgment. It was too good to be true. Maybe she'd imagined it. But she knew it was Avi's voice. He'd been just a boy when the "tragedy" broke over their heads. An easygoing boy, not brilliant, and precisely for this reason interesting. He was about to take his father's place on the farm after completing his army service. When her son Amir was born, Shoshana met Uncle Yaakov on Prophets Street. He sneezed and said solemnly, "Avi's volunteered for the paratroops."

Gone to meet his death, she said to herself. She'd heard of young men like that. They marched up front, knowing that nature had not endowed them with the qualities of leadership. They had stubborn perseverance instead of animal-like reflexes; they leapt a fraction of a second too soon, hesitated momentarily when they shouldn't. They "thought"; but in the critical moments of battle one must not think. And Avi had been full of thought when he went off to war. He went dragging a heavy load, his sister's scandal. The reprisal operations against the P.L.O. were a nightmare for Shoshana. After each one she would buy a morning paper and an evening paper, skip the headlines, and go straight to the obituaries. She didn't tell Fuad. He would have said that she had a murderer for a brother. Once she saw his face in *Yediot Aharonot,* the evening edition. He was surrounded by his buddies in helmets and ammunition belts, and they were laughing with surprise at the camera. Avi's face, however, was serious.

She can't speak to Fuad about today's phone call either. After nineteen years her brother calls her baby, and she forgets all the suffering and goes out of her mind with joy. They abandoned you, called you a whore, Fuad would say, and now you're happy. He wouldn't understand. Wouldn't get it. His family had accepted her. His mother, Grandma Huria, made the trip from the village every Sunday to see her grandsons.

The doorbell sounded. "Yes," she called, hurrying to the bathroom again. "The door's open."

"Where are you?" asked Zalman Pachtner, Shula's father.

Shoshana wiped her moist face with a damp towel. "I'm in here." Her voice was muffled.

"You're in the closet?"

She came out and smiled at him. He stood like a beast of burden with his two shopping bags, waiting for her to relieve him of his load. Then he dropped into the armchair with a sigh. "Where's Marduch?"

"Went to work."

"Who's going to buy art supplies and notebooks on Yom Kippur eve? I thought I'd find him here." He spread the Yiddish-language edition of the Party newspaper over his knees, then folded it up again. "I suppose he didn't say when he was coming back?"

"I didn't see him. He left before I got here."

"Hard-working boy."

The old man wanted very much to see his son-in-law. At the age of seventy-one, Zalman had remembered that he was a Jew, and Judaism meant Yiddish and the poets and writers who had used Yiddish for their works. By now all of them were gone, murdered or forgotten. In Zalman's mind, the intervening years had become blurred and confused. The poets and writers were still young, it seemed to him, brimming with creativity; but no one bothered to listen. Only Marduch, who came from Iraq, Marduch whose eyes were like a gypsy's and whose skin was like an Arab's, showed an interest in Yiddish literature.

Shoshana was cooking something in the kitchen.

"Come in here," she called to him. She opened the freezer compartment, which was stuffed full of meat. Indignantly she asked, "Where am I supposed to put everything you've brought?" There was chicken liver, several slabs of beef, a shoulder, and three fish. "Just look here! I've cleaned the refrigerator and I was about to throw all this into the trash."

Zalman lifted the mesh bag and peered at it from this side and that. "That would be a shame," he said finally. "I'll take it all back with me."

For the life of him the old man couldn't figure out why the woman was smiling. Had it not been for the miracle that had taken place hardly an hour before over the telephone, she would have tried to salvage the bag. At the very least she would have asked what he meant to do with it. Instead she said to him, "I'll get you a cup of tea."

"Do you have cake?"

"Cookies."

"All right, cookies, if that's all you've got." But the freezer compartment kept bothering him. "What will we do with the meat?" he wondered.

"Take it home with you."

Zalman thought this over for some time. "No. There'll be screaming hell to pay. We hardly ever eat meat." Seized with embarrassment, he raised his finger twice to Shoshana, like a shy pupil, and then fell silent.

"Well? What is it?" She said to him.

"Maybe over in the wadi, over in Ein Nesanas, there might be people . . . "

"Of course there are." She smiled at him like a schoolteacher encouraging a pupil to continue.

"Can you give it to them?" Zalman never gave charity on his own, lest it humiliate the poor recipient.

Shoshana understood. "I'll take the bag to the wadi, too," she said kindheartedly.

He took the cup of tea from her and relaxed a bit. "You're a good girl, Shoshana."

"My cards are running right today."

"What?" The expression was unfamiliar to him.

"Today's my lucky day."

He placed a sugar cube in his mouth and sipped gently. "Ah." When he finished drinking, he got up. "I'll go take a look. Maybe Ido's woken up." He returned on tiptoe. "Like an angel," he whispered. "What's keeping Shula?"

"You don't know how many customers there are waiting at the beauty parlor."

"I'll wait for Marduch," he said.

Shoshana shrugged. The old man put on his reading glasses and opened the newspaper. After a while his nose appeared over the top of the page. "You can go home, actually," he said to her. "I'll keep an eye on Ido. Tomorrow's a holiday; you must have a lot to do at home." Then he remembered that she was married to an Arab, and he was embarrassed. He hid behind the paper and said, "If you want to."

"Thanks."

She walked down the stairs carrying two heavy bags. She didn't even notice her bad back. All she could think of was Avi's cry, bursting from the secret recesses of childhood. "Baby!" She stood on the sidewalk, flooded with sunlight, and watched the shining cars rushing along the road. Over her head the branches swayed in the breeze. Light and shadow dappled her face. "Baby!" Once she used to walk in pale blue shorts and a white blouse on the dusty path to Kibbutz Hulata. Yoram, shy as he was, clumsily grabbed her golden pigtails and pulled them like the reins on a horse, calling, "Giddy-up!" Her blue eyes came to rest on his sensitive face, freezing the blood in his veins. That night she fell in love with him, because he was the first boy in the village who knew enough to say, "Excuse me." They sat on the lawn at the neighboring kibbutz and watched a movie. That is, all the other kids watched the movie, while she and Yoram. . . . He sat rigid and straight, as if at the dentist's. She told him to come closer and although he obeyed, he was suspicious and tense; she was famous for her pranks. She rested her head on his warm shoulder, spreading her golden hair on his chest. He was afraid to breathe, he held his head high and his neck rigid; and she closed her eyes for a moment and chewed a blade of grass. The boy's neck ached. Her hair was like a heavy curtain; she listened to the beating of his heart and the cadence of his breathing, and then she moved and her head rubbed his cheek. When she looked up, her face met his.

She had heard that he was the only one in the village who did not spit at the mention of her name.

He was killed in the Gaza Strip.

Now, years later, his death did not dim her joy. She imagined Avi rushing to her mother. Tonight they'll all sit between the two cypress trees, Avi and Nahum and Mother and the two sisters-in-law and the children, and Avi will tell how Shoshi's still Shoshi, how she pulled his leg with her story about a lawyer. And they'll laugh uproariously, finding it incredible that a corpse could sally forth from the grave after nineteen years. And they'll talk about her amusing pranks in days gone by, and then one of the grandsons will ask whether they're talking about *that* aunt, the whore who ran off with an Arab.

Her mother will say: "Your Aunt Shoshana isn't a whore."

"But didn't she run off with an Arab?"

Nahum will break the deathly silence. "She didn't run off. Shoshana married him."

And the boy will insist: "With a dirty Arab."

Shoshana set one bag down on the floor of the bus, and with her free hand she prepared to pay the driver. As the bus took a turn she lost her footing; the change fell and she clutched at the nearest shoulder so as not to fall as well.

"Hey! Watch what you're doing!" a heavily made-up old woman shrieked at her, as if at a housemaid. Shoshana set the other bag down and screeched back: "What do you want from me? Lift your foot, would you? You're standing on my money!"

3

Fatkhi, the poet, had intended to set out from the village bright and early, but by the time the big Buick came roaring out of the dusty side street, it was almost ten o'clock. Today, for a change, Fatkhi's future brother-in-law didn't honk the horn. He brought the car to a discreet halt and, although he saw Fatkhi hurrying toward him, he called out impatiently, "Come on, come on!" as if it were the poet, and not he, who was two whole hours late. He was very excited, and when he saw that the poet was carrying a small suitcase, he hissed, "Go on, throw it in the back seat, hurry up."

The American car took off again, spinning its wheels briefly in the gravel. A shroud of dust rolled over the village square that faced the ancient well, and flocks of chickens and children scattered about. "You're a maniac," the poet said to Wasfy. "Why don't you grow up? You'll run someone over."

"Just keep your eyes on the road," cried Wasfy. "All we need now is for someone to ask for a ride."

The poet disregarded him. He surveyed the bunches of garlic drying on the balconies, the piles of watermelon putrefying in the sun. "We're not going out to conquer the world."

"You know what? If you live here all your life, you still won't know the first thing about your own people. Don't you know everyone's got a tongue a yard long? Half a minute after we get out of here, everybody will know we're running off to the West Bank."

"We're just taking a drive," the poet said. "We're not running off."

"Tell that to the police. Tell it to the Jew soldiers when they grab us. I told even the wife and kids we were going to Eilat."

"Because you live in a world of lies."

Wasfy wasn't offended. On the contrary, he studied the poet's handsome face as if from on high, the practical man gazing down at the innocent.

"Caution, man; it's just simple caution."

"Cautious about your wife?"

"Better trust the angel of death than trust a woman."

"Don't you think she knows?" the poet asked, amused.

Wasfy turned a dumb peasant face to him. "Knows what?"

Wasfy's play-acting made the poet laugh. "Who are you trying to kid?"

A gold tooth in Wasfy's mouth flickered. "That's the way of the world, that's life. A man's a man. Go explain that to a woman."

"No," the poet agreed. "She wouldn't understand that."

Wasfy turned serious. "I've had it with you, Fatkhi."

"I'm not your wife; you don't have to lie to me."

"Listen, my friend, I haven't asked you what you're planning to do in Jenin, so why are you picking on me?" And Wasfy added: "Another thing—I've had it with this Ramadan. All day long, everybody stuffs themselves, choking on cigarette smoke in the closet; then they go out in the street and pretend they're piously and patiently waiting for the sun to set. You call that fasting? They praise Allah and screw each other. It takes the soul of a snake to sit home today and play their hypocritical game."

"Okay, okay."

"And don't give me any more of your sermons."

"Enough."

They left Kfar Mandah, heading toward Nazareth, and from there they drove down to Afula. In the restaurant opposite the bus station, over cups of Turkish coffee, they argued, as usual, about the best route to Jenin. Practical-minded, Wasfy said, "Listen, sweetheart, let's go by way of Zandalah. It's shorter and safer."

The poet made a show of innocence. "Safer than what?"

Wasfy was a short fellow, rather a dandy in appearance. He wore large rings on his fat fingers. Since making the jump from senior mechanic to partner in the garage on Haifa Bay, he had acquired all sorts of gold rings, inlaid with multicolored stones. Now he rapped his ring indignantly on the Formica tabletop. "Here you are sneaking into Jenin like a thief and you want to do it on the main road. Come on, be sensible; we'll slip in the back way."

"I don't give a damn about them."

"But I do," his brother-in-law-to-be declared. "When I see the sandbags and the barbed wire, the steering wheel starts shaking in my hands."

"This is my country," the poet proclaimed.

"Waiter!" Wasfy called in a loud voice, and added in a whisper: "Just you go on playing the part of Abu Ali. . . . Wait, just wait till you get married."

"Then what?"

"Hiam's my sister, I know her. She'll know what to do with you. She'll cut you down to nothing." He showed the poet a tiny space between finger and thumb.

Fatkhi smiled, while Wasfy, in a grand manner, laid two pounds on the table and, seeing that the waiter was an Arab, said, "Keep the change."

"That's exactly what your coffee cost," the waiter said.

"Then this is a clip joint," Wasfy shouted, exiting the coffeehouse with brisk little steps. Fatkhi grabbed his packet of cigarettes and hurried after him.

The highway was ruler-straight. From a great distance Wasfy spotted a patrol car stationed at the Megiddo Junction. He lifted his foot from the accelerator. "Police," he said.

Fatkhi shrugged.

"Aren't you scared?" Wasfy said.

Only people who've never had a run-in with the police, Fatkhi mused, sweat at the sight of uniforms. Aloud he said, "I don't give a damn about them. Keep driving!"

But Wasfy didn't have it in him to accelerate again. He squinted across the familiar green hills of Israel and said, "Maybe we should turn right? Let's go back home."

"Turn left."

"Didn't you hear the radio?" Wasfy exclaimed. "Soon their Yom Kippur will be starting—there won't be any traffic allowed in from the West Bank."

"We're not coming from the West Bank," Fatkhi said, "We're going to the West Bank."

"Whoever said that poets are crazy certainly hit the nail on the head."

"Signal a left turn."

Wasfy pushed the turn signal down and tried with all his might to ignore the patrol car and the two cops inside it. He muttered under his mustache: "What if . . . ?"

"I'll tell them we're going to Jerusalem by way of the Jordan Valley," Fatkhi said contemptuously.

Wasfy, biting his lip and accepting his fate, turned left onto the highway where the police car was parked, invoking the shortest prayer he knew: *"Ya rab!"* Once past the police car, he looked in the rear-view mirror and heaved a sigh of relief. The patrol car stayed where it was. "You're a devil, Fatkhi, a devil! What I say is, laugh at danger, but from a safe distance."

Fatkhi loathed Wasfy's attitude. In fact, he loathed many things about his brother-in-law-to-be. They had grown up in the same village. Their childhood had slipped away in the watermelon patches of the Beit Netufa Valley and in the dusty village square facing the ancient well. In that parched square Fatkhi had yearned for the sea breeze that he loved so much. In that square he was humiliated and dishonored as a child—it had been hateful for him. Wasfy would walk down to the square from his stone house, and Fatkhi would climb up from his family's rusty tin shack. Fatkhi's father and mother and brothers had collected tin cans from everywhere, even piles of trash. Laboriously, feverishly they had tried to prepare for the winter of 1949, but the winter blew and dripped in on them through holes in the roof. Fatkhi couldn't remember his old stone house in the fields. He remembered only, rather dimly, that night when he curled up against his mother's breast and heard his father's voice saying, "Hurry, woman, hurry. The earth is shaking, the bullets are flying." A day and a half later, they arrived in Kfar Mandah, this village swooning in the burning sun, and began life as refugees in their own country. They were never permitted to return to their lands and houses in the fields. And they never forgot the smell of the sea and the shade of the mulberry tree.

Wasfy and his friends made sure that Fatkhi would not forget. Wasfy was a chubby, good-natured boy. It was a comfort to take refuge in his shadow, except when a spell of bad temper would come over him and his hand would shoot out and grab Fatkhi's ear. His eyes would blaze above his swollen cheeks and he would spray words and spittle into Fatkhi's face. "Go back to your holes! Who wants you and your people here?"

Since then many years had passed. Every one of them had taken its toll on Fatkhi's father, on his body and his soul. His eyes burned in his lean face, but he did not relent. He bought land in the new village, he built his own stone house, but his heart was like a knot, a bundle of memories, the most vivid of which were of the smell of the sea and the shade of the mulberry tree. As time went by, Wasfy was inclined to let bygones be bygones, but Fatkhi nursed the dying embers in the depths of his soul. While his family's status in the proud village was still very low, he set his sights on none other than Wasfy's sister, Hiam. The other boys saw what Fatkhi had in mind, and more than once Wasfy flew into a rage. In order to defend his family's honor, he was obliged to roll about in the dust of the square, his heavy body crushing this thin young boy with the flashing green eyes. A few years went by, and Fatkhi had his revenge. Despite its wealth, Wasfy's family was compelled to humble itself before Fatkhi's in the engagement ceremony. Fatkhi had become the glory of the village. Moscow and Berlin lay at his feet; the blondes of Tel Aviv, shivering from the thrill of it, took him into their beds. His poems reverberated all the way from Cairo to Damascus. He was a noted intellectual, yet for his wife he chose none other than Hiam, who, having completed her elementary education, had been swallowed up again in the bosom of her family.

Wasfy, relieved to have passed the police car without incident, now settled into his favorite position while driving—one arm resting on the Buick's windowsill. His purple shirt blew in the autumn breeze, the stone in his ring glittered on the steering wheel. In the aftermath of their little adventure his face showed a youthful expression. He loved to talk while gesturing with the hand that was supposed to be gripping the wheel. As they passed Kibbutz Givat Oz, he pointed at the Israeli landscape behind them and the view ahead. "Look, Fatkhi, look how the sons-of-bitches divided up the land. They took the fat part for themselves, and left these poor wretches with the stones."

Fatkhi said nothing. As far as he was concerned, Wasfy's remark was phony, meant only to impress Fatkhi. This was Wasfy's way of fawning. Actually, he couldn't care less about the fate of "these poor wretches." So long as he can gorge himself on the fat of the land, it's all right with him, Fatkhi brooded. He's got two Jewish business partners, and from time to time it pleases him to burst in on Jenin in his gleaming Buick, proud, arrogant, conquering. He enters town in this palace-on-wheels, rolling into the poverty-stricken alleys of the refugee camp, and opens up his trunk before the eyes of the ragged onlookers. From it he pulls out gifts for his brother's widow, her children, and, especially, her young daughter, Amal.

They were driving close to cabbage fields that drew their water from open ditches. Fatkhi picked up his suitcase, rested it on his knee, and took out a brown necktie and a pale jacket. Wasfy's foot let up on the accelerator. He turned red in the face and whined, "You promised me, Fatkhi, you promised me that this would be a pleasure trip. You said that we were going out for a breath of air. That's why I lied to my wife and told her we were going to Eilat. I believed you, man, I took your word."

"What are you getting excited about? I'm not going to do anything."

"You're planning something. Yes, you are. I'm not blind. I can see you're changing clothes. You're putting on a disguise. Didn't we agree just to go out and enjoy ourselves a bit? Feel up a pair of nice young tits? Screw something firm for a change? A necktie! A European jacket! If you have your way we'll sleep on something hard tonight, all right—behind bars."

"You're raving, Wasfy."

"What am I, a child?" Wasfy shouted. "Here you are putting on a jacket and tie. You're making a fool out of me. I wasn't born yesterday. What do you expect me to do, keep my mouth shut? Allah protect me!"

"From what?"

"From your schemes, your politics. What are you getting disguised for? Come on, tell me."

"I'm not getting disguised," the poet said, taking a moderate tone. "What I'm doing, my friend, is removing my disguise."

"There is no God but Allah!" Wasfy exclaimed. "Do you think we're sitting in your Party clubhouse philosophizing? You want to convince me that day is night? Here you are dressed up like a waiter in a hotel and you tell me you've taken off your disguise. Don't make fun of me, man, don't make fun of me. I'm going back home."

Wasfy had already signaled a left turn. He slowed, looking for a place to turn the car. Fatkhi put his hand on Wasfy's arm. "You're right. I shouldn't have spoken that way. Go on, keep driving. I promised, and I keep my promises. Nothing bad's going to happen to you. I'm not planning anything."

"So why the get-up? Take it off."

"No. Now I'm dressed as I should be."

"What! All strangled in a tie and jacket in this heat? Is that what you call being dressed right? Where's your common sense, man?"

"I'm dressed like people my age are here," the poet said.

"You're putting me on," the mechanic said. He was bitter, exasperated.

"I don't want to show up in Jenin looking like a foreigner."

"You mean in these pants and this open shirt I'll be coming into my brother's home like a foreigner? Allah! The Communists have scrambled your brains, Fatkhi."

The poet would dearly have liked to tell Wasfy that in his American car he did indeed look like a foreigner, a detestable stranger in the refugee camp—but he didn't dare. "Listen, man, sometimes they see us from a slightly different angle, in a different light. Don't you remember our last visit?"

Suddenly Wasfy was furious. "May Allah shrivel the womb that bore them! I wanted to spill their guts onto the road and piss on them. . . . They ripped the mirror off and smashed the rear window. You know how much the repairs cost me? Seven hundred pounds!"

"We escaped by the grace of God," Fatkhi said.

"*Wallah*!" Wasfy shouted, the words and spittle spraying

from his fat mouth as they had done when he was a child. "You call that a mourning procession? We're a nation of maniacs. Even when we're in mourning, we go around raving like trash. Gamal Abdel Nasser's dead? So he's dead. Allah's mercy be on him. It's quite all right to march around with black flags and palm fronds and pictures. I swear it is. Tell me, Fatkhi, did I say anything different then? Actually, when I saw the black flags, I was so moved I couldn't speak. I turned off the radio and there were tears in my eyes. And who wouldn't weep for such a man, such a man's man? But how could I know that these were maniacs? What did the car do to them? What in the name of Allah did it ever do to them? They just saw it and right away they went crazy. As if I had run over the dead man's coffin. They threw the flags away, they forgot the pictures. Fatkhi, I tell you in Allah's name I can still hear them pounding on the car. They wanted to demolish it and us too. Well, the blood went to my head. I felt like screwing them but good. And I would have, too, except you stopped me. Afterwards I cried. Sure I did. They passed over the car like a storm and left it on the road like, like . . . You're a poet, you understand. . . . If you had a daughter, say fourteen years old, beautiful as the moon itself, dressed like a bride, and she went out for a walk, and all of a sudden a bunch of hoodlums jumped her and raped her, and you arrived to find her writhing in the dust. . . . Great Allah, that's how I felt!" Wasfy spat three times out the window. "And now for their sake you're getting dressed up like a waiter in a hotel? I'm surprised at you."

The poet flushed. "You haven't got the smallest particle of pride," he murmured.

Wasfy straightened his shoulders. "No pride? Try me. Try . . ."

"You're not proud of your people."

"Of these apes?" Wasfy said with astonishment. "You can

see for yourself. It's no wonder the Jews screw them good and proper."

The poet was trembling. "Because of types like you."

"Listen, man. I know a little history myself. Before the Jews, didn't the English ride us pretty good? And before the English didn't the Turks give it to us in the ass for a few hundred years? And before the Turks weren't we right down there kissing the feet of the Mamelukes? We're apes, that's all there is to it. Hitler came along and beat his drum and we danced to it. Now we're up to the very same thing with your Russians. . . ."

The poet had many arrows in his quiver, but he let none fly against his antagonist and relative-to-be. He was stifled by the dust of childhood eddying in the village square. He heard the rusty tin shack creaking in the wind. The people living up in the stone houses never provided the slightest crust of bread for the people in the leaking shacks below. Instead, they treated the wretches to the backs of their hands, while licking the boots of the Jewish conquerors. No wonder that up to now the English and the French and the Italians and the Jews knew nothing of true Arabs. For the most part they had dealt with mugs like Wasfy. Angered by these thoughts, Fatkhi would have loved to poke his fist into Wasfy's face. Instead he said to him, "Wasfy, do you know you've slowed down right opposite the military governor's headquarters?"

Wasfy's anger had evaporated. The Buick glided past the memorial to the German pilots of the First World War that stood on the main street of Jenin. Wasfy parked opposite the humble town hall. "Let's go to a restaurant," he said.

"You've forgotten, today's Ramadán. All the restaurants are closed."

"Closed to dopes like you. I know a good restaurant here where the back door is always open for me, even on fast days."

"I'm not hungry."

"Lamb roasted over charcoal will revive your appetite, man," Wasfy assured him. He had forgotten his fears. Wasfy got out of the car and walked around it as if meaning to attract the attention of the peddler of Ramadan pastries and of the peasant who was sauntering by with his donkey. The pastry-peddler pushed his cart up the slope of the main street without offering Wasfy his wares. Wasfy waved to the poet and called out, "Come on, my friend. You must be hungry."

"I don't want to," Fatkhi hissed.

Wasfy's rotund face darkened. "Stubborn, eh? You're going to have a swell family life with Hiam. . . . She's stubborn too. But listen, man, I'm really hungry."

"Then go over to the camp and take your brother's family out to eat."

The poet assumed that in spite of their poverty and distress, Wasfy's relatives in the camp had great pride and self-respect. He doubted whether Wasfy, that coarse brute, could comprehend the complex spirit of man. But then the poet relented somewhat, realizing that people were even more complicated than he himself might reckon. A hungry man is a hungry man. Nourishment is nourishment, even when besmirched with dust and spittle.

Wasfy got back in the car and reached for the key, but didn't start the engine. He thought it over, then leaned back and said: "You think I'm stupid, don't you? Invite them to the restaurant, you say. I know what you're driving at. By Allah, I understand very well. But you're mistaken. I'm not worried about the money."

"You don't understand," the poet said indifferently.

"Listen, kid, why don't you just shut up? Have you ever considered how they'd feel in there, in the restaurant? Not because they don't know how to use a fork, no, it's not because of that!" Wasfy's voice gained in volume and heat. "They're just as clever and quick as your fine friends in the Party. Take them to a restaurant two or three times and they'd even learn how to wipe their lips oh so neat with a paper napkin. They're perfectly capable of doing that, and you're dead wrong if you think that I'm afraid they'll embarrass me. You know what? You pal around too much with Jews and Christians, and they've muddled your brains, man. How can I explain it to you?" He leaned over to take a packet of cigarettes from the dashboard. Then he remembered that he was still on Main Street, where smoking was forbidden during Ramadan, and with a sigh he put the cigarettes back. "I was in the marketplace here a year and a half ago. It was the beginning of the fruit season. There was a pile of peaches in one of the stalls. Big golden peaches, as big as your fist. Well, a woman dressed in black, a woman from the camp, came walking up to this stall. She stood there and kind of dreamed. Then finally she got up the courage to ask the grocer the price. This was just when he was weighing some fruit for a guy who was dressed up in a *Franji* tie and jacket, like you're wearing now. The grocer didn't answer her. He must've thought that was all it would take to drive the wretched woman away. It embarrassed him to have the *Franji* see him serve such a filthy customer. Maybe the woman was expecting and craved peaches. Maybe she wanted to bring some home for her children. She asked again, this time louder. He answered, but without looking at her, the way you'd talk to a dog. 'They're not for you,' he said. 'They're too expensive.' Well, you know what? That refugee woman wasn't impressed, and the grocer had to make things plain for her. 'Eight pounds,' he told her. Eight pounds, just like that, twice what the *effendi* was paying. Just to scare her off. Fatkhi, you know me. I'm a pretty good poker player. But by Allah, that woman amazed me. She played her lousy hand like a professional. 'Four and a half pounds!' By Allah's life, that's what she said. . . . You should have seen the grocer go crazy. He almost kicked her. He made the marketplace ring with his screams. 'Get out of here, you dirty . . . ever since the Jews arrived you've been crawling out of your holes like rats. The Jews just pour their money down on you, and you have the nerve to show up here!' Listening to him, you'd have thought the bastard lived in the Sultan's palace. She looked like a black cow running away from him. Great Allah! I felt like turning his stall upside down. These refugees are Arabs, you hear? They're genuine Palestinians, too. You and your kind speak in their name, you use big words, but you despise them. The minute we arrive in Jenin, you make sure to get disguised like a waiter in a hotel, so you can look good for the *effendis*. And you tell me to take them out to the restaurant. The owner wouldn't dare say anything while I was there, but his eyes would tell all. The food would turn to poison in their mouths."

In the face of the mechanic's excitement, the poet remained unmoved. He was thinking about the village square. He remembered Wasfy's stone house and his own family's ramshackle tin hut. "There's nothing better," he said, with unconcealed cynicism, "than to stuff yourself with broiled liver in a restaurant and then go over to the camp and blow fat belches in peoples' faces."

"Jackass!" Wasfy hissed. He heaved and said, with all the pride of a short man, "I thought we'd eat first by ourselves, then order a meal to take out for them, a great bundle as big as a camel's hump. It'd be good to see them eat it in their own house, away from the eyes of waiters."

Fatkhi would have preferred to think the matter over, but he blurted, "All right—let's go."

When they were finished eating, Wasfy asked, "How are you going to get to Zuheir's place? It's a ways from here to Kabatiye."

"I don't know yet."

"Day or night, any time you want, I'll take you to him."

"I don't think I'll go to Kabatiye."

Wasfy was first surprised, then suspicious. He was afraid that Fatkhi would change his mind, putting an end to their little adventure. He took Fatkhi's hand and started coaxing him. "But didn't we arrange everything? Didn't we fix things so we could have a good time and relax here a few days? Yes, we did. And now you want to go home already."

"I didn't say I wanted to go home. I just think that if I went to see Zuheir in Kabatiye, I'd put him in danger. I'll call him and wait for him here."

Wasfy's chubby face lit up with pleasure. "You'll stay at that dentist's house, in Jenin?"

"Yes, I guess so."

"Good, very good. So now you're not in a hurry any more. You'll come along to the camp, right? Look, you're going to be a member of the family soon, and they haven't even met you. When Hiam and you got engaged, what did I say? I said the engagement party wouldn't be a real party if we didn't invite my late brother's wife. That poor woman, what kind of a life has she had? What's she ever seen? What I said was, why not cheer her up a bit? But you know what? They haven't got any luck, those people. Two days before the party, she gets sick."

Fatkhi didn't know whether to believe him. He had long since learned that his future brother-in-law believed his own lies. "Tell me, how was it that you and your family stayed in the village after the war and your brother wandered all the way to Jenin?"

"That's a long story, Fatkhi," Wasfy said. "But how come you don't know? Doesn't the whole village . . .?"

They were sitting under a smiling portrait of Gamal Abdel Nasser. The air was saturated with the fragrance of sizzling onions and broiled meat. Besides Fatkhi and Wasfy, there was not a single soul in the restaurant. From the kitchen, which was separated from their table by a curtain, came the sound of dishes being washed. Outside, the street and the town slumbered. Fatkhi let his gaze float down the length of the street. A rickety bus jerked along in the direction of Nablus.

A middle-aged man with an erect carriage and a smile on his lips, sporting a bow tie and a red *tarbush* with a gaily dancing black tassel, sauntered slowly down the sidewalk, acknowledging the greetings of the barber and the butcher. A peddler pushed a cart laden with fat Jericho bananas.

The smells were different, the air was different. Even the dust was scented. The sun was munificent, the breeze as mild and kind as life itself.

And everything was Arab . . . .

"Fatkhi!" Wasfy exclaimed.

Fatkhi came back to himself. "What's the matter?" he said, still smiling.

"I'm telling you a painful story, and you look as if I were singing a lullaby."

Just then, an Israeli army truck raced by honking, shattering the tranquility of the Arab street. Fatkhi's illusion turned out to be fleeting. "Come on, let's go," said the poet.

Wasfy stared at him. "*Ya rab!*" he said. "You know, you're hard to take."

Fatkhi's handsome face darkened. "Come on, let's go," he repeated.

"Wait a minute, can't you? The owner's cooking the food to take out."

Fatkhi's necktie was choking him, and his throat was parched from the smoke of the onions and grilled meat. He got to his feet, forcing Wasfy to his. The owner danced attendance on Wasfy. "Perhaps one more cut of liver? It's fresh young lamb, it melts in your mouth. I'll wrap everything in plastic. Look, I'm setting the *pitot* here so they won't get wet from the tomatoes. . . . "

The poet slightly resented the fact that, from the moment he and Wasfy had entered the restaurant, neither the owner nor the waiters had paid any attention to him. In spite of Wasfy's coarseness and rough manners, in spite of the stigma of his dalliance with the Jews, it seemed to Fatkhi that the owner and the waiters saw him as one of their own, a prodigal son who would always be welcome back in the family. Fatkhi, on the other hand, despite his tie and jacket, remained an outsider. They respected him more than they did Wasfy, but they saw him as a strayer. This feeling of being an outsider oppressed and pained the poet, and as they went back out to the American car, he kept wondering what the reason was, but found no answer.

Wasfy approached the car with little steps and saw to it that the owner of the restaurant himself set the large bundle on the back seat. Fatkhi wondered if he would have dared to degrade the man so. But the man saw nothing wong in it. He served his customer with evident pleasure, his services having been purchased for a good price. All at once the poet realized that, had he really considered himself a part of his people, had he thought like them, he, too, would have seen nothing wrong. The man lifted the corner of his apron and wiped the Buick's side mirror. He and Wasfy spoke about the car in affectionate terms. "She's a real fucker," the man said admiringly. "I'll bet she takes hills like a breeze!"

Wasfy was ecstatic. "She's a bitch," he said, smiling shamelessly. "A real bitch, I tell you."

Fatkhi, distressed, stood to one side and listened. Just a short time before he had blessed them all, these Arabs and their air and the donkey stink and the shriveled trees and the red *tarbush* on that nameless man. With something close to dismay he watched as Wasfy, who shortly before had cursed them all, now stole these Arabs away from him. He opened the door to the car and got in, wondering why this was happening.

Wasfy smacked his lips and started the Buick. As they drove off he said, "What's this face? Has the food turned to lead in your belly? Wasn't it good?"

Fatkhi kept silent while Wasfy rested his left arm on the open window and drove into the refugee camp. Immediately the clay walls closed in around them. Sewage streamed down the middle of the alley. Chickens scrambled about among barefoot children. Women swathed in black raised their tired eyes as the car drove by, Wasfy leaning on the horn. A couple of thin, hairless dogs sluggishly consented to get out of the way. The Buick passed several dim grocery stores, from which there came the reek of bottled cooking gas and rotten vegetables.

They stopped at a stone hut. An oven for baking bread and a kitchenette were attached at either side. Wasfy gave a prolonged blast on the horn and then waited, smiling like a happy child. Immediately, the plywood door of the hut was thrown open and a mob of urchins, shouting joyfully, burst forth into the alley. Three or four of them tried to get into the car. "Uncle Wasfy's here!" they cried. "Uncle Wasfy's here!"

There were about ten children in all. The poet asked Wasfy, "Are they all your brother's?"

"No," answered Wasfy. "Just two sons and Amal. It looks like their mother isn't home and the bastards have invited all the other bastards in the neighborhood to wreck the house." He turned with a severe expression to the oldest of his nephews. "Namir, where's your mother?"

"She's gone to the shop to get flour and oil. What did you bring us, Uncle Wasfy?"

"Lots and lots of things," his uncle assured him, the childish grin spreading over his round face once more.

"What a wonderful smell . . ."

"Something tasty, very tasty," Wasfy said, stroking the boy's close-cropped head. "And where's Amal?"

"Allah's curse be on her. She's never home," Namir answered in an angry voice, like a professional informer. "The street is her home, and strangers are her companions. She never thinks of returning before sunset."

"Namir!" Wasfy yelled. "Go and find her. Don't come back without her."

The boy's nostrils flared and quivered. His gaze was fixed on the bundle resting on the back seat. "Where will I find that bitch? She forgets that she's a woman already."

Wasfy opened the door and got out to confront the boy. "Go and turn the camp upside down until you find her. If you don't want your bones broken," he threatened, "don't come back without Amal."

"And what about this?" The boy pointed to the bundle in the car.

"What! Your sister goes astray and all you can think about is your belly? You scum!"

"Don't worry, Uncle Wasfy. When I grow up I'll kill her. That bitch won't dishonor you."

"Get going already!" Wasfy yelled.

He got back in the car to find Fatkhi openly lighting a cigarette and averting his eyes in embarrassment. The poet felt he had to say something. "How old is she?"

"Almost fourteen. And pretty. Go try and protect a pearl like that in a garbage dump like this. Fatkhi, don't believe what her dirty brother said. That's the way they talk here. She's a good girl, a very good girl."

In the meantime, the mother had appeared at the end of the alley. Her reflection showed in the rearview mirror over Wasfy's head. She walked erect, striding powerfully through the dust, a sack of flour on her head. When she noticed the car she quickened her pace. Next moment she was standing at Wasfy's window, so close that he couldn't open the door. "Wasfy! Light of my eyes! A thousand greetings to you, dear cousin!" she cried with genuine happiness, not bothering to remove the sack from her head. "Why are you sitting there in that stuffy car? Why don't you come into the house? What's this? Are these manners, dear cousin? Are we strangers? You know that this house is your house."

Wasfy laughed with pleasure. Then he put his fat hand on her stomach and pushed her away gently, so he could open the door. "Never mind," he said. "We just arrived. Amal isn't home."

The woman threw up her hands. "What can a helpless widow like me do?" She looked Wasfy up and down, as if his squat body was a minaret, and said, "You're a man. But this poor house doesn't have a real man."

Her gaze delighted the mechanic. "Sister-in-law," he said, "that's why I'm here. We were in Jerusalem," he lied, "and we said, let's stop by in the morning and say hello before we go home to the village. But it looks like we stayed in Jerusalem longer than we planned. Now we're stuck here until Sunday."

"Yes, dear cousin, we heard the Jews close the roads on their fast day. But that's good, my dear, that's good. You'll be our guest. Ach!" she cried, and froze. "The house is poor and wretched. I'm dying of shame."

Wasfy's shoulders heaved and his eyes glistened. "Sister-in-law," he rebuked her, "don't you know me yet? There's a feast here in the car fit for a king. I've brought it for all of you from a restaurant. Take a whiff, go ahead." And he took her head and tried to push it toward the window. In their excitement they both forgot the load she was balancing. The woman's forehead struck the roof of the car, and Wasfy was splattered all over with flour and oil. Suddenly his glorious purple shirt did not look so splendid. A cry of woe escaped the woman: "*Ya wili! Ya wili!* I'm so stupid. Look what I've done to your best clothes. . . ."

Wasfy recovered with superlative speed."Never mind, sister-in-law. It's just an old rag. I've got dozens of shirts like this in my closet. Come," he said, walking back to open the trunk.

Now, as the staring neighbors gathered, he began in a loud voice to tick off the riches he had brought. Cries of admiration rose from all sides, and Wasfy relished them. "Inside these newspapers there are fresh fish. This dress is for you, sister-in-law, and winter shoes for all the children, and this sweater is real wool. And this package is for that damned Amal." He straightened suddenly and shouted, "She's still not home!"

The woman gulped hard—it took her a moment to recover. "Amal!" she cried, "Amal!"

"But I told you she wasn't home," Wasfy said, irritated. "Who knows where your daughter is off to."

"Namir! Said!" the woman started screaming. "My sons, go fetch your sister."

"I already sent Namir to get her. This really is too much."

The woman turned to her brother-in-law with a reproachful smile on her lips. "Such thoughts about Amal? She is the diamond in the Sultan's crown. I'll kiss her footsteps. . . . Your brother, oh, that poor man, he never saw her in her glory."

Wasfy was not to be pacified so easily. "And meanwhile the whole camp has its way with her."

"God forbid!" The woman trembled.

But the poet, sitting in the car, saw that they were both enjoying their little charade—Wasfy, the zealous guardian of public morals, and his sister-in-law, well acquainted with his real character and blessing her stars for his generous mood today. The woman was still attractive. Her body was supple, her limbs delicate, her green eyes astonishing in her sunburnt face. She met Wasfy's eyes without the slightest shame, moistening her full lips with a quick tongue and gracefully arching her shoulders.

Amal appeared, hurrying in front of her brother. The poet, who had been left alone in the car, expected the girl to approach Wasfy in all humility. But she had grown up in a refugee camp, where she was already a woman. She knew her own value, and she also knew that Wasfy, for all his moralizing, was a man like any other. She wore a long dress, no bra over her well-formed breasts, and a gleaming pin in her hair. "Uncle Wasfy," she cried in a coquettish voice. "What a day this is! This world's turning upside down and people are going out of their minds. Abu Uleka's come home."

Wasfy, who was no taller than the girl, relented and smiled. "And who's Abu Uleka?"

"He's the one the Jews expelled two years ago. He's come back with a pistol in his belt. In three different places, in front of witnesses, he's sworn that he's going to kill Samih."

"God forbid!" Amal's mother murmured.

"Pistols, witnesses, oaths, killing," Wasfy said with a smile. "Let them devour each other. What do we care?"

The girl bridled. "What are you saying, Uncle Wasfy? Samih is Aziza's husband and Aziza is Abu Uleka's daughter. They married while her father, that brute, was away." Her eyes were shining. "They fell in love but her father was against it. When he started up with the Jews and they kicked him out, over to Jordan, Aziza and Samih went and got married. Now that hangman Abu Uleka has come to murder poor Samih. Everyone says that tonight he'll breathe his last."

Wasfy's plump face was still wreathed in smiles—he greatly enjoyed the look of the excited girl. "It's a simple matter, very simple," he said. "They go to the police and turn him in."

Wasfy's relatives, plus three or four of the bystanders, gasped as if the visitor from across the border had uttered a blasphemous heresy. "Turn him in to the Jewish police?" Amal shouted.

Wasfy was no fool. He raised his hands at once, accepting the justice of her reaction, and intoned one of his sententious sayings. "Those who play at love must pay."

It was then that the woman noticed the poet stretched out in the car. She pointed at him and asked suspiciously, "Who's that?"

Wasfy opened the door and pulled Fatkhi out. "This is Hiam's fiancé. He's a big shot. He travels to Berlin and Moscow like you all go to the market. He writes poems and appears in the newspapers. He's so important and famous that even the Je·vs applaud when he tells them that they're sons-of-bitches."

Fatkhi was sorely tempted to strangle him. With every word that Wasfy uttered, the yawning chasm between Fatkhi and the refugees grew wider and deeper. The bystanders hawked up phlegm, and the children regarded him with obvious suspicion, as though he was a dangerous, violent man whose very touch was to be avoided. Only Amal, impelled by her emergent womanliness, studied his handsome face with her pensive eyes, a look of distress darkening her young features. Now her mother said in an injured tone: "That's what happens when you marry into the upper crust—you forget your poor relations."

This embarrassed Wasfy. "Sister-in-law!" he scolded her. "What can you be thinking?"

"Your poor brother," she said mournfully. "How he dreamed of seeing his baby sister Hiam. And when she gets engaged, they don't even bother to invite his wife and children to the feast." All the while she was throwing the poet hostile glances as if he were to blame for her having been neglected and forgotten in this way. Had Hiam been engaged to marry a peasant, some ordinary *fellah*, they wouldn't have kept her, the refugee, hidden from the merrymakers.

The poet's tongue, accustomed to addressing mass meetings, faltered now. "Madam," he began, blushing at the high-flown language, "Wasfy told me that he invited all of you, and we certainly would have been happy to have you."

The woman was startled. "Wasfy invited us?" For a long moment she stared at her in-law. She was a practical woman, a woman of the refugee camp. It would not be wise for her to embarrass her benefactor in public. Better to exploit his lies in her own favor. So now she struck her forehead and murmured, "What a stupid woman I am. Really I am. Of coure he invited me. Now I remember."

"You were sick," Wasfy prompted.

"I was sick," the woman repeated obediently, while her children gravely nodded.

The poet felt like a fool. "Wasfy, I've got to be getting to the dentist's."

"What's the matter?" the woman exclaimed. "Have you got a toothache, *Ya baba*?"

Ya baba! The poet turned pale. This was a form of address that the poor used only in speaking to urchins, or to upper-class men whose manhood had been sapped by a pampered upbringing. He bore the woman's insult silently and returned to the Buick. He hated Wasfy.

4

Magid charmed the townspeople of Jenin. They said, in the coffee houses, that his smile instantly calmed all their fears. Tough guys who would rather face a loaded pistol than a syringe had nothing but praise for Magid, especially for his cunning way of keeping the syringes out of sight. He himself liked to tell comic stories about it. He and the poet were sitting in the dentist's living room, waiting for Abla to return from some Party meeting. She was a teacher, and on Fridays, when the schools were closed, she would see to most of her Party duties. The dentist smiled over his cup of coffee.

"One day," he recalled, "a well-known hoodlum from Nablus came into the clinic, a guy who would kill for a penny. His mug would scare you more than a pair of extracting tongs. Well, his mouth was so swollen he had trouble speaking. He came in, grabbed the patient who was in the chair, and threw him out. I was boiling mad. The patient he had thrown out was a sensitive type, Abla's uncle. But once this hoodlum sat himself down in the chair, his courage immediately failed him, and his eyes rolled in terror. I told him I couldn't pull the tooth because of the awful infection. 'Pull it out!' he yelled. I came closer, examined him, and again and again told him it was impossible. But now I couldn't get away from the chair.

That bastard grabbed my balls and roared, 'Now I've got your life in my hands and you've got mine in yours. And no lousy injections, either.' Fatkhi, he was ready to butcher me. So I said to myself, As Allah is great, I'll screw this gangster once and for all. 'It isn't just one tooth,' I lied to him. 'Never mind,' he shouted, 'start pulling, and like I told you, no needles!' I said to him: 'You know what? Why don't you inject me, so you'll see it's not as terrible as you think. Then I'll inject you.' He liked the idea. I guided his free hand—the one on my balls didn't relax for a second—and he stuck the syringe into my jaw. He must have considered me either a hero or a magician. Then it was my turn. I jabbed him, Fatkhi, I jabbed and jabbed until his mouth was just a block of wood, and then I started in with a vengeance. I ripped out half his teeth to make sure he wouldn't have many more opportunities to visit me. But do you know what? That murderer, who can hardly chew anything today, thinks I did him a great favor. Every month or two he's here. You see that box of grapes over there? He brought it just this morning from Nablus."

The poet grinned. "I'll bet he lifted it from some poor grocer."

"Fatkhi, you should know this—when a murderer wants to give you a gift, he doesn't steal it. He pays good money for it."

Fatkhi grinned again. "Not a bad idea, grabbing your balls—what a pair of hostages!"

Magid became serious. "You use the same tactics, my friend."

"How's that?" The poet was astonished. "Me?"

"You count on our friendship to force me to lie to the Party, man."

"I had to come, Magid."

"You've disobeyed orders, and now I'm in cahoots with you, against my will."

The maid was collecting the coffee cups. She stole several

glances at the handsome poet and then minced light-footedly from the room. "That piece is from the camp," the dentist said. "She's in love with you already."

"Be serious, Magid."

"All right, I won't report on this visit. But if it gets out, we'll both be in the same boat, sweetheart."

"I don't care."

"Allah! Allah!" Magid cried. "What, have you had enough of life among the conquerors? I've heard your nights in Tel Aviv aren't as boring as all that. And you're engaged to a real beauty. What else do you want, Fatkhi? Are you bored?" The dentist knew that this wasn't so. Deep in his heart, however, Fatkhi thought he was sneering at him.

Abla arrived. Her face radiated shrewdness, and her shapely body made up in part for her homeliness. "Fatkhi," she cried, in the tone of an unself-conscious woman. "How many boats did you lose at sea today? You look so miserable!"

"Magid is persecuting me."

"He's a professional sadist."

"I speak to him in all seriousness and he tells me to go to Tel Aviv."

"Don't pay any attention to him. It's only jealousy—the pure jealousy of a man who used to live in a refugee camp. The money may pour down like rain, but at heart Magid will always be a refugee."

"Actually," Magid said, "I am at peace with myself. You're not fair, Abla. I buried the refugee inside me. It's been years since he gave up the ghost."

"Every day you strangle him to death, and the next day he comes back to life. Whenever you're asked where you come from, you still say Jaffa."

Her husband smiled. "And you?"

"From Ramle," she laughed.

"Although she was born here, in Jenin."

Fatkhi knew that every child in the refugee camps learned to respond this way when asked where he was from.

"Have the children eaten?" Abla asked.

"They ate and they're playing outside," her husband answered. "And we're dying of hunger."

"How can you have any appetite after poking around in so many stinking mouths?" she teased him. "Besides, you're getting as pot-bellied as a shopkeeper and as bald as a druggist, Magid. Look at how Fatkhi keeps his great figure."

The poet was perturbed, but Magid joked, "That's his second weapon in Tel Aviv."

"And what's his first?"

"Poetry."

Abla laughed and turned to go. At the door she said, "Don't let him get you down, Fatkhi."

"I want to see Zuheir," he said.

"I know, I know," she said. "You wouldn't have bothered to come just for us."

"Abla, this is really important."

Her homely face turned serious. "In connection with the Party?"

"No," the poet answered. "A personal problem."

"Listen . . . "

"Abla," her husband interrupted. "I've already told him, I've explained to him a hundred times that Zuheir can't solve other people's personal problems now."

"That's right." She looked clear-eyed at the poet. Abla was one of the few women in Jenin who dared to look a man right in the eyes. "Zuheir's changed. He's like another man since the Jews pardoned him."

"But I want to see him."

Abla was annoyed by his childish stubbornness. "We've told you that Zuheir isn't Zuheir any more. I don't know if he'll be willing to meet you. He stays in Kabatiye, and when people come to see him he makes it plain that they're not wanted."

"Is he sick?" the poet asked.

"He's another man," the woman said vaguely, without going into detail. "And he refuses to be shaken out of it."

"I've got a Jewish friend," Fatkhi said. "A revolutionary from birth. He sat in jail for years. His name is Marduch. Once we had a talk about ex-prisoners. . . . He said that there were all kinds. The strangest ones are those who were on the point of breaking but didn't break. They start to fold up inside. They close all their shutters. They tremble at the idea that they might have to relive their experiences. . . ."

Abla, hearing this, furrowed her narrow brow and took her upper lip between her teeth. Under her nostrils a hairy little track sprouted. "I'm not as smart as you and I'm no great expert in psychology. But when you look at Zuheir you get the feeling that it's not only his hands that are trembling. Something inside him is shaking. . . ." She added mysteriously, "It's not fear; it's more like the way a car shakes and vibrates when it's about to go off the road."

Magid wiped his glasses with a handkerchief. "Maybe," he said thoughtfully, "maybe they ought to meet. They'd pour out their troubles to each other."

Again Abla took her lip between her tiny teeth. "And what are your problems?" she asked the poet.

"I can't find myself," he said, and immediately regretted his frankness.

"You can't find yourself?" she marveled, without the slightest sympathy. "But you're to be found everywhere. Even in Beirut."

"In Beirut?" The poet was bewildered.

"It seems you haven't seen the latest issue of *Al-Adib*."

The poet shook his head.

"Abla!" Magid said.

"You're not doing him any favor," she answered. "Why hide things from him?" And she went to the bookcase and took out the magazine.

The couple left him sitting in the armchair. The magazine was heavy in his arms and he let it drop onto his knees, and as he did so it seemed to pull his head and shoulders down with it. The open window darkened in the afternoon light and the town outside seemed to die. The house was perfectly still. In his ears the poet, like a deep-sea diver, felt a growing, painful pressure. He had discovered an act of treachery, and his lips murmured the reproach of a lover betrayed—No, Fakhri, no! His anger had not yet come flooding over him. Made up himself of layer upon layer of rage and hatred, the poet could not be angry with his one and only childhood friend, his friend since he had been weaned from his mother's breast. No, Fakhri, no! he moaned, and the pressure in his ears grew.

Just yesterday it was, a few weeks ago, or perhaps several months had gone by already—oh hell, the time wasn't important—they had sat on one bed in Moscow like two high school girls, spilling out their hearts. There had always been this rapport between them, free and pure. Fakhri had said that he would not return to Israel on a Party assignment, he had had enough of the fetters of discipline and yearned to rid himself of all the stains of Israel that were on him. He was going to travel by way of Damascus to Beirut, where he would find his place in the Palestine Liberation Organization. They were both stirred. That Moscow evening was clouded by the poet's impending separation from his friend, the literary critic who esteemed him so highly. "We'll meet again somehow," they pledged one another, like a young girl and a soldier on a railway station platform.

And thus, in the pages of this literary magazine, his bosom friend sends him greetings: "A traitor slipping craftily into the enemy's lap . . . a poet who casts his inspipid verse before the murderers of his people . . . an intellectual whore fallen into captivity in the parlors of the poison-mongers . . . "

No, Fakhri, no.

Unreasonably, hoping against hope, he looked again at the byline. Maybe he'd lost his mind. Maybe his eyes deceived him, he thought, even though he knew beyond doubt that this was his friend's flashy style. "The spiritual murder of a People." And under the title: "by Fakhri Biadsah."

No, Fakhri. . . .

There was a sound of dishes and knives and forks being set on the table. Now he became aware of Abla's clear voice: "Fatkhi, come and eat."

The poet raised his shrouded eyes to the open window, as if meaning to leap through it into the silent afternoon streets, and beyond them to the brown fields and the horizon . . . as if he wished to flee all the way back there. When he realized what "there" meant, he trembled. There meant Israel, the Israel he hated.

Magid's comforting voice sounded through the open door. "*Ya, Sheikh*, come and eat already. You're a creative artist, you should be used to falling down and getting slapped in the face."

He left the living room, the magazine still in his hand. He approached the table and dropped into a chair. The paper rustled on his knees. "Fakhri," he murmured.

"He got you good!" Abla said merrily, her eyes sparkling beneath her narrow forehead.

"You don't understand," the poet stammered.

"But you signed—isn't it true that you signed? So what are you getting excited about?"

"When their children were killed on that bus, all hell broke loose. Here you work single-mindedly, Abla, and you forget our problems. You forget that we're caught between the hammer and the anvil. We work among Jews. I envy you. I envy Fakhri. How easy it is for him to say whatever comes into his head, sitting in Beirut. Don't forget that in Israel the Party itself is made up of Jews and Arabs: We have to keep them in mind. When they demanded that we express our regret over the death of those children, when they demanded that we condemn that action, we turned around and demanded that they condemn the Israeli army's aggression in Lebanon, and they agreed.

"The death of the children," Abla murmured. "In your statement it said, 'The murder of the children.' We're murderers in your eyes, Fatkhi. Go and explain that to Zuheir."

Magid concentrated on his food. From time to time he cast a smiling glance at the poet, who was preparing to repel Abla's assault.

"I will explain it to Zuheir! And how!" The poet was afire with emotion, not to his advantage.

Abla tore at her food. "You mentioned your Jewish friend. What did you say his name was?"

"Marduch."

"Does he also make you walk the tightrope between the thieves and their victims?"

"He was shocked. As far as he's concerned, children are children. He has only one child himself, a retarded child. Fathers like that are crazy about anything having to do with children. If I lived here permanently, things would look simpler to me."

The woman refused to let up on him. "When do you envy us—when you go to Moscow, or when you go to Tel Aviv?"

"Abla!" Magid cried. "Let the poor man eat."

"I don't know," the poet answered evenly. "I'm an outsider in Tel Aviv. In a certain way I'm an outsider in my village, too. I come here and visit the refugee camp, and I'm an outsider here as well. I'm a stranger, Abla, a stranger in my own country."

Revolutionary women detest agonizing, especially in men. She promptly assumed an even more judgmental tone. "The Jews have turned your head, sweetheart. You're so taken up with them that you've forgotten that you're a member of the Party. You go into the refugee camp in a coat and tie and you want them to bow down to you. You've forgotten that there's still a class war being fought in the world."

Fatkhi had no more stomach for this conversation. "Will I see Zuheir?"

Magid smiled good-naturedly. "You seem to be very sure that he'll solve your problems."

"Will I see him?"

"All right," the dentist agreed. "Go rest now. Abla's spoiled your appetite."

Fatkhi went off to the living room. One wall was completely covered with books. He leafed through several and then dropped into the armchair. It was not only his appetite that Abla had spoiled. She had hurt his manly pride. And she had done it intentionally. No female made fun of him like that. He remembered their first encounter well. She had gazed at him, stared at his clear face and green eyes. Her shapely body twisted and her face became homelier than ever. He had thrown her a gallant smile. She warded it off, and immediately closed herself off to him.

Since bursting forth from his village, Fatkhi had been with many women, all kinds of women; but the ones who closed themselves off always frightened him. In time he adjusted to the strange behavior of strange women, convinced that these were usually women saddled with impotent husbands, who feared that Fatkhi would notice the hunger in their eyes. They always behaved aggressively. And in those few who finally let their guard down, aggression changed into the most frightful self-abasement.

Abla is famished, he decided vindictively. He stretched out his legs on the floor polished by the maid from the camp, and hung his head back. A light breeze fluttered the curtain behind him and a bird chirped on the branch of the pomegranate tree outside. Suddenly he relaxed. A smile came to his lips and his eyelids dropped. A sweet fatigue spread over his limbs. He did not trouble to open his eyes even when he sensed Abla's children standing in the doorway. Now he heard their hesitant voices.

"The guest is sleeping," said the little girl.

"He's from Israel," said the boy.

"A Jew. . . ."

"Shhh!" Her brother, alarmed, silenced her, as if fearing that she might stir up a force that no one could control.

"Does he have a gun?"

Her brother thought silently for a long time. "He's got one, but he keeps it where you can't see it."

"Where's Mommy?"

"She went upstairs," her brother answered. "She went upstairs after lunch."

"I didn't see her."

"Daddy went upstairs, too," he added.

"Why?"

"What do you mean, why?"

"Why did Mommy and Daddy go upstairs?"

"Dope!" Her brother, triumphant and superior, sneered at her. "I told you last week."

"What did you tell me?"

"He screws her. Every day he screws her and afterwards he lies on his back."

"I don't like to lie on my back," the girl said.

The two of them took their leave. The breeze through the window had died and the bird on the pomegranate tree had fallen silent. The poet's smile faded away, and his face flushed as if someone had slapped him. The couple making love upstairs were like a weight on his shoulders.

He begrudged Abla her pleasure. Characteristically, he sought consolation in words. She's got a squashed-in nose, he said to himself. It spreads out over her mustache and her ratty teeth. Her hair is bristly. Her eyes may be clear, but they're small. Her ears—they're like a couple of torn rags. She probably gives off a bad smell from her mouth when she gets excited.

It angered him that he had had to defend himself against her. She had sat there on the other side of the table, tearing at her food like a rat, spanking him as if he were a naughty schoolboy. Wrathfully, he got up and left the room, found the bathroom, rinsed his face. He made his way out of the house muttering, "Let them go to hell! All of them!"

"All of them" meant the Israeli troops, the Arab spies, the couple making love upstairs, and even the bird singing on the pomegranate tree. The poet crossed the road and walked along the main street. He found a coffee house drowsing under the eucalyptus trees and sat down on a wicker stool. Behind his back, the soft click of the backgammon dice abruptly ceased. An aged shopkeeper in billowing black trousers was leaning against a tree trunk. He gaped at the poet with extreme wariness, as if he were a lizard. On account of Ramadan, the coffee house was nearly deserted, and the few customers were not offered drinks. One of the backgammon players said in a husky voice, "We thought we'd be spared their disgusting faces until Sunday."

Fatkhi gazed along the main street. There were no Jews there, neither soldiers nor civilians. The shopkeeper stooped in his filthy trousers and breathed heavily. Then he quickly straightened and examined Fatkhi with some trepidation, as if afraid that the poet had changed position. When he found everything as it had been, the old man cleared his throat and called, "Boy!"

An idiotic looking waiter, barefoot and gangly, came to him and said, "Eh?"

The old shopkeeper pointed at the ground under the poet's feet. "Go see what that crow wants here."

"Eh!" said the waiter.

Tiny hammers beat in Fatkhi's temples. The waiter hopped toward him, swinging his shoulders, and stopped two paces from his chair. Looking as if he were quite ready to run for his life, he shouted, "Eh?" Suddenly he bared his teeth and, smiling disparagingly at all the world's dangers, fired the provocative challenge, "Shalom!" in Hebrew, no less.

Fatkhi was not amused. He measured the "boy" who stood shifting his weight from foot to foot and said angrily, "Get lost."

His perfect Arabic pronunciation pleased the waiter but heightened the shopkeeper's suspicions. The backgammon players behind Fatkhi's back reacted as if some sacrilege had just been committed. The backgammon box was slammed shut in a small avalanche of wooden counters and dice. The husky voice murmured querulously in the clear air and an unctuous voice said, "Someday they'll start climbing to the top of the minaret on Fridays and preaching to us out of the Koran. Allah protect us from the devil!"

If Wasfy were here, the poet thought to himself, he'd know how to get out of this stupid fix. The poet had fled the dentist's house without his jacket and tie. His short-sleeved shirt was open down to the third button, and his pants indubitably carried an Israeli trademark. The idiotic waiter still stood there, grinning impudently. The poet lifted his arm in a sudden movement, as his mother used to when she shooed chickens from the courtyard. "Get going already! I told you to get out of here. . . ."

Husky-voice came to life again. "Allah! Allah! He'll be shitting on your mat and giving orders inside your house soon."

"I'd like to screw him good," hissed the unctuous voice.

Where's Wasfy when I need him? Fatkhi thought, getting to his feet. He had to behave responsibly, accept the yoke of Party discipline. He mustn't provoke a disturbance in this town.

He rose, meaning to go. Even as he deliberately lit a forbidden cigarette, something to salvage whatever remained of his pride, he was thinking that it would be best to withdraw.

He took two steps and the waiter retreated. But now the unctuous voice stung him in the ear: *"Tuz!"*—a contemptuous challenge to which any self-respecting man must respond.

The poet burned with an all-consuming flame. The image came to him of Fakhri carrying a Kalatchnikov machine gun on his shoulder and a pen in his right hand. Fakhri, who permitted himself to call the poet an "intellectual whore." Legs trembling with anger, Fatkhi approached a young man with long sideburns, whom he believed owned that unctuous voice that had whipped him and burned him with *"Tuz."* "You're a creature that stumbles in the darkness," the poet mocked him in flowery Arabic.

The young man was startled. "What does he want from me?" he asked his friends. His was actually the husky voice.

Fatkhi threw caution to the winds. "I'm an Arab, the son of Arabs, from Beit Netufa!" he proclaimed. He wanted to say that he was a refugee driven out of Mazraya, but he couldn't take back what he'd already said.

A lean young man with wicked eyes got to his feet and said in his unctuous voice, "And what brings you here, *Ya baba?*"

Again, *"Ya baba."* Back in the refugee camp he could not respond to the woman's scorn. Here, with the young man's mug before him, he answered harshly enough to put him in his place: "That's none of your business."

They were too close to one another. A sickly-looking man sitting some distance away intervened. "Let him go, boys. He's obviously come looking for a woman."

The young man backed off to his stool and spat out, "I guess they're human too!"

But the husky voice flared. "That's what really gets me. The Jews piss a whole shower of money down on them and then they come barging over here to buy our girls and daughters. I tell you, in another year or two, all we'll have left to fool around with will be she-donkeys."

The unctuous-voiced young man bleated with laughter. "Go

to Nablus, kid," he said to the other man. "The Turks grabbed even your grandfather's she-donkeys—so why shouldn't the Jews do the same to yours?"

"You think that's a joke, eh?" the husky voice growled.

In his left ear Fatkhi heard another "Eh!" The waiter touched his shoulder and held out a cup of filthy tea. Fatkhi ignored the idiot and ran off to the main street.

Entering the dentist's home, he was enveloped by silence but found no rest. From one of the other rooms there came the children's light voices and the maid's soft laughter. Abla was sitting in the armchair next to the bookshelf, working industriously on her students' notebooks. When he came in she hurriedly removed the reading glasses that gave her homely face an owlish expression, and asked in a velvet voice, "Don't you nap in the afternoon?"

You can hear the satisfaction in her voice, thought the poet. Her movements were less abrupt, her eyes clearer. Fatkhi knew these signs well. Although certain that he was not jealous, he was tempted to annoy this female taking her ease in the armchair. "I took a walk outside," he said.

"This place is too small," she said good-humoredly. "Everybody knows everybody else."

"I was sitting in a coffee house and I almost got into a fight." He felt a strong desire to shatter her composure.

"You can't cope with our young men." She laughed a short, feminine laugh and added: "You won't find a single gentleman among them. When they need to, they can really sink their teeth in."

"They were convinced that I was a Jew."

"I'll bet they saw you come into the house," she said with equanimity. "That should calm them down."

The poet gave up. "I'll go and take a nap."

The teacher let her maternal generosity flow over him. "You're tense, Fatkhi. The room upstairs on the left is prepared for you."

As he climbed the stairs her gentle voice called out, "Zuheir's coming tonight."

5

The mud huts and stone houses of the refugee camp, distant and cut off from the town, huddled together layer upon layer. It seemed to Wasfy, as he went out in the dark to the Buick, that the alley was narrower then it had been during the day. The starry sky spread out over the town and the camp; the road between them was deserted. With the fading of the light Wasfy had grown excited. Circling the Buick, scheming and plotting, he kept coming to a dead end. There were four people in that small hut where he meant to stay for two whole days. There was a wide mattress that had belonged to his sister-in-law and his late brother, which was hidden behind a rickety cabinet, and there were three small, mildewed mattresses laid out for the children in the entrance to the hut. Toward nightfall, Hamadia, his sister-in-law, had specially dragged out the wide mattress for the guest, spreading over it a blanket which, in her opinion, was clean. She had announced that she herself would sleep on a mat. Amal protested, saying that *she* would sleep on the mat. Wasfy had landed himself in a ticklish position. While mother and daughter kept guard over each other, he would toss and turn, all alone on his stinking bed.

Despairingly he wondered whether he ought to sleep in the

Buick, on the roomy back seat. He had had a momentary illusion of feeling at home in that narrow alleyway. During the night, he would get up to drink from the pitcher of water in the hut, and when he finished he would leave open the door of the hut and the car door. Any woman or girl who wants to can come and join me, he thought, but then he cursed, knowing that neither of them would come out on her own initiative. The alley suddenly seemed less like home—a quarrel had broken out between two neighbors, several steps away from the hood of the Buick. It died out in shouted insults and the slamming of rickety doors.

Wasfy snatched up a rag and wiped the windshield with bad-tempered energy. Little Said approached him, silent as a shadow, and asked in an awestruck whisper, "Uncle Wasfy, may I?"

Wasfy's voice betrayed his bitterness. "No joy rides tonight. You and your brother are going to sleep right now."

"Uncle Wasfy, I just wanted to try the horn. You know, just a short beep . . ."

"That's not allowed!" Wasfy barked. Suddenly he had a bright idea. "Come here, Said."

The boy, like an animal that has known more kicks than caresses, approached him suspiciously. "Yes," he murmured.

"When do you all go to sleep at night?"

"At night," Said answered, confused.

"You're as thick as a jackass. When at night?"

"A little after sunset, Uncle Wasfy."

"And are there thieves here?"

"Yes." Said trembled and clenched his fist. "Lots. There are lots of thieves. But Mommy locks the door real tight."

Wasfy smiled, encouraging the boy, and said, "But you're a man, you're not afraid of thieves."

By now the boy didn't know what his uncle wanted from him. He nodded his head yes and shook it no. "Namir isn't afraid. He tells Mommy that he's afraid, but it's just to fool her. Actually, he steals himself."

Wasfy stroked the boy's head affectionately and said to him, "Go call Namir."

The boy's eyes gleamed. "Are you going out with us to steal in your car?"

"Go and bring your brother."

In a short time both brothers were standing before him. Namir was tougher than Said. He had matured early in the evil atmosphere of the camp. His obsequiousness made Wasfy flinch. Here was a youth who could kill.

"My son," Wasfy said, "you work from time to time, don't you?"

"Sure. All kinds of . . . I'm a porter in the market now."

"How much do you earn each day?"

"Sometimes as much as five pounds."

"Tonight you and your brother will have more profitable work."

The youth got up on his toes, craning his neck to check the alley behind his pint-sized uncle's back, as if on the look-out for his mysterious assignment. "Yes, Uncle. We're ready."

Wasfy grinned. "You haven't even asked what kind of work it is."

The boy did not trouble to hide his astonishment. "What's the difference?"

"I want you both to keep a watch on the car tonight."

The boy's expectancy vanished. "Is that all?"

"This car is worth a lot of money, Namir."

"Yes, Uncle," the youth said, turning toward the hut.

"Where are you going?"

"To get the knife, Uncle."

"No knives!" Wasfy cried. "No fooling around, you hear? You and your brother will just sleep here, in the car."

"Is that all you want?" the youth said, disappointed. Such a pleasurable assignment, like a wonderful dream come true, obviously wouldn't pay much.

"You'll get twenty pounds, and your brother ten."

The youth froze. He tried to say something, but all that came out was "Mother!"

Wasfy burst out laughing. "You'll sleep on the back seat, and Said on the front seat."

"We'll get your car all dirty," Said said.

"True, true. That's why I want you both to go and wash up real good."

"The faucet in this alley is busted," Namir said. "We'll go to the next alley."

Both of them went running into the house. Little Said came out at once. "Mommy says your coffee is ready, Uncle Wasfy."

"I'll drink it here," he said, his spirits improving.

The boy was startled. "Outside?" If you're offered a delicacy in a refugee camp, you gorge yourself indoors, far from covetous hands and the evil eye.

"Yes, outside," said his uncle.

"As you wish," Said said, although he had his doubts. Already the wafting fragrance of the coffee filled the hut, and the flimsy door was not enough to keep any passing stranger from sniffing the riches inside. And now this peculiar uncle wants to take his coffee outside, no less. Said poked his little head in the door of the hut and called, "Mommy, Uncle Wasfy wants to drink his coffee outside. Namir, where are you?"

The two brothers went off into the foul murkiness of the alley and Amal came out, carrying a couple of stools and a tray with cups and a coffeepot. She placed one stool close to the wall, the other next to Wasfy, and she set down the tray. "To your health and pleasure, Uncle Wasfy," she sang. The distant glow of a lantern flickered in her eyes.

Wasfy, making himself comfortable on the stool, leaned against the wall and looked up at the girl. Her thighs stretched her dress and her breasts hovered over him. "Have both of you had your coffee yet?" he inquired, dry-mouthed.

"What, before you, Uncle Wasfy?" Her belly quivered slightly. She rubbed one knee against the other, stooped and moved the tray a fraction. Her warm, glittering forehead nearly touched his head. Quickly she straightened up, moved away, and stood on his right, so that his awkward body, bent on the stool, was between her and the door of the hut.

Despite his confusion, he understood what these maneuvers signified. "I won't touch the coffee," he declared, "until you drink some first."

Her voice was steady and clear. "Uncle Wasfy!"

"By Allah!" her uncle swore. "You're a blossom, Amal."

"Uncle Wasfy . . ."

"I'll pour you some into this cup and you'll drink first."

"Uncle Wasfy!"

He poured the coffee with a trembling hand. With his free hand he tucked up the folds of her skirt and groped at the warm, firm, soft skin, and that hand trembled also. "You're a jasmine flower."

"I'm afraid . . ." She arched her body.

"Afraid of Uncle Wasfy?"

"No," she answered in her steady voice. "Abu Uleka is prowling the camp with a pistol in his belt, and there'll be murder tonight. I'm afraid."

"You've got nothing to be afraid of." Wasfy now had trouble speaking. "I . . . I . . . I'm here." His fingers burned, finding her firm curves naked under the dress.

"Oh, that's wonderful, just wonderful, you bitch." Her mother's voice thundered from the threshold. "Your uncle went out to enjoy his coffee in the fresh air and you're pestering him."

Wasfy's hand fell like a stone. He would have said something, but he knew his voice would betray him. Above him he heard Amal's steady voice. "But Mother, he's our guest. Someone's got to serve him."

What a devil, what a devil, Wasfy said to himself.

Hamadia pretended to be satisfied with this explanation. "Very nice, daughter. Now I'll serve him."

The girl relaxed. Hamadia, dressed in black, bent to pour the coffee for Wasfy. It had a different taste in his mouth now. When Namir and Said returned, he told them what the sleeping arrangements were to be. At first they stretched out on the empty seats with some trepidation, reaching out to touch all that gleaming luxury, and then they became children again. Their laughter could be heard through the open windows, and from time to time two pairs of astonished black eyes peeked out.

Hamadia, shaking her head, murmured, "My orphans, my orphans . . . ." Then she gave her attention to her guest, suppressing her unhappiness. Her teeth flashed in a brave smile. "Namir's a man already," she said to Wasfy. "He's left school, and now he brings home a little food. It was silly of me to dream. Is school for the likes of us? Are you comfortable, dear Wasfy? Should I bring you a cushion? Yes, yes, a cushion. Amal, my daughter, bring your uncle a cushion to rest on."

The girl returned and handed the cushion to her mother. Wasfy had expected Amal to place it behind his back herself, but she had turned modest, her eyes avoiding his. When he took out his wallet she moistened her lips with the tip of her tongue, and said nothing.

"It's not necessary," the mother said, her voice shaking.

"Winter is coming," Wasfy said in a burst of generosity. "All of you need things—you need lots of things. Here, one hundred, two hundred . . . three . . . "

Hamadia stood, took his hand, and kissed it. "Amal," she cried, "take your beneficent uncle's hand and kiss it." As the girl hesitated, her mother took her small head and pushed it down. Amal's soft lips fluttered over the mechanic's rough skin. The girl fled into the hut. Simultaneously, Hamadia remembered that she and Wasfy were in the alley of a refugee camp, surrounded by prying eyes and pricked ears. "Come," she said to him. "Come, you're tired, you have to rest. I've prepared your bed."

Wasfy obeyed, letting her carry the two stools and the cushion and coffee things. Once inside the hut, she lit a kerosene lamp. In the meager light, the poverty struck Wasfy such a blow that his lust cooled somewhat. Amal already lay under a blanket, a shadow heaped up on the floor. She and her shadow aroused only pity in him. Hamdia knelt in the corner and set down her load. She took off her scarf and her black hair shone in the dim light. She smiled at him and sighed. "Do you need anything?" she asked in embarrassment. "You must be used to all the comforts of the rich, and we—all we've got is a beggar's house."

"Good intentions are the main thing, sister," he said affectionately.

He stretched out on the wide mattress, and she on Namir's mattress. He tossed fitfully on his bed; she sighed softly. Amal was perfectly still. Her breathing was inaudible. It was as if, under that blanket which covered even her head, nothing was alive. Wasfy felt warm. He gave his bare thigh a hard slap, and Hamadia started and sat up on her bed. "What is it, my dear?" He could hear her voice trembling.

"The bedbugs are swarming. They're drinking my blood as if they wanted to take revenge on me."

Once," the woman whispered, "once, the bedbugs used to gorge themselves on us. But now, my dear, there aren't any bedbugs. Amal, Amal! Isn't it true that there aren't any bedbugs?"

The girl did not react.

The woman rose carefully on all fours and touched her daughter lightly on the shoulder. "Amal, isn't it true that there aren't any more bedbugs in our house? The child's sleeping," she added in a whisper, returning to her bed.

"Why are you sighing, Hamadia?" Wasfy asked in a trembling voice.

The woman fell silent.

The man was filled with anger. "Have you decided to go to sleep, too?"

"How could I sleep?" she said in a strangled voice. "How could I sleep while you're suffering?"

"Great Allah, I am suffering. That's right. I'm suffering."

"I can see, my dear, I can feel."

"And the girl?" he asked.

"Amal!" she called again. "The child's sleeping like a baby," she said in an expectant voice.

"Where's the water?"

"Here, the pitcher's next to me. I'll get up and bring it to you."

"Why bother?" He was sitting up on his mattress. "I'll get it myself."

"My dear, you're our guest. I'll bring it to you myself. It's dark here and you're liable to fall, God forbid."

She approached him, the cup shaking in her hand. He reached out and asked, "Where are you?"

She said nothing.

His groping fingers touched her face. Her cheeks were wet with tears. "You're crying, woman." He was startled. He took the cup from her trembling hand and placed it on the floor, far from him. "Why are you crying, woman?"

She knelt, sobbing silently. She kept sobbing as he grabbed her and she embraced him. Her misery inflamed him. For the first time, he slept with a woman without treating her coarsely. He was soft and gentle, and she wept. There was even something strangely joyful about those tears. They were like the autumn rains, releasing an intoxicating aroma from the earth.

He lay on his back beside her and whispered, "Tell me why you're crying, woman."

"Your brother," she whispered. Her weeping ceased.

Wasfy was crestfallen. "My brother," he growled angrily, as if he had been tricked, fooled. "Have you been thinking about my brother this whole time?"

"No, no. Just now. It was on this same mattress that he wept with the winter rains and the summer stars. That poor man. While the children slept he would weep and say that you had forgotten him."

"We always remembered him. All those years we said what bad luck he had. It pained us greatly."

"He used to sit by the radio listening to the Jewish broadcasts . . . He thought that maybe you all would send greetings. There were others who even got letters."

"You know, woman, everyone has his own troubles to think about."

"Am I blaming you, my dear? He was the one whose heart used to bleed. He knew about the family-reunification scheme. He was sure that because of the fields, you were all happy that he was so far away. . . ."

"That's not true."

"But that wasn't what bothered him most. He had a sort of foreboding, a premonition. He used to say that the Angel of Death would come before he would see you all again. And that grieved him. It wouldn't have mattered to him that you had meat in your pot, while he had weeds in his. He gave up his right to the roof that sheltered you all. It only hurt him that he would die without ever seeing your faces again. Strangers told him when Hiam was born, and also about your father's death. How he laughed with joy and wept with sorrow."

"Don't blame me, woman. I was only a child myself."

"And is it your fault that he was at his uncle's house in Tiberias when the Jews got there?"

"I'll do everything for you that Allah would allow, Hamadia. I'll take care of you all, Hamadia."

She tried to thank him with her body, but he was limp now. Dimly he realized that his hands weren't clean. At that moment, however, all he wanted to do was to go to sleep. The woman's tears have thinned my blood and taken my manhood from me, he thought. The people in the clay huts around them were sunk in a deep sleep like a threatening mire. Wasfy found it difficult to breathe. The woman was still stretched out at his side, ready and willing to satisfy his desires, whatever they might be. But it wasn't clear to Wasfy himself exactly what he wanted. He was frightened by the camp—that sleeping, sharp-eyed monster, that bogeyman. The ghost of his dispossessed brother frightened him. He wanted to get up, to escape, but his limbs were bound to the mattress by invisible cords. This is where my brother gave up the ghost, he thought in a panic, and I'm going to die here too. His brother is a black skeleton. Foul bandages are wrapped around his bones like flesh and skin. Someone's pulling the skeleton along on a rope like an animal at the fair. Roars of laughter all around. He's hungry and his bones shake and knock against each other. No one understands what's happening, except Wasfy. His brother is terrified. Tortured by unfeeling strangers, he wants to go home, but his brothers won't have him. They're helping themselves to his portion, they're happy that the Jews have thrown him off the fat brown land, that land that's like a woman's backside. So he had gone and hid deep inside his wife, this woman. And Wasfy hadn't known, he hadn't known at all. It was only when he entered Hamadia that he found him there, inside her. And now Wasfy tries to escape, but his brother's bones close in on him: Hamadia is a trap, a murderous snare. He chases the prancing Amal and slips and falls into Hamadia again, and it's like falling into the grinding jaws of a trap. Woman, what did I do to you? he cries in silent agony, but she keeps grinding away. Woman, I'm not a man any more! he says, and she weeps for him and for his brother. Wasfy begs for mercy. Now I too shall be doomed to wander. There's no place in the village for a man who's lost his . . . the kids in the street will laugh at me. I'll have to leave my home and business and children and flee, barefoot and disgraced!

"Where am I?" he shouted.

Hamadia was bending over him with a damp cloth in her hand, wiping his face. Amal, sitting wrapped in her blanket, stared at him with revulsion. The kerosene lamp was burning again, casting its yellowish light between the black walls.

"Amal, my daughter," Hamadia whispered. "Your uncle's sick."

The girl shrugged. "Sick?" Her tone was insolent, contemptuous. Her mother understood what she meant. In a refugee camp, a weak man arouses only revulsion.

Humbly, as if she herself were in part responsible for the man's weakness, Hamadia said, "My daughter, get up and make some tea for him."

The girl rose as silently as a shadow. Wasfy was certain that he was dying. A ball of fire burned in his intestines, his belly was about to burst like a balloon. He pushed away the woman who was crouching over him and sat up on the mattress. In the feeble light of the lamp he slowly came back to his senses. It's the ulcer, he said to himself. And he got to his feet, ignoring Hamadia's pleas not to. On his way out he sputtered at Amal, "I don't need your tea!" He went out to the Buick and took two pills. He returned, chewing them, and gulped some water from the pitcher. "Turn out the light!" he ordered softly.

Mother and daughter, somewhat calmed by the sight of the man regaining his courage, returned to their beds without a word. But Wasfy knew that his standing had been damaged in their eyes beyond repair. His money would be of no use any more. He got up again and went to the door.

Hamadia rose in alarm. "Are you leaving our house in the middle of the night?"

"No!" he said angrily. "I'm going out to get a little air."

"At this time of night?" Amal asked, a bit of her earlier respect for him returning to her voice.

"Did you think I was afraid of the jackals? Go to sleep. . . . "

"Don't go too far," Hamadia advised.

"Do they eat people here?"

"Who knows?" Amal chirped.

He laughed. He lit a cigarette and sat down at the foot of the girl's mattress. "You're a devil," he said, trying to make up to her.

Her mother sighed and said, "Don't I know it."

Amal drew her legs away from him. Wasfy's voice was self-confident in the gloom of the hut. "She's a troublemaker, this child, eh?"

"I wish some man would come along and take her from me already."

"And if I take her myself?"

For the first time since Wasfy's arrival, Hamadia laughed. "I wouldn't even ask you for a dowry," she said. "I'd tie her up by the legs like a chicken and hand her over and wish you good health and a long life."

Wasfy put his hand on the blanket. The girl stiffened. "And what would the princess have to say about that?" he said.

She kicked him with her bare leg and then immediately drew her foot back.

Wasfy burst out laughing. "This she-donkey kicks. She'll have to be trained, Hamadia. But I'll build her a big house. I'll give her silk clothes and gold jewelry. If she wants a maid, I'll get her a maid."

Hamadia was taken by the fantasy. "Only munificent Allah above and you down here will get us out of this hole." Then she reflected and added mournfully, "You're making fun of us,

Wasfy. You're deceiving two gullible women. Where you are, over with the Jews, they allow only one wife—and you're married."

"Who mentioned anything about the Jews? Can't I build a home here? Is there no land? Is there no stone? The money will be in your hands, Hamadia, and everything will be registered in your name and in the name of this bitch," he added affectionately.

As his fancies grew, his lust stirred, then raged. Under the blanket he felt the girl's body relax.

"May Allah hear your words," Hamadia murmured.

The darkness was dense with the dreams of starving people. Now Wasfy's groping hand met no real resistance. He was dumbfounded by the texture of the girl's delicate limbs, but he had to keep speaking so as not to arouse her mother's suspicions. "You're both going to leave this damned camp," he said. "Over on the outskirts of the city, on that pretty road going up to Nablus, a nice piece of land can be bought . . ."

From the depths of the camp there came a scream like the moaning of the wind.

Wasfy's rough fingers froze on the girl's delicate flesh. She leapt to her feet. "Abu Uleka has murdered his son-in-law, Samih," she cried.

"You're staying in the house," her mother cried. "Don't you dare budge from here."

Outside, someone passed by, barefooted. A door slammed. Namir's tense, boyish voice cut through the darkness: "Uncle Wasfy, Samih's been finished off, may Allah have mercy on him. I'm guarding your car."

"Good, my son, good," Wasfy answered dispiritedly. "Light the lamp, Hamadia." As if the light could help him extricate himself from this web he'd been thrown into.

In the light of the burning wick Hamadia's face shone forth, framed by her dark hair. Her eyes were dim. The big house, the silken clothes and the gold had vanished as all dreams do.

Only the filth remained. "My dear," she pleaded with Wasfy, "get up, flee. You don't belong here."

He had already grabbed his packet of cigarettes and his matches. "Flee? Why?"

"Because around here, it's murder and no questions asked. The Jewish police will come around and ask what a stranger from Israel with a car like yours is up to in the camp."

"Am I a stranger, then, Hamadia? A stranger already?"

"In their eyes you are. They'll forget about the murderer and the dead man and the whole camp will talk only about Hamadia and the man who slept in her house while her sons slept outside."

"You're my brother's wife, Hamadia."

"Will you stand before my brothers and tell them that, when they come rushing up here from Jericho? They'll come with pistols, and if not pistols, then axes. Get up, my dear, get up and flee."

Wasfy had already figured how he might beat a hasty retreat. He'd drive to that dentist's house where Fatkhi was staying. But until Sunday morning it was impossible to return to Kfar Mandah. The Jews had blocked off the West Bank roads until the end of Yom Kippur. He lit a cigarette and studied the silent Hamadia. "I'm staying here."

"What a hero!" Amal puffed up her cheeks. Her curiosity was aroused. "Aren't you afraid? They'll come and get you . . ."

Wasfy ignored the girl's teasing and turned to her mother. "You don't know the Israeli police. If I flee, that's when they'd start looking for me and get me. They'd get me even if I were a bird in the sky. It's better to stay where I am."

"They arrest people for less serious things."

"Let them arrest me. They won't eat me."

Hamadia shook her head with relief. "Admit it, my dear: You're one of them, you're hand in glove with them, you're partners with them. That's why you're not afraid."

"And the killer?" he asked, ignoring the obvious innuendoes.

Hamadia sat up cross-legged, her dress falling in a dark circle around her. "What about him?"

"He shoots, he kills, and that's that?"

"It's poor Samih's bad luck. This Abu Uleka is very cruel. He'll sleep in the camp tonight and before dawn he'll pick up and go."

"What's happening here, Hamadia?"

"No one's heard, no one's seen. If he asks they'll give him a place to hide. With us, no one goes looking for trouble. It comes by itself."

"What a world!" Wasfy groaned.

Hamadia nodded. "I can see that the Jews have spoiled you all."

"You can't just go and kill like that," the man protested.

"Why not? If you're strong and you've got a gun in your hand and people bow down before you, what reason have you got to be afraid?"

Wasfy thought aloud, "He's liable to come and order me to help him escape in my car. He'd have the gall to do that."

Amal revived. "Yes, that's right! Mother, Abu Uleka might very well come around with a pistol and order Uncle Wasfy to be his driver."

"This is what he'll get from me!" Wasfy raised his middle finger in the air.

The girl burst out laughing. "We'll see," she said.

"Amal!" her mother warned her.

Wasfy got to his feet. "Namir! Said!" he cried. "Come, come into the house. From now on I'm guarding the car."

Namir was upset. "And the money?"

"You'll both get it, you'll get it. I won't rob you of your wages, my sons."

He picked up a stool, went outside and sat on it, resting his feet on the Buick's front bumper. There was shouting in the refugee huts around him, but the doors remained shut. A wolf was on the prowl in the alleyways and no one wished to meet him. The bumper gleaming in the starlight gave Wasfy confidence. He blew his nose and said to himself, I'm the only one outdoors. The only one. The idea worked on him like magic—he gained stature in his own eyes. The only one!

"Good evening!"

Wasfy was terribly frightened—it seemed to him that the stranger's voice had come from right under his feet. The man had stealthily approached and crouched beside him without Wasfy's noticing. "You're Abu Uleka," Wasfy whispered, dry-mouthed. A terrifying thought passed through his mind: Hamadia and Amal and Namir with his knife had heard the stranger's voice, yet the door to their hut remained closed. The stranger might murder him, and not one of those vipers, to whom he had been so generous, would lift a finger to help him.

The stranger's laugh sounded like a grunt to Wasfy. The man struck a match and held it up to his face. "Do I look like Abu what's-his-name?"

Wasfy saw a shock of black hair, a narrow forehead, very thin mustache and flashing teeth. "No, you're too young to be Abu Uleka." But he didn't relax. Something about the young man's appearance, especially his grin, was not to Wasfy's liking. But for the sake of politeness he offered a cigarette to the stranger.

The young man lit up and exhaled, then crushed the cigarette between his nimble fingers. "An American car," he said. "One of the best. It's obvious you've got the best of everything."

Now Wasfy detested this impudent young man. "You work and you sweat," he moralized, "and you make it. Yes, you make it!"

"There are those who sweat and those who are called upon to spill their blood." This young man had all the right answers. "By the way," he added, touching the tip of his foot to a tire, "this is American, too."

"Ah!" Wasfy groaned. Now he wanted to get rid of the young man as quickly as possible.

"I'll bet it cost a fortune."

"Fortune's not the word."

"So what is?" the young man coaxed him. "Tell me. Maybe I'll understand." It was enough to hear his voice to know he was grinning.

"Listen, kid. To a guy growing up in this dung heap, what's the difference between fifty thousand and a hundred thousand? I could just as well tell you a million." Wasfy's patience with his uninvited guest was growing short. He fished out three cigarettes from the pack and sputtered, "Take them and get lost."

The young man ignored the cigarettes. "A million," he mused out loud. "You're exaggerating, my friend. Really, I'd be sorry if she were worth a million. Fifty thousand—okay. A hundred thousand—it's possible. But a million?"

In the dark Wasfy saw that the young man, while speaking casually, was taking various objects from his pocket and arranging them in the dust between his legs. "What's this?" Wasfy asked.

"A bomb," the young man explained in a soft voice. "A simple incendiary device. I'm going to burn your car, my friend."

Wasfy was suddenly dizzy, but in spite of this he shouted, "You're crazy!" And he even reached out toward the objects that the young man was arranging in the dust.

The young man, grinning broadly, gave Wasfy's hand a sharp smack, as if he were a child about to touch toys that were not his. "If I were crazy, would I have been able to tell the difference between a million and fifty thousand, my friend?"

"Why are you planning to burn my car?"

"Orders are orders. That's what they told me, my friend, very clearly. Go burn that Jewish car that came into the camp."

"Idiots! Damned idiots! Jewish car! What are you talking about? The car's mine, every nut and bolt is mine. I paid a fat bundle for it. Allah's curse be on all of you. . . ."

The young man seemed surprised. "And we were so sure that it belonged to the Jews."

"Why?" Wasfy shouted.

"What we say, and of course we're right, is that the Jews rob the Arabs of everything. They take an Arab and leave him naked and barefoot. They even steal the land from under his feet. They wreck his house and put a cane in his hand and tell him to hit the road. That's how every one of the refugee camps came to be. So here comes an Arab, cruising into camp in his toy palace, with the warm fragrance of broiled meat and fish coming from inside. Money flies right and left. My dear brother, only a Jew with a Jewish brain could behave in such a vulgar way. It's like a cheap propaganda movie that tries to show how good the Arabs have it over there in Israel. Try to put yourself in our place and think as we do: Isn't this Arab a Jewish agent? He was even cunning enough to leave children in the car, since he knew that the children are our flesh and blood and we would never hurt them. See for yourself—everything planned in advance."

"Nonsense, nonsense," Wasfy mumbled.

"Stop your tricks," the young man warned him good-humoredly. He was arranging his things in a neat row, making Wasfy more anxious than ever.

"But this car is mine, I swear to you on my father's grave. Wait. Wait here a minute," he cried, getting to his feet.

The young man caught him by the shirt and sat him firmly back down beside him. "Where are you going?"

"I wanted to show you the papers."

"The Jews are experts at forging papers. On paper they can prove to you that the air you're breathing belongs to them."

"How can I convince you?"

The young man deigned to take a cigarette from the packet,

which had fallen to the ground. "Very simple," he said. "Just tell me what the car is really worth, and stop messing around."

"How will that help me?"

"It will help us to figure the percentages, according to the value."

"Percentages, value!" Wasfy shouted. "What is this, an insurance company?"

The young man burst out laughing. He slapped himself on the thigh and then slapped Wasfy on the shoulder. Despite the strange circumstances of their meeting and their different outlooks, it seemed that the young man had taken a liking to Wasfy. "You're really something," he marveled. "An insurance company! Allah! No wonder you've made it like you have. You've got a sharp brain working in that head of yours."

Wasfy was still agitated. The young man had not yet drawn in his claws; Wasfy was still in danger. But his initial alarm had passed, and with it the urge to appease his antagonist by truckling to him. "What do you want?" he asked impatiently.

"Like you said, we're a kind of insurance company. The difference is this: Anyone who hasn't been favored by Allah with the intelligence to insure his goods with us, gets them burned on the spot."

"How much do you want?"

"Now you're talking like a man!" the young man said. "How much is the car worth?"

"It's used."

"Yes, that's obvious," the young man agreed.

"It's in hopeless shape," Wasfy exaggerated.

"Don't overdo it," the young man warned him.

They were both glowing from the pleasure of bargaining. Wasfy slapped the gleaming bumper. "By Allah, these American cars are like rich old broads. You understand. With every year that goes by they lose half their value."

"How old is she?" the young man inquired, absolutely understanding.

"Three, three and a half."

The young man clicked his tongue in surprise. "Tsk! Tsk! Tsk! And I thought she was almost a virgin."

"That's because I take care of her devotedly, like a jealous husband."

"Sixty thousand, then," the young man blurted.

"What? All you see is the new paint job. The carburetor's shot already. The tires are worn. At the most," he pursed his lips scornfully, "at the most, twenty thousand."

"You're pulling my leg," the young man said, scolding him affectionately. "Just look at her—she's a beauty."

"Have you ever seen old millionaire women? From a distance, they always look like beauties. But have you ever tried sleeping with them?"

The young man became tense around the mouth. "Have you?"

Wasfy looked knowing.

The young man took the hint. "Oh, come on!" he pleaded.

"In Tel Aviv," Wasfy began with great reluctance "there's a street parallel to the sea with one hotel after another. One afternoon I go there in this," he indicated the car, "and I park it and walk down to the water. I come back up about the time the sun is setting into the sea, twilight. I go up to the door of the car and suddenly I hear something like a cat screeching. Well, inside the car was this broad with blonde hair down to her ass. She was sitting there in sunglasses, in the dark. The glasses rested on her cute little nose, she was smiling, and I could see the pearly teeth between her rosy lips."

"Yes, yes," the young man said, growing excited. He reached for Wasfy's cigarettes.

"Wasfy, I said to myself, this whore's going to cost you a fortune. But so what? A chance like this comes once in a lifetime. I put my hand on the door handle and she started screaming again. And then I realized that she wasn't a whore and she wasn't sitting in my car."

"I don't get it."

"She was sitting in a car that looked just like mine. What am I saying, looked like? A real twin. I explained things to her and calmed her down. She understood, even though she spoke English and I spoke half-Arabic, half-Hebrew. The only English yours truly knows is *yes*, *no*, and *pleez*. But it seems that was enough for her. She came over to my car and we went to The Caliph."

"What's that?" The young man did not want to miss the slightest detail.

"That's a nightclub where the broads dance on stage with their tits and ass hanging out. We drink, and then we dance. What a body! And how she danced later, too, on her bed in a hotel room, with all the lights turned down low. What a night. . . . " He licked his lips. "What a night. . . . Comes the morning, I open my eyes and what do I see?"

"What?"

"Have you ever seen olive skins after all the oil's been squeezed out of them in the press? They look the same, but man, the stench! And the whore wants more! Before breakfast, no less. Well, yours truly put his hand over what was left between his legs and took off like the devil was after him. . . . "

"Tsk! Tsk! Tsk! Forty thousand, then."

"What do you mean?" Wasfy shouted.

"Based on one percent of forty thousand, you'll have to pay only four hundred pounds."

Deep in his heart Wasfy had already accepted his fate. But he was still curious. "Where does it go?"

"To the Palestinian revolution."

"Talk sense, man. I don't understand such things."

"With this we buy weapons, pay our fighters, and, if they fall in battle, compensate their widows and orphans."

"I'll give you a check."

This angered the young man. "And maybe you want a receipt for income tax?"

"Man, I don't have much cash."

"I believe you," the young man said.

"So you'll take a check?"

"Forget it. We're not idiots. Do you think we'd put our heads into such a stupid trap?"

"What then?"

"Give the check to Hamadia. Make it out in her name. And it'll be too bad for you if . . ."

"Man!" Wasfy interrupted. "I'm a poker player. I know how to lose."

"You're a man," the young man complimented him, getting to his feet. "I knew right away that you were a man. I hope you'll visit us again."

"With cash in hand."

The young man smiled. "Don't be sore."

"I don't like being screwed like this."

"Don't complain, man. You made a good deal."

The world being what it was, Wasfy knew that the young man was right. "Take the cigarettes," he said.

The young man vanished in the darkness. A thoughtful smile played over Wasfy's lips. But he burst into the hut raging mad. "Hamadia, they've robbed me!"

"But how, my dear?"

Amal smiled cunningly. Wasfy grabbed her under the arms, his thumbs pressing cruelly into her breasts, his fingers wrapped around her back. He nearly lifted her from the floor. "Daughter of the devil!" he shouted. "You know that wretch who robbed me."

"Let the girl go," her mother howled. "She's not the guilty one. It was Sabri. He's asked me twice for her hand and I'm still considering."

"I'll kill him, by Allah. I'll kill him."

The girl gazed at him for a long time.

Her mother sighed. "What for? They're doomed anyway. The Jews wipe them out, one by one. They walk among the living with death carved on their foreheads. Why should you soil your hands with his blood, my dear? He'll die soon enough anyway, and no one will even know where he lies."

"That's what they deserve."

"And the check?" Amal said.

"You're his accomplice, you bitch!" Wasfy shouted.

"You're mistaken, brother," her mother said, appealing to him. "You gave your word, and it would be best to pay. They'll make trouble for us. They'll look for you even over among the Jews, over there, and they'll find you."

"This visit has already cost me a fortune," the guest grumbled. "Can we finally sleep now, like human beings?"

"Here's your mattress, my dear, you've got it all to yourself."

"Uncle Wasfy," Namir said, "should we go out again to guard the car?"

"No, there's no need. Go to sleep, damn it!"

And he turned toward the wide mattress. Hamadia stretched out close to her daughter. The kerosene lamp went out and Wasfy snored.

6

In her house optimism was a kind of ideological obligation, yet Abla lived in a compromise with the opposite principle: Eat and drink today, for tomorrow . . . Her childhood had been wasted in the outcast refugee camp. Growing up, she had borne heavy burdens—her homeliness and her fate as a refugee. And yet, ever since girlhood, she had won most of her gambles. She had set her sights on becoming a teacher in the girls' secondary school, because she knew that there she could reach the limit of her abilities without prejudicing her reputation as an Arab woman. It was a crazy dream for a girl from an uprooted family, but she made it come true. Her most successful gamble had been her choice of the impoverished Magid, against her family's fierce objections. About a week after the engagement he went off to Lebanon to study dentistry. Her mother cursed, her friends browbeat her. His letters became more and more infrequent, but Abla kept sending him money that she set aside from her salary every month. Her father was beside himself. "Isn't it enough that we didn't get a bride-price from him, not a single penny? On top of that you have to support him while he plays in the bordellos of Beirut?"

Her parents pleaded with her to break the engagement. They went to Nablus and brought back Uncle Gamal, a notable. He entered their refugee hut, not bothering to conceal his disgust at the stench and the dirt. He had to hurry back to his stone villa in Nablus that same day, but before he left he ordered Abla to accede to Aziz's urgent suit. Aziz had come especially from Kuwait to take a wife. Hearing this bachelor describe his car and his apartment, where the air conditioner hummed day and night, made Abla's family drool. Her highly respected Uncle Gamal could not understand her obstinacy. Terrible suspicions stirred her father's heart. One night he caught her in their hut. Abla stood in the corner, staring at the iron bar which, in his fury, her father had snatched up in the courtyard. He threatened her. The tip of the bar, stained with dirt, was pointed at her chest—it flashed like a spear in the light of the kerosene lamp.

"I'll kill you," he screamed.

She turned pale but didn't believe it. He loves her, he's proud of her. Her two older brothers are a shameful disappointment to him, one a gambler, the other a thief. And his other children are still young, midgets with enormous appetites. Standing in the murky corner of the hut, she was filled with compassion. "*Baba,*" she said, keeping her eyes fixed on the bar, "don't excite yourself . . . your heart, *ya baba.*"

Tears of frustration and shame gathered in her father's tender eyes. "I should have a heart attack right now—it would be a relief." The heavy bar trembled in his hand. "Abla, I'll dig my grave here with my own hands. I'd rather die than listen to what all the snakes around here are whispering."

She didn't dare touch him. She only touched the clods of earth on the tip of the menacing bar. For the first time since she was a young girl, she looked straight at him with her clear eyes. "What are they saying about me, *ya baba?*"

"Why do you reject Aziz?"

"I'm engaged to Magid."

"Magid! He threw a ring on your finger and then disappeared. He's a shadow that's slipped away, my daughter. Aziz offers you a roof over your head and a life of plenty."

"I'll wait for Magid."

The bar rose again over her head. "What has Magid done to you?"

She was astonished. "What could he do?"

"Are you still a virgin, Abla? Maybe he took your virginity, and you're afraid of another man discovering your shame."

"Mother!" Abla cried out in distress.

"*Ya boie!*" came her mother's answering wail.

Abla's eyes flashed. Her compassion for her father vanished. "Come," she said. "I've got five dinars here. Take me to Doctor Adib Al-Ashkar and he'll examine me." She raised her hands to her face and wept. "Tomorrow, *baba*, you'll follow my coffin proudly. After we come back from the doctor I'll kill myself, *baba*."

The gossip around the camp ceased. Samira, the old woman who lived opposite them, concluded, "That damned Magid slipped her a love potion and bewitched her. The poor girl's hopelessly infatuated with him."

But Abla, at eighteen, knew that this was no pure love affair. She was inclined to be a rebel, not a romantic. Magid had kissed her only twice—his unschooled lips touched her temple once before the engagement, and after it those same bashful lips had once grazed her expectant mouth. Nevertheless, guided by common sense, she decided that Magid was meant for her. And so it was. She never reminded him of the money that she sent him, month after month on the wings of the wind to a strange fog-enshrouded land, because she was sure when she did it that she was investing in her future. She never told him—neither in the heat of quarrels nor in the languid aftermath of lovemaking—about the iron bar that had threatened to crush her chest. While he was still in Beirut, she had already sketched out his shingle in her imagination, and built herself a villa and visualized him sitting in the clinic, his patients fearfully clenching their jaws. Bit by bit she planned their life together, down to the most routine matters. At the same time, she learned to take pleasure from what was at hand. And now that she and Magid were surrounded by flowerbeds of dreams come true, she was afraid of a tempest that could destroy everything. Magid was a Party man, and she was just as active as he. They were in danger of expulsion from their house and their homeland. In her role as mistress of the house, Abla carefully saw to it that this threat did not dampen everyday joys and pleasures, nor deprive the family of its comforts. Even the refugee maid who lived in their house was dressed in Abla's hand-me-downs.

Now, with supper over, the children vanished to their rooms and she and Magid and Fatkhi went to the living room, where Ibitsam, the maid, served coffee. The tension between the poet and Abla had eased. Once more Abla was the female showing deference for his poetry and his manly charm. Fatkhi knew his weakness. Other poets became addicted to drugs or sought their salvation in drink. Fatkhi couldn't live without adulation. He was a declamatory poet, a poet of the stage—his poems were not meant for the printed page or anthologies of verse. Adoring looks, applause, and cheers were his reward and his inspiration.

Outside the open window, night was falling over the town. The chandelier in the living room cast a soft light. The last bus had long since departed Jenin. The road to Nablus was lost in the dark horizon. The coffee houses emptied. A dog barked. The sky scattered a myriad of stars over the pale stone houses, and someone in the main street cried as if trying to embrace the whole universe, "Allah be exalted and glorified!"

Fatkhi took the gilded cup from the tray that the maid held out. Her dark brown skin was flushed, her head bent. Suddenly Fatkhi realized that from the moment the Buick had come honking into town that morning, this maid was the one and only creature to have viewed him with respect. He wanted to repay her, but in Abla's presence he didn't dare flirt with another female, especially a younger one. But he did smile. He smiled at the chandelier, at the coffee, at the open window, and at the road from which there arose on this Yom Kippur eve only Arab voices and Arab smells. A house like this was what Fatkhi yearned for and, at that moment, realized he would never have. A house, a home, is first and foremost a wife. Hiam, despite her beauty, despite her latent, virginal ardor, would remain an adolescent peasant girl even at sixty. Her intelligence was limited, her manners as crude as Wasfy's. Fatkhi would have an obedient slave, not a spouse. Daphna, the *sabra* student from Tel Aviv, was more like Abla. But this student was as Jewish from head to toe as Abla was Arab. Both of them, like palm trees, would only blossom and give forth fruit in their natural surroundings. Fatkhi had been in love with Daphna before his engagement and was still in love with her. He knew that she also loved him, but she thought of him as a sort of malady that overcame her, from which she expected one day to recover. She didn't want to marry an Arab who refused to covert to Judaism, anymore than Abla would allow the air conditioner owner to drag her off to Kuwait.

Fatkhi hadn't come across any Israeli Arab women as promising as Abla and Daphna. In spite of his childish, petty urge to screw Wasfy by marrying his sister, Fatkhi had looked for someone else. For years he diligently searched for an Israeli Abla or an Arab Daphna. Twice he found what he was looking for—or almost. Once at the University of Haifa, once at the Workers' Bank in Nazareth. But both girls were Christian. And he wanted to be an Arab poet. He needed a Muslim woman.

"Boo!" Abla cried boisterously, right into his face.

He looked up at her, and, seeing her mustache bristling, he laughed with embarrassment.

"Do you compose poems even here?" she said.

"Excuse me," he said.

Magid came to his defense. "He must be dreaming of his fiancée."

"Look who's talking," Abla cried. "Since when are you an expert on dreams about women?"

Magid, shy when it came to women, took off his glasses and polished them with his handkerchief. He blinked and stammered, "In Beirut I had plenty of time to become an expert."

Abla applauded. "Bravo! Bravo!"

Her voice merged into the ringing of the doorbell.

Magid was surprised: "That can't be Zuheir. But he said he'd come . . ."

He did not finish the sentence. The ringing continued without letting up, beating on their temples. The hand pressing on the button outside was unrelenting. Fatkhi was seized by a spasm of nervousness. Abla nearly screamed. Her mouth opened so wide that her mustache disappeared. "What's happening?" she cried.

Magid put his glasses back on his nose. As the ringing persisted, he heard Ibitsam's footsteps on the stairs and shouted at her, "Wait there!" To his wife and the poet he whispered, "It must be the Jews."

Despite his pallor and the knocking of his knees, the dentist got to his feet and steadied himself with imposing dignity, as if he were being observed by dozens of strange and hostile eyes. He approached the door. "Who's there?" he cried, managing to conquer his fear.

"Open up! Open up at once!" came the urgent reply in Arabic.

Abla and the poet glanced at one another, puzzled. What they had heard was the terrified cry of a man running for his life. Despite the fear that permeated it, the voice clearly carried authority and the presumption of obedience. They heard voices and froze. The door creaked open cautiously, and there came the tramp of boots in the entrance hall. A thick voice was heard, the quick sound of metal, a deep groan. The door was slammed so violently that its frame shook. Again the tramping on the floor, and someone who could never learn to whisper said loudly, "Careful! Careful, I tell you . . ." And then that same voice, miraculously tender, addressed someone else. "Patience, a little patience, my friend. With Allah's help everything will be all right."

As Abla and the poet watched, a strange procession made its way past the living room door. At its head walked Magid, safe and sound, leading a group behind him in the dark. Now and again he turned around to give directions. After him came the outline of a heavy figure, dressed in a coat despite the warm night, stooping forward and walking backward, a wounded man, a giant Negro. A thin red trail was drawn on the tiles in the wake of this procession. When the group reached the room near the kitchen, Magid was heard to plead, "Gentlemen, dear friends, what do I know about such things?"

The voice that couldn't whisper ordered, "Do what you can. But do it well and quickly."

Suddenly the black giant appeared in the living room doorway. He appraised Abla and the poet with a crushing, contemptuous look. Then they heard him carefully open the outside door, stand for a moment in watchful silence, then ease the door shut. He returned to the living room with a pistol in his hand. Abla did not know him.

"What happened to him?" she asked, pointing at the room next to the kitchen.

The black man glanced at the poet, amazed that it was the woman who posed the question. "Something," he said.

"You don't need that pistol in this house," Abla said coolly.

The black man was sufficiently astounded by her brazenness to ask, "Have you got an understanding with the Jews, woman?"

Realizing that the weapon was meant for imminent danger from outside, not for them, Abla relaxed a little and even allowed herself a shudder. She appealed again to the man. "My husband can't help you much with such a serious case."

"Your husband?" he said sharply.

"Yes."

"And who's this?" The black man pointed at the poet with his pistol.

"A guest."

"A guest," he repeated, as if trying to find a hidden meaning in the word. "Where does he come from?"

Abla realized that she had gone as far as she could. She sat there, sweating. "A guest. It's not important."

"I asked where from!"

"From Israel," she murmured.

The muzzle of the pistol rose toward the poet's head and the black man shouted, "Abu Yusef! Abu Yusef!"

The man in the coat came quickly, pistol drawn, his watchful eyes seeking the source of the trouble. He asked no questions, waiting for an explanation.

The black man pointed with his pistol. "This one's from Israel."

"Get up!" Abu Yusef ordered.

The poet got up out of the armchair, his mind in turmoil. Facing the cocked pistol, he smiled and said, "I am an Arab," happy for the first time in his life to say he was an Arab.

Abu Yusef ignored the poet's smile and turned politely to Abla. "Ma'am, I know your husband and trust him. But who is this?"

"No need to be afraid," she answered, straining to master her trembling jaw. "This is Fatkhi, a well-known Communist poet."

Magid's glasses flickered over Abu Yusef's shoulder. "What's happening here? What are these pistols?"

Abu Yusef turned sharply. "You get back to him, right now!"

Magid closed his eyes behind his glasses, shook his head, and said, "He's dead."

Abu Yusef would not believe it. With his pistol he indicated to the black man that he should keep an eye on the poet; then he hurried to the next room. When he returned his face was wracked with anger. "Why?" he asked.

Though the situation was complicated and his fate unclear, the poet was moved by the sorrow and pain on Abu Yusef's twisted face. "Your brother?" he asked.

"More!" Abu Yusef hissed. He turned to Magid and asked again, accusingly, "Why?"

Magid spread his arms out helplessly. "You brought him too late. I don't understand such things. An operation might have saved him."

The poet had a foolish thought. Jewish doctors operated on Israeli soldiers, saving many lives. He would read about this in the newspapers, and reflect on the paradox—they cut into the flesh in order to save it. "Don't you have a surgeon here?" he asked in a sympathetic voice.

"A surgeon," the man growled contemptuously. "It is obvious you come from Israel." And he turned to Magid with renewed anger. "I turn my back for a moment, and he gives up the ghost. How?"

"Understand me, man. He was dying when you brought him."

"All the way he was trying to say something," Abu Yusef mused out loud. "I felt he wanted to say something important and I made him shut up. And now he's dead."

"I think I heard what he wanted to say," Magid whispered.

"What did he say?" Abu Yusef looked at him, his eyes filmed with tears.

"Abu Uleka. Does the name mean anything to you?"

"Yes! Yes!"

"He said that Abu Uleka must be punished."

"Is that what he wanted?"

"That's what he said."

"That was his dying wish," Abu Yusef cried with relief, as if this information could salvage something of the dead man.

"Abu Uleka," the black man reflected. "What had he to do with Abu Uleka?"

"Plenty!" Abu Yusef said emphatically, as if afraid that the dead man's memory might be lost or blotted out. "Tonight, in the camp, Abu Uleka betrayed the revolution and murdered a hero."

"We are Allah's and to Allah we return!" the dentist cried bitterly. "Are you all drunk, or are you crazy?"

"No," Abu Yusef said, adopting an explanatory tone. "Ziad was hurt in an accident. But everything mattered to him. His wish will be carried out. It will be carried out before daybreak." Abu Yusef's gaze fell on the poet. He thought silently for a long while, and then ordered Magid, "Tell him to leave the room. And he's forbidden to leave this house without permission."

"Anyhow, he's got nowhere to go at this time of the night. He's our guest, and he'll go up to his room."

The poet sat at the foot of the bed on the top floor and smoked. He was now an accomplice in the eyes of the Israeli law. An accomplice, on account of his presence in this house and the things he has seen and heard. If Israeli soldiers come bursting in, he'll be arrested along with the others. There'll be an uproar in the Hebrew newspapers and teeth gnashed in the Party. He was here in clear violation of Party orders, but despite that the Party would be obliged to defend him.

He smiled bitterly. In spite of everything they did not want him downstairs. On the contrary, they suspected him. They threw him out unceremoniously, they wanted him to have no part in what was happening. He heard their footsteps, and Abu Yusef's voice speaking authoritatively. The dentist too was speaking, in an angry, critical tone; but the poet could not make out what they were saying and didn't know whether they were discussing what was to be done with him or how to dispose of the body.

Once more he reflected on his situation. He was a material witness. He had even heard the commanding officer's name. What if Abu Yusef came upstairs now and asked him just one question? What would he say if this officer demanded an immediate decision on his part—are you with us or are you going to make trouble for us? They wouldn't let him go just like that, carrying their secret with him; he already posed a threat to their lives.

Are you ready to carry a weapon, to kill?

I'm ready.

You're ready to kill anyone, whether you know him or not, if your superiors order you to?

I know . . . I don't think . . . What do you mean?

You'll be told, go to such-and-such a place and kill so-and-so.

Anyone?

Man, you can't ask questions.

Even Marduch and his wife and their retarded son?

Who are they?

Israelis, friends of mine.

Jews?

Yes . . . Jews. But they're fierce defenders of the Arabs.

Jews!

I told you. They're Jews of an entirely different sort.

There's only one kind of Jew. They all sit on land that's been plundered from the Arabs. This Marduch and his wife—do they hover in the air, or do they walk on stolen land, land which is not theirs?

You can't put things like that.

The revolution puts its principles clearly. When you're firing a gun there's no room for fine distinctions. Any doubt at all just serves the enemy.

Marduch isn't the enemy.

Can he bear arms?

Yes. Actually, he serves in the Israeli army at least one month a year.

He fights in the ranks of the Jewish army.

Yes, when he is mobilized. He's a soldier and must obey orders.

You mean he obeys orders that compel him to kill Arabs. And you, an Arab, are afraid of hurting Jews.

I meant Marduch and his family.

Traitor!

Don't throw accusations around! It's true that I've never held a gun in my hand, but I've fought for the Palestinian cause for many years, right in the enemy's stronghold, while you loafed in coffee houses and played cards.

What have you done?

I've written poems.

How many Jews have you killed with your poems?

You're stupid.

Get ready, boy.

You're talking nonsense.

You're going to die.

Idiots! I've got many more poems to write yet. Wait! Do you imagine that the revolution doesn't need poets? What a bunch of numbskulls. Since when does a poet have to carry a gun?

It's nothing new, sweetheart. Antar did it before the advent of Islam.

I'm not Antar.

You're a Zionist worm. The Jews have robbed you of your manhood. *Ya Allah*! If I were you I'd be glad to have done with such a demeaning life.

There was a soft knock at the door.

The poet trembled but girded up his remaining courage and got to his feet. He didn't want to die sitting down. He'd face them on his feet. With great dignity he said, "Please come in."

Ibitsam's young body slipped into the room. She blushed and paled by turns as she stood before him. She was barefoot, dressed in one of Abla's hand-me-downs. The top three buttons were undone, revealing a rigid, plum-dark nipple. "Oh my friend," she murmured, "a man's died downstairs."

At the sight of her nipple and the fear in her eyes, the poet's own fear and turmoil abated. "You should be ashamed of yourself, girl."

"This is the first time I've been in a house where there's a dead person. And he's been murdered. I saw the blood from the stairs, so I came to you, sir. I was afraid to go back to bed in the childrens' room." She was having a hard time stopping the flow of words. She came closer to him, looking into his eyes. As she swung her arm to indicate the horror downstairs, she happened to uncover her brown breast with its dark upstanding nipple. She kept approaching, talking all the while, until it seemed to the poet that she meant to pass right through him and disappear somewhere behind his back. Beads of sweat glistened on her forehead; he felt her breath on his face—in another moment she would be upon him. Compelled to bar the way, Fatkhi put out his hand in self-defense, and his palm came to rest on her naked breast.

The girl started backward, panic in her eyes. She sobbed softly. "*Ya boie. . . . Ya boie. . . .* What have you done?"

The poet was ashamed.

"*Ya boie. . . . Ya boie. . . .* Are you like that?"

Fatkhi returned to the bed and put his face in his hands. He shook his head and murmured, "Forgive me, really, forgive me." He looked up, trying to convince the girl that he was sincerely sorry, but she had already disappeared from the room. For a moment he wondered whether his senses might have deceived him—perhaps Ibitsam hadn't been in the room at all. He put his hand to his nose, the hand that had touched her breast, and smelled an odor of thyme and sweat.

He got to his feet and turned off the light. Standing in darkness, he studied the street, placid under a starry sky. Zuheir, the poet cried to himself, Zuheir you mustn't meet those armed strangers downstairs. What a mix-up, what a mix-up. . . . He was sorry for what he had done. He should have mastered the perverse mood that had come upon him and returned to Israel. This was a senseless, stupid trip. He had come to find his roots, and instead he was learning by degrees how much of a stranger he was here. And by this fruitless trip he was liable to bring new tragedy down on Zuheir, who had already experienced more than his share of trouble. Zuheir had been released from prison just two months earlier, having served four years. He had been just skin and bone when he entered the Israeli prison. First the English had drained his vitality; after that the Jordanians crushed him and sent him to the desert for ten years. When he was brought into the military court, even the Israeli officers shrank from the sight of this broken creature who spoke in a cracked voice. What the man urgently needed was a nursing home. He had no teeth, his hair was white, his veins as gnarled as the trunk of an ancient olive tree. The courtroom buzzed at the sight of this old man, forced to stand for long periods on his feeble legs. The military judges were astonished to learn that he was not even forty years of age. Everyone was certain that he would be released on probation or fined. It seemed that even the judges agreed. They put their first questions to him gently. But then that Jewish woman, selected by some idiot in the Party to defend Zuheir, leapt to her feet. She saw Zuheir as a banner, not as a man on the verge of collapse. With female fury she wrapped herself in this banner and assailed the judges until she made them furious, too. She rejoiced in her victory. The courtroom became a battlefield. Slogans, insults, cheers. The woman panted; there was huge applause. Zuheir, crushed, was sent to prison for another four years for handing out leaflets—an irrelevant sentence so far as the woman lawyer was concerned. The important thing was that once again she had denounced the occupation and the army.

Now, thanks to the poet, Zuheir was in danger again, this time immeasurably more serious danger. Fatkhi stood beside the window, praying: Don't come now. Break a leg and don't come; don't come until they leave. . . .

But now, through the open window, he saw two men leave the house, supporting a third between them. A car was waiting and they disappeared into it and drove toward the center of town. Fatkhi was about to run downstairs. He thought they had taken Magid hostage and left Abla with the dead man. Just then he heard Abla's voice. "What if they catch them?"

The answer came, not from the dead man, but from Magid himself. "All the Jews have vanished from the streets on account of their fast. The town is all clear."

Fatkhi went downstairs. In the hallway he saw Ibitsam bent over the floor, scrubbing the blood from it. The water was turning red in the bucket, and she was so disturbed as she dipped the rag into it that she didn't notice him. He passed behind her on tiptoe and entered the living room. Abla was gloomy. "I'll get you a sleeping pill," Magid said to her.

"What for?" she growled.

The dentist shrugged.

"Ibitsam," Abla called. "Ibitsam, where have you gone to?"

"Here I am, ma'am," the girl answered in a shaky voice.

"Have you gone to sleep, by the grace of God?"

"No, ma'am."

"Come here."

The girl stood before them, her hands dripping with water. "Yes, ma'am." She was close to fainting—she could hardly speak.

"What are you doing?"

Ibitsam stood staring at her mistress, trying to overcome her nausea. "I'm . . . I'm cleaning up."

"Have you seen a ghost?" Abla spoke roughly to her. "Who woke you up and pulled you from your bed? Why did you get up to clean in the middle of the night?"

"She's washing the floor," Magid explained cautiously.

"Blood!" Ibitsam screamed.

Abla supressed a terrified shriek. "Allah protect us!" she whispered.

"Did you want something from her?" Magid asked.

"I wanted a little tea. But with the dead man's blood on her hands . . . leave us, my child."

Ibitsam stayed rooted in the doorway and didn't move. Her hands had ceased dripping. She searched out the poet's eyes and mutely pleaded with him. "I'm afraid," she said, glancing in terror over her shoulder toward the hallway. "I'm dying of fright."

Magid took pity on her. "Come, my daughter, come. I'll stand by you. Finish what you're doing right away. Afterward you can come and sit with us. There's nothing to be afraid of, my daughter. You see, there are two men here."

Her gaze left the poet. With her eyes glued to Magid's glasses, she went out with him to the hallway.

"What luck that Zuheir didn't arrive while they were here," the poet said, dropping into a soft armchair.

"Zuheir?" Abla said, stunned and uncomprehending.

"It's turned out all right," he tried to reassure her.

The woman made a sweeping gesture about the living room with her bare arm. "Does this house please you?" she shouted.

The poet was repelled by hysterical women. He hated disruptive emotions. During his childhood in the village, he had seen women going out of their minds, quarrelling noisily. But only when he moved to Tel Aviv did he meet up with true hysteria. He would not have imagined that Abla could act like this—to him it was as if a homely exterior had no right to house an hysterical temperament. He squeezed his knees together and wrapped himself in silence.

She raised her voice. "Don't you like it?"

"Sure, sure."

"An architect from Alexandria came to visit his in-laws and I got a crazy idea. At first he didn't want to see us. He was talking in terms of tens of thousands of dinars, but his wife's parents pleaded with him and he agreed to have a look at the land. We told him we could pay up to five hundred and he almost fell down laughing. He was modest, he didn't tell us what he was really worth back in Alexandria. But a capricious mood came over him; he was like a great painter acceding to the naïve request of ignorant peasants. And we were not ignorant, Fatkhi. We poured all our refugee dreams into this house. Inch by inch, from the foundations to the roof, this house was built with pink stone and cement and years stolen from the grime of the refugee camp. And here it is now, full of light and air. Nice, right?"

"Right," he hastened to agree, cautiously, as her husband had done earlier.

"It's a dream!" she cried tearfully. "Today it's a dream, and tomorrow, my dear man from damned Israel, tomorrow it will be a heap of ruins. Tomorrow the roof will kiss the foundations and the bedrooms will open shamelessly into the street."

The poet was alarmed. "What are you talking about, Abla?"

"Tonight we gave shelter to armed men. Tomorrow or the next day your Jews will come with dynamite and detonators and the dream will go flying sky-high."

"Abla, they aren't going to denounce you."

"They'll be caught. They'll fall into the hands of the Jews. They'll tell."

"Don't exaggerate."

"Do you know what a wicked idea I've had? What really filthy wish I'm wishing?"

"No."

"I'm wishing that the Jews don't take them alive, so they won't be able to talk."

"Abla."

She wept. Her homely face was rinsed with tears. "Most of them don't have a very long life to look forward to. A year or two and they're wiped out, and that's if they're very careful."

"Enough. Enough, woman."

"I'm a godless witch, aren't I? Godless! Allah!"

He didn't have what it took to get up, take her hand, and calm her. "You're tired," he said.

Her eyes flashed. "What do you Israelis know? For twenty years we thought you were living in hell, and we wept for you. Look how fat you got, while we sat here eating dry weeds."

Fatkhi was offended. "My parents and brother and sisters were thrown off their land also. A bulldozer came and flattened our house. Abla, we were refugees inside Israel."

"Not like here, not like here."

"What do you know," he said bitterly.

They fell silent as Magid entered the living room, carrying a tray of tea cups and smiling bravely. Ibitsam followed him like a shadow. She sat on the floor beside the bookshelf, resting her hands in her lap as if trying to hide them.

7

That night they waited up for Zuheir, who didn't come. The poet closed his eyes, grumbling to himself. What an unnecessary, idiotic visit. At dawn, he awoke to the chirping of birds and the cries of the peddlers. He groaned. Another stinking day.

He went downstairs and found Abla devouring her breakfast at her usual daunting speed, in the company of her two children. "The children and I are hurrying off to school," she said. "I thought you'd want to take it easy in bed like Magid. I told Ibitsam to bring coffee up to your room in another hour."

"Good morning," he said, going to the window. He told himself, I shouldn't condemn her. Just because she's gorging herself doesn't mean she's a monster. A few hours ago, right here in her house, a man gave up the ghost—and that's that. She grew up in a refugee camp. There, especially in the beginning, food mattered most. People died off like flies on a frosty night. Nevertheless, the sound of her munching and chewing disgusted him.

"Ibitsam," she cried, tearing at the bread and noisily gulping her tea, "Ibitsam, give the guest some coffee."

He raised the cup to his lips. Abla studied him with her clear, intelligent eyes. "You're an Israeli, everything about you is Israeli," she said, not in an accusative tone, but matter-of-factly.

But the poet did not want to be an Israeli here. "Are we starting that again?" he grumbled.

She paid no attention to him. "A man is dead—may Allah's mercy be upon him. At least he knew what he sacrificed his life for." And she drank from a cup of yogurt.

The poet looked at Abla's mustache. "What happened to Zuheir?" he said.

"How should I know? Forgive me, I'm in a hurry. Magid will look into it during the day."

He remained on the ground floor with Ibitsam, who was fussing in the kitchen. He wanted more coffee but was afraid to ask, lest the girl misunderstand him. He noticed that today she was wearing a simple peasant dress, buttoned up to the neck. He stood next to the window, smoking. The Buick drove down the main street, honking its horn, frightening three donkeys and two peddlers. It came to a halt just below the window, and although Wasfy saw the poet, he could not contain himself and blew the horn again. "Fatkhi! Fatkhi!" he sang out.

"Man," the poet complained, "a little quiet."

From inside the car dark heads and glittering eyes blossomed. Hamadia smiled foolishly in the back seat, like a grown-up forced to sit on a seesaw. She suppressed a laugh and put an affectionate hand on Wasfy's shoulder. "You're driving the whole town crazy . . . Everyone's going to be talking about us."

But Wasfy's elation knew no bounds. "We're going for a drive!" he shouted through the window. "Guess where!"

"To the Dead Sea," Namir and Said cried. "To Ein Feshka."

The poet said nothing. Wasfy said, "What's with you? Are you sick or something?"

His round, dwarfish body tumbled out of the car, he hurried

up the stairs and beat on the door as if there were no doorbell. "Open up, open up, man!"

Ibitsam rushed from the kitchen to open the door for him. As she led him into the vestibule, he fell silent, awestruck. But when his future brother-in-law appeared, he hitched up his pants, mustache bristling, and began flirting with the girl. "You're a dream, a real dream," he said, stretching his neck to examine her hindquarters. "What's a pearl like you doing in a place like this? Allah, Allah, what a beauty. . . . I'm going blind from it already. By the life of the Prophet—would you do a favor for a poor man? A favor, and let him put a blind man's hand on your shoulder? If you do, I'll let you lead me all the way to my grave."

"What nonsense," the girl said. But his prattle was having its effect on her.

"And I'm sure that your angel hands can brew the most refreshing coffee."

As Ibitsam disappeared into the kitchen, Wasfy took a few steps toward the poet. "Guess what I did last night."

The poet, sure that Wasfy was about to brag of his amorous exploits, said contemptuously, "Save your stories for the kids in the village."

"No! A thing like this mustn't get out of the family, Fatkhi. I implore you by the Prophet Mohammed. If they find out they'll rip my balls out, *Ya, Sheikh*."

The poet's curiosity was aroused. "What is it? Did you rip off some gasoline from an Israeli army truck?"

The mechanic's eyelashes drooped in sorrow. "So that's what you think of Wasfy. As far as you're concerned I'm a leprous dog. Well, listen, man—from now on, me and Arafat are shoulder to shoulder."

"What?"

Wasfy stood in the middle of the room, legs spread wide and chest puffed out. "I gave him a check for four hundred pounds!"

The poet laughed. "Drawn on a branch of the Bank of Israel."

"Go ahead and laugh." Wasfy shook his head pityingly. "The money's already in his hands."

"You were with Arafat last night?"

"Don't be so literal. Maybe not Arafat himself, but an important agent of his."

The poet was inclined to believe him, but a kind of jealousy led him to bait the man. "I'll bet it was just some imposter making fun of you."

This angered the mechanic. "It's about time you got to know Wasfy. I'm careful about what I put my signature to, and I'm careful who gets it. Hamadia and Amal know this agent."

"He came and asked you for a contribution?"

"What, I should wait for him to put out his hand? I put the checkbook on my knee and took out my pen and told him to name a sum. Four hundred pounds. Too bad I won't be able to tell this story around the garage."

"Are you going for a drive with that whole bunch?" The poet pointed at the impatient passengers in the car downstairs.

"Poor bastards! Day in and day out they choke on the smoke and stink of this hole. They deserve to breathe some fresh air."

"Allah be with you."

"You're sending me away already. What's the matter, you're afraid I'm going to get somewhere with that pearl? Ah, here she comes. What coffee! You're my sugar, you're the light of my eyes. What garden did you bloom in, my springtime rose?"

"You're crazy," laughed the girl.

"No wonder. If the Muezzin, way up in his minaret, caught sight of you, he'd fall straight to earth."

Ibitsam, for the first time since the night before, addressed the poet. "Please. Throw this old guy out of here."

"Wasfy," the poet began.

"All right, all right." I didn't mean to stand in the way of true love."

Fatkhi raised his arm in protest, while Ibitsam, red-faced, ran off, almost bumping into the doctor, who had come down in a dressing gown. Seeing Wasfy, he started in at once to scold him. "When will you people understand that I don't see patients here? There's a clinic, there are reception hours."

A man like Wasfy could not let such a chance go by. Making a mournful face, he put his cup on the table and said, "Allah's curse on this tooth. The pain—excuse the expression, Doctor—the pain goes all the way down to my ass. You call this a tooth? Some demon must have found himself a home in my jaw." And he approached the dentist, stretching his mouth open with his fingers.

Magid was about to examine him, but Fatkhi, laughing in spite of himself, thrust his future brother-in-law to one side. "Don't believe this ape. He's Wasfy, Hiam's brother. Magid, Wasfy. Wasfy, Magid."

They shook hands good-humoredly. The mechanic went out to the Buick and was on his way.

Half an hour later the poet was alone in the house with Ibitsam—that hillside house and garden. The town, roused by the cries of the peddlers, the twittering of birds, and the roar of motors, now subsided apathetically into the languor of the daylight hours. The house, embracing this blessed quiet, slumbered too. The poet, sitting next to the window with Teh Hussein's book, *The Days*, imagined Ibitsam hurrying about the house on the tips of her bare feet, silent as the breeze in the branches of the pomegranate tree. The unseen girl's presence troubled him. She had washed the dishes in the kitchen noiselessly, as though the dishes and water had turned to air in her hands. Then, hearing the pillows and mattresses being energetically beaten upstairs, he sighed with relief. Ibitsam was a hardworking girl, however, and the upstairs rooms quickly became quiet again. As the poet's eyes skimmed over the blind Egyptian's rhythmic sentences, he heard the girl's feet padding on the stairs.

In Tel Aviv, the women came to him in heat, their glands swollen, confidently expecting him to carry out his mission in life; hadn't his forefathers kept harems? He reveled in their jucies like a rabbit in springtime. Later, trying to find himself in their eyes, he would come up against thick darkness. As the years passed, he got used to considering them as instruments, just as they saw him. With the exception of Daphna, who learned to hide her feelings, they all treated him like kindergarten teachers taking a new child to their hearts. They were surprised, some even made fun of him, if he dallied the slightest bit before getting out of his clothes. He quickly learned to play the bull as it charged into the ring; he was trained to appear untamed. He could not look with equanimity into a woman's eyes, though he openly eyed their crotches. Shula, Marduch's wife, probably wore tin panties to ward off his X-ray vision. He had been amazed by his fiancée Hiam's absurd resistance when, finding her alone in her parents' home one day, he tried to take her, Tel Aviv style. As for Abla, she had immediately waved a "No Entry" sign before him. Here, sweetheart, you're among Arabs, real Palestinians. It had truly infuriated him yesterday morning when she had gone upstairs. He didn't need her, yet he had developed certain reflexes in his groin. An optometrist, thrown in with a group of people, can see immediately which of them are squinting.

And what, Fatkhi asked himself, is my profession? His identity card stated that he was a journalist. He thought of himself as a poet.

He hated Tel Aviv.

And here, in Jenin, in this Arab region whose Arabness was all the more conspicuous on this Yom Kippur morning, Fatkhi, an Arab with so many Israeli layers loaded onto his soul, was trying to find his way.

Here in Jenin they considered him a stranger. In the refugee camp, the coffee house, the restaurant, even in this house. He was frightened, because he too saw himself as an alien, a young man who has come back to his tribe after living abroad in the great world, full of experience and good will, but speaking a different idiom, bound by other modes of thought. His friend Fakhri, meeting this danger in good time, had moved to Beirut, and from there he now poured pitchers of boiling water righteously down on Fatkhi and his own past, in contrition for his sins.

"Sir, shall I make you something to drink? I'm going out to the market."

Ibitsam stood alluringly, one foot raised as if she were about to dash off.

He was disgusted by everything. "No, nothing, nothing from your hands!" Immediately he realized that he had been unintentionally crude and biting.

The girl gazed at her hands, which rose as if of their own accord. Her lower lip trembled and her foot dropped to the floor. "Is it because. . . because. . . ?"

"I meant," he said, by way of excusing himself, "that I wasn't thirsty."

"It's because of my hands," she insisted. "I swear to you that I washed the blood off. Many times, sir. First with laundry soap and then with the mistress's special soap. I put toothpaste on them this morning and then washed them again with the mistress's soap. They don't smell any more." She lifted her hands again, but hesitated to smell them.

"We are Allah's and to him we shall return!" Fatkhi groaned. "That's not what I meant, Ibitsam. Blood is like any other kind of filth—once is enough to wash it off."

Again he realized that he had blundered.

The girl said with alarm, "That poor man's blood is filth? You've got a heart of stone."

He gave up. "Could you tell me what you want?"

"I'm afraid. All morning I could feel him following me around the house. He was a boy. . . "

"He's dead."

"And his blood is on these hands."

"Girl, you're talking nonsense."

"You yourself are afraid to drink from anything I've touched."

He looked at her and said, "Ibitsam, go make coffee for me."

"Really?"

He nodded his head.

"Coffee?"

"Blindness on your heart!" he cursed her.

Ibitsam was pacified. The curse proved to her that she was now pure in his eyes. She turned, her back and her young rump expressing her gratitude to him. But when she returned, carrying a coffee pot and a cup on a tray, her face was frozen. "There's an old man at the door," she whispered, "and he wants to see you."

"Me?"

"So he says."

"He specifically mentioned my name?"

"Yes, sir."

"What does he look like?"

"What does he look like?" she repeated with horror. "He's got one foot in the grave."

"That's him," Fatkhi said, overjoyed. "Go to the market as you were told, and I'll bring him in."

"Can I visit my parents in the camp?" she asked.

"Go on, go on. I'm not your employer."

He hurried to the guest, opening the door and his arms as well. But the man standing at the threshold shied away from the embrace as if he were made of china. He put out his wrinkled hand, murmuring in a tired whisper, "Peace be with you, my dear fellow." And he gazed at Fatkhi with melancholy eyes.

Fatkhi put his hand under Zuheir's arm and led him to the easy chair in the living room. "How are you? How do you feel? So you troubled yourself to come all this way on my account, my good friend." He knew that he was prattling like a peasant, but because of Zuheir's appearance he couldn't stop talking. "How's your health? I'm grateful to you, comrade. Your presence honors me. By Allah! whoever sees you will live. . . ."

Zuheir raised a hand toward the open window. "It's cold."

He was dressed in a woolen garment under a jacket, and a *kefiyeh* on his head. His week-old beard was like frost.

Fatkhi went over and closed the window. "Tea. I'll give you some right away. You need tea."

"No sugar."

The poet's wry face showed his surprise. "No, *ya Sheikh*."

"Diabetes."

"I was sure that you came dressed this way so as not to be recognized."

The guest blinked, saying nothing. The poet returned with the tea. He had an encouraging, youthful smile on his face—he was ingratiating himself a bit. The old warrior's mournful face cast gloom. He knew that the poet was expecting to hear fine words from him, magic formulas. On another occasion he might have been prepared to sprinkle a little incense on the head of this confused young man. But the trip from Kabatiye had weakened him. "Sit down," he said to the smiling poet. "What do you want?"

"Just to bask in your brilliance, my friend," the poet said, caught up in village etiquette. All the fateful questions he had prepared now escaped him.

"I assume that your Party comrades over in Israel sometimes get sick."

"Sure, sure, no one's immune." The poet himself was bursting with health.

"Where do they go?"

"To the hospital, of course."

"It's very expensive."

"It's paid for by health insurance."

"And the really sick?"

"People in your condition we send to the best hospitals in the Soviet Union."

"In Kabatiye . . ." Zuheir said, and then stopped. "Here," he tried again, and stopped. "What's troubling you, man?"

"I don't know where I am."

"You're there, and we're here."

"I've had enough of being an acrobat. It doesn't work. I manage, but it doesn't work—an Arab and an Israeli at the same time."

"Is it so different in Tel Aviv?"

The poet, noting the irony, blushed and fell silent. Then he said, in a plaintive voice that sounded childish to him, "It's stifling."

Zuheir closed his eyes, then opened them. "You're still young," he said. His eyelids drooped and he dozed off. The poet picked up Teh Hussein's book again, which had remained open on the table. Again its style enchanted him. The Prophet Mohammed, at the start of his career, was approached by people who challenged him, saying, if you really are the prophet you claim to be, show us your powers; perform miracles, like the prophets who preceded you. But the Prophet Mohammed was no trickster. He was not about to perform miracles on command, he told them. The only "miracle" that he took credit for was the Koran itself, with its lucid language and rare, inimitable style. And indeed, over the course of many generations, only two other writers succeeded in performing such a miracle—the poet Abu al-ala al-mari of the tenth century, and the Egyptian Teh Hussein. Fatkhi smiled.

They were both blind. Abruptly the smile died on his lips. This Teh Hussein, acclaimed in all the Arab countries of the twentieth century, had taken a European wife without damage to his reputation. Sadat himself was married to a European.

Why not Daphna?

He thought about her as if Hiam were no obstacle. Sitting in Arab Jenin, browsing through modern Arabic literature, gazing at this enfeebled Arab leader sitting opposite him, the poet wandered in thought to Tel Aviv. He wondered why he hadn't given Zuheir even a hint about the Jewish girl. He had no doubt that she loved him, although she had never used the word.

"I'm me!"

She hadn't been proud of this outburst. Daphna had seen too many mixed marriages. She had seen these couples struggling, caught between two peoples, like a man with a broken leg who can't find a position to alleviate his pain. "Their children," she said once, referring to Shoshana's and Fuad's children, "are orphans, without a guardian or any institution that would take them in."

"She'll marry a kosher prick," he said to himself with a villager's resentment.

"Show me the way," came the dry voice, bordering on a cough.

The poet jumped. "The way where?"

"To the toilet, man."

"Oh. This way." Hastily he put the book on the table and averted his eyes, so as not to embarrass the leader who was making his third very determined attempt to get up out of the armchair. The leader's face resembled that of an old bull, sunk in mud.

"Thanks," Zuheir groaned bitterly, having been extricated from the armchair.

"Don't mention it," the poet said automatically, not knowing where he had gone wrong.

The leader put his hand on the door to the toilet and looked up sadly at the young man. "Wait here."

"Sure, of course." The poet nodded uneasily.

And despite himself he heard the groaning behind the door, the sporadic dribble and gush. When Zuheir came out he said with a kind of gloomy satisfaction, like someone whose prediction has come true: "Blood."

They walked slowly back to the living room and settled in their places. The poet sensed, to his distress, that the silence between them had turned hostile. He re-examined all he had done and said since Zuheir's arrival and found nothing amiss. He picked up the Teh Hussein book, trying to persuade himself that he did not care about the gloomy eyes resting on him, the eyes of an old man warming himself in the sun. Ibitsam returned—her head appeared for a moment in the doorway to the living room, as if inquiring whether the guest was still of this world.

Fatkhi heard Abla's businesslike footsteps, and with great relief he shut the book. She threw her bag down in the hall and burst joyfully into the living room. Her laughter died in her throat. "My darling," she cried. "Good God!" She looked accusingly at the poet, approached Zuheir, and put her shoulder under his arm. The two of them stood upright under her power alone. She set the sick man down on the couch, and then her eyes drilled into the poet's. "Why?"

Fatkhi spread his arms in utter bafflement, upset at the injustice done to him.

"Let him alone," Zuheir whispered.

"That's what he's learned from the Jews," she grumbled.

Zuheir had known much trouble in his life. "Don't blame everything on the Jews," he said to her. "He's got European manners. When his friend stumbles, a gentleman closes his eyes so as not to embarrass him. The Europeans love the satisfaction of self-control. Well, shit on that self-controlled culture."

"Culture? What kind of culture is that?" Abla shouted. "Sick people have to be taken care of. . . . He's gone so modern on me, he's afraid to take pity."

"I didn't know." The poet, ignoring Abla, went over to Zuheir and sat on the couch, his body touching the sick man's. "I've always considered you a great man, even that time in court when our lady lawyer crucified you."

"By Allah, that Jewish woman really did crucify me. That bitch deserves to burn in hell."

The poet's hand rested on Zuheir's frosty beard, and he smiled at him. "I've got a favor to ask of you, man. Save me from this woman who's about to crucify me."

A smile began to glimmer in Zuheir's sad eyes. "Abla, he's still young."

Though he refused to admit that he had done anything wrong, the poet was happy to see that he was forgiven.

The telephone rang and Abla hurried to answer it. She returned and said that Magid was delayed at the clinic with a difficult case and they would eat without him. The children sat around the dining room table while the adults ate in the living room, Zuheir from a tray near the couch. Again the telephone rang. Abla hurried off with her mouth full, listened to one sentence over the receiver, and returned, her face pale and the food still bulging in her cheeks.

"What's happened?" Fatkhi asked.

She swallowed without chewing, bringing tears to her eyes. "Magid says something big is happening. He's coming right away."

The two men stopped eating. Something big: These words might mean a fire, a conflagration, but also many other things besides. A petty quarrel, a riot, an armed clash, even a war. The three of them pricked up their ears; they vibrated with the earth below them. Only now did they notice something unusual. There was a heavy, continuous rumble coming up from the road to Nablus. Military trucks, armored personnel carriers, and civilian cars were rushing along, as if to an urgent rendezvous with the devil.

"Turn on the radio!" cried Zuheir.

Abla nearly tore off the dial. The rumble from the street was swallowed up in marching songs.

"Quick," said Fatkhi. "Turn to the Voice of Israel."

The woman stared at him, surprised and pale, wavering between the desire to curse him and the urge to obey. Zuheir's nod tipped the balance. Carefully, as if she feared that her fingers would be burned, she turned the dial. The external world retreated and stood still. They listened with their ears, their hands, their hearts and their brains. Past and future came crashing together.

Zuheir dropped down on his back, his eyes closed, putting off any further worldly demands. "Something big," he murmured.

When Magid came in, Abla said, "Zuheir has to be taken home right away, by the safest route there is."

For a moment, her husband said nothing. Possibly, he thought to himself, she was simply worried about the sick leader. But Magid was a refugee himself, and he knew that deep in her heart, Abla considered Zuheir a kind of time bomb, getting ready to go off in a world that was itself close to exploding. Magid stood looking at his wife. The tiles she stood on, the solid walls, the marble, the furniture, the carpets—these were her body's extra limbs. Even the bravest soldier is frightened of returning from battle crippled or blind. Perhaps for the first time, Magid was forced to disagree with his wife on a fateful issue. "Zuheir's staying here. This house is safe. Safe," he repeated, intoning the word with all the devotion of a believer.

Abla had the fixed expression of a captain whose ship has entered a storm, who must see to it that every superfluous object is thrown overboard. She turned to the poet and said, "And you?"

"Wasfy!" he cried.

"Where is that ape?" Magid asked.

"At the ends of the earth. He went off with his brother's family to the Dead Sea. He's bound to be arrested with them there."

"He won't come back alive," Abla declared.

The four of them shrank as the roar of a jet plane ripped the sky. Abla, standing near the window, cried, "Look! Look! There's a fireball up there."

"Is it flying this way?" Magid asked coolly.

"No, toward them."

Magid squinted into the sky and said, "That's a burning plane."

Abla turned back to the poet. "Well! Your good-for-nothing brother-in-law's done for."

Her expression annoyed him. "Wasfy will always return safe and sound, even from hell."

"You don't know the Jews, my dear poet."

"I know Wasfy."

She shook her head dubiously. "We'll see. And what if . . ."

"I'll ask the Jewish soldiers for a lift. I'm an Israeli, after all."

"She didn't mean to insult you, Magid intervened. "This is a very serious matter, Fatkhi."

"I'll wait for Wasfy outside."

"No you won't!" Abla said in a threatening voice. "That's all we need."

At that moment Wasfy came gliding up to the house in his Buick, sleek and mute as a dolphin, without any honking of the horn. Hamadia and her children, who had been so gay in the morning, now resembled wilted plants. Wasfy waved through the window. He called out in his usual thundering whisper: "*Ya Allah*, man! *Ya Allah*! The world's turning upside down. Let's drop off these people and get back home."

"No," the poet told him. "We're driving to Haifa. There

must be an arrest warrant waiting for me at home, like there was in the last war."

Wasfy groaned. "It must be great to have a few nice cunts to burrow into whenever the going gets rough."

For the first time in many years, there was a clear note of scorn in Wasfy's voice, scorn for the poet. But Fatkhi, seeing Wasfy's upraised chin, let it go. Perhaps, he thought, it's driving through a country once again in flames that has done it to him.

8

A heavy night had descended over Haifa, taking the city by surprise, seizing it by the throat. Shula had been certain that something would happen before nightfall, but those few people still in the streets were going home, taking with them the suspenseful expectation that hung in the air. Shula stood on the balcony, clenching her jaws in an effort to master the trembling in her cheeks. The primeval night fell with unusual suddenness, swallowing up the streets. The sea was lost in the sky, and all the settlements along the bay were blotted from the face of the earth. Anxiously she awaited the dawn, knowing that there was a long night ahead of her. The darkness terrified her. It seemed to burgeon and billow and rise from the earth itself, like dense fog, burying everything and penetrating her body.

A whistle cut through the darkness down on the street and an authoritative voice called out: "Turn that light off!" But instantly that lonely voice lost something of its rough confidence and added: "Please . . . "

Shula's first impulse was to flee into the apartment, but the "please" checked her. She heard something of her own loneliness in that stranger's voice, and wished that the man in the street would come closer. She leaned over the railing, her eyes searching the thick darkness, but she couldn't see him; she began to doubt his existence.

Upstairs, someone rolled up a window, and Shula looked up expectantly toward the fourth floor. The pensioner asked, "Shula, is that you?"

She was glad to confirm her own existence. "Yes, yes. Good evening, Tuvia."

"Is it hot in your place, too?"

The voice from the fourth floor was a kind of lifeline, and she grasped at it, afraid that it might be hauled back up. "Nice and cool, actually," she said.

"Here it's like an oven." He exhaled violently, as if he were inside an oven. "It's all because I was so lazy this year. When the summer started I thought I'd whitewash the roof, but I put it off and put it off, and now the summer's almost gone. There's no sense doing it now. Right?"

"Yes, you're right." And she wondered, was he asking to be invited over?

Two floors above her, Tuvia's heavy head was outlined against the stars. He, too, was ruminating. Then he said, "Have you heard anything from Marduch?"

"Nothing. I'm sticking by the telephone."

"Everything will be okay. It'll all be over very quickly."

"I hope so," she said wearily.

"The air-raid siren caught us in the middle of a game. I left the board on the table and told Hannah not to touch the pieces until Marduch comes back. We'll wait for him to finish the game. He'd beaten me twice before that, but this time around I've got a good chance."

Shula felt ashamed. The pensioner had not said all this in order to comfort her—he actually believed it, while she, a young woman, was beset by fears and anxieties. Suddenly she said, "How's Hannah?"

"Her temperature's gone up a bit. That's natural. Your temperature always goes up in the evening when you've got the flu. But it'll pass."

In that case, I can't invite him down, Shula thought. Tuvia said something. "What?" she said.

"How old is Marduch?"

"Forty-something." All at once she laughed. "But he doesn't know his birthday. It saves me the trouble of birthday presents."

"Forty," Tuvia said presently, as if weighing the years in the palm of his hand. "There are younger men who serve in the rear. What's he doing in a combat unit? And in the Sinai, no less."

"He's in the artillery. Actually he's serving in a mortar battalion now. That seems to be important in the army."

"And the heat bothers him."

She was touched that Tuvia remembered this. "Yes," she said.

"It's hard to believe that he comes from back there, from Iraq," the pensioner said. "I've heard that it gets to be one hundred and thirty degrees there. And in spite of that he's sensitive to the heat."

"Maybe it's because he was put in chains. For eleven years he was kept in irons." She blushed in the dark, as if she had revealed her innermost secret thoughts to a stranger. Perhaps it was her loneliness, or the way the pearly lights along the bay had been blotted from the face of the earth, but she couldn't stop herself. She added in a kind of tremulous stammer, "He was seventeen years old. They chained him in irons and sent him to a fortress in the desert. . . . "

"God!" The pensioner groaned, striking his palm on the windowsill. "Listen, he'll come back all right. He'll come back, I tell you. I'll move the chessboard into the corner and tell Hannah not to touch it until Marduch gets back."

Shula laughed. "You said that already, Tuvia."

The pensioner was silent. "Good night," he said suddenly, and went into his apartment.

"Daddy! Daddy!" Ido shouted.

"Yes, Ido," she cried, rushing to his room. On the way her left shoe slipped off. She kept running, haltingly. "Yes, yes, I'm here."

She found him sitting on his bed, hugging his big head in his thin arms. The only things that showed his age were his voice and the size of his head. "Where's Daddy?" he asked. "I want Daddy."

She sat down beside him and pressed his head to her breast. Then she looked into his frightened eyes. But she could not drive away his fear while she herself harbored such deep anxiety. Only Marduch knew how to calm the child, and at night Ido called only for his father. Shula removed the blanket and hugged his small body. "Daddy went to the army," she explained, keeping her voice as steady as she could. "You saw him go to the army."

"Where's Daddy?"

"Ido, when you go to the army you don't come home every night."

"So let the army come to us."

If her son had not been ten years old, Shula would have smiled at this. "That's not possible," she said. Instantly she recalled that Marduch was strict about never giving the child vague answers. "Ido, my sweet," she said. "There are lots and lots of people in the army, and lots of cars and big camps, too. They can't all come to us. We can't get them all into the apartment. Isn't that right?"

"So where's Daddy?"

"Daddy went to the army. He said you should be a good boy and sleep in your bed. And he told me to take care of you."

"Why was there a siren, Shula?"

"Daddy told you. You remember what he said."

"I don't remember."

"The siren tells us to go down to the shelter."

"I don't want to go down to the shelter. There's stairs and it's dark there. Why do we have to go down there?"

"Daddy told you why. You've forgotten, Ido. We have to be careful about the airplanes."

"The Arab airplanes?"

Shula nodded.

"Fuck the Arabs."

"Ido!" Shula was angry now. "I don't want to hear that again."

"So why do they set off the sirens?"

"Not them. Not the planes, Ido. We set off the sirens."

"Fuck the Arabs!"

"Go to sleep, Ido," she ordered, her patience at an end. Though she saw the fear building again in his stupid eyes, she could not deal with him as Marduch did. She put him down and covered him—briskly now, like a governess—and saw the fear in his wide eyes turn to panic. His lips trembled, but he was afraid to sob. His limbs froze and his shrivelled body was outlined under the flimsy blanket. Shula stood and turned her back to him.

"Shula," her son said in his mature voice. "Shula, why are you crying?"

"I'm not crying."

"That's a fib."

She knelt suddenly and put her head up against his. "Ido, I'm your mommy! Marduch's your daddy, and I'm your mommy. You understand?

"You're Shula."

"Why?"

"Daddy doesn't hug me like this. He lies down beside me. You're Shula! You're Shula!"

She kissed him and he didn't move. "I love you too."

"So where's Daddy?"

It occurred to her that he was putting her to a test. A baseless, unreasonable suspicion, she told herself without conviction.

"Shula, don't you want to tell me where Daddy is?"

"Daddy went to the army." She almost smiled. She was being tested. She was giving him the answers that his confused mind wanted to hear over and over. She said to him, "Ido, my sweet, do you want something?"

"Yes, Shula, a record."

She put a record on. The music acted on him like a drug. His large ears, indeed his whole body, opened wide to it. She saw his limbs thaw under the blanket, the fear melt from his eyes. His eyelids drooped, the long lashes yellow and beautiful. He asked in a childish voice, "There won't be another air-raid siren, will there, Shula?"

"No, there won't," she promised.

"Good." And he dozed off.

She left the room on tiptoe and then limped until she found her lost shoe. It seemed to her that she had forgotten something, and she stopped in the dark and made an effort to remember what. Supper? No, not that. In fact, she had not eaten, but it wasn't that. She closed the shutters, placed a dish on the floor and a burning candle on the dish. Then she sat in Marduch's armchair, near the television and gazed at the flame.

She did not remember when it was that she had begun, as it were, reliving Marduch's past. He himself tried with all his might to evade his past, to forget it. Few of his acquaintances would have believed, even if he had told them, that for eleven years he had been buried in the desert. But she believed it. More than that—the chains crunched her wrists and ankles, seared her skin in the heat of summer, and gave her chills in the bitter cold of winter. On more than one occasion she had tried to cast off the burden of her empathy, to escape from these horrors of the past—especially when it seemed that Marduch himself might be liberating himself from them. She would vow to cease her questioning and prying, but after two or three weeks she would forget her resolution, and she would embrace Marduch and squeeze another detail from him, and another. But her requests were not always granted. Whenever he felt inclined to pour out his heart, Marduch abstained from speaking. However, when he found her in a receptive, accepting frame of mind, he would begin. The sentences were ready, the words all picked out, as if he had recounted these things many times over in his innermost soul.

Perhaps it was because he knew how to pick the right time that his past affected her the way that it did. It frightened her. It seemed to her that his soul, the soul of a living person, would transfigure her. She knew that to believe in this metamorphosis was absurd, yet here she was, living his life with such intensity. One day they were driving to her parents' home in Kiryat Haim. At one of the bends in the road she said to him, "Do you remember the army truck we saw here? The one that turned over?"

Marduch was astonished. "Shula, you didn't see that truck."

She smiled. "What are you talking about?"

"Only Ido was with me. You were at a meeting and I was driving to your parents' with the kid."

She could not believe it. She remembered the oil that had spilled out over the highway, the soldier crawling out of the ditch behind the overturned truck, Marduch getting out of the car and going over to the soldier. The soldier was young, not more than a boy, and it still made her smile to recall Marduch's maternal expression as he touched him on the forehead. Marduch asked him if he wanted anything and the boy asked for a cigarette. Marduch gave him a light, and Shula remembered very clearly how the match flared in the dusk. She could still see the overturned vehicle, its wheels pointing upward, its rear end filthy with a thick layer of dust and oil, and down the middle the axle shining as if it were brand new.

"You want to drive me crazy," she said.

"Shula, you're the one who wants to confuse me! When I came home with Ido, I hoped he'd tell you. I didn't want him to forget such an experience, to run away from it. You got excited when I questioned him about what we had seen on the road. . . ."

So Shula had not witnessed the accident. She was shocked, and then frightened. This is bondage, she thought. And because she was not resisting it, she became more frightened than ever. Yet she made no real effort to free herself. As time passed she grew accustomed to this strange connection, and even derived pleasure from it.

The air was quite still in the apartment with its closed shutters, and the candle flame stood motionless. In that dim candlelight, a curious daze came over Shula. Her body fell asleep, while her mind stayed alert and watchful. Just now she had no wish to remember that peculiar experience from her double youth—hers and Marduch's. She tried to blot it out, although generally she stood by him in his difficult moments. But not in this. She took an upright posture in the armchair, dug her fingernails into her hand, and tried not to remember the details. She opened her eyes, swung her head around, shifted in her seat. She took a sleeping pill and immediately spat it out in the sink. It was the first night of the war. She mustn't fall asleep under the influence of a pill with a child like Ido in the house.

She remembered—she had to.

It's because of Rami I'm remembering, she said to herself. She would have borne Rami a son whose laughter would gladden the heart. Since hearing of Rami's divorce, she had been thinking about her womb a great deal. All these years she had felt that Ido was a sign of a morbid condition. On one occasion, a couple of tears had fallen from her eyes right into the Sabbath cake, and she had said to herself: Such a sick creature could only have spring from a sick womb. But since hearing that Rami had gotten rid of his wife, Shula had become more and more confident about her womb. Her womb was pure, fresh. From now on, Marduch was the guilty one.

"Marduch, I've been wanting to ask you a question." She was stretched out on the wide bed, her body touching his.

"Go ahead and ask."

His voice seemed fearful to her. "There's nothing to be ashamed of," she said. "And I don't want you to get angry."

"What an introduction!" he laughed. But his body moved away from hers.

"I wanted to know whether . . . in your family . . . forgive me, this is very important, important for our future together . . . I wanted to know, was there anything like this before?"

He sighed with relief, and this reaction grieved her, made her bitter. How could a father be so at ease with himself, knowing what the future held in store for his only son?

"No," he said, decisively. Then he began speaking more hesitantly, although with precision. "In a culture like the one I grew up in, these things are difficult to detect, especially when they're not too severe. A person may be born and grow up and marry and have children and die, without anyone suspecting that he might not have all his wits about him. Not many children got the sophisticated kind of toys they have here—toys that may entertain them and make them happy, but also reveal their weaknesses. Not every adult had to learn how to use the logarithmic tables, either. They didn't administer Rorschach tests and I.Q. tests. So perhaps there were cases like this in my family, and no one noticed it."

Shula, listening silently, saw that he was shaking again. He had been lying close to the wall, and now he got up, taking care not to touch her as he crossed over. He found his cigarettes in the darkness and sat down to smoke on the other side of the room. Shula took a certain satisfaction from her sense that he was doing this because he felt unclean. "Why don't you say something?"

His voice sounded very far away. "Maybe . . . maybe it's my fault."

Try as she might, she could not overcome the tremor in her voice. "What do you mean?"

He lit another cigarette, using the butt of the last one. "When they stripped me and tied me to that metal chair, I didn't know what they were planning to do. It was in the summer. Four or five in the afternoon. The walls radiated the heat they had soaked up during the long hours of the day. The interrogators were tired before they began. They knew from the start that they had tough game this time, because I was a kid who was afraid of his own fear. I was so afraid that I hated them, and for them that's worse than anything. Hatred gets in the way of a smooth interrogation. In our group we had spoken very little about this. It was bad for morale, so the subject was taboo. But at night, there were two things I thought about—girls and this. I was preoccupied by the question of how I would stand up to the ordeal when they caught me. I asked myself what right I had to recruit kids for such dangerous missions if, when the time came, I would deliver them over to the monsters with my own hands. Once I tried to bring it up with my brother, but he became annoyed and changed the subject. So I decided to cope with it by myself, and I wracked my brains to anticipate all their moves, every trick and contrivance they would use, to prepare myself for a spiritual test. But when they sat me naked in the chair, and tied me to it, there was no way I could imagine what they meant to do. I don't remember anything except that when they finished with the straps the terror let up; yes, suddenly it let up. I could still feel their groping fingers as they took off my pants, I could see the lust on their faces, yellow teeth digging into dry lips. They cried out with all their being: What a pity, what a pity! I was like food set before starving men, but they had strict orders not to gorge themselves—they could only have a taste. So I calmed down a bit when they put me in the chair; I knew then that they wouldn't touch me the way they really wanted to. I was scared to death of that."

Shula plumped the pillow, doubled it up, and leaned back on it. She had hoped, secretly, that he would forget her question. She was happy enough that he was talking more. He lit a third cigarette. She said, "And so they chained you up and left you. A person could go mad that way."

"No," he said, "they didn't go away. They don't believe in psychological methods there. It doesn't suit their way of thinking. Their culture has always believed exclusively in physical means, and it still does. Even their heavenly Garden of Eden, the reward of the righteous, is sensual. Flowing rivers, shade trees, beautiful girls, nice boys . . . listen—Allah promises nice boys to pious believers. But let that go. I heard a noise behind me and I didn't know what it was. The officer facing me smiled with pleasure. I couldn't turn to see what caused this noise. My hair stood on end and my skin . . ."

"Enough!" Shula cried. "Enough!"

"Why?"

"I don't want to hear any more." And she plumped the pillow again and straightened it. "Enough. Let's go to sleep."

Marduch didn't move. "You asked a question and I'm going to answer it, Shula. You asked a very important question."

"I didn't ask any question. Forget what I asked. Let's go to sleep."

He stubbed the cigarette out in the overflowing ashtray. Then he got up, went in the dark to the kitchen, returned with a glass of water, and sat down. He took a sip and put the glass down on the table and lit another cigarette. "This is important," he said. "It's very important for our future, as you said. Maybe they put me out of commission. Worse than that—maybe they turned me into a creature capable only of begetting children like Ido."

Now she wanted to hear it all. "What do you mean?" she asked.

"That strange noise, coming closer to me from behind, was a primus stove. They put a burning primus stove under that metal chair that they had tied me to."

She touched him and pulled him toward her bed and he hardly noticed her. She held his head in her hands and clasped him to her breast. This horror was with him always, even in his sleep. She realized that she was the first soul ever to force the terrible abscess of his youth out into the open. His lips grazed her nipple. She stifled a cry and kept listening to him, as she had listened from the moment he had opened the gates of his past to her. Marduch took his head from her grasp. His eyes drilled through the darkness, finding hers. "Shula, I'm still bashful. As a man, I mean. Even with you I'm ashamed sometimes. But that's not the reason I wouldn't let you see me from behind. The primus stove burned a long time. I screamed and screamed and fainted and screamed again. The flame of the stove may still be burning. Through me it reached Ido."

Shula fled to the bathroom. She locked herself in and wept bitterly. She hadn't the courage to admit to him that she had asked a vengeful question. She knew that he was still sitting there, his feet bound to the chair with ropes that she had tied, and she couldn't go out to him and loose those bonds. She heard him get up and slowly walk toward Ido's room. The child woke up and asked for something, and Marduch went to the kitchen and returned. She heard music, and then the creak of Ido's bed as Marduch climbed into it and stretched out beside the boy.

9

Since Marduch told her very little about what he did in the army, Shula did not know much about mortars. She tried to imagine what he was doing at that very moment, but couldn't. The vague announcements from the Israel Defense Forces' spokesman had planted in her the suspicion that the enemy had breached several strongpoints, and that elsewhere a strong current was about to become a tidal wave. Strange things had been happening. That morning, Tuvia had come out on the balcony and announced that Hannah was still sick, and in the same breath he said to Marduch, "Look how many people are going to the beach. I don't remember a Yom Kippur like this."

Marduch was just then trying fruitlessly to teach Ido the basic moves of checkers. He folded the board and ruffled the child's beautiful hair, sadly, affectionately, "No," he said to the pensioner, who was standing on his balcony in a blue undershirt. "They're not going to the beach."

"Out for picnics, then," Tuvia said.

"Look who's in the cars. No children, no women, and the drivers are nervous. Except for a few pedantic German Jews, no one's bothering to stop at the stop sign at the end of the street."

"So what's going on?" Tuvia said, and did not wait for an

answer. A moment later he rang their doorbell. "This is queer," he said.

"It's the army," said Marduch.

"On Yom Kippur?" Tuvia marveled.

"Do you feel like a game of chess?" Marduch asked.

"Come up to our place," the pensioner suggested. "I don't want to leave Hannah by herself."

Marduch complied, and so it was that when the air-raid siren went off, he was upstairs. Hurrying down, he heard the radio in his own apartment. "How did you think of turning the radio on?" he asked Shula.

His approval pleased her. "I thought that if there's a siren, they'd start broadcasting for sure."

Tuvia came down to their place again, in his blue undershirt. Standing, they listened to the I.D.F. spokesman's first announcement. Marduch said, "The Egyptians have crossed the canal and invaded Sinai."

The pensioner became angry. "You're talking nonsense."

"Listen carefully. The announcement said explicitly that the fighting is in the Sinai."

"But how could they pass the Bar-Lev Line?"

Marduch grabbed a stool, went over to the closet, and pulled out his uniform.

Shula looked on silently. At that moment she wasn't thinking about the siren, or the war, or her fears. Marduch was a private, just a private, and privates didn't go to the assembly points in uniform. Officers went there in uniform, but not privates. It's because of his scars, she said to herself. She remembered wanting to say that he had nothing to be ashamed of. She had wanted to tell Tuvia, the neighbor, and little Ido that Marduch was entitled to be proud of his scars, because he had not broken. He had stood up to the torture without betraying his comrades. Communists her age in Israel hadn't experienced even a fraction of the terrors that Marduch had undergone. Haim, the Technion student, had his ear crushed at a demonstration. The incident was an historic event. "He graduated from the Technion two years after they hit him in the ear. . . . That's no way to talk about him! You don't know what he went through." His scarred earlobe was a mark of distinction. Haim lay in Rambam Hospital surrounded by flowers, receiving a parade of admirers of both sexes. When he recovered, he took Shula to Mount Carmel and demanded that she immediately sever her relationship with Rami, and that she make love with him, Haim, right there on the dew-washed rocks.

Marduch, standing on the stool, waved his army shirt at Ido and cried, "Catch it! Catch it, son!"

Ido wriggled with laughter. He lifted his arms but couldn't catch the shirt. Marduch kept the trousers. Shula, gloomy-faced, pulled the clothes out of his hands. "Give them to me. I'll press them for you."

"What for?" He had gotten used to taking care of himself in prison. "I'm a super-deluxe presser," he boasted, clutching at the clothes.

"I told you to give them to me."

Her anger surprised him. He surrendered, and in his confusion gave Ido a mischievous wink, but Ido didn't understand such subtleties.

"So it's war," Tuvia had said. His soiled undershirt stretched out over his belly, gray hair grew on his stooped shoulders, and his left eye was inflamed and red. His bald head glistened with sweat. Two buttons were missing from his pants, and Marduch didn't know why he recalled his father, who was meticulous about his clothes. He had not thought of him for a long time. He had died during Marduch's sixth year in prison, without forgiving either him or his brother, blaming them for the family's ruin. He never once came to visit him in prison. Marduch put his hand on Tuvia's shoulder and said, "It's war."

The pensioner walked to the door as if he were making his way across a shaky roof.

Ido needs a man, Shula said to herself, gazing into the candle being consumed by the flame. Suddenly she understood that this thought expressed all the fears and anxieties and aches and sorrows that war brings in its wake.

Again she was reminded of Rami, but she wasn't worried for him. He was a veteran professional in the tank corps, a lieutenant colonel. As if rank immunized against death. Marduch was more vulnerable than Rami. She imagined him now, running with his eyes closed, obeying some meaningless command, into a cloud of smoke that concealed God-knows-what.

She thought of supper again but didn't get up from the armchair or move at all. She sighed and said, as she would whenever she was fatigued, I've got to get up and get things ready for kindergarten. But clearly kindergarten would be closed tomorrow. "Shula, get up!" she said out loud, as Ido did sometimes, but she did not get up. And then she realized that she was waiting for Marduch to take her by the arm and pull her out of the chair, out of her bitter gloom. At that moment, however, Marduch was rushing bodily to the front line, which she imagined as a fiery front traversing the hills, an unbroken wall of flames.

"Enough!" she said and got up to go to the telephone.

I should call my parents and ask them how they are. Maybe there was something they needed—although she couldn't do much for them. Marduch had left her the car, but she couldn't drive in this darkness—besides, she couldn't leave Ido alone in the apartment. You're paralyzed already, she sneered at herself. Even making a telephone call was a problem for her. Perhaps because she wanted to keep the line open for Marduch—nonsense, she said, and put her hand out to the receiver. Just then the telephone rang. She snatched the receiver and shouted, "Yes, yes, hello!"

"What's happening to you?" Shoshana asked.

"You scared me. I was waiting for a call from Marduch."

"Did they take him?"

"Yes. He sat and waited for them. They called him up at three-thirty."

"So there's no sense in our coming."

Shula said nothing. She remembered that Marduch had invited Shoshana and Fuad and the poet for this evening. The three men loved Arabic verse and enthusiastically played a game that Shula could not stand. The first player opens with one stanza of a poem, his friend takes up the next stanza, and so it goes, stanza after stanza, poem after poem, for hours at a time.

"Shula, are you there?" Shoshana said.

"Yes, yes. What time is it?"

"Nine-fifteen."

"So early? I thought it was already past midnight."

"I wouldn't have called you at midnight."

It seemed to Shula that they were using the line too long. "Come over, then," she decided.

"But you say Marduch isn't home."

"You mean if Marduch isn't here you don't want to see me?"

"You really want us to come?"

"Shoshana, don't drive me crazy. I'm telling you to come."

"All right."

"Wait a minute. What about Fuad?"

"Well, what about him?" Shoshana asked.

"Isn't it dangerous for him to go out now, at night?"

Shoshana laughed disparagingly. "We went through worse things than this in Czechoslovakia."

Shula wanted to get off the line at once. "I'm waiting for both of you. Bye."

"Bye."

Shula was troubled. She wanted to take a shower, not having washed since the day before. But what if Ido woke up? Or the siren went off? Or Marduch called? Everything looked so complicated. She went to the bathroom, bringing a dressing gown in addition to the dress she meant to wear, and she left the door open. She put her hand out to the faucet, wondering about what Shoshana had said—we went through worse things than this in Czechoslovakia . . .

Shoshana and Fuad and their three sons had lived for about two years in Czechoslovakia. Fuad was summoned to serve on the editorial board of a multilanguage weekly published there. This job was just for show. The editorial board's cadre was appointed, the copy was sent down from above, and Fuad's functions were undefined. Actually, this was a sort of extended vacation given as a reward to outstanding Party members. Fuad had a handsome salary and a good apartment in Prague, a car at his disposal, and all this in addition to the adulation due him as a persecuted hero.

When he returned to Israel, Shula and Marduch heard Fuad speak at the study groups and meetings organized in his honor. He sang the praises of the Socialist system. But his spontaneous smile had disappeared. Instead he wore a sharp, cynical grin, a smile for the cameras. When Shula mentioned this to Marduch, he dismissed it. Shoshana, on the other hand, kept strangely silent.

On their return to Israel they suffered from poverty. Their son Amir grew his hair long and adamantly refused to participate in Party activities. Shoshana was forced to go out and look for work. Finally she came to do the housework for her friend Shula.

Many years before, swept up in a romantic tempest, Shoshana had been caught in the dilemma that every Jewish girl who marries an Arab must face—should she continue living as a Jew, or change everything and live as an Arab? Or should she seek a path between the two extremes? Shoshana had tried all three choices, retreating from each one of them, borne down by failure.

In the beginning she and Fuad rented a modest room on

Sirkin Street. Shoshana introduced her dark-skinned husband as a new immigrant from India and continued teaching in the Jewish school where she had worked for years. Amir was circumcized according to the canons of Jewish religion and law, even though her husband was a Christian. Presently the truth was discovered. She was immediately dismissed from her teaching post. The small room on Sirkin Street became an abomination to the Jewish neighbors. Many stopped greeting her. Some did not conceal what they thought of her. The grocer stopped serving her. When she complained, he threatened her with a jar of pickles—"Get out of here, you apostate, you whore; you're a traitor to your people!"—and the black skullcap slipped off his head. And he was a good, sensitive man, well liked, who never cheated on weight and was known for his affection and absurd concern for pregnant women.

Amir would come back from nursery school with a scared expression, all dirty and muddy. Shoshana ignored the first scratches that appeared on his arms, but her heart cried out at the sight of the caked blood on his face.

"What's this?" she asked.

The child climbed up on the rocking horse. Crimson-faced, rocking violently, he screamed, "Kill the Arabs, every one! Kill the Arabs, every one!" With the tears brimming in his black eyes, he continued chanting these words intensely, until his mother plucked him from the horse.

So the age of delusion, as Shoshana called it, came to an end.

Next she tried the second way. She gathered their belongings, went to Rama, Fuad's birthplace, and moved into his widowed mother's house. Now commenced the period of bitter reality, as Shoshana called it. Industriously, diligently, she learned Arabic, prepared oriental dishes, served as the head of the women's organization of the large village, and burned all the remaining bridges between herself and her people. She even began speaking to Amir in Arabic, to his astonishment.

Many doors opened for her, but not many hearts. In kindergarten Amir was set apart from the other children. They considered him a Jew, as the children in the Jewish nursery had considered him an Arab. As for Shoshana, her free and easy *sabra* manners got her in trouble with the village elders. Fuad's political enemies capitalized on this.

From the very beginning of his career in the village, she heard things said that the Party angrily denied in meetings and in the press. Ugly things, things she had previously discounted as malevolent fabrications, were the daily bread of her new kinfolk. They expected that she, a woman "who left them and came over to us," would share in and partake of their bitter hatred. When she refused, she was condemned behind her back. Shoshana was shocked; she felt that she was standing on the verge of a dark abyss.

That was when Naim was born, her second son.

There was no respectable job in the village for a Party official's wife. The lower-class women worked in the fields; not even Shoshana's sworn enemies imagined that she would debase herself to that degree. When she told Fuad that it was impossible to get along on a Party functionary's salary, and added with a smile that she had no choice but to go work in the fields, his reaction was: "Have you gone mad?"

"What's the matter? It's work like any other."

"You're staying home."

Shoshana, a third-generation tiller of the soil from Yesud Hama'alah, took umbrage. "I'm not asking you," she said.

"You budge from this house and I'll break your legs. We've got enough trouble already with rumors about you. When the teenagers get together in the alley, they talk about you like a slut."

So Shoshana spread her wings again. Her decision to take off, to return to the twentieth century, was absolute. They went to Haifa, to Wadi Ein Nesanas, where Arabs and Jews lived together. She didn't think of moving to Abbas Street, where many of the better-off Party members lived. An Arab comrade burdened with an ostracized Jewish wife could not live there. In the Wadi, that somber neighborhood, their third son, Victor, was born.

The trip to Czechoslovakia saved them for a time, or so many people believed. Thus Shula was surprised to hear Shoshana say, "We went through worse in Czechoslovakia."

"Daddy! Daddy!" Ido screamed, and Shula hastened to him. She stroked his head, "Ido, you'll wake the neighbors."

He looked at her with hostility. She shuddered—she saw in him Marduch's eyes, gazing at her. "Don't scold the child if he gets frightened at night," he always told her.

One night she was curled up in Marduch's lap, listening to the music that carried Ido into the world of forgetfulness. "Aside from all his other problems," she said, "doesn't it bother you that he's such a coward?"

She couldn't see Marduch's face. His finger found her eyebrow and caressed it, then his hand slid down and clasped her hip. She thought that he was embracing her, and leaned her head back on his shoulder, but he was holding on to her. He said, "I'm a coward, too. From childhood I was taught to be one. Back there, over generations and generations, our people became rabbits. That was the law of survival. Without cowardice we would have been wiped off the face of the earth long before. When we were children we were fed stories of ghosts and spirits, murderers and cops. We were terrified of the dark, of an empty street, of a thick mustache, of a muscular forearm. And we would scream in our sleep. Maybe I passed this on to Ido."

"You think everything that's wrong with Ido is your fault. How awful to feel that way."

"No," he had said, "it's good. Otherwise we'd think of him as a terrible burden. We'd hate him."

Ido shrank from her. "Where's Daddy?"

"He went to the army."

"I want Daddy."

"He'll come back."

"Now?"

"No, in another couple of days."

"Then where's Daddy?"

"I told you."

"What did you tell me?"

"That Daddy went to the army."

"Shula, I want to do wee-wee."

"Come, I'll take you." And she helped him get up and then shrieked, "Ido!"

The child cringed. "I couldn't help it."

"Come to the shower," she said, gazing into her son's beautiful, obtuse eyes.

"Daddy carries me."

"You're big and heavy and I can't carry you."

"So let Daddy come and do it."

She decided not to pay any attention to his questions. She grabbed his hand and pulled him to the bathroom and stripped him in the tub, and he stood submissively, fearful of the mother who had borne him. She was moved to pity. She toweled him dry and dressed him. The child put out his hand, but she stooped down and lifted him in her arms. At first he drew his head back in fear, but then her fragrance subdued him, and with a smile on his lips he rested his head on her shoulder and closed his eyes. Shula kissed him and he opened his eyes and looked at her calmly. She wanted to call Marduch to come and see Ido's smile—but at that moment Marduch was rushing to the front.

"Do you love Mommy?" she asked, arrested by her son's sober look.

"Daddy says that Shula's a good mommy."

She put him in bed and he pulled the blanket over himself. The doorbell sounded, and Ido leapt up. "It's Daddy!"

"Just a minute," she called toward the door. And she ordered

Ido, "Lie down and be quiet. These are guests and I want you to be a good boy. You promise?"

The boy nodded and was silent. She went to the door. There stood Tuvia the pensioner, sheets of black paper in one hand and a box of tacks in the other. "Oh, it's you," she said.

Tuvia showed her the paper. "It was left over from the last war. Who would have known that we'd need it again so soon?"

Ido rejoiced on his bed. "Tuvia, *ahalan!* Have you come to visit us?"

The pensioner's happy voice contrasted with his gloomy face. "Of course I have! It's your friend Tuvia."

"*Ahalan*, Tuvia!"

The pensioner walked past Shula and into Ido's room. "I've come," he said to him, "to keep a guard on the apartment. We'll put black paper over the windows and we won't let the war come inside."

"Fuck the Arabs!"

"Ido!" Shula upbraided him, and said to Tuvia, "He's excited and he can't fall asleep. I'll have to give him a sleeping pill. Maybe you could put up the paper tomorrow?"

"Oh, it's really nothing at all." And he looked at her dress and her hair and said like a bothersome father, "The way you've dressed up, someone would think you're about to go out."

Something in his expression amused her. "We had invited some friends over for this evening and they called and I told them to come. I was afraid to be by myself."

The pensioner, standing on a stool, murmured, "As if I weren't here."

"Hannah's sick."

"It's only flu. Now of all times!"

She laughed. "You don't plan things like that."

The box of tacks fell out of his hand. Shula picked it up and gave it to him. He put some tacks in his mouth and said, "Go calm the boy down."

"He doesn't trust me. He's driving me crazy. He only wants Marduch."

"I'll sleep here tonight."

"Hannah's sick."

"I put the telephone next to her bed."

"It's out of the question. Thanks very much."

"Ah, I forgot that you've got guests tonight."

Shula burst out, "You're as bad as Ido!"

He sat on the stool and spat the remaining tacks into the palm of his hand. "What do they want from us?"

"Who?"

"Your Arabs. How many wars do we have to fight? My grandchildren. Yesterday they were just kids. They always forgot to say hello, they were in such a hurry to ask what I had brought them. They were the most beautiful blessing of all. I told their mothers, to hell with good manners. It's a pity. I used to walk with them in the dark, hand in hand. They always had bruises—from the seesaw, the curb, the bicycle, trees. And now shells are raining down on all of them."

"Tuvia," Shula cried, seeing his hand squeeze into a fist with the tacks inside. "You'll cut yourself."

He opened his fingers and stared at his palm. "I'm sorry. I came to cheer you up and now look at me babbling."

"Never mind."

"I don't dare say anything to Hannah. She's sick. I thought, why bother her? I hide in the toilet and listen to the news there. I flush the water all the time and hold the transistor radio to my ear. She thinks I've got diarrhea and tells me I've got to go to the doctor tomorrow." He got up. "I'm going. If you need . . ."

"Thanks a lot." She had closed the door after him and was turning away, when suddenly his face reappeared. "Did you really mean what you said on the balcony, about the chains?"

She nodded, regretting that she had let Marduch's secret out.

"I thought it was just a figure of speech," Tuvia said.

"I found a photograph among his things. He probably forgot to tear it up. You can see everything there."

"And he never told me."

"He wasn't imprisoned for Zionism. No one's interested in what he suffered. And if he did talk about it, people would not be sympathetic."

"Don't be cynical, Shula. It's wrong. Goodnight."

"Goodnight."

10

Fuad knocked just once on the door, so as not to wake Ido. When he was in a good mood he would devote some time and attention to the child, patiently answering his repetitious questions. He entered the apartment with a transistor radio over his left cheek, saw the windows blacked out with paper, and said angrily, "You're already prepared for war."

"The neighbor did it," Shula said, as if apologizing. "He just left."

"That strange old man."

"He's not strange" his wife Shoshana said. "He's very nice."

Fuad ignored her. "It's stifling in here," he said. "Let's sit on the balcony."

Shula glanced at the telephone. "I'm waiting for a call from Marduch," she said.

"He won't call tonight," the visitor declared. He stood in the middle of the living room, twirling the radio dial to Damascus, the BBC, Jerusalem, Cairo, and again Jerusalem. Tonight there was a lot of music, marching songs, between the announcements in Hebrew, English, and Arabic.

"You go out to the balcony," Shoshana said to him. "Shula and I will sit here."

"We'll all go out," Shula said. "It really is stifling in here. And we might wake Ido. Tonight he's completely crazy."

"Not just him," Shoshana said. "At home everyone's gone off his head."

"That's enough!" Fuad ordered.

"Will you drink something?"

"Coffee and cold water," Fuad said.

"Go out to the balcony, go on," Shoshana cried and went into the kitchen with Shula. Her eyes were mournful in her broad, open face. Her demeanor was brisk, her voice subdued. In spite of all the hard blows she had taken, she was still far from giving up hope. On the contrary—she was like a prize fighter getting ready for the next round.

"What's happened?" Shula asked.

"It's war."

"Between you two?"

"Right in the family," Shoshana said. "All of a sudden Amir's decided that he's a Jew, and his two little brothers are playing the part of the poor, screwed Arabs, no less. Their father descends from the heights only when their shouting drowns out the news. Then he jumps up from the armchair and yells at them, and my miserable Arabs and Jew turn on him and open their own yaps. It's been like that since the siren went off this afternoon. They almost tore the house apart."

"They'll calm down. All of us are tense."

"Sure they'll calm down," Shoshana said, "but the older boy worries me. He sees the fellows running off to their units and he's dying because he's not invited to go and die with them."

"You should be happy that they're all with you."

"Happy!" Shoshana shouted. "He'll be all messed up, I tell you. What's this Jewish business all of a sudden? All these years they've been spitting at him. Ever since he was a child he's been hearing about his Jewish whore mother who sleeps with an Arab. Suddenly he's Jewish? You should hear him. He says he's going to the recruiting station—that's the way he provokes his brothers—he's going to get into a tank and race off to the desert. He and his brothers both know that if he went to the recruiting station he'd get a kick in his Arab *fellah*'s behind. At the most they'd stick a Civil Defense whistle between his teeth and tell him to go chirp on it in Wadi Ein Nesanas. . . ."

"Did this start today?"

"That's what's so funny about the whole thing. It was in Czechoslovakia, no less, that he decided he was a Jew, an Israeli patriot. He went with the Czech students to toss rocks at the Soviet tanks. I almost died, I went there and dragged him away. His friends thought I was a Russian bitch. Maybe because of this lousy Russian face my nice parents gave me. When they saw me pulling at their big hero who threw stones at the Soviet tanks, they jumped me. What a scene. My son covered me with his body to protect me from his friends, but they didn't understand. He shouted and no one paid attention. The Russians stood on their tanks and laughed—they thought it was a riot."

"Let's go to the balcony," Shula said.

"All right," said Shoshana.

Fuad's silhouette stood out against the moonlit sea. Shula set the tray down on the ledge and looked at the man's haughty head. His lips were full, his eyes bulged slightly, his hair was kinky; these features emphasized his masculinity. Fuad was still the attractive man Shula remembered as a young girl. The first time she saw him, he was standing on a stage flooded with spotlights and covered with red flags. Shoshana, who was next to her, said, "Look at him—that man was born to improve the human race."

But there was more to Fuad. Marduch had immediately noticed his unusual personality, and a warm friendship sprang up between them. At that time Marduch was lonely and looking for a friend.

I was dumped, by surprise, against my will, into this country. I don't know if you can understand this, Shula: The good and bad in your life, the sum total of your existence so far, all took place here. More than anything else, a person is a social creature. He may roam in search of pasture, livelihood, better conditions, but he does whatever he can to move within a human framework—his clan, group, family, friends. I believe in peoples more than in nations.

While I was in jail, a regiment of ignorant soldiers stormed the capital and in a few hours accomplished something that had taken us twenty years to prepare for. The soldiers smashed the old regime and broke the chains that shackled me. After a couple of days they broke down the prison gate and said: Leave. You're all free men. Don't stand there like idiots. Go!

Go. . . .

We were asked to go back to the people. The soldiers needed intermediaries between them and the masses. The comrades were delighted to go back to the people, but first of all they wanted to go home. So we all drove off to Baghdad in great clouds of dust.

I arrived in our neighborhood at twilight. The air was burning hot and full of the best smell of the river. When I got out of the car, the sight of the roses and flowerbeds on the avenue made me euphoric. After all that time in the desert, here was water. I caressed the jasmine, I buried my face in the flowers and breathed them in. On the other side of the fence I saw a frightened girl. She was screaming, "*Ya baba!* There's a thief hiding by our fence."

I smiled at her, and waving my arm gaily, I quickly entered our street. I took a few steps, and then I remembered that actually I had nothing to look for. There were strangers living in our house. So I said to myself, I'll go to my people. Only a desperate man could say such a thing.

Who were my people?

The masses celebrating in the street would tire and return home. None of them would take me in. I don't say this with any bitterness, Shula. I didn't do what I did for the sake of any particular person. When the crowd broke up into individuals and every individual went back home, no one owed me anything. I hadn't asked the interrogators to strap me into that iron chair; I didn't demand that the judge give me prison with hard labor. These things were done to me against my will; they were nothing to boast about. Others fought better than I and came out all right. They served the cause more effectively. They were free and gave more. No, I had no claim on the crowd celebrating in the street.

To find my people, and also perhaps some shelter, I went down to the old city where the remnants of the splendid Jewish community were huddled together. A few thousand remained after the great exodus to Israel—strange, queer people, poor souls clinging with their fingernails to the past. Do you know what they did to me?

Why am I laughing?

When they heard that I had just this minute left prison, they gazed at me with pity. They wanted to give me food and drink. And in fact I was thirsty and hungry and tired. But not one of them dared to take me into his house. Now do you understand why I'm laughing? I admired courage and I still admire it. I don't consider it a defect. These Jews were the pitiful fragments left over from a mighty body. They were suspicious of me, as cowards are. In jail I almost forgot the Jewish dialect, so I appealed to them in the Muslim dialect. The women wanted to help me, the men wanted to throw me out. Finally a compromise was reached. They took me to the synagogue, and there they brought me all kinds of delicacies. In the middle of this feast, soldiers started pounding on the synagogue gate. The beadle fainted. My Jews had denounced me. That's the nature of any human periphery. I won't lie, I won't tell you that I understand and forgive them. Even now, whenever I remember them, I want to throw up. It's not decent for a man to condemn his own people, but it's even worse to condemn those whom his people rules. I ask you, Shula, how many informers are there in the Arab villages, here in Israel? Many, many. They betray their brothers, not out of fear or cowardice, but for a little measly cash.

I'll say this for the soldiers—they let me finish that wonderful meal. I stuck the peaches and plums in my pockets. There's no fruit in the desert.

From the synagogue to a military prison. I told them I was a veteran freedom fighter. They hesitated, made telephone calls, conferred. A Muslim fighter? Very desirable, if he'd support the military coup. A Christian revolutionary? Maybe. But a Jew? They treated me well, but they wouldn't let me contact the comrades. They dealt correctly with me for two weeks. They even took me to the river for an enjoyable swim when I told them I missed it. They found it strange that a Jew should miss the river.

After two weeks they told me they were sorry, but the holiday was over. I had to leave the country. "Where to?" I asked.

"To Israel, of course."

"Why?"

They winked and smiled at the crafty bastard, and even in the plane they kept slapping me on the back.

You understand? I felt nothing for Israel. As far as I was concerned it was deportation, another exile, another arbitrary order determining my fate.

I arrived here without a penny, without family, and worst of all, without a language. At the age of twenty-eight I found myself stuttering like a moron. You know what really killed me? The girls.

Until then I'd never been with a woman. For years I'd been in prison, dreaming sometimes more about women than about freedom. And here they poked fun at me. My stammering made their tits shake with laughter. That destroyed me. Well, I can understand it now. I remember the first months with you. You yourself called me Tarzan. I couldn't dance, express myself clearly, or take a girl's arm in mine. I remember how you laughed when you saw that I didn't even know how to kiss. The fact is, I thought of myself as a kind of miserable Tarzan, flung into the main square of a noisy city.

No. The Party didn't help me much. I didn't feel at home among the Jewish comrades. They sat around abusing their country. I had no desire to be a wretch among professional wretches. I said to myself, I'll go to the Arab comrades. So I went up to Haifa. Have you ever gone to a strange, new place, a place you've never been before, and suddenly it seems that you've seen it already? It's a strange feeling. That's why some people believe in reincarnation.

I went to the Arabs in Haifa, I saw the Arabs in Jaffa, I visited the Arabs in Umm-al-Fahm, I stayed in Kfar Yassif, and it seemed to me that I had seen and spoken to them before. I came back and lay down on the sofa in the Party clubhouse in Haifa and I thought, Marduch, you're going crazy. The desert sun and the loneliness here have addled your brains.

Then suddenly I remembered where I had seen them before, where I had spoken with them. It was in the ancient quarter of my native town. They were the remnants of that strong body that had picked up and departed. Shula, don't let this get around, but even the Party members among them repelled me. They're small-minded villagers who found the Party a sure means to achieve their petty aims.

But not Fuad. He's different. His head glides above the mud, the suffocating mud, like a swan's. The others have found some strange way to enjoy being suffocated. I respected Fuad because he really suffered.

"How did you get here?" Shula said, sitting between Fuad and Shoshana. "No problem on the way?"

"No," Fuad said. "Not yet."

"Fuad," Shula said, "your radio is driving me crazy."

"Important things are happening," he said, his bulging eyes shining in the moonlight.

"This isn't a soccer game," his wife protested. "It's a war."

"And what a war."

"You're happy," Shula said, sadly.

"Yes," he declared, candid as usual.

"And the thousands who will die don't matter to you?" Shula was amazed. She wasn't thinking of the thousands, but of Marduch and Rami.

"They matter, they matter," he said, "but they're not the main thing."

"Monster," his wife murmured.

"Be quiet, woman!"

Shula's curiosity was aroused. "I'd be interested to know what the main thing is."

Fuad sipped the coffee and licked his lips contentedly. "This time we started it. We fired the first shot, Shula. We leapt into the fire."

"Who's 'we?' " Shoshana asked bitterly.

"You'll be married to me fifty years and you still won't understand who 'we' is. I hope, Shula, that Marduch's in the rear."

"If I know him, he won't be far from the fighting, not if he can help it."

"He's a man."

"Is that what men die for? To prove that they're men?"

"Yes, yes," Fuad cried, moving his chair in his excitement. "When you've got a whole chorus around shouting that you're a eunuch, you're a coward, you're a woman—why then, you drop your pants and draw out a long . . ."

"Fuad!" Shoshana cried. Shula blushed.

He rested his arms on the railing and planted his strong jaw in his hands. Gazing at the sea, he said softly, "Forgive me, Shula."

"Never mind," she stammered, embarrassed.

Shoshana broke the silence. "Fuad, all you need is for someone from the political bureau to hear you say that."

Fuad looked so long and searchingly at his wife that she felt butterflies in her stomach. Then he said, "You're all right, Shoshana." Again his anger flared. "You know very well what I think of the people on that committee."

Shula opened her eyes wide. "Fuad, what's going on? You're on the committee yourself. . . ."

"Not much longer, not much longer."

"Marduch said nothing about it to me."

"And he won't."

"He tells me everything," she cried, and immediately regretted it. Her words sounded so childish.

Fuad smiled and asked, "Did you read Fatkhi's poem yesterday?"

She smiled. "I don't read Arabic."

Fuad said, "What good are you?"

"Bring it to me, I'll keep it for Marduch."

Shoshana was resting her legs, clad in black slacks, on the balcony railing. "Fuad's already learned the poem by heart. This guy," she went on with a hint of pride, "reads a poem once and knows it by heart. Ever since yesterday he's been dying to do two things: murder the poet and talk with Marduch. Poor guy, the war came along and deprived him of both pleasures."

"I don't understand poetry," Shula said.

"I don't either," Shoshana said, then shouted, "Shula, the telephone!"

Shula had already leapt from her chair. "Maybe it's Marduch!" she cried. The two guests hurried after her and stood on either side, their faces tense.

"Hello!" she cried in a trembling voice.

"Shula?"

Her face fell. "Yes, Amalia."

"You sound disappointed."

"I was expecting a call from Marduch."

Fuad dropped into an armchair. He waved his arm and said, "That bitch?"

"Fuad, please . . ." Shula rebuked him.

Amalia's shrill voice could be clearly heard. "Who's over there?"

"Shoshana and Fuad."

"Isn't it enough that you've sent your husband off to this filthy war . . .?"

"Amalia, I did not send Marduch off to any war," Shula flared.

"You have to entertain those two characters on top of it?"

"What are you talking about?"

Fuad waved his arm again and said, "Hang up on her."

Shula was close to tears. "Fuad, Amalia," she stammered.

"Listen, comrade," Amalia said in a commanding voice. "Throw them out at once."

"They're my guests!" Shula shouted.

Fuad jumped up and grabbed at the receiver. "Give her to me! What did she say about us?"

Shula turned pale and shook. "Shoshana, please, calm Fuad down."

Amalia's voice beat against her ear. "What is that lunatic shouting about over there?"

"Nothing. Amalia, why did you call? If you wanted to drive me crazy, I can tell you you've succeeded beautifully."

"Why the sarcasm?" Amalia said.

Fuad would not be pacified. "Don't get involved!" he told

his wife. And he advised Shula, "Just hang up. Don't answer that witch."

"Fuad," Shoshana pleaded.

"Listen, my friend," Amalia said in her chilly voice, "throw those two out of your house. That's an order. Emile and I are coming over to your place in fifteen minutes, you hear? I don't want to find them there."

Shula held the receiver away from her body, as if it were something repulsive. Staring at her guests, she murmured to them, "What do you think of that?"

Shoshana hurried over and put an arm around her shoulders. "What does she want?"

"She wants me to throw you out. She and Emile are coming over soon. And she says it's an order."

"Order my ass!" Fuad interrupted. He grabbed the receiver and barked into it: "Let me talk to Emile."

Amalia was a veteran teacher in a school for disturbed children. "Comrade Fuad, get off the line. Let me talk with Shula," she said patiently, in a measured voice.

But Fuad was no backward young boy. "You know where you can stuff it. Give me Emile at once."

"You'll pay for this. You'll pay for your crudeness and your deliberate failure to carry out Party orders."

"Shut your mouth and give me Emile."

"Get off the line!"

"If you don't give me Emile, I'm hanging up."

"Wait," she screamed. "You can speak with Emile, but don't kid yourself. I won't let such shameful behavior pass."

"Emile?"

"Yes, Fuad," Emile said in a marvelously quiet voice. "What's this hullaballoo?"

"You chose that cunt from all the women on earth—but that doesn't mean I have to take her crap. Throw her out of the room and talk with me yourself."

"Fuad," Emile said, with all the serenity of a man relaxing

in an easy chair. "You shouldn't be offended by her way of speaking."

"I *was* offended by that mouse of yours, but that's between me and her. I want to know what's going on."

"Well, in a manner of speaking . . ."

Fuad interrupted. "Man, what's happened to you? Where did you get this 'well, in a manner of speaking?' That Jewish woman's turned you into a Jewish merchant, but you'll never be greasy. You're a simple Christian and you'll die one. At worst she'll take you to some chicken slaughterer and chop off a piece of your prick."

"Fuad! You go too far!"

"Then don't give me any of your stinking 'well, in a manner of speaking.' Get to the point."

"That's the trouble. I can't over the phone."

"Idiots!" sighed Fuad, the Party man. "If they're tapping your telephone, your wife's hints have already woken the dead. She may be the daughter of a Knesset member, but she goes too far. I'm hanging up, Emile. And I'm not budging." He placed the receiver in its cradle. Ido, who was sitting on Shoshana's lap, gazed at Fuad with shining eyes. Shula was in an armchair—meticulously scrubbed and combed, yet wrinkled and worn out. Fuad gave Ido a smile.

"*Ahalan*, Fuad!" the child cried.

"*Ahalan*, Ido."

"Why haven't you gone to the army?"

"In your Israel, Arabs don't go to the army."

"Fuck the Arabs!"

Fuad, overcome with laughter, choking on it, took Ido in his arms and said, "Fuck the Arabs!"

Ido waved his arms, bursting with happiness. "*Ahalan*, Fuad!"

Shula protested weakly. "Encourage him, that's right. That's all he needs."

11

When the doorbell rang, Shula did not have the strength to get out of her chair. She looked helplessly at Shoshana, who said, "I'll get it."

The room, with its windows sealed, was hot and smelled of cigarette smoke. All Shula wanted was to go out and stand on the balcony and gaze at the bay, all alone, without even Marduch. She'd forgotten Rami and her womb. She just wanted to be left alone. Everything disgusted her—Fuad's chattering in Ido's room, Shoshana's heavy footsteps, the telephone crouching silently, like a malefactor. She blew her nose and felt the tears welling in her eyes. She got up, went to the bathroom, turned on the tap, and heard Shoshana's astonished voice. "Fatkhi, what are you doing here? Fuad, Shula, look who's here. . . ."

Then she heard Amalia's sharp angry voice. "Shut up! Shut up!"

The door closed, and in the hall Emile said in his placid voice, "Shalom, Shoshana."

Shoshana was furious. "No one overdid it in describing your wife," she said to Emile, insolently.

"Shut up, I told you," Amalia ordered.

"Listen, sweetheart . . ."

Emile interrupted her. "You don't understand, Shoshana. No one understands. Where is everybody?"

"They all disappeared. They ran for their lives when they heard your wife was coming."

"With the greatest respect," Emile said, almost losing his composure, "where are they?"

Shula appeared, face washed, eyes shining. "Shalom, Emile, Shalom, Amalia," she said and turned to the poet and shook his hand. "Marduch asked me to invite you over tonight with Fuad and Shoshana. Here you are, though they said you'd disappeared from Haifa; and it's Marduch who's missing."

Fuad came charging out of Ido's room. Without greeting the newcomers, without a glance at anyone, he kept going toward the balcony, saying, "Emile, come here."

Fuad was a veteran Party official. Emile was about to follow when his wife's voice froze him. "Emile, don't you move! Who is he to order you around? Stay right here."

Fuad stopped as if he had collided with a wall. He rubbed his forehead and turned around. His dark face had become even darker. "I demand an explanation," he said in an intense whisper.

The poet took one step toward him and stood there, smiling reproachfully. "Fuad, what's the matter? You haven't even said hello to me."

Fuad glared at him for such a long time that the smile froze on the poet's lips, and he shifted his suitcase from hand to hand in confusion. Shula, Shoshana, and Fuad noticed it with astonishment, and Fatkhi set it down on the floor. He forced a smile.

Shoshana said to him, "Where are you going on a night like this? There isn't even any public transport."

"I'm not going anywhere," the poet answered.

Emile, relaxing in the armchair, said, "Could you all calm down and listen like human beings? We couldn't explain over the telephone. Comrade Fatkhi has come to hide here. He's got an administrative detention order hanging over his head. Ladies and gentlemen, war has broken out. They'll arrest him as they did during the last war."

Fuad's voice had a distinct note of scorn in it. "And who decided to put Comrade Fatkhi in mothballs?"

Amalia cried delightedly, "I told you."

Fuad raised his arm. "Amalia, I'll take care of you later. Emile, answer me—who decided?"

"It's an order from above."

"Above?"

"The political bureau."

"Who took the order?"

Emile was surprised. "What difference does that make?"

Amalia warned her husband, "Don't tell him anything."

"Really, I don't understand why it's important," Emile said defensively.

"I'm telling you that it is," Fuad insisted.

Emile's irresolute gaze shifted to his wife's face. Finally he gave in and said, "Amalia."

"Just as I suspected," Fuad said, concluding his interrogation.

Amalia approached him until her face almost touched his and he was obliged to step back. "What do you suspect?" she said.

"My dear lady, you're an agent of the secret police."

"What?"

"Fuad." Emile smiled as if someone had made a joke. "Fuad, really. . . ."

"You," Amalia hissed, "Nobody trusts you, and you accuse me of having links with the secret police?"

"Not just having links, my dear lady, but of rendering real service, over many years."

In the uproar that followed, several things happened at once. Emile, blessed with a sweet disposition and an abhorrence of violent confrontations, treated the whole affair as a tasteless joke. "Fuad, sweetheart," he began, but when he saw his wife's glazed look, he realized the worst was yet to come. He thought, however, that he could stop what was happening, or at least put a brake on things. It was necessary to confront Fuad and say a few harsh words to him—but if Emile held back, it wasn't because he feared the leader. He was alarmed by his own rising feelings, yet he said in a quiet voice, as if nothing had happened, "Amalia, I'll get a glass of water for you."

Amalia's lips trembled. She stared at him for quite a long time, as if she did not understand what he was saying. Then she braced herself and said with disdain, "You're so happy to see your wife get screwed."

These words might perhaps have concluded matters for the time being. But Emile stood before her, grinning like a naughty boy. She screamed, and the two other women jumped and hurried off in opposite directions: Shula to Ido's room and Shoshana to the balcony. Shoshana leaned over the balcony and scanned the moonlit street. As Amalia was being embraced by her husband and led to the armchair, she saw Shoshana making her way back from the balcony. Amalia beat her fist against her husband's chest and extricated herself from his grasp. "What did you do out there?" she demanded of Shoshana.

"I went to see whether they followed you here," Shoshana said quietly. Fuad rewarded his wife with a smile.

"Why should they follow us?" asked the poet, who had been forgotten.

"Let's all sit down," Fuad suggested. Miraculously, they all obeyed him, and even Amalia seated herself in the armchair, as far away as possible from her husband. By now she had lost some of the glamor of her blonde, tall figure, posturing on a platform, shaking loudspeakers with her assured voice. She fingered a tiny handkerchief, and in her eyes there was nothing but hatred. Turning to Fuad she said in a rough voice—the voice of an injured woman, not a teacher—"Fuad, tonight you've gone too far."

"There's a reason."

"I want to hear it," her husband said.

The poet relaxed a bit. "Comrades," he said, "please don't attack each other personally."

Fuad, ignoring this, turned to Emile and spoke as though Amalia weren't there. "Listen, my friend. For years now I've suspected that something stunk in the Haifa branch."

"What stinks," Amalia exploded, "is that they've kept you in it much too long."

"Emile, will you hear me out?"

"Of course."

"Then make your wife shut up."

"Amalia . . ." Emile pleaded.

"You've got nothing to say about this," his wife interrupted.

Fuad went on. "After every important debate in Haifa in the last few years, a full report has reached the newspapers just a little too quickly. Your wife sits in the secretariat."

"There are other comrades in the secretariat," Emile protested.

"Just a minute. Let's go back to what happened tonight. You received a secret order—why didn't you telephone Shula yourself?"

"They know my voice. We wanted it to sound like a social call."

"So for that you chose your sweet wife? Come on, let's be honest: On the first night of a war a Jewish voice on the line is better than an Arab voice like yours."

"That's racism," Amalia protested.

"No, it was a reasonable calculation," Fuad said. "And you, Amalia—what did you say in your Jewish voice? The strange innuendoes . . . the demand that we be thrown out before you came . . ."

"Because you're not considered trustworthy any more," Amalia spat out.

"My dear lady. If the report is correct that they're about to arrest Fatkhi, then tonight they'll be coming to arrest me as well. And whose brilliant idea was it to have our poet walk the streets at night with a suitcase in his hand? No Arab with any common sense would do such a thing during a war."

Fatkhi, wounded by Fuad's scorn, said coldly, "It wasn't anyone's idea. It just happened, we didn't think about it."

"Comrade, you're allowed to float in the clouds. You're a poet. And Emile we know is as naïve as a little child. But Amalia brags about her sharp wits. If I know her, her approach is practical—very practical."

"How would you know?"

"Oh, I've known you a long time, Amalia. For years I've been following your career. When all the comrades who taught in government schools were fired, no one lifted a finger against you."

Emile laughed. "They didn't fire everyone."

"That's right, they didn't fire everyone, only those stupid teachers who acted in accordance with their beliefs. But didn't you think it was strange, Comrade Emile, that your wife carried on teaching Jewish nationalism even though she was married to an Arab who was considered a security risk? They even kept her job for her after she went to Poland and poured fire and brimstone on the government and all its organizations. Do you want to tell me that all this didn't arouse your suspicions?"

"Really," Emile stuttered, "really . . ."

"Just keep on stammering," his wife snapped. "He's slinging mud all over me. He's jealous, because they fired his wife; and you smile like an idiot."

"It all adds up," Fuad said. "Someone made a deal with her."

The poet wore a closed expression. Wondering whether he

ought to get up and find another shelter, he touched the tip of his shoe to his suitcase. He looked at Shoshana—her smile astonished him, for it seemed inappropriate to such a serious discussion. He cast a questioning glance at Amalia, and his look enraged her again. She turned red in the face and said to him, "You believe Fuad!"

"You can say what you like about Comrade Fuad," he answered with great seriousness, "but I've known him since I was a child. I disagree with many of his ideas, but I've never caught him lying."

"Then you've changed your mind about him," she said angrily. "Or have you forgotten what you said about him on the way over here?"

"Comrade Amalia, please . . ."

Fuad's massive head moved back and forth like a spectator's at a tennis match. Amalia raised her hands in disgust, and Fuad said in an almost tender voice, "Well, Comrade Amalia?"

"I don't have to answer your dirty innuendoes."

"They're not just innuendoes," Shoshana said.

"And what are they, in your opinion?" Amalia asked. "You're both eaten up with envy. They didn't fire me because they were afraid of making a scandal. They were deterred by public opinion."

"That's strange," Fuad said. "Here's a regime that doesn't mind challenging the whole world but trembles when it comes to firing Comrade Amalia from school."

"It would have reached the Knesset."

"Because of Daddy?" he asked.

"Yes!"

"We've finished," Fuad said, his eyes smiling.

Emile was perplexed. "What have you finished?"

"The conversation with your wife."

"You've accused her of serious things."

"I've finished," Fuad repeated.

Amalia groped on the couch in search of her purse, then

remembered that she had come without it. She got up and turned to her husband. "Emile, let's go home."

He obeyed with an embarrassed smile. "Good night," he said.

"Just a minute," Fuad said.

"Now what?" said Amalia.

"The thing you two raised all the fuss about in the first place—Fatkhi. You brought him here and now you're dumping him and taking off."

"I suppose you want to send him out into the street," Amalia challenged him.

"I think the lady of the house should be asked."

Amalia faced him. "Do you doubt her readiness to obey Party orders?"

"Her husband's gone off to war and she's by herself with a small child."

"Fatkhi can take care of himself."

The poet sat, gloomy-faced.

"It's not that simple," Fuad said, staring at the poet until Fatkhi became uneasy. "He's a young man and, thank God, he looks quite healthy. What is Shula supposed to say if someone sees him in her place? In wartime she can't say that she's hiding an Arab in her house."

"She doesn't have to say anything," Emile said.

"People see, they hear, they talk."

A silence followed and Amalia took advantage of it to say, "So you do suggest putting him into the street."

Fuad laughed. "I was only hoping to have a companion in prison with whom I could discuss real poetry."

For the first time, the poet blew up. "Comrade Fuad, I respect you, but your insinuations hurt. What do you have against my poetry?"

"Did I say anything against your poetry? I just said that we've got a problem and it has to be solved."

"I suggest," said Shoshana, "that Shula say that Fatkhi is a relative of Marduch's, a new immigrant who hasn't been drafted yet."

"That's believable," Fuad agreed. "Now we just have to ask Shula."

"You still doubt her loyalty," Amalia spat out.

"Shut your mouth," Fuad rebuked her. "Get out already. Emile, get her out of here."

"You'll hear from me yet."

"I hope not."

"Let's go say good-bye to Shula," Emile said.

"No," Shoshana said. "You're liable to wake Ido. He's nervous tonight."

"How considerate!" Amalia exclaimed, and left the apartment with her husband in tow.

A heavy silence ensued. Even the sparks of affection in Shoshana's eyes went out now. The poet sat isolated from the couple, sunk in a feeling of insult. Fuad's tone and his deprecating insinuations had stunned Fatkhi. Wasn't he the best Arab poet between the River Jordan and the Mediterranean Sea? There was no doubt about it. His poems had been translated even into Mongolian. He had been accorded respect and honor, not only by members of the Party, but by people who loved the Arabic language and Arabic culture. And now Fuad—Fatkhi was sure of it now—was deliberately insulting him. He lit a cigarette and pictured Zuheir prostrate on the sofa, and Ibitsam's blood-stained hands. He looked at Fuad's massive head and for the first time, he hated him. His soul, the torn soul of a peasant uprooted from his land, was in turmoil. They despise us, he said to himself, they mock us. These Christian intellectuals are like the Jews. They consider us stupid villagers. They've been in bed with the Jews for so long they stink of it already. Their blood is polluted. Fakhri's right. We march blindly in the footsteps of the Christians, who themselves follow in the footsteps of the Jews. If I could go back to Jenin . . . Now he had answers for the questions

Zuheir hadn't asked. Now he could look into Abla's eyes. He had many things to say to them. Abla and her sarcastic remarks . . . she was better than this leader searching for the path, the golden mean, between the darkness and the light. No such path existed.

Nevertheless, he had to admit that Fuad was one of the few people in Israel who understood and loved Arabic poetry. He had trouble understanding, therefore, why Fuad had chosen to attack him as a poet. Fatkhi, like many poets of his generation, took his nourishment from praise. The slightest slap in the face could finish him. He kept sitting, smoking, wrapping himself in silence. Finally he could stand the pain no longer. "Fuad," he said, realizing that he was debasing himself, "what have I done to you?"

The leader stirred, a slight smile came to this thick lips. He gazed at the dead television screen and recited softly:

When the barbaric army of occupation
Came to my village
A thistle bloomed on the roof of my house
And the trenches gouged the fields of my youth
Like the wrinkles on an old woman.

Come, let's hurry and embrace the ancient olive tree
Come, let's gather the corpses of the trampled flowers
Come, let's trace a picture in the dust of an abandoned windowpane
A picture of my village
Invaded by the barbaric army of occupation.

Shoshana crushed her cigarette in the ashtray. She threw her husband a pleading look. "Fuad, really, enough for tonight."

The poet, pale, leaned toward Fuad. "Don't you like it?"

"It's disgraceful," Fuad hissed.

Fatkhi shook with anger. "A very interesting critique."

"Would you like to have a real critique?"

"Yes! Yes!"

"Good." A strange excitement began to show in Fuad's bulging eyes. He turned to his wife. "You won't be bored?"

Shoshana laughed. She knew that at this point he wished he could send her away, dismiss the Jewish woman. "I'm beyond boredom. And anyway, what does it matter?"

"You're right," he said, turning to Fatkhi. "As a poet, you're a petty thief and a miserable imitator of Nazim Khawat. As a revolutionary—well, I still have trouble sorting you out. Are you lost in a dream, or are you just an ignorant villager? Since when does a revolutionary embrace the past, since when does he go around hugging ruins? Mohammed Umru al-Kais did it better than you, and that was before the advent of the Prophet. He wept tears over the desolate ruins, but his fake tears were beautiful, as beautiful as pearls. You ought to be implanting hope in the hearts of your readers and listeners—but where is it? And no doubt you're convinced that in Moscow they adore your poetry. All they want is to whip Israel. They make the country out to be one big concentration camp, and along comes a courageous poet who dares to challenge the barbaric army. . . . Why barbaric, Fatkhi? Who needs such exaggeration?"

"Every army of occupation is by its nature barbaric."

"Let's suppose it is. If all you wanted was a ticket to Russia, then I can assure you that you've succeeded. But I'm obliged to tell you that as an Arab, you've got the soul of a hunted animal."

"Fuad, enough!" Shoshana cried. "Sometimes you are really mean. I don't know how your colleagues on the editorial board can stand you. I'm leaving you both and going to Shula."

Fuad looked at her. "This means more to me than anything. What does this boy know about the Arabs? He doesn't know his people's past. Don't bother looking for the proud Arab in his poetry, the fighter—you won't find any. The Arab he depicts is the one that the females in Tel Aviv carry around in their heads—the Jewish girls who drop their panties for him from time to time. He's rewarded very nicely for retailing this image: it gets him another lay. This image of the miserable Arab, bowed down, persecuted, dispossessed of his land, wretched, trembling, shaking from fears and nightmares, so in need of some pitying Jewish female to take that deprived little boy in him under her protection. It's nauseating. . . ."

"You're disgusting," Shoshana told her husband, and went out to Ido's room.

"Have you finished?" the poet asked Fuad.

"I've finished," the leader said, surprised by the strange glimmer in Fatkhi's eyes.

"You don't understand the poem, man. There's no weeping over ruins here. The poem leaves the ruins behind, Fuad. We're starting from scratch. All the bridges have been burned. I see the Jewish army as barbaric, and the people who created it as my enemy. This is a war to the end. You may marry a Jewish woman and amuse yourself with the dream of brotherhood. I don't believe it. Brotherhood is a slogan for fools. It's us or them."

"I'm an Arab too," Fuad said.

"With a Jewish way of thinking. You're more comfortable in Haifa or Tel Aviv than in an Arab village."

"I didn't realize we had a new kind of racism growing under our feet."

"Call it whatever you like. This is a war to the end."

"What end, Fatkhi?"

"It's our land."

"And Marduch? You've come to hide in his house."

"There'll be a place here for people like Marduch."

Fuad laughed. "And in the meantime he goes rushing off to kill Arabs."

"That's a problem," the poet admitted.

"You're an idiot!" Fuad exclaimed.

The poet sighed.

"So you're about to take up arms," Fuad said. "We're nothing but babblers, so you're turning to the gun."

Fatkhi nodded his head in agreement. Fuad fell silent.

12

Fuad closed the door to the balcony and turned on the light. Blinking and sleepy-eyed, smiling with embarrassment, Shula came out to greet them. A short while before, Shoshana had found her sleeping a troubled sleep on Ido's bed, her fists clenched like a baby's, one fist in her mouth. She was moaning and stammering incomprehensibly. Shoshana sat on the floor and caressed Shula's other clenched fist. It twitched and opened and then grasped Shoshana's hand, while Shula slept on. When at last she opened her eyes in the meager light of the small lamp, Shula stroked Shoshana's hand with such tender gentleness that Shoshana became uneasy. Shula's fingers expressed gratitude, happiness, hope, and even the beginnings of desire.

They had both blushed when Shula awoke fully and sat up in confusion. "I thought . . . I was sure . . . and now he's gone off to war." She glanced at Ido's calm face and got off the bed. "I'm awful. I've got guests and I run off and go to sleep."

"Amalia and Emile have left already," Shoshana said.

In the living room Shula smiled brightly at the poet, as if to make up for her bad manners. "You won't believe this," she said with captivating frankness, "but I dozed off. I just fell on the bed and went to sleep."

Fuad smiled easily, thinking, what a woman! At first he did not know why the thought had come to him, but then he understood. She was still sleepy-eyed, her expression delicate and lovely. It was a face that attracted a man's touch, yet a face that would repel a man's touch.

"Marduch bought a terrific watermelon. I'll get some for you all right away."

Fuad thought to himself that he would gladly accept anything from her. Aloud he said, "That's a great idea."

His wife hoped he wouldn't make a fool of himself. She found him disgusting when he let himself go in the company of other women.

Shula was confused, like a teenager thrown in with adults. She cried out, with excessive gaity, "Fatkhi, you must be famished. I never even asked you whether you've eaten supper. I'll fix us all something to eat. Marduch brought some delicious Greek olives."

"Sit down, Shula!" Shoshana ordered. She had noticed her husband's eyes bulging. "We've got a serious problem. Wake up."

"I'm awake."

"Not awake enough to understand what's happening here."

Suddenly Shula was seized by vertigo and faintness—she had a vision of Marduch dead. "When?" she whispered.

Shoshana was puzzled. "What do you mean, 'when'?"

"Did the news come while I was sleeping?"

"Shula, you're asleep!" her friend shouted. Shula had awakened with a headache. Again she smiled with embarrassment and said, her eyes gleaming, "I must be going crazy."

"If you don't quit it," Shoshana threatened, "I'll pour water over you."

"What do you want?" Shula said.

Fuad answered, "We're afraid that Comrade Fatkhi is about to be arrested. They make these arrests every time there's a war—preventive detention, they call it. During the last war they arrested me and Fatkhi and a lot of others. The Party has decided that this time, for the first time, a number of comrades will not turn themselves in. You've got to admire the decision—it takes some courage, after all. Till now they knocked on the door and off we went to jail, like sheep. It's been decided that Fatkhi won't go this time. That explains Amalia's strange behavior. He came here . . ."

Suddenly the possibility seemed real to her that Marduch might be killed by a Soviet bullet, fired from an efficient Soviet machine gun, fruit of the creative labor of a Soviet factory, that had traversed seas and continents in order to kill him—Marduch, traitor to the Soviet Union. More than once he had told her, "Those poor Kurds—they're being wiped out by Soviet planes." He would say such things only at night, whispering them into her ear. She saw him stretched out on the sand, a Soviet bullet in his heart and an Egyptian fly on his face. Two Arabs and a Jewish woman are come to comfort her. The Arabs, who loved the Communist in him and hated the Jew, had asked him to hate the Jew in himself, or at least to be ashamed of it. He hadn't done it. He had hidden the Jew, sheltered him in silence. Marduch is a Communist because he was a Jew back in Iraq, just as Fuad is a Communist because he is an Arab here. Fuad was expected to wear his Arabness like a crown, Marduch to estrange himself from his Jewishness. But he had refused. And now comes the Soviet bullet to solve the problem, to kill the Jew in Marduch and exalt the memory of the Communist. Now Shula cried out to herself: Let him alone; he's only a child burned with a primus stove, who's afraid that someone might see the scar.

Shula had ceased to pay attention.

I was sure something would happen that night. I'd had such feelings on many nights before, but never so strong. Karim and I would ease the fear by stuffing ourselves with food and going to the movies. Both of us were always hungry, maybe because we were young. It was always open house at Karim's, whereas my house was almost impenetrable. My father was always furious at me; whenever he met me he'd go crazy. He was already old and exhausted. My brother, who had a good job, had been caught and sentenced to twenty years, and the burden of supporting the family had fallen on my father. He was more enraged than grieved by my brother's imprisonment, and he cursed me and let out his rage on me because I was within reach. Sometimes he locked the door in my face and Mother would have to coax him to open it.

One night I came home with a toothache. For the first time in my life I realized what a toothache was. That evening we'd been distributing leaflets and we'd almost been caught. I ran through the alleys like a maniac until I lost the men who were chasing me. While I was running I forgot everything, but when I stood before the locked door, the toothache and hunger and fatigue were suddenly too much for me; a strange longing for a warm touch and a kind word overcame me. I stood before the locked door, still trembling from the fear of the chase. I imagined my father waiting in ambush on the other side. Now that he's dead I don't hate him. He did what he did because of the family and because he was old and tired. Others hated him for the wrong he did to me and my brother. But I remembered him gratefully for what he was to me in my childhood. I stood at the door, hungry and frightened, waiting to be a child again. I remembered his touch when I was a child. Maybe it was because I wanted to be a little boy again that I lied to him. "Father," I whispered through the locked door separating us, "Father, open the door. Father, the police are coming for me. They'll be here soon. Father, let me in—I'm sick."

I heard him rush away from the door and thought that what I had said had moved him and that he'd gone to Mother so that she could persuade him to let me in. I was so dizzy, I fell down on the stoop. When I was young, I had many dizzy spells. I don't know why. Suddenly, I heard the door to the balcony opening above me and father came out; for some reason he looked enormous. "Police!" he roared. "Police, come and get him . . . he's here, the Communist!"

It just wasn't a Jewish thing to do. It was cold that winter. Up and down the street people threw open their windows and listened to my father shouting. They all rebuked him, but the hardest words of all came from his friend, our neighbor, Abu-Yitzhak. "Shut your mouth, Abu-Shlomo!"

"Police!" my father kept shouting in the freezing air. "Come and get him. He's here."

Abu-Yitzhak lost control of himself. "I hope you don't see the light of dawn, you atheist. Finished, everything's finished between us. From now on I don't want to see your face."

Behind my father, my sisters stood wailing. My mother had caught him by the shirt and was pulling him indoors. He smacked her arm and kept screaming at the scandalized neighbors.

Opposite us lived the Hagag family—Zionists, not only sympathizers but real activists, and hostile to me. Now their son Bachuram came out on the balcony and stood facing my father and shouted, "You should be ashamed, Abu-Shlomo. Isn't it enough that they took one son away from you?"

"Let them come and take the second, too. Police!"

The Zionist leaned over the railing. "Marduch," he called, "come up here. I'll open the door for you."

That killed me. I turned my head toward the great and mighty father standing above me and whispered, "Father, father . . ." And I went.

I'm not a saint, Shula. Of course I was angry then. I was in a rage, and I made many vows. But inside, I mean deep down, below the level where transient hatreds are born and pass away, I felt only pity for my father. I think it was then that I grew up. A boy who pities his father isn't a boy any more.

Close to midnight I knocked on my friend Karim's door. It had begun to rain. But Karim's door was open to the slightest knock, day or night. We would have gluttonous feasts at his house when we were terrified. Sometimes we'd be ashamed of gorging ourselves, but his mother with her smiling eyes would laugh with pleasure, and his father would go out into the courtyard and stroll about rubbing his hands together. It was there he would later stand before tanks and attacking horses, seek shelter from the bullets, cover his head against the rifle butts. And Karim and I would keep gorging ourselves and then we'd go out to see a movie. Even when there wasn't a good movie playing, we'd buy tickets—and they were expensive. We bought them with Karim's money, of course—we'd sit and watch the worst junk.

Are you tired, Shula? I didn't mean to tell you about that night. What I wanted to tell you about was my last night of freedom back there. We'll go on with it some other time, why do you insist? Do you think I enjoy it? It just comes out. When I'm next to you, beside you, I feel as if I were daydreaming. No, no. I feel as though I were speaking with Karim. He and I used to talk a lot. They killed him in jail. I can't speak with him anymore.

On that last night I was sitting in a coffee house in a palm grove. There were stools and chairs and tables laid out under the fronds and the air was full of the fragrance of the river, the water pipes, and the grilled fish. All around sat the members of the cell and I conducted the meeting while we pretended to play backgammon. We often held meetings like that. It was easy to make a getaway from such coffee houses.

That evening I had a palpable feeling of danger. During the day I had learned that an arrest warrant had been issued against me, meaning that my name, address, and activities were known to the secret police. They had gone to school and taken my photo from the office. They had me. I went to live in the house of a comrade who was not under suspicion. I didn't give a damn about the photo they had, I just shaved my head and took off my necktie. The feeling of danger was because of something else, because of Marhoun. We had just taken this guy into our ranks and right away I suspected him. I don't know why. Marhoun had this doggish, devoted way about him. He would happily take on the most dangerous missions. That joyfulness bothered me. His way of laughing didn't fit in with the image of a revolutionary, either. His strange laugh, rising up out of his belly, repelled many of us, and so did his talkativeness. He loved to gossip. He came from a devout Muslim family and knew the Koran by heart. One day he invited me over to the Left Bank of the river. He said he'd brought together some fifty people who frequented the tea house in his neighborhood. Marhoun wanted very much for me to see him in his glory. The crowd welcomed him with shouts of joy—this was at odds with the somber atmosphere of an underground movement. The men gazed at him with a mystical devotion that seemed strange to me. We sat in the middle by the light of a kerosene lamp, and those on the periphery pressed in close in order to see Marhoun better. Even the waiter stopped working and he and the proprietor joined the circle. Marhoun cleared his throat, and his sweet song melted the hearts of the tough men around him, who thirstily drank in every word that came from his lips. I was horrified. Marhoun would chant chapters from the Koran and embellish them with selected passages from Marx and Stalin. From time to time he would interrupt the melody and offer a few words of exegesis—on the mysteries of the dictatorship of the proletariat.

I admonished him after the crowd dispersed, late at night, but in vain. From then on I didn't trust him, and I warned the others about him. You couldn't put him off, though. He never took offense, or at least he never showed it. I myself treated him harshly, unjustly. "Marhoun," I said to him once, "I'll speak frankly with you. I'm sure that you wouldn't stand up to torture. If they so much as poked a nail in your flesh everything would come spilling out. Understand me—from now on you're just another member of the cell. Our friendship is over. Through me you might meet other comrades and place them in jeopardy."

Marhoun broke into a belly laugh at the sight of my severe expression. He said, "I understand you. You meet with really important comrades."

"Just take care that you're not caught!" I warned him.

But he was caught. And he did give the interrogators my real name and other details. I cursed the day I met him; I was so furious that I hoped they would cut him to pieces. I waited for the day I could lay my hands on him.

That evening I was in a hurry to finish the cell meeting, because I didn't want to arrive late at the house that was providing my refuge and have to knock at the door. The comrades left while I, as usual, stayed for a little while by myself. As I was about to get up, the barefoot Negro who took care of the water pipes passed by me quickly and whispered with a gloomy expression, "The police have surrounded the place. Run for your life!"

I froze. Fear paralyzed me, but I was also afraid that if I ran, I'd draw the police after me. I saw them all around. After a little while a car came to a stop in front of the coffee house and two officers got out with a man whose head was bandaged. It was Marhoun. He stumbled and his escort prodded him forward, poking him in the ribs with their red clubs. One eye was puffed shut and the other was sunk in a blue ring. His underwear stuck out of his dirty pants. He was barefoot. From the way he walked I could tell his feet were in bad shape.

*Falakot?**

No. The interrogators would break bricks and spread the pieces over the courtyard, and force the prisoner to walk over them for hours at a time, till they were covered with blood.

Marhoun limped and very slowly came closer, studying the faces of those sitting in the coffee house while the two officers poked their clubs in his ribs. Out of the fear that came flooding over me there rose up an island of hatred for Marhoun, who was bringing death down upon me. Suddenly the fear of death and the hatred receded, and in their place came another, more terrifying fear, that of healthy, normal people for monsters and bogeymen. Just then Marhoun was a bogeyman. His face, under the filthy bandages, was a congealed dough of blood and flesh and mud. He was crouched over, limping along on bruised feet, approaching me. I felt not the slightest pity for him, only the instinctive fear of a child about to be grabbed by a monster. There were about ten paces still separating us, and I was hoping that he would collapse and croak or faint before he reached me. He had come to turn me in. I couldn't stand it, I almost got up and turned myself in before the monster arrived. But my legs had turned to stone. He stopped. He had recognized me and as he stood beside me, one slitted eye turned to me. His breath made a peculiar wheezing sound. "God damn you!" I shouted, but the cry remained in my heart. Marhoun stood; he said nothing. His hand did not rise to point at me. The sweat poured off my shaved scalp, over my face. I did not have the strength to wipe it off. Marhoun's

*Whipping on the soles of the feet.—Bastinado.

eye-slit kept glimmering at me. His arms drooped lifelessly by his side. The realization dawned with a shock that Marhoun wanted to torture me. It was then that I knew, too, that he would not turn me in, and this not out of self-sacrifice or heroism, but rather because of the harsh things I had said to him. Of course he had not planned it beforehand. I'm sure he was completely shattered and had come with them to the coffee house to identify me. But once he saw me, he was seized by a strange desire to spit in the face of one who had told him ahead of time what stuff he was made of, one who had claimed to know who would suffer martyrdom for his comrades and who would betray them. As I sat before him, sweating and trembling, he saw the look in my eyes, the fear, and he held his tongue. One of the officers poked him again with his club and Marhoun gave a tortured wheeze. His eye-slit lingered on me for another moment, then he hobbled on toward the other stools.

No, I don't know what happened to him. I heard that when his interrogation was over they took him to some remote prison, and then I lost interest in him. I wanted to erase him from my memory. He had routed the haughty, conceited revolutionary that dwells inside every do-gooder.

I plodded back to the house where they were giving me refuge. As I turned the corner I saw the police gathered at the door and I understood that this, too, was Marhoun's work. So I went instead to my uncle's house, and just as I was climbing up on the roof to sleep there, I heard knocking on the door below. "Marduch!" my little sister shouted from the street, "Marduch, they arrested Father and he gave them the addresses of everybody in the family. They'll be here soon. Run!"

I leaned over the railing and asked her, "Did they hurt him?"

"Just a few slaps. Mother's with him now."

"So they're holding him hostage."

"Yes. Run away, Marduch, quickly."

"I'm going to give myself up," I told her. "They have to let him go."

"Dust be on your head!" my sister cursed, down in the street. "If you do that, Mother will die. Run!"

She wept, but it wasn't her weeping that touched me; it was my uncle's hand, striking the back of my neck with a stunning blow. He was pale. "You brute, you atheist," he cried. "Isn't it enough what you've brought down on them? Do you want to kill your mother on top of it?"

He helped me over to his neighbor's roof and from there I climbed down to another alleyway. He was waiting and walked in front of me to his son's house, where he stayed with me quite a long time, until my sister appeared again, shouting in the street. I was weak, but we had to go at once; my sister said that the police were chasing her. My uncle pulled me up onto another roof. We picked our way down a dark staircase. "We're going to Simha's house," he said.

"No," I said, stopping on the stairs. Simha was a distant relative, and her sons were activists in the Zionist underground. I thought of them as votaries of a cult, members of a mystical sect that smelled of religiosity. We had never even had a real debate. In those days the Zionists weren't hunted down with the same ferocity as the revolutionaries. I despised them, and they considered me a tightrope walker who performed acrobatic stunts at the behest of foreigners. "No," I said vehemently to my uncle, "they won't dare endanger themselves for my sake."

My uncle flared up angrily and almost struck me again. "What do you mean they won't?" he asked, shocked. "Have you forgotten so completely who you are? You're a Jew, Marduch, a Jew. What have the Communists done to you. . . ? They won't dare, you say!"

I had no choice but to give in. I was exhausted, my eyes were closing as I walked. He took my arm and didn't let go. We entered the old marketplace; my uncle rapped on a splintered door and shouted in a voice that could be heard up and down the alley, "Simha, Simha! Open up. I've brought Marduch. The police are after him."

It was as if Simha had been sitting on the roof, waiting. Her head was outlined against the stars, she said, "Of course. I knew he'd end up like this."

The neighbors had been sleeping on their roofs on this blazing hot night, and now they made a tumult of shouting voices. Half asleep, I was separated from my uncle. Simha saw me tottering and she caught me by the shoulders and pushed me into the staircase. I don't remember anything but the cool touch of the mattress. I fell asleep at once. When I woke up, two things penetrated my consciousness with an inexplicable burst of joy: gleaming rays of sunlight and a cascade of black hair. The young girl was lying so close to me, I could smell the fragrance of her hair.

I knew, before I even saw her face, that I would love her. Maybe because of the wonderful joy flowing in my blood. I was still free. I wasn't afraid of anything, except my encounter with Simha's sons. I had met them, but not her daughters. The sons got up, looked me over, greeted me with nods that seemed to express only curiosity, and hurried off to work. I waited to see the girl's face. After a long while she shifted the blanket a bit, but without revealing her face. I was sure now that she was embarrassed to show herself to me, and I was about to turn and let her get up unseen, when she let the blanket fall to her chest and gazed at me with her black eyes, without flinching. Suddenly a smile brightened her enormous eyes, her cheeks and her mouth; and her dark brown skin was flooded with rosy light.

In jail, this smile endured for many years. Despite the desert sand storms, it lost none of its brilliance.

Shula got up and walked to the balcony, not responding to Fuad's request that she give refuge to an Arab. Shoshana and Fuad looked at one another in surprise, but the poet was not in the least perturbed. He was certain that he was a valuable asset to the Party, and not solely on the basis of his own feelings. They said as much in the Party, and he believed what he heard. It did not occur to him that Shula's silence could be interpreted to his discredit. It was between her and the Party. It was neither his business nor Shula's that war had broken out between the Jews and the Arabs, that he was an Arab and she a Jew, that her husband was shooting and being shot at somewhere out in the desert.

But these very things were on Shula's mind as she stood on the balcony. War was hateful and terrifying. Gazing at the moon cruising through the crystalline sky, her head spun. For years she had been indoctrinated with the notion that Israel's wars were wars of aggression. But no one in the Party had said in so many words that the wars the Arabs waged were just. If they had, every Party member in Israel would have been obliged to strive for the military victory of the Arabs.

Not only the leadership but also the Jewish rank and file comrades avoided coming to terms with this problem. Shula had not dared ask the others for their opinion. But she and Marduch did not want the Arabs to win. They didn't delude themselves—an Arab military victory meant a holocaust. Here the leadership played a double game, to add to the confusion. Incessantly, with subtle hints, they inculcated the idea that an Arab victory would be a disaster, and in order to prevent it Israel had to make concessions before it was too late.

But as Shula saw it now, it was already too late: War had

broken out in all its fury. As a revolutionary, she had to help the Arabs confound Israel's aggressive military moves, but the leadership had not given her a clear diagram. As a Jew, however, as a mother and the wife of a soldier, it was her duty to do all she could so that Israel's armies would not be broken, its border would not be crossed—so that the flood would not wash away her home. She knew very well what Fatkhi and Fuad, sitting in the living room waiting for her answer, had in their hearts. They were demanding and taking for granted that she would give refuge to the poet, and this at a time when they were hoping and praying for the destruction of the armies of Israel.

The armies of Israel.

What were the armies of Israel?

The roads leading to Nazareth and Safed and Nahariya were bright with the lights of military vehicles ignoring the blackout in their haste to get to the front. The roads were like strings of pearls glittering in the hills, while the village and kibbutzim along the way were sunk in heavy darkness. Were these engines of destruction the armies of Israel? Or were the generals, winning battles in the south and the north?

There, in the darkness, was also her parents' house in Kiryat Haim. She shook her head. They could say what they wanted at Party meetings, write what they wished in the newspapers—right now the armies of Israel were Marduch, lots and lots of Marduchs who had left their homes for the hills and the desert.

Had they gone of their own free will, or had they been forced?

Had she been certain that Marduch had gone to war out of fear of being punished, she would have gone back to the living room and without a qualm given the Arab poet the refuge that was requested. But in all of Israel's wars, what punishments had been dealt out to those soldiers who sought to evade napalm, mines, burning tanks, rockets, and bullets? Paltry punishments.

It wasn't for fear of such penalties that Marduch had gone to the desert. If a man like Marduch believed he was right, he would not be deterred. She knew that very well. Hadn't he put on his uniform and gone to wait downstairs? Three times he had come back upstairs and kissed Ido and stroked her face, then returned downstairs to wait. Tuvia the pensioner had laughed at him. "What are you afraid of? They won't finish the game before you get there." Marduch's expression was not of someone going out to play a game. He had had more than his fill of such games.

Shula gripped the railing of the balcony and repeated through clenched jaws, "Marduch's gone off to fight." This simple revelation shocked her. Marduch had gone off to war in order to avert catastrophe. Marduch had gone off to the mortars with the brazen-faced intention of winning.

Giving refuge to an Arab poet like Fatkhi would be like a bullet in Marduch's back. Yet in spite of everything she wasn't sure what she ought to do. With a pang in her heart she recalled the young girl's hair on the roof of that house, far, far away. Why had he told her this? Why did he have to tell her of the strange upsurge of love for this girl whose face he had not yet seen?

Marduch, who had been persecuted for so many years, had sanctified the concept of "refuge" for Shula. He had told her of that night to show that to give refuge to a fugitive was the most virtuous of acts.

Shula returned to the living room and said, "Fuad, you and Fatkhi can move the spare bed from Ido's room into the empty room."

Shoshana inclined her head and looked sadly at her friend. Then she hurried after the two men. "Be careful," she said. "Don't wake Ido."

Once she had decided, Shula was relieved. Hurriedly she went into the vacant room and moved aside books and notebooks and chairs to make room for the poet's bed. From the closet in the other room she took out sheets and a summer blanket. Then she announced, "Now Shoshana and I will make supper for everyone. It's almost one o'clock. You'll stay over, too, Shoshana. I don't want you and Fuad running around in the streets on a night like this."

Shoshana was happy. "The two of us will sleep together," she said lightly, "and Fuad can fend for himself on the sofa in the living room. But I have to call the children. Amir's certainly not asleep. He's listening to the news on three transistor radios." She was already standing by the telephone, when there was a soft knock on the door. They all froze.

Shula came out of the kitchen and called out, "Who's there?"

"It's me, Shula," Tuvia said. "I saw you standing on the balcony and I said, I'll go down to see her for a bit. Did I scare you?"

Shoshana whispered to the poet, "Go! Go to your room and close the door behind you."

"No," Shula said. "He's staying here. It's better that Tuvia see him now."

"What's that?" Tuvia asked through the door. "Who are you talking with in there?"

"With my guests."

"In that case I'll go back upstairs. I didn't want to intrude. I couldn't sleep and I thought you were alone."

Shula opened the door. "Come on in. I'm making supper and you can eat with us."

He greeted Shoshana and Fuad with a nod, his gaze lingering on the poet.

"This is Fatkhi," Shula said. "He arrived just this evening. A cousin of Marduch's."

The pensioner approached him, put out his hand, smiled, and said, "What's this, young men go around visiting in the middle of a war?"

The poet was struck dumb. Shula said, "He's a new immigrant. He came to Israel only a week ago. We invited him to come tonight—we didn't know there'd be a war."

The pensioner kept smiling. "Marduch never mentioned having a cousin who was a new immigrant." Tuvia did not say it maliciously; only to let his neighbor know that she was a poor liar. When she blushed, he regretted what he had said. "Go, go make supper. I'll just drink some tea." As soon as Shula was in the kitchen he turned to the poet. "So you don't understand Hebrew."

Fatkhi smiled his superb smile and nodded.

The pensioner looked intently at Fatkhi and then said to Fuad and Shoshana, "Have you heard the latest news?"

"No," Shoshana said in a hostile tone.

"The air force bombed and destroyed all the bridges the Egyptians put over the Suez Canal. Now the Egyptians are caught in a trap."

And he turned his back on the poet and sat down next to Fuad.

13

Shula opened her eyes and thought, Marduch still hasn't called. That's not like him. He always calls in. During the first few months of their marriage she thought it was just love. Whenever he went out of town he would spend more on long-distance calls than on the trips themselves. Once, when he had to stay for four days in Tel Aviv, sitting on a Party committee, he would call her at seven in the morning and seven at night. On the third day he could not call at the usual time, and he woke her at midnight.

"Shula," he said, "I'm sorry, you must have been worried."

"I miss you a lot," she tried to calm him, "but I didn't worry. I knew you were busy . . . and anyway, you're a big boy now."

From the tone of his voice she knew that he was disappointed. She realized then that all these calls to her were being made by a young boy who wanted his existence and whereabouts known, who wanted to be worried about. Marduch, by some miracle, had not grown old in that jail in the desert—instead, he had remained a young boy. Within those fiery walls he had found the shaky security of a prison society. Upon leaving prison he had, in effect, been orphaned. His friends thought of him as forged in fire, and even she thought of him that way in emergency situations that called for resourcefulness. But during the calmer moments of life Marduch remained a boy. He revealed his weakness only to her, and in roundabout ways.

She turned over on her bed and met Shoshana's blue eyes. Her friend laughed softly and said, "How is it to wake up and find a woman in your bed?"

Shula smiled reluctantly and said, "Like it was when I was little."

"Kiss my ass," Shoshana murmured. "When you were little! Your husband's gone to war and I'm being screwed by an Arab."

"Shosh," Shula interrupted her. "Marduch still hasn't called."

Shoshana looked at her, the sorrow and bitterness gone from her face. "Tell me, do you really want him to call *now*?"

Shula blushed. The question troubled her. Deep inside she had her doubts, and they perplexed her. "What shall I do, Shosh?"

Shoshana gazed at the ceiling and said, "Don't tell him."

"I can't. That's disgusting."

"I knew you'd feel that way. That's the reason I agreed to sleep over. Don't be a fool. Only a murderess would tell her husband, when he's dodging bullets and shells, that a strange man is sleeping in his house. By the time he learns of it after the war, he'll have forgiven you. He'll have seen so many corpses and death throes and so much blood, he'll be happy just to be alive. For those first few days he'll be willing to forgive all the sins of this lousy world. In the beginning he'll be forgiving and understanding, and he'll laugh at your worries."

"What do you mean, in the beginning?"

"Later he'll start making sarcastic remarks, in a joking way of course, so that you'll be even more hurt than if he accused you straight out, and you'll laugh and stammer, and that'll bother him still more and make him joke more and more . . ."

"Thanks a lot."

"That's nothing," her friend said with satisfaction. "Marduch meets many Arab comrades."

"What do I care?" Shula shrugged her shoulders, and realized that she had not undressed, that she had slept in her clothes.

Shoshana laughed once more. "My dear, you don't know how men think, especially Arab men. If you swear on all the holy books, you'll just increase their suspicions. Look, Shula, you've got a pretty face and a great body and you're letting an unmarried man sleep in your house at a time when your husband can't suddenly burst in and see what's happening in his nest."

Shula turned pale with anger. She leaned against the backboard of the bed. Her disheveled hair fell in waves over her breasts. "You're awful," she murmured.

"It's the way of the world. I just wanted to explain to you what kind of fix your friend Amalia's got you into."

"Nonsense. Fatkhi isn't some bum off the street. He's a poet, an important personality."

"He's many things, but first and foremost he's an Arab man."

"Meaning what?"

"I'm married to one," Shoshana explained patiently. "They're jealous of their manhood and their honor."

"So everything's fine."

"Everything's lousy."

"You got up on the wrong side today," Shula said.

"Do you want to listen?"

"No!" Shula said, her eyes flashing.

"By the way, do you know that Fatkhi's engaged?"

"No." Shula was surprised. "He was sitting here with us a few weeks ago, speaking with Marduch. He said he was a confirmed bachelor, he wasn't cut out for married life."

"He's engaged to a girl from his village."

"Fatkhi with a village girl?"

"Exactly. A simple girl whose pure soul hasn't been infected by higher education and who hasn't set foot in a Party clubhouse."

"You can't stand him," Shula said.

"That has nothing to do with it. Listen, let me tell you something about this revolutionary. Scratch a little deeper and you'll find a Muslim villager, a typical nationalist. It is not important what I think of such a combination—what's important is that Fatkhi himself hates it. He hides his identity behind revolutionary bangles and beads. And it's not just Jewish girls who fall in love with him—a lot of Arab virgins melt when they see him, too. But he thinks they're unfit, and so do many other Arab comrades. A girl with so little common sense as to work with men loses her reputation. She's looked at with desire and lust, but no one takes her seriously. She's tainted. Fatkhi knows what he wants. A pure virgin like Hiam."

"So I've got nothing to be afraid of," Shula said with relief.

"So you think. Fatkhi's friends in the village and on the editorial board and at the clubhouse will come over and poke a friendly elbow in his ribs. They'll whisper in his ear. They'll say that while they laid low during the war, he was enjoying a cozy shelter. Your poet will have to decide—your honor or his. Understand me, if the choice were your honor or his life, perhaps he'd hesitate. But your honor against his—that's serious. If he denies it, that is, if he succeeds in convincing them thay they're mistaken, they'll consider him a hopeless case, a dishrag, a sick pervert. Shula, he'll be forced, against his will, to answer with a wicked smile and a half-hearted denial."

Shula tried to treat it as a joke. She smiled and said, "What should I do?"

"You've already done it."

"Should I get out of the house?"

"Don't be a child."

"Then come and stay here, Shosh."

"I'd do that, but my man is an Arab, too. He'd cut off my legs. Especially if they arrest him."

"The two of us will be together."

"Yes!" Shoshana cried. "Then they'll be sure we're having nightly orgies with the great poet."

Shula didn't know whether to laugh or to cry. Although she refused to take Shoshana seriously, her anger mounted. "Did Amalia know all this when she brought him here?"

"No. It's not fair to blame her that much. She's no expert in these things. Her husband's an Arab, it's true, but she's been able to fix him very nicely indeed. Emile's pasteurized, sterilized, and brainwashed. Amalia does things thoroughly. Her man's not an Arab any more. From time to time a little Arab bark sneaks out, but one freezing look from Amalia sends him right back to the doghouse. As an Arab he's lost his identity. The Arab comrades don't dare say so in public, but among themselves they agree that he isn't a man anymore. Amalia has no idea what a man or an Arab is."

"All this nonsense makes me want to throw up."

"Then do it fast. I hear your Ido waking up."

"Damn," Shula grumbled, getting up and going out to the living room, where she met Fuad's eyes, protruding and red from lack of sleep. He was lying on the sofa with his ear stuck to the transistor radio. From the poet's room as well she could hear the energetic voices of the news announcers. The sour odor of urine filled Ido's room. The child lowered his eyes with shame, his body huddled under the blanket. "Where's Daddy?" His question was like a supplication.

"I've told you twenty thousand times that he's in the army."

"I want Daddy."

"Get up!" she ordered him.

The child's miserable body rolled up into a ball under the blanket. "Tell Daddy to come."

"Idiot!" she hissed, in a rage. "Look, can't you understand, your father's gone off to war. This," and she pointed her finger at him, "this is what he left me with at home."

The child had a frightened look; he seemed unable to speak.

Suddenly he said, with remarkable speed, "Daddy—school—Shula—airplanes—fuck the Arabs—Shula—peepee-shit—all the girls—Shula—all the girls . . ."

She stood over him, the anger still raging in her. "When you finish your morning prayers, tell me."

Suddenly the fog receded from his eyes. "You won't hit me, will you, Shula?"

She was shocked. "Who hits you in this house?"

"They hit at school."

She put a motherly hand on his large head, and this time he didn't recoil from her touch. For a second she was proud. She lifted him in her arms and went to the bathroom. In the living room the child waved at the man stretched out on the sofa. "*Ahalan*, Fuad."

"*Ahalan*, Ido," Fuad answered in a thick voice. He put the radio down on the armchair and called toward the bedroom, "Shoshana, is your sleep so sweet?"

"What do you want?"

"Coffee. My mouth is dry."

Shoshana and the poet burst from their rooms simultaneously. Shoshana looked at Fatkhi's pajamas and the undershirt beneath it and remembered from her first days with Fuad that he too would sleep in underwear beneath his pajamas. She went into the kitchen with a sad smile on her lips.

The poet sat beside Fuad on the sofa. "Have you heard?"

"I've heard."

"What do you say?"

"I'm confused," declared the leader.

"It can't be a lie," the poet whispered.

"It's still too early to say."

"Man," the poet exclaimed, "an Egyptian flag on the eastern bank of the Suez Canal. Kantara liberated. Do you understand? Jebel es-Sheikh is in the hands of the Syrian forces and they're rushing like the devil toward the Sea of Galilee. What's going on here?"

"Who would've believed it?"

"Surely not you." Immediately he remembered that he was a poet. "The myriad tears shed since '48 were not in vain. I feel that I was not born for nothing. I have a reason for being. It is good to be here!"

"Where?" Fuad asked. "Dressed in pajamas and hiding in the house of an Israeli soldier who's killing your brothers?"

"With all due respect, Fuad, you're always inclined to spoil things. Tell the truth, how do you feel?"

"Like a grounded airplane. You heard Amalia yesterday. Understand this, Fatkhi—if the leadership ever learns that you're sitting beside me now, talking confidentially, you'll fall under suspicion."

But the poet had confidence in his own reputation. "Don't exaggerate. Don't spoil this morning, Fuad. Today's a holiday."

"Let's hope so."

After breakfast, Shoshana dressed Ido. Shula said to her, "Today he'll be with me. The schools and kindergartens are closed anyway." And she sat down at the kitchen table to write out a shopping list on a scrap of paper. "Fatkhi," she said, "I'm going to the store. Do you want anything special?"

The brisk tone of voice confused the poet. He looked at her and thought, I'll have to spend a lot of time with her. He said, "Nothing. Thanks a lot. Nothing."

She sensed that somehow she had offended him. During the first days with Marduch she had had this same feeling. From this "Thanks a lot" she had known that Marduch was hurt. She said, "Listen, Fatkhi, I'm a very bad cook. If it wasn't for Shoshana we'd eat rubbish in this house. At least you could ask me to bring you whatever you're used to."

"Cigarettes and beer," he said

"Ido, you're coming with me to the store."

"I want to go to school."

"There's no school today."

"Maybe you need me today after all?" Shoshana asked. She was afraid to go back to her house.

"No, really."

Shoshana turned to the door. "Shalom, Fatkhi."

To her surprise, the poet shook her hand firmly. Then he gave Fuad a hesitant glance. Finally he embraced him, hugged him fiercely, and kissed him on both cheeks.

Fuad burst out laughing. "What's with you, my friend?"

The poet, still in pajamas, lit a cigarette and said with great feeling, "Who knows when and where we'll meet again. . . ."

At the door Shula warned the poet, "If the phone rings, don't answer it."

Fatkhi thought her concern was for him, not realizing that she didn't want a strange man answering Marduch. She locked the door after her and the four of them went down to the sunlit street. This morning no one remarked on the sunshine. The streets were full of amazement and fatigue. Haifa had waited impatiently for the break of day, but daylight had brought no relief. The pensioner's head and shoulders were outlined over the railing of his balcony. Shula looked up, expecting him to greet her, but he didn't say hello as he usually did. "Good morning, Tuvia."

"Have you heard anything from Marduch?" was the reply.

"No. How's Hannah?"

"She'll be all right."

That's not just coolness, Shula thought. The old man was distancing himself from her. It angered her. She grabbed Ido's hand and went toward the car, taking leave of Shoshana and Fuad. She did not go to the local store. Cigarettes and beer. The grocer knew she didn't smoke. He was sure to ask, with his salacious grin, "Who are you hoarding cigarettes for?" And the beer. She never bought beer. Marduch detested beer.

His guts turned over inside him at the sight of the foaming liquid.

I'll tell you, Shula. I don't just hate beer, I'm terrified of it. It's simple conditioning. Of course, I managed to overcome it. I try to overcome many things. It's hard to root out such terrors. I used to like a beer from time to time. One evening Karim and I were sitting in a casino on the bank of the river. All around us the world shimmered enticingly. There were white sailboats skimming along the blue water, palm trees set off by the dusk on the opposite shore, colored lights blossoming between the branches of the trees, the fragrance of roses and young women. Karim and I were going crazy. Actually I was the one, as usual. I raised an authoritative finger and called out, "Boy!" Casinos were different from ordinary coffee houses in two respects: In a casino there was no radio, and to call the waiter you didn't shout *"Ya walad,"* but "Boy"—with that British kind of arrogance.

We liked beer, because in the novels we read people drank chilled beer. Of course by the time we finished sitting around, late at night, Karim's pockets were empty, and he chewed me out and said that because of that pissy drink he wouldn't be able to buy the works of Sartre. He was crazy about Sartre, he read him in the original and he believed that he was destined to be a writer himself. In fact he did write a few things, nice, small things. I wanted to cheer him up and so I said, "Come on, at least we can act like drunks."

The idea enchanted him. He asked how.

"We'll walk along the street and bark in the gay effendis' faces."

We scared the wits out of several gorgeously outfitted gentlemen. A bleary-eyed cop approached us with awe and reverence, thinking we were well-to-do kids, and asked us politely to behave as befit our lofty station. Karim straightened to his full height. He was an impressive lad, one of the ideologues of the underground. "Go home," he ordered the cop," and tell Father to send the car to pick us up."

The black bristles quivered on the cop's leathery face. "And who is the gentleman's honorable father?"

"Naif Sansal!" Karim declared with great self-importance.

This was the chief executioner, who supervised the torture in the C.I.D.* dungeons.

The cop disappeared like smoke, and we took off our shoes and went down to the river. Opposite us, in midstream, was the island, and on it bonfires and pillars of smoke bearing the fragrance of roast fish. I didn't know then that I was to meet Naif Sansal in the near future and that it was beer, no less, that he would serve me.

At that time this murderer was dying to discover the underground's printing press. At night he would hoist his belly up on a bicycle and sneak silently into the city's remotest corners, listening for the heartbeat of the underground. The printing press was his obsession. For some reason he was sure that I knew where it was. He was right, and perhaps he could have got what he was after. I was terrified and felt guilty for getting caught in the stupidest way. Shula, you can get a revolutionary to say anything if his conscience isn't clear. But Sansal made two big mistakes.

First of all, he tried to get at me as a Jew.

I was shoved into a room and found myself face to face with Sansal, who was sitting in an armchair. He got up at once and gestured to the soldier to close the door; then he ordered me to sit down. At first he didn't speak, just stared at me with infinite loathing, as if there were a disgusting smell coming off me. And in fact I reeked of the urine that had formed a pool around me while I was chained in the basement. Then he spat, not on me, but on the floor, because his loa-

*The secret police.

thing was genuine. "Another Jew," he hissed contemptuously. "A Jew stays a Jew—plays at revolution and pisses in his pants."

That was good, Shula. Really good. For the first time I felt something other than the terror that had gripped me ever since they laid their hands on me. A wonderful feeling was rising in me—anger. Not a personal anger, but a kind of collective anger, larger and greater than me. More than anger, it was indignation, and its roots went very deep. Generation after generation, we had been degraded. Iraq had known many conquerors and cultures, but they all, conquerors and conquered alike, saw us Jews as scum, miserable wretches, cowards.

And we believed them. They convinced us that we were cowardly creatures. Over the course of time we ourselves fostered this image. We said it was indispensable for our survival. Better to live as a dog than to die as a lion. They spit on our beards and it never occurred to us to explode with rage. It seemed a natural, necessary part of a dog's life.

Then our situation changed; it grew intolerable, and we were forced to adopt a cult of courage. Sometimes, perhaps, our cowardliness had been justifiable. But now things were different; there was a new world in which only courage would do, where the old cowardliness would mean our destruction.

A small handful of Zionists emerged. Of course, it wasn't they who initiated the change. At that time they avoided direct clashes with the establishment. All they wanted was to leave everything behind and emigrate to Israel. I won't be cute, I won't pretend it was the Jewish revolutionaries who brought about the change. The new Jew came into the world when our fathers left their ancient alleyways and ventured into the mixed neighborhoods. I played hide-and-seek, climbed trees and stole plums with Muslim and Christian boys. When I grew up no one could tell me: "You're a grown-up Jew, and from now on you've got to learn to bow and scrape like your ancestors did."

I was a member in good standing of the neighborhood gang, and I took part in dangerous attacks on the adjoining quarter. I'd return with the others, either defeated or crowned with victory. All the revolutionary doctrine just provided an ideological infrastructure. What it meant to me personally was, I'm an equal among equals, and if anyone tells me different, I'll tear his eyes out.

Sansal's blunder exposed his ignorance. Either he didn't know that a new Jew had come into being, or he didn't want to believe it. All he wanted was to lay his hands on a Jew who knew where the printing press was. He was imbued with the thousand-year-old certainty that he'd be able to extract each and every secret from the first Jew who came his way. And that confidence incensed me.

Presently he mastered the revulsion that my Jewish body stirred in him, only to focus on my Jewish name. He said disdainfully, "Marduch . . . what a disgusting name. It's got a stink of Sabbath stew coming off it."

Yes, yes, Shula. I told him, "Sir, you don't even know the history of your own country. Marduch is al-Shumairy's name."

That was more than he could take, and he called out, "Mansur! Said!"

Two cops came in. They knew their job. They hauled me out of the chair and shoved me behind the door. With all their might they pushed against the door, as if they meant to crush me between it and the wall. I thought my bones were about to be smashed. And while I was trapped this way, struggling to breathe, Sansal started his monologue. "Fuck his mother! Jewish insect, son-of-a-bitch. Leprous mouse. Just yesterday you were worms, and you'll be worms again. Newspapers, articles, rallies, demonstrations. Great God, have you forgotten who you are? With my own eyes I saw a filthy Jew raise his hand against an officer. Who ever heard of such a thing? Why, at the very first whistle you all used to scurry off to hide in your holes, every one of you would go looking for his mother's cunt to push his head into. How dare you threaten the government. . . . Where did you learn that?"

And I, squeezed between wall and door, tried to take in some air just to answer him. When he told the two cops to let up so that the leprous mouse could come out of his hole, I fell to the floor and answered him. One of the cops came and slapped my face, and I kept answering him. The three of them grabbed me and stamped me, and still I kept answering him.

And then Sansal made his second mistake. He started on me with the maximum, the worst—the primus stove and the iron chair.

When I had lost my voice from screaming and I was near to fainting, he and I both knew that anything further would only be brutality for the sake of brutality. I was hoping that my end would come quickly, and he was trying to delay it as long as possible.

That was two or three days after Tisha b'Av.* The city was scourged by fiery summer heat, about one hundred and twenty degrees in the shade. The sun was like a savage ball of fire in the cloudless sky, and everyone fled from it to the cellars or the shade of trees. People hurrying home would dash from one patch of shade to the next, as in other countries they jump from shelter to shelter in the rain. The teacher in fourth grade had said that on a summer day, the palm tree drank more than one hundred and twenty glasses of water in order to survive. I hadn't believed him. After all, the trunk of a palm tree is dry and hard, its foliage is sparse and resistant to heat and drought. A man's body, on the other hand, is covered with a thin, half-transparent skin. This poor integument was all that separated me from the death in the sky when I woke up on the roof of the C.I.D. building. I was naked, and the

*Jewish day of fasting and mourning in commemoration of the destruction of the First and Second Temples.

burns from the primus stove tormented me. I don't know how many minutes or hours I had lain out there. My eyelids were swollen shut. My body was covered with blisters. I don't remember when and how they took me down from there. I only remember the cold touch on my lips. I tried to open my eyes but it was impossible. I heard a voice ordering me: "Drink! Drink! Drink!"

It was a bottle. I sucked at it like a baby. I was shaking as if from cold and I sucked until I realized I was sucking air. Right away another chilled bottle was put to my mouth. And again the voice commanded: "Drink! Drink!"

I didn't have the strength to swallow. I was drinking from the elixir of life and collapsing at the same time. I think that with the fourth bottle I understood what the beverage was that was bringing me back to life. It was beer.

I gulped and collapsed and the commanding voice goaded me tirelessly. Beer and more beer. Chilled, cold, moist beer, its wetness penetrating my body and filling it. Even my hair, it seemed to me, was filling with beer. And I wanted more and more and I couldn't swallow and in spite of that I drank and I drank. I was sure that I could drink without a mouth, without a throat, without a stomach to take in the stuff. I would have drunk like a palm tree drawing water from the bowels of the earth.

And suddenly everything stopped. The beer, the voice, the trembling, the exhaustion and even the agony. I lost consciousness, I lost track of time. Intermittently I would wake up and sink into delirium. In that sealed room, under my swollen eyelids, the sun kept blinding me with its white rays. Through the pain that gnawed at my body, through the short spells of unconsciousness, the sense of accomplishment grew stronger. My body contained an unruly, oceanic tide that struggled to break out, to free itself from its confines. I thought I was dreaming. How could my tortured body contain such a great ocean, a tide struggling to break through this poor skin without success? It was a long time before I understood Sansal's little prank. I tried to urinate and couldn't. They had tied up my genitals with wire. All the bottles of beer that I had drunk were trapped inside me and I couldn't void them.

"Shula, you said we were going to walk to the store."

"We're going to drive, Ido. We're going to the supermarket."

The determined expression on her face, together with the fact that they were not going to the familiar grocery, made the child uneasy. He fell silent and stared about the streets, astonished and wide-eyed.

The beautiful city rising from the sea had turned ugly overnight, grown old and hesitant. The city rose after a sleepless night, preoccupied and gloomy, yet overflowing with benevolence and generosity. Strange, Shula thought to herself, that the people don't seem angry. Rather, it was as if they had come out with one desire in their hearts: to make things easier for one another. It was good to breathe this air. So it seemed until she entered the supermarket. Inside, a storm was raging. Greedy hands were snatching at the shelves and emptying them. Shula grabbed hold of frightened Ido's hand and steered a course between bared teeth and sweaty faces. She collected the items she needed and, unsteadily, took two bottles of beer for the poet.

Ido was wailing. The uproar and the crowd terrified him. Shula stooped and picked him up. By the time she had escaped with him outdoors, out of the commotion, his eyes were shut, his face was creased, he was exhausted. She sat him down on the seat next to her and started the car. "Where do you want to go?" she asked.

"To Daddy."

"We can't. You want to visit Grandma and Grandfather?"

"Yes! Yes!"

She felt jealous. Ido preferred her parents' company to her own. For the thousandth time she wondered: Can such a child have any idea of his mother's despair?

She found her parents having their customary breakfast—sliced tomatoes, yogurt, and tea. Her mother wore her testy expression. Her father's eyes smiled, as always. Ido loved his grandmother's withered bosom. Her mature, confident manner attracted him. He knw that somewhere inside this tough old-timer, deep inside this veteran activist, there flickered an ember of tenderness reserved exclusively for him and his mother. Her abstract love embraced the whole world, but shrank from any personal contact. Ido and Shula were the exceptions.

"Did you bring a newspaper with you?" her father asked.

"What do you expect to find in their newspapers?" his wife asked.

"News, just news."

"Lies, that's all you'll find. Do you have to read their lies every morning to know they're still lying? Shula, he's driving me crazy with his radio. I thought last night that he'd fallen asleep and I turned it off. But no! Our great expert opened his eyes and shouted that he was listening. How can he swallow their lies, day and night?"

"How is Marduch?" her father asked.

"He went to war."

"Say that they took him," her mother cried.

"He put on his uniform while he was still home waiting for them."

Her mother was irritated. "He's simple-minded. Your Marduch's simple. But don't you play their games the way he does."

"Who are they?"

"They! They! Those criminals."

Only Marduch knew how to cope with her. Shula would bridle at her extremism and become entangled in noisy quarrels. "Who started this war?" she demanded loudly.

"Listen! Listen! She's still casting doubts. Even their radio had to revert to Cairo's story. Didn't they admit that the navy went to attack . . . what's that place. . . ?" and she turned irritably to her husband.

"Ras Zafrava."

"That's it! Ras Zafrava." She shifted the teacup as if this place name had cleared up all the uncertainties. Ido was sitting on her knees, playing with the buttons on her shirt. Her left hand petted him tenderly while her right pounded angrily on the table.

Shula saw only her mother's right hand, and she felt compelled to hurt her. "It seems," she said almost in a whisper, "that there's an arrest warrant out for the poet Fatkhi."

"What?" her mother shouted.

"Just what you heard."

"Now you know why they needed this war. They're trying to destroy the progressive Arab leadership."

"They won't destroy Fatkhi,"

"What do you know!" her mother said. At that moment it pleased her to have this leadership destroyed, if only to see her theories borne out.

"He's in a safe place, Mother."

"There's no safe place in this country."

"There is, Mother, there is."

"Marduch's naïveté is getting to you."

"Mother, I've given the poet shelter in my apartment."

Shula remembered her childhood horse. It was a chestnut, with a bright white spot on its forehead. It would pull Grisha's wagon over the dunes of Kiryat Haim. On more than one occasion Grisha picked Shula up from the sand and sat her in the wagon beside him, way up there in the heights. From there she could see the horse's great and marvelous back, trembling and laboring as the animal pulled the wagon. She still remembered the horse's expression: not when the snake rose up to strike at it; not while it galloped blindly, overturning the wagon; not even when its head struck a tree. What she remembered was its look in the split second between dropping to the sand and dying. The expression on her mother's face was like the one on that horse. But her mother didn't die. Only her right hand, rushing about on the tabletop, lost its vitality. With exaggerated care she gave Ido over to her husband, always ready at times of crisis. Only then did she hiss, "What kind of foolishness is that?"

"It's not foolishness, Mother." Already, Shula regretted the injury she had inflicted. "Someone up above was worried about the poet and Amalia brought him over to our house."

"But why did that woman bring him to your house, of all places?"

"Maybe because it's safe. Very few Jewish comrades are called up to the army, and it's just possible that Marduch's the only one who takes part in combat. So they thought my place would be safe."

"Your place would be safe . . ."

"Mother, I'll bring you a glass of water."

"I don't need any water," she shouted.

"It's not as dangerous as you think."

"What do you know, child. What do you know."

"Everything will be all right. I shouldn't have told you. Now you'll worry for nothing."

"Tonight you'll bring him over here."

"You're talking nonsense."

"Speak to her, speak to her," she appealed to her husband, gloomy-faced. "Explain to the child that she's playing with fire."

The father looked at his daughter. The smile in his eyes was undercut by anxiety, but he didn't open his mouth.

"Say something!" his wife pressed him.

"Mother," Shula said, "you're panicking for no reason."

"A child," her mother murmured. "A little girl . . ."

14

The poet felt as if he himself had gone to war—he was a soldier without uniform. If his rifle and uniform hadn't reached him, this was only because the proper arrangements hadn't been made. Fakhri, his friend who had gone off to Beirut, had the right idea, not Fuad, who tried to make his life in the Jewish state.

Fire!

All other means had been exhausted. The time for killing had arrived. Anyone who did not shoulder his burden in the great military effort was a traitor to his people. The Arab armies, shouting "Allah is great," had surprised the Jewish state in its sleep. At this very moment Israel was lifting thousands of hands to rub the sleep from its eyes, and these hands were being chopped off, one after the other.

Fire!

The clumsy body, drugged with sleep, had to be destroyed before it awakened fully. It had to be smashed by all possible means.

Fire!

Kill, slay, slaughter. As quickly as possible and with every weapon that came to hand. There was no room here for the rules of the game as invented by English gentlemen. It was useless for Fuad to wrestle with moral problems. As a matter of fact, elementary human morality demanded that the venomous serpent be trampled underfoot with hobnail boots. Doing one's duty meant acting according to instinct. Sometimes simple instinct was the whole of human morality.

Fire!

Break the legs of an Israeli soldier. Strangle an Israeli soldier. Butcher an Israeli soldier. Slice off the hands of an Israeli soldier before he awakens and reaches for his gun.

Fire!

And yet, despite all this, the poet visualized himself not as a man who was going out to slaughter, but rather as one who was sacrificing his life. He stubbed out his cigarette, moved by an urge to cleanse himself. Barefoot, he proceeded to the bathroom. As he stood in front of the mirror shaving, he pondered matters in all seriousness. Everything had its price, even a poet. Of the Soviet poet Ilya Ehrenburg it was said that with his pen he contributed so mightily to the armed struggle against Germany that his value was reckoned as that of a full division. And he, Fatkhi, what did his value, his weight, come to? One Israeli soldier? An artillery piece? A tank with its crew? In war things were weighed with brutal simplicity. He knew his value as a poet very well. But today, after his talk with Fuad, he had no illusions. The poems he had written were, indeed, addressed to the masses, yet he had always managed to maintain certain standards. There had been bitter fights on this subject on the editorial board. He had refused to give in. His poems lacked that spark, the spark that sets off conflagrations. Soldiers marching off to war would not recite them. His poems were not meant to stand up to a hail of bullets. Fatkhi's generation—here was the ironic, the tragically ironic secret—his generation was for better or worse a product of Israel. Here, in Israel, the system did not educate children explicitly for war. The Jews, those bastards, spoke only of peace, yet they went to war every ten years. No one living in Israel, neither Jew nor Arab, ever thought of openly preaching war.

The poet carefully worked his razor over his handsome face. Let Fuad say what he wished, his poems were valuable. Fuad would not have committed to memory an inferior, a worthless poem. . . .

Forget personal considerations, the poet told his white-lathered reflection. His poems were among those that had rescued Arabic poetry and the Arabic language in Israel from the decline into which they had fallen after the 1948 war. Although his poems were full of lamentation and wailing, they had great importance. Before a revolution can begin, injustice must be exposed. People who didn't know they were oppressed would never think of stirring. And in these poems, the first step was taken. He splashed his face with eau-de-cologne, inhaled with pleasure and asked, so what is my value? At least a battalion, he answered at once.

But since he had no military training, he didn't know exactly what a battalion was, how many soldiers were in it, and what sector a battalion could hold at the front. And then he remembered his drive to the Haifa seashore. The traffic halted, the bell sounded, the signal light flashed yellow, the ground shook, and the air quivered as the train, loaded with monsters, hurtled by.

That's it, he cried to himself. A train loaded with tanks. . . .

The poet was as content as if he had already sabotaged that damned train, equivalent in value to a national poet. The tanks were scattered over the brown earth, twisted and smoking. The poet longed to take a shower. Nervous as a soldier going out to battle, he stripped and turned on the tap. The water was cold. Shula had forgotten to heat the boiler. The corpses of the tanks were scattered around him. Teeth clenched, he leapt into the frigid torrent, and as his neck shuddered from the icy impact, he remembered Marduch. He respected him. This fighter, forged in fire, was the Jew who was closest to him, closer even than those Jewish girls with their fresh skin and blonde hair in whose passion he had reveled. He believed in Marduch's friendship. Marduch, who found nothing wrong with being a Jew and an Israeli—unlike many Jewish members of the Party—had won the poet's heart with his sincerity. The others, he found, suffered from a bad conscience because they belonged to the Jewish people. They apologized for themselves, with a certain haughtiness. Actually, their apologies were a proclamation of superiority—we, the Jews, can treat you unjustly, Fatkhi, but you can't do it to us. Therefore we come and ask your forgiveness. Even Shula. How she had hesitated before consenting to take on a simple assignment—providing shelter to a comrade. There was nothing apologetic about Marduch's behavior. Perhaps that was why he alone had dared express revulsion at a number of P.L.O. operations. They were furious with him in the Party. Marduch said that a revolution had to be clean, and not only in its goals. They remained furious, but they respected him.

Fatkhi dried himself off with a towel that Shula had given him that morning, and he thought with relief: Marduch would have done the same thing as I did to that train if he were in my place.

Suddenly the empty apartment reverberated with the ring of the doorbell. The poet hurriedly dressed but did not answer. It's not Shula, he thought. She had locked the door and taken the key. She had told him that he was not to answer the telephone, but hadn't mentioned the doorbell. That meant that she was not expecting visitors. The poet kept silent. The bell rang insistently, annoyingly. Maybe it's the police—the suspicion dawned on him—and he regretted letting the train slip away without attacking it. Had he met Fuad while he was free he could have discussed the matter with him. But now, when they met in jail and he told him, Fuad would only laugh. Sitting safely behind bars, you dream of being a hero.

The stranger on the other side of the door let up on the

bell, and then stubbornly attacked it again. The buzzing, it seemed to the poet, roiled his insides. At any rate, it wasn't the police. Cops would already have been shouting and beating at the door. Nevertheless, he would not answer. Eventually the stranger would give up and go away. But that's not what the stranger thought. For a long time the poet listened to the heavy breathing, and it seemed to him that the stranger was standing there thinking things over. The poet stole to the door. At first he did not believe his ears. Someone seemed to be whispering at the keyhole. What was the queer stranger muttering? Maybe he was just some lunatic. Fatkhi was afraid that the fellow might start raising a fuss, and then who knows what might happen? Next, Fatkhi became persuaded that it must be some sly detective who had come to work on his nerves, to force the poet to reveal himself. He must be standing there, smiling, waiting for the poet to break down. Fatkhi withdrew to the sofa in the living room. It's my nerves, he thought, and then he understood the stranger's odd behavior. Whoever it was, he was diligently avoiding anything that might attract the neighbors' attention. In the beginning, he just rang, then he whispered in the keyhole, and even now he was neither knocking nor calling out.

Idiot, the poet scolded himself, maybe it's a friend. . . .

Again he approached the door. The whispering was clearer now, the voice slightly husky and cracked. "I know that you're . . . don't think that I'll . . . from here. I've come . . . something in Marduch's apartment."

Suddenly the poet remembered—it was the old man from upstairs, the pensioner. The poet was inclined to open the door now, even though he had not liked at all the way the old man had stared at him the night before.

"I have no key," he said into the keyhole, in English, as was proper for a new immigrant who understood no Hebrew.

"So you also speak English," the pensioner marveled. "All

right. I'll speak Hebrew and you'll understand as much as you like."

"I do not understand you," said Fatkhi, again in English.

"Fantastic!" Tuvia cried with admiration. "On the refrigerator in the kitchen there's a bowl. Inside it you'll find the key. Do you understand that?"

"Not a word," Fatkhi said in English.

"*Habibi*, that's too much, even for a new immigrant. Don't be too clever. The neighbors might come out. I'm not budging from here, even if there's an air-raid siren. Listen. On the refrigerator in the kitchen," the old man said in bad English, "there's a key," he said in Yiddish. "Go get it."

The poet was angry. Reluctantly he went and took the key and opened the door. Their eyes met on the threshold. The old man was holding a roll of black paper and some tacks. He pushed the poet aside gently and closed the door cautiously and surreptitiously behind him, as if he were engaged in something criminal. "I didn't finish the job last night," he said without looking at the poet. "I've still got to close off the windows in the kitchen and the toilet."

The poet spread his arms as if he did not understand.

"Listen, my friend, I'm not an idiot. You're an Arab. You've got light hair and fair skin, but you're an Arab."

The poet exploded, in Hebrew: "And do I smell bad?"

"No," the pensioner said. "You smell of woman's soap and some kind of sissy perfume."

"Eau-de-cologne," the poet said defensively.

"All right, eau-de-cologne, if you say so. But let me tell you, I prefer the smell of the Arab village—I've noticed it on some young men. But what's the use, even villagers are turning into women nowadays."

"I told you it was just eau-de-cologne; men use it after they shave."

The pensioner put out his hand. "My name's Tuvia."

The poet shook his hand. "Fatkhi. Very pleased to meet you."

"Really? Pleased? Very pleased? There might be a lot of things in this apartment that upset me, but I've always found sincerity. Now you people have forced Shula to lie. I won't forgive you for that. Where is she?"

"She went to the store," The poet answered irritably.

"Don't get into a huff," the old man warned him. "Come, help me with these windows."

Fatkhi followed him silently. The pensioner placed a handful of tacks onto Fatkhi's palm and fixed the black paper to the windowpane. "What's your profession?"

"Poet."

"That's a profession?"

"What's wrong with it?"

"Nowadays a poet who supports himself on his poetry alone must be either a parasite or a monk. How do you make your living?"

"I'm also a journalist."

"You could have said so before. Don't try to impress me with your poetry. My brother wrote poetry in Petah-Tikva and made his living from the orchards, until the mosquitoes ate up him and his poetry."

"The same mosquitoes guzzled my ancestors' blood."

"They lived together, they coexisted for the benefit of the mosquitoes."

"We would have wiped out the bugs without you."

"The bugs still lay waste to the Socialist valley of the Nile. We eradicated them long ago."

"Together with the natives."

"You hate Jews."

"And you hate Arabs."

"At least I don't prattle about the brotherhood of man," the pensioner said, drawing back a little and inspecting his handiwork with satisfaction. "See if there's cold water in the fridge."

"You can serve yourself. I'm not your flunky."

The pensioner, looking into the poet's excited face, said, "I've asked the same thing of Marduch many times, and he never answered like that. Do you have a feeling of inferiority?"

"Tell me, what do you want?"

The pensioner stared. "Nothing. Nothing at all."

"You already know that I'm hiding here."

"Of course."

"You came to make a deal. You must be thinking of getting some compensation for keeping quiet."

"Compensation? Absolutely not. Just a little Jewish satisfaction. Listen, my friend," he said, putting his hand on the young man's shoulder and causing him to recoil, "You're a *goy* and I'm a Jew. Your ancestors used to trample mine quite often. They did it so well that my ancestors' guts would come spilling out. Of course we mustn't forget that among your ancestors there were some decent folk, perhaps even many. Yet only a handful endangered themselves for some unimportant Jew, jeopardizing themselves by giving him shelter in his time of trouble. Marduch doesn't know it, but he's repaying a great debt. If I know him, though, he'd give his blessing to what Shula is doing for you. It's a pleasure, my friend, a pleasure finally to see a Jew giving shelter to a *goy*, even though I wouldn't say that your life's in danger."

"Is this what you came for?"

"I came to help Shula."

"It seems to me that you're finished now."

"Don't be rude. If Shula's given you shelter, she must be taking good care of you. So what's eating you?"

The old man's pestering annoyed Fatkhi, even though the poet had already come to trust him. The pensioner would not betray him, but his tone—that of a grown-up to a child—was insufferable. "This is my country," Fathki said. "This is my country more than it is yours. Don't you find anything wrong when I have to look for shelter in it?"

"No," the old man answered calmly. "Every young Jew would have to hide as well, if he took it into his head to shirk his duty in such dangerous times."

"Wait a minute," the poet said, breaking into a laugh. "You're either joking or you're mad. You expect me to grab a gun, run after Marduch, and kill Arabs?"

"He runs after you every other day of the year. He does many things for you under conditions that are just as hard. Marduch's a gifted young man. You know how far he would go if he ditched you people?"

The poet did not notice that he was clutching Tuvia's sleeve and pulling him toward the living room. He released him next to the sofa and sat down. Tuvia sighed, smiled, and sat beside him. The poet said to him, "It's clear you don't understand what you're asking of me—to betray my fellow Arabs who have risen up to liberate me."

"You're talking nonsense. You don't believe what you're saying. Not one word of it. Do you think that the people you call your fellow Arabs will come here as liberators? They'll slaughter not only us, but you as well."

"See what nonsense they cram you with."

"Listen, Fatkhi, let's talk as if we were two Palestinian fighters sitting in some camp in Southern Lebanon."

"An interesting exercise," the poet said, puffing out his cheeks disparagingly. Yet, against his will, his eyes flashed. "You can't be serious, at your age . . ."

"Completely serious. Look, we're two fighters in one of the P.L.O. groups. Just now we've come back from our morning training session and we're sitting down to relax a bit. Both of us are hoping that tonight we'll be assigned to a mission in occupied territory, and both of us are scared, because we're only human. You're a Christian, George is your name, and I'm a Muslim, Ismail, yet we're fast friends."

The poet had been taught not to get drawn into futile debates. A successful outcome had to be assured beforehand. Every conversation was a skirmish, a part of the greater battle. But the subject that Tuvia had suggested aroused Fatkhi's poetic imagination. Halfheartedly he said, "All right."

"Wonderful!" the old man cried, like an excited child. "It'll be a fine game. . . ."

"All right, Ismail," the poet interrupted impatiently.

"All right, George. Aren't you tired? These training sessions kill me. I'll let you in on something, George. I thought I was going to collapse before the last hurdle."

The poet laughed. "Because you smoke too much, Ismail."

"Yes, you're right. And at night I can't sleep. This suspense . . . you think they'll assign us to a squad tonight?"

"Forget it. They plan every operation days ahead of time. No one's approached us yet about any operation."

"That's right. But now there's a war on. This morning I saw a lot of vehicles breaking camp—I'm sure they're headed for the front. George, tell me about your relatives over there, in the occupied territories."

"I've got two sisters. They were babies when I left. Now they're married with children. Imagine if I met them . . . go ahead and laugh, but they've got it better than I have."

"How do your brothers-in-law make their living?"

"They're educated fellows. They've both made something of themselves. In that respect I'm not worried for my sisters. They knew who to choose. The husband of the older one's the principal of a school in Kfar Rina and the second's a well-known contractor in Nazareth."

"I don't want to hurt you, George, you're my best friend and I'm sure you're dedicated to the revolution. But let's consider the first brother-in-law—his case is clear. He's the principal of a school, you said. Most of the year he's busy making sure that Zionist schoolbooks poison the minds of Arab children. I don't want to say more than that. We've heard a lot about school principals in the occupied territory. They hold sensitive posts and they have to do certain things in order to keep these posts. They're collaborators of the worst sort."

"You exaggerate."

"And that's nothing, my friend, compared with the contractor. This relative of yours will have his case looked into some day. I wouldn't prejudge it by saying he's made a fortune helping to build the fortifications on the Golan Heights. Right now Arab soldiers are paying with their lives to break through what he built. I'll bet he rounded up Arab workers to build earthworks against Arab tanks. Do you know what a tank costs the Arab nation? All right, I don't want to charge him with worse crimes yet, but I'll bet he helped build homes in Jewish settlements, and air-raid shelters for Zionists in Haifa. These are serious crimes, George."

"You exaggerate."

"George, you're already defending your in-laws. You're going to find yourself in big trouble. Remember, you're my friend. I'm not casting doubt on your loyalty. Don't tell me that loyalty to your family is more important than dedication to the revolution."

The poet rose from the sofa. "This is a dirty game."

"Right," the pensioner acknowledged, "and reality is even dirtier. Listen, my friend, how many Arab police are serving in Israel? Go count the government clerks, the functionaries in the Zionist political parties, the owners of garages that repair army vehicles. I won't mention those who own villas and buy expensive cars and get rich in various ways. They'll all be brought to justice. You cry about all the spit you catch here in Israel, and I'm as angry as you are about that, but when the liberation comes you'll catch a hail of bullets."

"I don't want to hear any more."

"Look at you, for instance. Look what you're wearing. Go to the bathroom, get on the scale in there and compare your weight with that of the boys who grew up in the refugee camps, who are the soldiers of your revolution today. They'll be coming in the first wave of liberation—not your humanistic ideologues. And these lean boys will have machine guns in their hands. Go and tell them that you've been fighting for years for Jewish-Arab brotherhood. You'll get a bullet in the head. That's why you should have followed Marduch instead of hiding with his wife."

"Get out. I'm not listening to you."

"You're like a child, you don't know how to lose at games."

"Enough, I heard you."

"Say hello to Shula."

"Get lost."

After the pensioner left, the poet stood for a long time in the middle of the living room, repeating to himself, you lousy, lousy . . . Even after three cigarettes he was still disturbed. He returned to the train that was conveying those tanks, he shelled and pounded it. The tanks were smashed like plastic toys in a trash heap. Then he loaded the train with soldiers armed with submachine guns and again he shelled and bombed and crushed it. The corpses were strewn between the blackened bands of steel. He saw himself dying among the soldiers, his shirt torn, the blood flowing from under his belt. He felt no pain, and the blood, his blood, calmed his anger. His left arm had been ripped off, but his right arm and his pen were safe. He wrote his last poem on a packet of cigarettes. A love poem. Fresh and pure like Hiam, his intended, the only girl in his life whose face he had caressed but whose flesh he had not known. No, not Hiam. . . . The other one. Ibitsam. The girl from the refugee camp whose hands dripped blood. Now that the life was running out of his torn body he saw her breast rising behind her open blouse. A dark breast. The earth blazed and burned. And all this latent heat, in Ibitsam, in the earth, in the blood dripping from her hands, ignited into poetry.

The poet took off his shoes again. Walking barefoot over the shiny floor, he polished his poem mentally. The floor was pleasant underfoot, and the words streamed and flowed. Suddenly he rushed excitedly to the kitchen. On the refrigerator, beside the bowl with the key, was a pen and small pad of paper. He wrote down the poem as he stood beside the table, then tore off the paper. He read what he had written, stuck the sheets carefully into his wallet, and returned, fatigued, to the armchair. He sat facing the balcony, pacified and relaxed, as if he had made love. Until the need to speak troubled him again, and he went to the telephone and called Tel Aviv.

"Hello?" It was the mother's thick voice.

"Shalom. Is Dafna home?"

"No. Who wants her?"

"A friend from the university."

"She's not home. She was mobilized last night and she hasn't come back since."

"They mobilized Dafna?"

"Yes. She's serving in the Civil Defense. Should I leave her a message?"

"No, it's not important. I'll call another time."

"Who are you? A soldier?" The mother's voice was full of hope, expectant.

The poet did not want to disappoint her. "Yes."

"Ah, peace be with you," she blessed him a second time. "Where are you calling from? From far away?"

"From Haifa."

"This call must be costing you a fortune. Give me the number and hang up and I'll call you back."

"There's no need, really. I've got enough telephone tokens."

"It's too bad Dafna isn't home. She'll certainly be very sorry. I think she didn't come home on purpose, because of Yigal, her brother. He's up on the Golan, and with everything that's going on there . . . We're sick with worrying and off she runs, she has to get out of the house. What did you say?"

The conversation oppressed him. "Everything will be all right."

"Are you sure? Thank you, thank you so much. Take care of yourself. It's so good to hear your voice. His father and I haven't closed an eye since yesterday. What's the matter?" she shouted.

"Excuse me?"

"I'm talking to his father. He's mad at me for telling you. But you're a soldier too and you understand. Wait, wait a minute. I forgot to ask you what your name is. I have to tell Dafna."

"It's not important."

"What do you mean, not important! Dafna will want to know who called, and you're a soldier. Are you going up to the Golan, too? Take care of yourself. . . . Wait a minute! Here's Dafna. She's just come in. Ah, *habibi*, what luck. . . . Here, darling, a soldier from Haifa is calling you."

"Hello." The voice was tired.

"Shalom," the poet said with unconcealed joy.

"It's you?" She didn't brighten up as she usually did at the sound of his voice.

"Yes," he answered, disappointed. "I wanted to know how you were."

"All right," she said, and from the tone of her voice he knew that she wasn't deceived.

The poet did not notice the weariness in her voice, and was hurt by her indifference. "See you," he said in a tone that would end the conversation.

"See you," she said.

"Who knows when . . ."

"What's the matter? Are you going to war too?"

The contempt in the question scalded him. "No," he answered sharply. "I'm hiding in Marduch's apartment. There's an arrest warrant out for me."

"If there isn't an air raid nothing will happen to you."

The poet slammed down the receiver and his handsome face turned pale with rage.

15

"Where are you going?" Shoshana said when she saw Fuad hurrying past the bus stop, as if swept along by the momentum of the steep slope.

Fuad waved his arm toward the long line at the bus stop on this first morning of the war, and said, "I don't want to see their mugs."

Shoshana wanted to surrender to her exhaustion and fear; she longed to be one of the crowd gathered at the bus stop. From the moment the flames went up in the north and the south, the people standing here had forgotten their petty quarrels. Grazed by the wings of death, they had reverted to being one body. They were all in a hurry, but they weren't grumbling. There are no buses, one person explained to the other, because they're transporting soldiers—sons and husbands—to the front. Private cars were halting at the bus stop and generously collecting passengers.

The conversation with her brother, Avi, two days before, seemed like a dream to her now. Her family would not take her to its bosom. The people congregating at the bus stop would not have let her partake of their brotherhood, either, had they known who she was. Again she looked at Fuad. He was a foreigner, a suspect—an enemy. He walked about in the purely Jewish street, an enemy in the land he was born in. His bulging eyes were fixed on a point in the calm sea, as if he was about to go there. He was so dark, and so noble in his loneliness. Now, despite the pains in her back, she hastened to catch up with him and joined her arm in his, and stared as well at that distant point in the sea, ignoring the Jewish people, the Jewish buildings, the Jewish cars. Fuad's tense neck relaxed, as if thawing in the rising sun. Lowering his eyes, he gazed at her broad face—his smile showed that he accepted her within the circle of his loneliness. He raised his arm slightly so that his elbow touched her breast, and so they walked within their loneliness through the foreign city. For some reason Shoshana felt good. From deep inside, a youthful, forgotten smile floated to the surface. Fuad's arm was rubbing her breast. They both felt the contact through the fabric and for a moment they ceased being husband and wife and reverted to man and woman. When he spoke she noticed his flirtatious tone, harking back to the old days. "Later I'll go down to the office. . . ."

Later.

Shoshana pressed quietly against his arm. After half an hour had gone by, they stood in Prophets Street, reconsidering this "later." Shoshana extricated her arm from his, and the sea breeze swept in between them. Behind her was Wadi Ein Nesanas, in front of her Fuad's solid body hiding Hassan Shukri Street and the police station. His lustful smile pleased her; it made her want to slap his face. She was a girl from the farm again, and she asked in a rough voice, "What if they take you?"

He tried to smile and failed. "It won't kill us."

Deep inside she longed to stay a farm girl and to tell him in a mischievous tone, come, let's play a trick on them. These remnants of mischief pleased him, as they had pleased him about twenty years before. He collected his smile and withdrew his body, putting distance between them. "I have to," he said. "Today of all days I have to. What's the matter?"

"Shit!"

"Listen, woman, it's as if you had a religious husband. Instead of the synagogue, he goes twice a day to the police station."

"Kiss my ass!" she hissed. "Go then."

"Woman, don't curse in the street," he answered irately.

"What should I bring you if they decide to arrest you?"

"The three books I put on the top shelf." He had already put distance between them; now he was a stranger, concentrating on his own needs. "The shaving kit," he added, "and a lot of underwear."

His laugh startled her. "Stop that filthy laughter. I know there aren't any women there." Her blue eyes flashed.

"I'm going to pay my respects at the police station," he reminded her.

"Go! Go!"

"Tell the children that I'll break their bones if . . ."

"Go already. Your bulldog threats don't impress them any more."

"Don't fight with them. Ignore them."

"Shalom," she said, turning and walking away toward the melancholy Wadi Ein Nesanas.

He stood for a long time with his back to the police station, watching her as she crossed Solel Boneh Circle. I've got to make her see a doctor, he said to himself, and then turned to the police station.

At the door he breathed deep, as was his habit twice a day, and tensed his neck. A proud smile came to his thick lips. He greeted the duty officer and noticed three cops, their buttons dull and their uniforms untidy, shuffling along the corridor. The duty officer was tired, too. On the dirty bench sat a villager, his eyes shifting from the duty officer to the street to the strip of clear sky that was visible from where he sat.

The man seemed to think that Fuad could come and go as he pleased in this strange trap that he had been thrown into. "*Ya Sidi*," he cried in Arabic—it was a shout of joyful relief. He jumped off the bench, approaching Fuad. "*Ya Sidi*, as Allah is great, they're just holding me here, holding me for nothing."

"Sit down," the duty officer told him in a tired voice. The villager, misunderstanding Fuad's smile, was doubly convinced that he was an Arab police officer. He waved dismissively at the Jewish cop. "Shut up for a minute," he said, turning again to Fuad. "As God is my witness, this is the first time I've forgotten that damned identity card. Tell me, *Ya Sidi*, isn't it just a piece of paper and a blurred and faded picture of your servant? Am I a criminal already for not carrying that lousy picture on me? Here, look at me. This face is my face. We are God's and to Him we return! Is Mustapha Ahmad al-Uradi a terrorist just because he isn't carrying his picture with him? And I tell you, cousin, if you'd seen the picture you'd be shocked. Some ape pulled a fast one on me, stole four pounds and gave me a monster's mug. By Allah, I looked at the picture in the identity card and I didn't recognize myself."

"Sit down already!" ordered the cop.

The cop was ruining his story, and Mustapha Ahmad al-Uradi would not stand for it. "I told you to shut up. He sits up there on his throne like a crow on a tree, ordering people around." Mustapha Ahmad al-Uradi, contemptuously ignoring the cop, poked his thick finger into Fuad's shoulder. "So tell me, *Ya Sidi*, why should they have such a false, lying picture? By my God al-Kaba, the next time I come to town I'll bring a mirror with me. So they'll see my mug. I'll ask Allah's refuge. So I'm a terrorist! I'm a *fellah*. Afifa says I can't light a kerosene lamp. She tells her neighbors that my hands shake. Liar! Allah punished me with a wife who has an idle body and a quick tongue. But between you and me, do I know what a bomb looks like? What do you say? Let's put an end to this comedy and go home like men."

"Sit down!" the cop scolded him. Mustapha Ahmad al-Uradi looked at Fuad with astonishment. How dare a cop who looks like a crow scold in the presence of an officer, even if he is an Arab! Suddenly the villager's eyes lit up with understanding. "Are you caught in this trap too?"

Fuad nodded.

The villager wrapped himself in sorrow and returned to his bench. "Allah be with you," he murmured for politeness's sake. Obviously he had wasted his breath talking to this useless fellow, and he turned in the direction of his village and cried out bitterly, "Afifa, Afifa! Allah will break your head on the earth. Didn't I tell you—the ground is shaking and the sky is burning. Is this a day to go into town?" Now he turned a bewildered look on the exhausted duty officer and took a rusty tin box from his pants pocket. He wanted to roll a cigarette but feared the cop's reaction. He rested the container on his knees and cried out to no one in particular, "Now what?"

Any other day, Fuad would have told the villager to go ahead and smoke, if only to provoke the gleaming buttons. But today he was cautious, on his best behavior. He offered his pack of cigarettes to Mustapha and got up hastily to give him a light. The two of them sat quietly on the bench; then Fuad dropped the matches on the floor and got to his feet. When he returned, he sat some distance from the peasant. The sweat and the smell of goats overwhelmed him. Mustapha's restless eyes saw through the effendi's maneuver, but he took it with equanimity, as Fuad would have expected. "And what brings you here?" Mustapha asked.

"Communist," Fuad answered pithily.

"In our village the Communists come and go and no one arrests them. They talk a lot. Ever since they began shouting, the roosters have been hiding among the hens. Aziz's son came out from behind a flock of goats, brushed the earth from his knees, wiped his nose with his sleeve and went off to Moscow.

When he came back to us he was a doctor. What did you really do?"

"It's a long story, uncle."

Mustapha stubbed out his cigarette on the floor and absentmindedly opened the tin box—he was very curious about Fuad's long story. But Fuad had grown weary of the conversation. He left Mustapha still waiting and approached the duty officer. "Do I have to wait?"

The tired cop lifted his head. "Who told you to wait?"

"I'm Fuad."

"So? I recognize you."

"Can I sign and go?"

"What else? Maybe you want an escort to your doorstep?"

Turning to go out into the street, he met Mustapha's eyes. The peasant, his mouth defiled by Fuad's cigarette, sucked in his cheeks as if he were about to spit. He was sure now that he had been deceived. A splendidly dressed Arab enters the police station, signs the register, and departs, and no one stops him. He must be hand in glove with the Jews. The peasant was so angry he could not contain himself. "That's how it is," he said. "When you sit at the table you forget your brothers."

Fuad, standing at the door, muttered, "Idiot . . ."

On his way to the office he tarried beside a newsstand. The giant headlines reflected confusion, shock, the loss of self-confidence. He did not smile; he felt no relief. Walking along freely in the sunshine, in the sea breeze, he was pierced with humiliation. Trying to rally his spirits, he remembered the poet hiding with a woman, but he received no pleasure from Fatkhi's misfortune. As usual, Fuad strode powerfully, his head raised, his bulging eyes scanning the street authoritatively, seeming every inch a leader. But to himself he was saying, you're an old man already, Fuad, an old man.

A new generation, a disrespectful generation, the offspring of Mustapha al-Uradi, had sprung up around him and was showing him up for nothing right in his own stronghold, the offices of the newspaper. Once he had been a true revolutionary. His great weapon was his brilliant, stimulating intellect, his world-embracing view. Now he was surrounded by dwarfs, who grasped at crumbs of stolen thought with their peasant paws. They had all the self-assurance and dogmatism of the illiterate, all the arrogance of the armchair heroes, all the fanaticism of the narrow-minded. And they were crawling over him like ants.

I'm a corpse, he told himself.

His nostrils trembled, as if his own smell were choking him. He kept marching to the office. That was where they had gathered together to hatch their plots. Fatkhi the poet had been their leader. Now they despised and disregarded even the poet. He wasn't sufficiently radical for them. Did the poet ask why, perhaps? That was a bad habit. Ants didn't ask such destructive questions. They scurried and rushed, turned and turned again, circling here and there, back and forth, until finally they reached their goal. They could not feel surprise, they could not feel remorse. Their heads were made for butting at obstacles, for determining where their path was blocked, where another route was needed.

There was no escape for Fuad. Like all who made a career of revolution, his fate was sealed. He marched straight to the anthill.

And once there, to add to his rage, he found that no one had doubted that he would arrive safe and sound, even though in the last war he had been locked behind bars, and even though, for several months now, he had been forbidden to leave Haifa and required to report twice a day at the police station. In spite of all this, they were expecting him, and they were out for his blood.

"How did you know I wasn't under arrest?" he asked them.

The Politbureau representative, a lean fellow, straightened his tie. His severe expression indicated that something fateful and conclusive was about to be decided one way or the other.

Fuad loathed the fellow. He stood by the window looking at the street below. Fuad was experienced, an old-timer. Such performances and stunts would not crush his spirit. Nevertheless, he was disturbed.

The Burnt-Out Case, a man his own age, was sprawled in a chair facing Fuad. The ants had already burrowed through him completely, with their tunnels and caves. He sat behind a massive desk, fidgeting nervously. For five years now he'd been stuffing himself with great quantities of tranquilizers and bicarbonate of soda.

Three of the poet's protegés were gathered beneath the portrait of the late deceased leader, whispering and laughing among themselves. They were lively young men. Fuad despised them, and they responded to his scorn with cruel insults. They called him "Mister Cambridge" because he knew proper English, yet his articles in Arabic had to be carefully edited. They would correct his mistakes in red ink, so that even the typesetters at the printing press would know his limits, his failings. A year before, the boundaries between Fuad and these young men had been clearly delineated, once and for all. The younger of them had burst out during a tumultuous debate, "You're an Israeli Arab, and we—we're Palestinian Arabs."

"Idiot, I was an Arab before you were born."

They were not impressed.

Fuad went to his desk in silence and sat at it. An irrelevant thought passed through his head. How many times a month do they shower? Their necks were filthy, their nails black; they gave off a smell of rancid cheese.

"Comrade Fuad," the Politbureau representative began.

Kiss my ass! thought Fuad.

"This meeting has been called to clarify several aspects of your personal behavior . . ."

"My personal behavior is my own affair," Fuad interrupted.

"There are no personal affairs within the ranks of the Party," the largest of the young men said with a grin.

"Does that include embezzling funds from the paper?" Fuad hissed.

The young man didn't even blush. "Don't change the subject, Comrade Fuad. And besides, I ordered an independent accounting and presented my findings."

Fuad groaned. It would take a gifted writer to describe such people, he thought. "Balzac!" he said out loud.

"Balzac? What kind of nonsense is that?" the young man asked.

His friend touched his shoulder to calm him down. "The old man's senile already."

The Burnt-Out Case leapt to his feet and threw a dictionary to the floor. "I can't stand any more of these idiotic meetings. . . ." With an abrupt motion he wiped the spittle from the corners of his mouth and dropped pale-faced into his chair.

A young boy entered, carrying a coffee tray. As he approached, he picked up the dictionary from the floor and presented it, along with a cup, to the Burnt-Out Case. The three young men sipped their drinks noisily. The Politbureau representative lifted the cup with a delicate, feminine motion, bringing it up to his mouth as if it were a flower.

"Where's the water?" the Burnt-Out Case shouted.

"Right away," the boy whispered and went out.

"When we scheduled this inquiry for today," the Politbureau representative explained, "we didn't know that a war would break out."

"If this inquiry is so important," Fuad said, "the war can be postponed."

"It's important," the Politbureau representative said, "very important."

"You want to get out of it," one of the young men cried.

Fuad ruminated. Since the '67 war Mustapha Ahmad al-Uradi had seen to it that four of his own representatives would sit on the paper's editorial board, to oppose Fuad and the Burnt-Out Case. Hassan had got to his feet four years earlier and said that it was only accidental that he was an Israeli, that he had been forcibly separated from his family in Gaza in '48, and all he wanted was to return there, with his wife and children. No one had stood in his way. They explained to him that the Party would have to expel him. The ceremony was festive, with handshakes and embraces. His place was taken at once by one of the young Muslims, a fellow fluent in the language of the Koran who knew all the required slogans by heart. Fakhri, the literary critic, could not retire to Gaza and so found shelter in Beirut. Immediately Mustapha al-Uradi sent another villager to take his place. In an issue of the paper two weeks before, this young man had published a poem entitled, "We Are Coming Back!" The poem's grating nationalistic tone upset Fuad, and his displeasure showed. The young man acted without delay. He collected Fuad's observations on the Soviet invasion of Czechoslovakia and took them to the Politbureau. Fuad didn't care. The Party was a rising power among the Arabs, and as such could accommodate all sorts of people, strange people. They'd tolerate him as they tolerated the Burnt-Out-Case. But he hated the accusing finger waving in his face. He knew from the start that the whole affair would end in bitter recriminations. Things might have passed quietly, had it not been for the tension gripping him that day. One of the young men went too far: He leaned on Fuad's desk, grinning at him, and whispered the P.L.O. slogan, "We Are Coming Back!" as if Fuad were the high priest of the Jewish state.

This was a clear threat to Fuad. The Burnt-Out Case was behaving with unusual self-restraint. He took a sip of water and whispered, "This is hooliganism."

For Fuad, this self-restraint was an ominous sign. He promptly got up, pulled the Burnt-Out Case to his feet, and snapped over his shoulder, "We'll have this inquiry some other time."

The Politbureau representative protested. "I came especially from Jerusalem."

One of the young men said in a loud voice, "Mister Cambridge is evading things."

"Bastards," the Burnt-Out Case muttered outside. "Bastards." Energetically he wiped the froth from the corners of his mouth and, waving his arm in the air, said, "If you ask me, they put us into the same cage with those apes against our will. Some days I just feel like getting up and leaving."

Fuad smiled. "You do that a lot. They go looking for you at the printer's, and you're nowhere to be found."

The Burnt-Out Case gave him a reproachful look, as if Fuad had some traits in common with the apes, and kept silent until they came out into the main street of Haifa. "So it's war," he said. Folding his veiny arms behind him, he sailed off into his own world. "You don't understand, Fuad. I feel like leaving, once and for all. They sent you to Prague. I'm nailed up in this place and I'm suffocating. Everywhere you turn you see fools. In the street, at home, in the office, in the Party, and among the enemies of the Party, too. Jews and Arabs alike. I hate them so much that I've begun to hate myself. It's a slow death. Incurable chauvinism on one hand and arrogant pride on the other. Pui! Pui! Pui!" he spat devotedly, as if praying, and wiped the corners of his mouth again. "Have you ever seen two dogs mating in the street? They twist and howl but they can't break apart, they can't put an end to their agony. One pulls this way, the other that way. That's the Jews and the Arabs in their shitty fix . . . and some morons take pleasure from this awful show."

"You're tired," Fuad said gently.

"No. That's not it. You remember what al-mari said about birth. You're born against your will. Take a child in a refugee camp and a Jewish child growing up here. These two kids can't wait to grow up enough to receive the finest guns so they can go out and slaughter each other. Aren't we like dogs?"

Fuad had ceased paying attention. It was several years since he had paid any attention to the ramblings of his comrade, debilitated by decades of Party infighting. The fire that once had burned in him was now completely extinguished. He had surrendered; he was prepared to state, without shame, that his soul was twisted with hate. As a revolutionary he was a lost cause. But the Party expelled no one, not even lost causes. The Party was built of layers upon layers of generations, of various and peculiar types. Almost all adjusted to the strange situation.

At a distance Fuad and the Burnt-Out Case saw the figure of Hanna, a clerk in the Ministry of the Interior. Fuad left the Burnt-Out Case and approached his friend with unconcealed joy. Hanna was a fisherman in his spare time; he chased good-looking women; he was a great gourmand and a master of the humorous anecdote. By all the criteria of the Party he was one of the enemy. Not only because he had taken an important post in the apparatus of the Jewish state, but also because he was downright devoted to that state. Flouting all the rules, he believed that the state had improved his lot. That was his worst sin. There was a candid smile all over his plump face as he greeted Fuad. "Well, now what?" he asked.

"It's war."

"A serious one?"

"A war that's going to decide a lot of things, Hanna."

Hanna ran his fingers over his neck, smiling. "Should I get a rope ready for myself?"

"And deprive a lot of other people of the pleasure? Don't be so selfish, man."

"I'm heavy, *Ya Sidi*, very heavy. I'd like to save them the trouble. And I've got a bag of tricks, Fuad. What if I decide to piss on their heads when they're stringing me up?"

"Not a chance. You won't be able to undo the buttons. Your

hands will be tied behind your back—that's the way they do it. You'll just wet your pants."

Hanna inspected his knuckles. Fuad's vision did not please him. "No. I'll pick the rope myself anyway. And now tell me, do you think I ought to interrupt my vacation and go back to the office?"

"Are you already asking me what to do, you bastard? Telephone your boss."

"He told me to stay home."

"So stay there."

"The wife's crazy and the kids are running around wild. Samiah went to school."

Samiah was frightfully beautiful. She was the first Arab girl to study for honors at the Technion. Hanna knew it was a weakness, but he never tired of boasting about his daughter. He was possibly the only Arab in Israel who carried a photo of his grown-up daughter in his wallet.

"Man," Fuad said, "You should marry her off. The Technion is full of horny Jewish boys."

"Listen to the revolutionary! *Habibi*, Samiah is the crown on her father's head. By the way, I was sure they'd arrested you."

"It seems they don't consider me dangerous any more."

"And does the slaughter going on now make you happy?"

"Do you want to fight?" Fuad cried, angrily.

Hanna smiled. "War or no war, today's Sunday. For three weeks now I've had a bottle sitting at home. I got it as a present and I'm looking for someone to share it with."

Fuad refused: "Not today."

"With chicken livers and *kubeb* on the side," Hanna added.

"I don't feel like it."

"By Allah, you're an old man."

"I've already been told that today."

"Leave the Party and you'll live longer."

"And serve the Jews like you?"

"I serve them?"

"You lick their asses morning, noon, and night."

"If you knew how much the Arab villagers owe me, you'd be ashamed to talk that way."

"You've been permitted to throw the poor devils a few bones."

For once, Hanna exercised self-restraint. "Listen, man. The flames are going up all around us. Who knows what'll happen tomorrow? Come, let's do a job on that bottle."

"I'm tired."

"You're an old man."

"You already said that."

"And I'll say it again."

16

Victor and Naim were as dark and clever and bursting with life as Fuad in his youth. Amir, the eldest, on the other hand, had a lighter complexion and an even temper. Three days before the war broke out, he turned sixteen. His parents, who had gotten used to the tricks of the two younger boys, were occasionally dumbfounded by the surprises that Amir sprung on them. At the age of fourteen he had declared that from then on he would earn his bread with his own hands. Fuad, who had never had a liking for manual labor, asked ironically, "And what will your lordship do to support himself?"

"A glassmaker wants me to work for him."

Fuad was enraged. As a leader of a revolutionary organization, he felt ashamed to show that his eldest son's inclinations came as a disappointment to him. He shouted, "Go find someone else to make fun of. School or work. Both at the same time is impossible."

The youth proved that it was perfectly possible. Every month he would throw a sum of money on the kitchen table, having first allotted some petty cash for his own needs. In his studies at the municipal high school, he outdid himself. Yet Fuad would not be reconciled. He complained to Shoshana, who advised him to have a father-to-son talk with the boy. So one day, when Fuad was in a good mood and the boy was calm and even somewhat cheerful thanks to some accomplishment at school, Fuad said, "Son, I want to talk with you. Victor and Naim, get lost."

Amir turned serious. The two little ones, offended, left the room and lay belly-down near the door, eavesdropping.

Fuad said to Amir, "You're grown up already and you must have considered your future."

"Of course."

The father sighed with relief. "What do you want to be?"

"A doctor."

"Wonderful."

The two urchins lying on the other side of the door could not see the glowing smiles on their father's and brother's faces. Fuad and Amir had never been so close as they were at that moment. It was obvious from the boy's voice that he was doing everything he could to repair his damaged relations with Fuad. "Father," he shouted, "I'll do it. I'm not counting on any miracles. Do you believe me?"

"Certainly. You're very gifted. Everyone knows that. But have you thought of all the difficulties?"

"I've thought of every one of them. Boys . . . other boys go to the army for three years. They won't call me up. Isn't that right?"

The disappointment in the boy's voice surprised his father. "No," he said, "I don't think they'll call you up."

"So I'll work like a donkey and save a lot of money, a lot. And then I'll go to Jerusalem."

"Don't be naïve, Amir."

"I've already weighed everything, Father."

"Look, you're a gifted boy, but I'm sorry to say you're not very practical. You're living in a Zionist state. The same way the army's closed to you, the doors to medical school will be too. Don't forget who you are and where you come from."

"I'm not forgetting, Father. I'm not forgetting for even a minute. They don't let me forget."

Fuad straightened. "Who?"

"Your Arabs and Mother's Jews."

Everything that was upright in Fuad's body and soul crumbled. When his fingers had thrust into Shoshana's golden hair, when his body had soared high with hers in the wonderful act of creation, he had not imagined the weight of the burden that would lie on the frail shoulders of his offspring. He said in a dry voice, "They won't take you."

"I'll manage, Father. I'll try with all my might."

"And I thought you were a realistic boy."

The youth smiled sadly. "There's another way. I'll go to Italy."

"Why?" Fuad shouted. "Why do you choose precisely the hardest ways? Are you a masochist? Do you need to prove something?"

"I'm telling you all the possibilities."

"And you're purposely ignoring the only practical, simple possibility available to you."

"I don't want that."

"I promise I won't be angry with you. Tell me."

"It would be just like going to Yesud Hama'alah and pleading with Mother's family to help me."

"You don't have to get down on your knees before the Party. You wouldn't have to disown your principles to go to Moscow and study medicine for free."

"I've seen the boys in Umm-al-Fahm and Shafram, the ones who are getting ready to study in Moscow. I talk with them, Father, you don't. You think they're revolutionaries. That's a detestable lie—complete hypocrisy. They buy themselves an airline ticket by mouthing Party slogans. Once I was talking with one of them at a demonstration in Nazareth. He provoked a cop, hoping he'd be arrested, and he was very disappointed when the cop ignored him. He lost several points in the race. And you know very well how whole clans in the villages turn into vote contractors at election time, when one of their members has been promised that he'll return from Berlin a doctor."

"And in the meantime, these peasants study medicine and you'll remain a glassmaker's apprentice."

"I detest them. They sell their consciences."

"As Arabs they don't have to."

"I would be forced to."

"You're as stubborn as a mule."

"That's the way you see it."

"Idiot!"

"I can't argue with you."

"Shut up, you impertinent bastard."

"You're angry because . . ."

"Get out! Get out with all your complexes. You'll die a laughingstock. Remember what I'm telling you."

About two months earlier, Amir had come home wearing a knapsack on his back that was filled to bursting. He had a lovely, barefoot young girl in tow. Standing before his father, holding the girl's hand, Amir said in a grave voice: "This is Suzi. She's my girlfriend and from now on she'll be living with us in my room."

Fuad was stunned, amazed. "Where did you find her?"

"We met at the Sea of Galilee."

"How are you, Suzi?"

The boy, noticing his father's bulging eyes, said icily, "Suzi speaks only English." An insurmountable barrier went up between Fuad and the girl.

Suzi, it turned out, was the daughter of an English Jewish woman who married an Australian Christian in France. "Birds of a feather flock together," Shoshana said with a sigh, taking the girl under her wing.

Although Fuad was a Christian, all three sons had been circumcised. They were never told anything about their identity at home, nor were they taught any particular ethnic customs. When Amir was in kindergarten in Haifa, he and his mother celebrated the Jewish holidays. When the family moved to Fuad's village, they all celebrated the Christian holidays. And when they returned to Haifa, they ceased observing any holidays—one day was like the next, none holy, all profane. The children found themselves treading a tortuous path between two peoples. The parents, as Party members, were inclined to identify ideologically with the Arabs. But the grounds for this were political, nothing more. Fuad considered himself an Arab, one who was proud of his origins, and Shoshana declared herself a Jew—an ostracized Jew, but a Jew nonetheless. The children sought their identity without the interference or involvement of their parents.

Yesterday, when war broke out with the screech of sirens and the thunder of jets, Amir had stood to announce that he was a Jew. Naim and Victor had painted the Palestinian flag in watercolors on a large sheet of paper. About an hour after the shells began to whistle on the Golan Heights and in the Sinai, the war exploded in all its fury in the cramped apartment in Wadi Ein Nesanas.

When Fuad came back home, he promptly went to take a shower. On his way to the bathroom he said to his wife, "If you're not working today, maybe you can cook up something good and we'll eat like human beings."

"What would you like?"

"Stuffed vegetables," he said, closing the door behind him.

Shoshana found Naim and Victor glued to the Arabic-speaking radio. Their black eyes flashed and from time to time they hummed a song that was unfamiliar to her. "Where's Amir?" she asked.

Naim answered in Arabic, "He went out early with his whore."

The sound of little Victor's laugh maddened Shoshana—she kicked his behind and slapped Naim on the face. "In this house," she said, breathing heavily, "you watch your dirty mouths, both of you."

Victor screamed at her, "You bitch, see what you did to him . . . blood!"

She was tempted to hit Naim again, to hit him over and over with all the bitterness that was stored up in her heart, but his wounded look stopped her. He said nothing, but his dark eyes were unsubmissive. She dropped into a chair and broke into tears. "You're terrible, both of you. You're terrible," she sobbed.

"Jew," whispered young Victor.

"Shut up!" his bleeding brother shouted at him.

"She's a Jew," Victor said, pointing at his mother. His voice expressed the shock of recognition.

"I'll kill you," Naim threatened him.

Shoshana blew her nose. She tried to touch Naim's shoulder, but he recoiled. She said to him, "Go to the kitchen and wash your face. I hurt you something awful."

Naim obeyed, but the younger one wasn't about to let up. "Don't, don't wash off the blood. She's afraid that Father will see."

"Do you want me to kill you?" Naim shouted.

Shoshana heard the tears in his voice. But he and his brother revived immediately when Suzi and Amir came home. "What's that?" Shoshana asked, pointing at the brush and paint can that Amir was carrying.

"We were painting car headlights next to the funicular."

"Traitor," Victor fumed.

"Wait," Naim warned him, "just wait. One day we'll smear you with tar and stick feathers all over your ass."

"Fuad," Shoshana implored her husband, who was sitting, washed and shaved, on the balcony, reading a newspaper with a transistor radio humming in his lap. "Fuad, I'm going out of my mind. If you don't come and make them shut up, I'll leave the house."

Fuad, his leisure disturbed, entered and encompassed everyone with an angry glare. Naim and Victor shrank at the sight of him. Amir turned pale and took the silent Suzi's hand. "What's going on here?" his father asked.

Intrepid Victor was ready to commit suicide. "She," he said, pointing at his mother, "she hurt Naim."

Fuad's bulging eyes were riveted on his younger son's face. "Who's this she?"

"She." The boy pointed at his mother again.

Fuad struck his newspaper against his thigh and shouted, "Answer me!"

"Mother," the boy murmured.

The father's eyes almost popped out of their sockets. "A curse on your head!" he swore. "Don't be a coward. Tell the truth. What did you call her while I was in the shower? I heard it all. Answer me, damn you."

"Jew," Victor whispered.

Fuad's face turned ashen. In the deafening silence he ordered his son, "Go, bring the carpet beater."

His knees knocking, the boy obeyed. Once he had disappeared onto the kitchen balcony, Shoshana pleaded, "Fuad."

"You shut up!"

The boy returned, gave his father the stick, and turned his back to him.

"I don't want to dirty my hands on your stinking behind. Take your trousers off yourself."

Victor, surprised, turned round to his father with tears in his eyes. He hadn't imagined that this time his father would flog him on his bare buttocks. For the first time he pleaded. "Father, in the shower. Not here, in the shower. Please." He was ashamed in front of Suzi. The first blow fell on his face while these words were still on his lips. Fuad beat him like a man fed up with himself, a man longing to flagellate himself. Suzi wept. Shoshana, with her strong hands, tore the stick away from her husband.

Naim, who had kept silent until now, fixed his gaze on Amir. "It's all because of you. Are you happy now?"

Fuad turned on him and snatched him up as if he were about to smash him against the wall. The boy's legs jerked in the air, and Amir and Shoshana caught at them. Fuad's back was close to cracking—finally he had to give it up. He took in everyone with his angry stare and said, breathing heavily, "Listen you dogs . . ."

"We're not dogs," Amir said insolently.

"All three of you are dogs. You buy that filthy hatred outside and spill it out at home. That's what's happening here."

Victor, chastised, asked, "So why do they want to take you to jail?"

"First of all, they still haven't arrested me and it looks like they won't. Second, they arrest me from time to time because I'm a member of the Party. The British used to arrest me too." Naim, down on the floor, said, "But they don't arrest the Jewish members of the Party."

Fuad had no answer. No one in the room had an answer to this. Suzi approached Naim, who was hurt, and put out her hand to help him up. The boy drew back from her. He considered her a Jew, too. She smiled at him affectionately. She didn't know his language and he didn't know hers, therefore they needed some more primitive contact. The boy was enthralled by the warm enchantment in her blue eyes, her open, smiling lips, her fingers caressing the big toe that poked from his sandal. Young Victor was ticklish, especially on the soles of his feet, and he broke out giggling at the sight of the girl tickling his brother's foot. The laughter communicated itself to Naim, stretched out on the floor. Fuad escaped to the balcony and Shoshana to the kitchen. Amir stood isolated and alone, realizing painfully that from now on his brothers' laughter would not be his. He went and secluded himself in his room.

In the kitchen, Shoshana was filling marrows and tomatoes

with rice and ground meat and trying to cling to her love for her three sons. That love was now like a sword hanging over her head. Her eyes were tearing because of the chopped onion. The future looked frightful. She spread a thick layer of jam over chunks of bread and called out, "Naim, Victor, come in here." They abandoned Suzi at once, hurried to the kitchen, grabbed the food and started eating. "Sit down at the table like human beings," Shoshana said.

"Can we have cocoa with milk?" Naim asked.

Victor hurried to be seated before his brother, crying, "Me, too."

From the balcony, Fuad was heard to groan, "That's all we need today. *Ya rab,* that's all we need."

Shoshana was frightened. "What's happened?"

"Come see."

Her two sons hurried before her. Over their black heads Shoshana saw two old women approaching on either side of the street.

"Grandma Huria!" Naim cried out.

Shoshana turned pale. Her heart pounded and she was gripped by dizziness. Grandma Miriam, who had come from Yesud Hama'alah wearing her Sabbath best, was tired and perspiring, but as unbending as always. She had never been in her daughter's house. She had learned the name of the street from her son Avi. Unable to make out the house numbers with her dim sight, she turned to Grandma Huria, who was walking along the opposite sidewalk and asked, "Do you live here?"

Huria, who did not know Hebrew, smiled apologetically. Miriam, the seasoned villager, still remembered a few words of the Arabic of her youth. "*Inte beterafe* [do you know] Shoshana and Fuad?"

A light went on in Huria's eyes. "*Hom waladee* [they're my children]."

They were facing each other across the black pavement. Miriam fished out a handkerchief and wiped off the sweat, thinking, that's the tone of a devoted maid speaking of her masters. Then she remembered that her daughter could not afford a maid. She must be a close neighbor, she thought. Suddenly the old woman's splendid posture seemed familiar to Miriam, and she was so moved by emotion that she forgot her Arabic. "You're . . . you're his mother."

Huria nodded vigorously and her sensitive features brightened in a smile. She too had understood and was filled with embarrassment. Miriam was tottering toward her on swollen legs. Huria stepped off the sidewalk, clearly expecting to be embraced. Miriam put out her hand, and Huria took it in her rough villager's hand. Finally, Miriam's pale eyes detected the longing and embarrassment and disappointment in the black eyes of Huria.

"Who's the old Jewish woman Grandma Huria's talking with?" Victor asked.

Fuad, seeing his wife trembling, whispered, "That's your other grandma, Miriam from Yesud Hama'alah."

The boy was struck dumb.

It was a lugubrious drama that Shoshana was witnessing from the balcony. A year before, her mother had had a hysterectomy, and Huria was very old. What an injustice! The first glimmerings of reconciliation could come only at the threshold of the grave, in the shadow of a terrible war.

Naim, however, saw a kind of beginning. His cut lip touched the railing, as if he were about to bite the concrete. The spectacle was beyond his comprehension. He was moved by a vague happiness and an undefined disappointment. Dropping on to the edge of his father's armchair, he implored, "Father, call them."

Fuad looked at him gaily and called out, "*Ya Mama*, bring my mother-in-law home."

At the sound of this strange cry, Amir too came out of his room, almost colliding with Suzi in his rush to the balcony.

Amir watched the two grandmothers approach the house

together. In his childhood, during the years when he lived with his parents in the village, he had loved Grandma Huria, her lullabies, her pastries. When he was sick she would pull his bed close to her widow's bed, and after Shoshana fell asleep she would take him in with her. What Amir remembered from childhood were the silvery olive leaves on the hills around the village and Grandma Huria's smell. He remembered the tiny earrings in her earlobes; the two pale pearls and the glittering golden hinges always pinched him. He had dreamt of finding them once, hidden among the burning stones outside the village. His friend Bassem—quicker and more nimble than Amir—saw them, grabbed one earring, and, catching hold of Amir's hand, robbed him of the other. A warm breath touched Amir's face, and laughter sounded in his ears. When he opened his eyes he breathed in the smell of Grandma Huria. She took the hand that was pulling at her earring and tickled his belly, laughing silently until he let go of her. "You'll tear my ear off, my sweetheart. You'll tear it right off." Even while scolding him she laughed. Immediately he dropped off to sleep again.

All this subsisted in his imagination like a remote spring; from that source, streams penetrated into the bowels of the earth to vanish underground, breaking through at last to the sea. The sea existed, despite the wilderness of silence and uncertainty into which he sometimes strayed. And the sea was Grandma Miriam. Uncles and cousins floated there, a nameless grandfather dove in the depths. The great moment came when he and his parents met his two uncles and his grandmother Miriam after the 1967 war, in the restaurant at the crossroad to Usfia. His grandmother and uncles sat at the table, their faces as frozen as if they had seen a ghost, exchanging a few words with his parents and looking at him with an air of depressed astonishment. He saw his grandmother's features soften and felt that she wanted to touch him. But she did not touch him. His uncles asked him matter-of-fact questions and he answered briefly. He found the sea to be cold. They recognized his existence, as they recognized his father's, but they did not accept him. His grandmother, sitting beside him, clandestinely opened an old purse and tried to give him two hundred pounds without anyone's seeing. Amir refused the money. His grandmother's manner reminded him of his mother. "Is money unclean, or are you just too proud?" she asked.

He had an urge to say that it wasn't money he wanted but an invitation to Yesud Hama'alah. He shook his head in stubborn silence.

"Anyway, the money's yours," she said.

Amir had not understood.

"You can tell your lovely mother—I'm signing over everything to you and your brothers."

What could be the value of a farm that he had never seen, that he had never walked on, where his mother's memory had been blotted out for so many years?

"Even that doesn't impress you." She grew angry.

"They say you grow wonderful apples," he said suddenly.

At first she thought he was trying to change the subject, and she was hurt. Then she thought he was hinting that he had never received a gift from her, and she felt embarrassed. "I'll send you a couple of crates of Jonathans."

"I've never seen apples on a tree up close."

She had not understood. For many years she had refused to understand, until suddenly understanding hit her like a blow. Amir had seen, sitting beside him, an old woman with swollen legs, a scalp sparsely crowned with white hair, false teeth clattering in her mouth like a trap, death in her womb. She had come a long way, a hard way. Because of his mother and because of him and his brothers and his father, Yesud Hama'alah was a grieved and bitter place. Amir suddenly knew that this magical term "the farm" did not represent a joyful place, but rather a gloomy refuge in which his grandmother had immured herself, shut off from the eyes of neighbors. He had dug so many years to reach the sea—now it broke over him in a torrent of terrible hostility. Amir raised his arm and placed it on his grandmother's shoulder. Although her daughter had mentioned his occasional strange ways, the old woman had never imagined this. She burst noisily into tears.

Now the two old women entered, and Huria took it upon herself to act as hostess. She led Miriam to the sofa and said to Shoshana and Fuad, "How are you both? There are all kinds of rumors going around the village. I don't know what to believe."

To the dismay of the little grandsons, she almost completely ignored them. They sensed that this had something to do with Grandma Miriam. When she went into the kitchen, they ran after her. Standing next to the stove she kissed them and, seeing the expectation in their eyes, smiled and said, "I brought things for you, yes, I did. Here, in the bag. But later. Wait until Mother gives them to you."

Shoshana came in and said firmly to Huria, "Out. You didn't come to wait on her. Go sit beside her."

Huria left without replying. Victor and Naim stood near the bag and didn't budge. "Grandma's brought goodies," Victor announced.

"Sit down at the table, both of you, and you'll get them."

Huria, in the living room, was asking Miriam for the tenth time, "How are you? Is everything all right with all of you, *Inshallah*?"

Amir was afraid that these customary polite phrases might be felt as hypocrisy. But Miriam had not forgotten her childhood, and answered tirelessly, "Good, by God's will. And how are you? How do you feel?"

Fuad, whose self-confidence was intact after twenty-five years of Israel's existence, was not in the least apprehensive; on the contrary, the bizarre meeting amused him. "Shoshana," he called out cheerfully, "tea for Grandma Miriam and coffee for Grandma Huria."

"I'm already making it for them."

Miriam's gaze rested on Suzi. "Who's that?"

"Amir's girlfriend," Fuad answered.

She turned to her grandson. "Why is she barefoot?" And when she saw the girl's blank expression she added, "Is she an idiot?"

"She doesn't understand Hebrew," Amir said.

"But she's not an Arab, I hope."

Amir was embarrassed before his father and Grandma Huria. He said, "No, she's from England."

"And did she come all the way from England barefoot?"

"It's a principle with her," the grandson said defensively.

"A principle!" his grandmother exploded, just like his mother. "What kind of stupid principle is that? There are nails in the street, burning cigarettes—do you know how many thorns I got in my feet when I was her age?"

"Did you walk around barefoot too, Grandma?"

"What a question! But not on principle. There wasn't enough money to buy shoes."

"Suzi believes that the old days were happy."

"She's telling me!" Miriam cried. Promptly she understood that her grandson had caught her out.

"You didn't get that cleverness from your dear mother."

The boy smiled. "Go," he said to Suzi in English, "go shake hands with Grandma Miriam and Grandma Huria."

The girl went first to Grandma Huria—the old woman got to her feet and gave the girl a forceful hug. Over Suzi's shoulder Huria said to Amir, "I didn't understand what you said in your language, but I understand that this is your betrothed." And when the boy did not deny it, she held the girl at arm's length and, looking into her face, said: "You've gladdened my heart, you two. May Allah make you happy." And she kissed the girl on both eyes.

Suzi blushed and turned to Grandma Miriam. "Suzi," she introduced herself.

Miriam shook her outstretched hand, not moving from her seat. It was evident from the expression on her face that the girl did not impress her. It was also clear to her that this was a passing fancy—why, the boy was just a fledgling. "So it's war," she said.

Shoshana offered refreshments. "How are things at home?"

"Terrible, just terrible. There aren't any men around, and the cows are mooing with pain. Their udders are swollen. Now those fancy ladies have to learn to milk a cow."

"And that's what's worrying you?" Shoshana was amazed. "The cows?"

"What's worse than that? The air-raid sirens go off and everybody disappears. They just manage to grab the babies and run to the shelters. Have you ever heard of anyone taking pity on a cow and bringing it into the shelter? You can go crazy inside. The shells are exploding and you hear the cows screaming in pain." She turned angrily to Fuad. "Why are you shelling the cows?"

"Mother," Shoshana cried, "did they shell the village?"

"The whole Golan Heights went up in flames. Yitzhak brought me to Haifa and he says that the boys are rushing up there, but it's like trying to dam a flood with your finger. He says they can spit in the Sea of Galilee, they're so close to it." And again she belabored Fuad: "Can't you people ever keep the peace?"

The smile finally dropped from Fuad's lips. "Did you come here to wage war on us?"

"Mother," Shoshana said. "Things are upside-down here. The children are killing each other—Fuad nearly murdered them. I'm asking you—don't make things worse."

All that Grandma Huria understood was that her son had been insolent to his mother-in-law, and she upbraided him in her language. "My son, that's not the way to talk to a sick mother-in-law. Look how tired she is. She made a long trip just because she was worried about you all."

"Let me be . . . ."

Amir took Suzi's hand and pulled her to the kitchen. "Now do you understand?" he said to her. "They can't even quarrel in the same language. And yet there are some idiots around who are ready to make speeches for hours about brotherhood."

"Your Arab grandmother's super," the girl said. "But your Jewish grandmother is harder than a rock. Maybe only an atomic bomb . . . ."

Amir went pale. "Why did you say that?"

"I don't know, really I don't. I take it back, forgive me."

"I'm not angry, Suzi. I was only surprised. I was thinking the same thing just then. And you don't understand what they're saying. Maybe you're lying? Maybe you understand Arabic and Hebrew too?"

"Don't be stupid. You still want to play at war. Come with me to Australia."

"Kiss my ass," he murmured in Hebrew.

"What?"

"No way."

"And the atomic bomb?"

"What's the difference between being killed by a sword and dying in an atomic explosion?"

"So come with me to Australia."

"Never."

"You're strange."

"And you? Why did you come here? You read, you know everything—why do you stay here?"

"I don't know . . . everybody's shouting in there and now we're shouting too, and the telephone is ringing."

Amir grabbed the receiver and yelled, "Hello!"

"Is Fuad home?" It was the poet's voice.

"Yes, just a minute. Father, it's for you."

Fuad took the receiver, glared spitefully at everyone, and said, "Hello?"

"Shalom, Fuad."

Everyone was silent. "What do you want?" Fuad said.

"How are things with you?"

"Rotten! I feel like going fishing."

"So they haven't arrested you!"

"No."

"Maybe I'm not wanted either. You people put me under house arrest for nothing."

"*Habibi*, it wasn't me who did it. Maybe most of the leaders put themselves under house arrest voluntarily. It's fantastic! A clever move. Sitting safely in some quiet hole when action means running a risk, at the same time keeping open their option of claiming, afterward, that they couldn't budge—they were being harassed."

"Are you suggesting I go out? I'm going crazy here, Fuad."

"It wasn't me who put you into an incubator, so I can't tell you that you're a big boy already, knock on wood, and you can go out into the dangerous street. That's the price you have to pay. Not everyone's a famous poet."

"Fuad, I've decided to do something."

"So do something, man. Don't wait for a permit from me."

"I want to take part in the war. By any criterion, this is a war of liberation."

"Great. Go take part in the war, then. How many Israeli planes can you put out of action with your poems?"

"It's impossible to talk with you."

"You and your friends are very shrewd. Did you prepare yourselves for a war of liberation?"

"Who knew it would come so soon?"

Fuad laughed. "So sit in Marduch's house, Marduch who's slaughtering Arabs, and play your war games."

"I've been thinking about that since this morning. It's maddening. I've been playing at war ever since you and Shoshana left."

"Have you liberated Acre yet? Tell me when you have. I'm dying to go there."

"Fuad, have you thought what would happen to your wife and children if . . ."

"Man, believe me, it's been a long time since I stopped thinking so far ahead. It's not healthy."

"That's no way for a revolutionary to talk."

"Is there a single revolutionary left in the revolutionary movement?"

"I don't know what to do."

"Go run to Marduch and ask him what he'd do in your place."

"What advice could he give me?"

The poet's voice was driving Fuad up the wall. "Man, at least he's giving off bullets, not just empty words. You're hiding in his house, dying of boredom and playing infantile games."

"Fuad, I want to talk with you."

"I've got to show up at the police station in the afternoon. Maybe afterward."

"Thanks."

"I came to take you all to the village," Huria said, almost in a whisper.

"Hurray for Grandma!" Victor rejoiced.

"Shut up," his father scolded him.

For the first time Shoshana saw her mother look at Huria warmly. Miriam stuck her hand into her purse, extracted several bills, and, taking Huria's hand, forced the money into it. "Yes," she said, "take them away from here. That's the best thing for them."

The money made Huria shudder. She tried to push it away, but Miriam's fist closed over her palm. "Not money . . . not money . . ." she murmured.

"How will you support them?"

"We don't want for anything in the village. Just so they come."

"Thanks," Shoshana said. "But we're not coming."

"You won't be hurt there," Miriam said. Huria nodded, her hand still linked to Miriam's.

"We can't," Shoshana said. "Fuad has to go to the police station twice a day, and he's forbidden to leave Haifa."

"So take the children and go."

"We're staying here."

"She's a stubborn woman," Grandma Huria said.

"You're telling me?" said Grandma Miriam.

17

Shula stood at the gate to her parents' derelict garden, absentmindedly picking at the bark of the old pine tree, whose resin shone like frozen tears between the cracks. Ants were running helplessly up and down the trunk.

"Are you sick?" her mother asked in a neutral tone, so as not to trouble Shula with her own concern.

"Why do you say that?" Shula said, knitting her eyebrows. Up to this point she had felt fine, but now, instead of picking at the tree, she found herself leaning on it for support, suddenly seized by dizziness. Quickly she stood upright and said, "I'm absolutely all right."

Her mother went over to the sprinkler that was dripping on the desiccated lawn, turned it off, and said, "I'm going to the clubhouse today. Maybe I'll visit you—I might spend the night."

"The clubhouse is closed today. Who can think of meetings now?"

"It's not the end of the world," her mother said. "We've gotten used to wars already."

Her mother's stratagem was too transparent. Shula said, "I don't want you going around the streets during the blackout."

"Don't worry about me, child."

"You're getting on my nerves," Shula cried, losing control, and immediately regretted it.

Her mother, as usual, took Shula's scolding in silence—this time she even managed to smile. "I hope you won't throw me out."

Shula took Ido's hand and said good-bye. On her way to the car, parked in the narrow street that resembled a tunnel arched over with green branches, she heard the loud voice of Goldschmidt, Rami's father. "Shula! My beauty! What a surprise. . . I haven't seen you for months. What's this? You're getting younger every day. How is Marduch?"

"He's in the army."

"Have you heard from him?"

Shula's mother, standing on the lawn, turned pale. "Degenerate!" she muttered, in anger and disgust. For the two hours that Shula had sat in her house, she and her husband had avoided asking the child precisely this question. "Degenerate." To tell the truth, Goldschmidt was a degenerate every day of the year. He played cards once a week on his balcony, he had refused for twenty-five years, politely but firmly, to accept the Party paper from Shula's mother, and he was crazy about large dogs—just like his son.

This likable, aging fellow was usually jovial, but today his good humor seemed excessive to Shula. He came up, touched her on the cheek as he had done since she was a child, shook his finger at her and said, "Let's have a little smile." He rolled his eyes toward Ido. "Look, even he's smiling."

"War."

His gaiety collapsed. "Did you think I'd forgotten?" There was a trace of bitterness in his voice. "I'm going to my shift at City Hall. Could you take me as far as the highway?"

Her gray eyes rested on him. Now she saw his cracked lips and the swollen pockets under his eyes and noticed the strong smell of tobacco. "I'll take you to City Hall," she said.

He made himself comfortable on the passenger seat and tried to smile again. Shula's foot pressed down on the clutch and her short skirt rode up. Goldschmidt stared purposefully, as if her pretty golden leg might give his smile some justification. She didn't dare ask. Turning into the street, she looked at him, and found that he had stopped staring. Only then did she pull her skirt down.

"His whole unit's up in the Golan," he said.

"Since when?"

He took a pack of cigarettes from his pocket and asked, "May I?"

"Yes, of course," she said, pulling out the ashtray. She could have sworn he had not heard her question. To this day she found it difficult to pronounce Rami's name before his parents.

"Why, Shula?"

She tightened her jaws.

Hurriedly he apologized. "I didn't mean to hurt you. I know it's a stupid question. And yet it still bothers me. All these years I've wanted to know, and you know him: It's impossible to get a word out of him."

She couldn't explain. She knew that the explanation she had on the tip of her tongue would not serve him—rather, it would have given him a sense of injustice. "Are you sure he's up on the Golan?" she said.

It was as if Goldschmidt hadn't heard her. "Everything was clearly understood. His mother and I . . . we didn't imagine that suddenly, like this . . . Parents who boast about their sons disgust me. But I can tell you one thing: Rami's . . . Rami's . . . we were so sure of his future."

"What are you talking about?" she protested. "He hasn't been lost. He became a soldier in the army. How many lieutenant colonels are there his age?"

Goldschmidt looked at her, and the pockets under his eyes nearly disappeared. "You're still proud of him."

"Yes," she said.

No one, on the face of it, had forced her to do what she did. But as she grew up, she found that freedom of choice was limited. Everything was against Rami, especially her mother. Shula had been a young girl blossoming within the confines of the Party, inside a kind of closed sect, growing up in her mother's bosom—impossible that all this would not leave its mark on her. Rami grew up on the same street, attended the same school, went on the same hikes, and yet for all that, they were separated by a great divide, as if she were an Orthodox Jew and he a *goy*.

One evening she was sitting in the Party's youth clubhouse, getting bored listening to the comrades' reports. One by one they got up and spoke, even those who had nothing to say. It was improper to remain silent during meetings. If a comrade did so, it raised doubts about his loyalty. As a result, even those who weren't talkative by nature were forced to drone on and on, making fools of themselves.

Arie, a restless boy, got up, left the hall for the third time, came back in, and sat down again. Emile was presiding. As a young man, Emile was already notable for his exceptional composure, but Arie's comings and goings perturbed even him. "Comrade, can't you sit quietly? This is an important meeting." All the meetings were important, actually.

"I saw a suspicious-looking guy when I came into the club. First I thought maybe I was seeing things, so I got up to check. He's still hanging around outside."

Emile turned pale—he was speechless. The boys smiled, pleased to see Emile, that fiery speaker, falter. A few of them wanted to go out and take a close look at the suspicious character. Two or three, despite Emile's warnings, had an urge to teach him a lesson. The girls giggled. Winking and dropping insinuations, they coaxed the boys back to their seats. Emile stood foolishly on the stage. Then Amalia got up and calmed her future husband. "It's Shula's boyfriend. He's a suspicious character, all right, but he's not dangerous."

Emile's self-confidence was shaken. "Comrade Shula, what kind of behavior is this?"

Shula said nothing.

Emile spoke to her mother. Several days later her mother said, in a gentle voice, "Child, I've been hearing strange things about you."

"About that suspicious character, I'll bet."

Her mother nodded.

"Just some nice Moroccan boy from the slums," Shula said lightly. "Of course he's involved a bit in the underworld, but believe me, Mother, he can be set straight."

"Leave that to the grown-up comrades with more experience. These characters—you can't imagine what they might take into their heads to do."

Shula silently picked up her book bag and went to school, and broke the good news to Rami Goldschmidt. "From now on you're a suspicious character. They decided it at a special meeting last week."

Their love had flowered in secret. Though Shula's mother guessed what was happening, she didn't reveal it even to her friends. Years later Shula realized that Rami had been the rebel, while she toed the line. Too late she began to suspect that she had been sent to the youth festival in Bulgaria only to separate her from Rami. She was seventeen years old. She had found sanctuary from the festival's noisy tumult and orchestrated happiness in the company of a skinny boy from Holon. For three whole days she forgot Rami. A week of happiness.

Had Rami joined the Party, everything would have gone differently. Even her mother would have accepted him, though his father was a hopeless "degenerate." But Rami thought along his own lines and loathed any ideological restraint. He believed only in what seemed right to him, and felt no need for the approval of others. He never pressured her to leave the Party, but he would mock her. "Shula, you're a prisoner. You hate them, but you're their prisoner."

Her mother insisted that the boy was a destructive influence. Shula had stopped jumping to her feet and applauding at meetings, and she was evading demonstrations. Very cleverly, her mother proceeded to demolish Rami's romantic image in the young girl's eyes. Whenever one of the debating wizards came over to their house, her mother would go out of her way to be nice to Rami, so that Shula would see by comparison how short his temper was, how rudely he shouted, how quickly he collapsed in defeat. For days afterwards Rami would remain silent, his spirit broken, a man tricked in an unfair game. Shula was worn down between him and the Party. Their honeyed kisses grew tainted by the bitter taste of treachery. In Bulgaria, with the boy from Holon, she learned the taste of other kisses. One evening she came home, washed hastily, spoke hardly a word to her father and mother, and hurried over to Rami's. "I never loved you," she said. "I just thought I did."

He was wearing only shorts, hoeing the garden next to his house. His hair fell over his forehead. His broad chest gleamed with sweat. In her absence he had grown a nice little mustache. Sparse black hair covered his arms and body and disappeared down into his shorts. He hoisted the hoe in the air and she said, "I've got a boyfriend."

The hoe dropped to his side and he sat down on the ground. "How long?"

"More than a week. It's serious."

To this day she could not understand how she had expected him to congratulate her. He looked into her eyes and said, "You're crazy."

She flared up. She was offended, but more than that, she thought he was showing contempt for the skinny boy from

Holon. "You don't know him!" she exclaimed. "He's something special, from the shoulders up."

Rami had something of his father's sense of humor. "Oh? By how many inches?" he asked.

It was hot. They were alone in the garden, and the soil exuded an exciting odor. She tried to visualize the face of the boy from Holon, but it melted away among the thickening shadows, between the trees. Rami sat on, his hair curled down over his forehead, the hoe on his shoulder, a hurt smile on his lips.

"Don't you want a last kiss?" she challenged him.

Rami didn't move.

"Are you angry at me?" she asked.

He kept silent.

"So that's it?"

He remained frozen.

She turned pale and approached him. Rami, confused, let his hoe drop to the crumbly earth and fell back absurdly onto his behind, his shorts collecting fresh clods of earth. She wanted him to stop fooling, to get up and say something.

"Well?" she asked.

Still he said nothing.

Shula turned, but at the garden gate her scalp prickled; she heard him say, "You know I love you."

She turned again and saw him still sprawled on the earth with a frozen expression. She could have sworn that her ears had deceived her. One could not say such things with such an expression. She didn't dare go back to him. Crossing the narrow street, she went into her house. She was certain he had said something, but she never dared to ask him what. They both waited years before they married. She had invited him to her wedding, and held up her face for a bride's kiss. He had ignored the gesture.

"Where are you going?" Rami's father asked her.

She blushed. "Home. I'm all mixed up."

"Never mind, it's really not important. Pull over here and I'll take a bus."

"What do you mean, a bus? I'll turn around and take you to City Hall."

"I don't want to put you to any trouble."

"Nonsense." As the car was going uphill, Shula said, "I asked you how long he's been up on the Golan."

"Almost a month."

"You mean . . . " she began, and didn't finish.

"They caught the first blow," Goldschmidt fingered his necktie and threw out his chest. "Rami will see it through," he said. "He can stand up to anything."

She was afraid to look him in the face. She stopped and said, "Here we are."

"Thanks."

"Don't mention it." Her voice was stiff, almost hostile. Suddenly she said, "If he calls . . . "

"Of course," he cried. "Of course I'll give him your regards. He always asks about you."

She got no pleasure from this lie. "Shalom," she said, and drove off.

Opposite the Municipal Court Building, at the end of Memorial Park, a crowd blocked her way. She shifted into first gear and sounded the horn. A wave of nausea passed through her stomach, her throat constricted, and she felt the blood rush from her face. No one paid attention to her honking. The noonday sun was hot, the air unmoving, and she was stuck in the crowd, her ears assaulted by shouts and curses. Someone struck his fist on the roof of her car and shouted right into her face, "Just because you've got a steering wheel, you think you can run people over?"

Sweaty shirts obstructed her view from all the windows of the car. Ido was howling, "Daddy, Daddy!"

Hunched over, an old man waved his cane aloft with his bony hand, trembling and shouting. He was obviously frightened: There was froth on his lips, and his Adam's apple rose and fell as he stammered.

"He'll get a heart attack yet," someone said.

A woman put her hand on his bony shoulder, but he pushed her away and screamed, "He was going to kill me!"

Several paces away Shula made out a group of men yelling, but she could not see the culprit they had caught. She wished she could extricate herself and flee for her life. In despair she leaned on the horn, closed her eyes, and kept them closed until someone stuck his head in the window and shouted, "What are you bugging us for?"

She saw a man's bald head. "Sir . . . ," she said.

Ido screamed, "Daddy! Daddy!"

The man flinched and said in a less aggressive tone, "Wait a bit. You can't drive through now."

"What's happened?" she asked.

"Some Arab thug threatened the old man. We ought to kill them. The uppity bastards. Wait here, wait a bit."

Having no choice, she turned off the engine. By now the old man looked very feeble, and his voice was weak—only his eyes still expressed fear. When he raised his cane Shula saw the blue concentration camp numbers tattooed on his forearm. She said to the bald man, "Put him in the car; he's going to collapse. Maybe he'd like a ride home."

But the old man would not get into the car. Shula closed her eyes once more, fighting nausea. "Where's the casualty?" a new voice near her asked. Opening her eyes, she saw a police sergeant.

The bald man pointed at the old man. "There he is, over

there. He thinks the Nazis are after him—he's gone out of his mind."

"So she didn't hit him?" the sergeant said, pointing at Shula.

"What? No! That Arab there, a curse on him, threatened the old man."

The sergeant turned away from the car and approached the stalwart group of heroes. As the ring opened, Shula cried, "Naim! Naim!" She quickly opened the door, ignoring Ido's screams, and hurried after the sergeant, just in time to see him land a slap on the boy's face. Someone in the crowd took this for a signal and honored Naim with a kick. The boy was close to fainting. His shirt was torn, blood oozed from his lip, there was a swelling on his forehead, and one ear was red. Shula threw herself on him, crying, "Don't touch him!"

Everyone was stupefied—even the old man fell silent. "You know him?" the sergeant asked her.

"Of course. His mother's a friend of mine."

"So he's a Jew," the bald man said, surprised.

"Don't believe her," another man broke in. "He's an Arab."

"But she knows him," a girl said.

"Kill him," the man insisted. "I say he's an Arab."

"Silence!" the sergeant commanded. He said to Shula, "Madam, can you take us to the police station?"

"What for?" Shula said, alarmed. "I told you his mother's my friend." Swinging Naim around, she urged him, "Tell them, why don't you say something?"

"Madam," the sergeant said. "It doesn't matter. I'm asking you to drive us to the station."

Shula, sitting in the car again with Naim and the cop in the back seat, thought, poor Shoshana. As they drove away, a woman in the crowd was heard to lament, "What a young generation we're raising." No one, including Shula, remarked that the police station was only a few hundred feet from the scene. "Where to?" she asked the sergeant.

"Drive home."

Shula, surprised and relieved, turned to look at the cop. "Really? You're letting me?"

The cop smiled. "I know this bad boy."

"You?"

"Madam, I'm an Arab from Wadi Ein Nesanas myself."

"I wouldn't have believed it, from the slap you gave him."

"I had to. First of all, he deserved it. Second, it was thanks to that slap that I could save this fool from being lynched. Let me out here, please."

"Thank you, thank you very much."

"Don't mention it. It's a good thing you happened to come by. They would've torn him to pieces."

"The poor old man was confused," Shula said, by way of apology for the insults that the Jewish crowd had hurled at the Arabs. "The old man thought the Nazis were after him again."

"It's not important what he thought. What Naim did was very bad. It wasn't proper for Fuad's son."

"You know him?"

"Of course."

On her way home she wondered how she could bring Naim—bleeding, shirt torn—up to her apartment. The neighbors would be curious. And the poet was hiding in the apartment. "Naim, maybe you'd like me to take you to your parents'?"

"No!" He shuddered. "Father's crazy enough today. We drove him and Mother crazy. And there are two grandmothers there besides."

Shula, preoccupied, did not follow up the matter of the two grandmothers. She said, "There's someone from the Party at my house who the police are looking for. You'll arouse suspicions, Naim—the way you look."

"No problem," the boy said. "I'll take off the shirt and carry your bag. Everybody'll think I'm a delivery boy."

She smiled in spite of herself, relieved because her nausea

had passed. The dizziness especially had worried her. Not during a war, she thought. Not now.

"Naim won't hit me, will he, Shula?" Ido asked.

The youth said nothing. Ido's question seemed to him an allusion to what he had done. It angered him that Shula had seen his humiliation.

"Your mother must be worried sick about you. When we get home I'll call and ask her to let you stay with us until this evening." In the mirror she saw his face relaxing. "You'll shower and put on one of Marduch's shirts. I can't match your mother's cooking, but you'll eat lunch with us—you like schnitzel and French fries?"

"I'm sick of rice and cooked vegetables."

Before he got out of the car, her eyes scanned the windows of the apartment house. Naim had already stripped off his shirt and wiped his face with it. There was no one on the stairs, and she breathed with relief. "Marduch won't like what you did to the old man," she said on the way up.

"He's a great guy!"

It pleased her to hear the boy say it. "Why?"

"He's an Arab Jew."

Shula knew that this was what the Israeli Arabs called Jews of Oriental extraction. "Just because of that?"

"No. Some Arab Jews are really . . . Marduch doesn't act superior with Arabs, maybe because he's known better Arabs than the ones around here."

"The Israeli Arabs aren't so bad, Naim."

"They aren't worth much."

"That's your father's opinion, too."

"I won't marry a Jew."

"You've got a long time to go yet."

"I know what I want."

When they entered the apartment, the poet came out of his room. He was angry when he saw the boy, and when he recognized him he cried in dismay, "Naim! What are you doing here?"

"Problems," said the boy. "Why do they want to arrest you? Did you do something?"

"Actually, I still haven't committed any crime. Last night the leadership decided I had to go underground."

The boy's disappointment showed clearly on his face. He turned away from the poet and on the way to the kitchen spat out, "Father didn't run away from them."

The poet was about to reply to this scornful remark, but Shula gestured to him to be quiet. He approached her and whispered angrily, "I don't understand this brilliant move. Why did you bring him home?"

Her lower lip trembled. She didn't want him to see her face. "There's a reason," she whispered, while to herself she shouted, I don't owe you any explanation. But Shula was not one for quick comebacks. In the kitchen, she put her arm around Naim's shoulder and felt his dark brown skin quiver at her touch. "Your mother must be worried. I'll tell her."

The youth, embarrassed, broke away from her. "We don't worry much, among us, but if you want . . ."

Shula dialed. "Shoshana, Shalom."

"Shula, you'd die if you saw what was happening here. The end of the world. My mother and Fuad's arrived together. Mother's drinking one glass of tea after the other and she's grilling Fuad over a low flame. You should see the two old ladies. They've joined forces against Fuad and he's going out of his mind."

"Shoshana, I wanted to let you know that Naim's at my place. I did a lot of shopping and he helped me. Is it all right if he stays here?"

"I'll lend him to you for a few hours. Maybe then there'll be some quiet here. Fuad will come over to your place this evening. Maybe I'll come, too."

Shula replaced the receiver and started when she saw the poet. He had been standing behind her, listening to the conversation. "Pardon me," he said. "Didn't you forget the cigarettes?"

"No, here they are on the table."

The poet took them and shut himself up in his room.

18

Shula threw open the kitchen windows. As she turned to the stove to prepare the meal, she felt a wave of nausea and dizziness—the second that day. She breathed deeply, filling her lungs with the sea air, but still she felt weak. She remembered that since yesterday she had not had anything to eat except a slice of bread and a cup of coffee. Right away she felt relieved. It's hunger, hunger and nothing more. She smeared a thick layer of butter on a slice of bread and bit off large bites, although she didn't feel hungry. To make doubly sure, she studied the calendar on the wall. Of course, she was not due until next week. She laughed, her fear receded, and then the sharp odors rising from the skillet struck her. She heard Ido's wild laughter from somewhere in the apartment, followed by Naim's laugh. A nice boy, she said to herself.

The mantle of female revolutionary did not suit Shula, who was sensitive and easily hurt. Actually, it oppressed her. But she had never had the courage to rebel, to shed the cloak openly. Only a true revolutionary was likely to act, to free himself from the gulf between conscience and the powerful forces hemming him in on all sides. Shula, like many of her kind, had been swept by circumstance into the whirlpool of activism, and lacked the courage to set herself free. She dragged her feet in the ranks, avoided the centers of activity, strove to find a quiet corner. Sometimes decades pass before such unrevolutionary souls manage to extricate themselves from the stream. Shula knew that she did not belong there. She had known it as a girl; she had known it when she was in love with Rami; she had known it when she ran from his garden at twilight. She had always felt like an outsider in the Party. With the advent of Marduch the process was suspended for a time. Instead, she developed a kind of defense mechanism—she could persuade herself that some things were to her liking and ignore whatever was not. Her contact with reality was limited and selective.

Once Amalia said to Marduch, in her caustic way, "Your wife's strange, almost crazy. She lives in a constant delusion."

They were standing in the courtyard of the Party clubhouse. It was after a tiresome lecture, and the comrades were helping themselves to piles of sandwiches and cases of soft drinks. The people nearest Amalia and Marduch stopped eating and glanced at Marduch. Two things he knew: that they hated Amalia, but trusted her, and liked Shula, but didn't trust her. He said to Amalia, with great seriousness, "Maybe. I'm no expert." He raised his head, looking her in the eyes. "But at least she's not malicious."

The echoing laughter had reached Shula, lingering in the hall.

Now she stood in the kitchen, enjoying the sea breeze. There was no bloody war raging now. Ido was in the company of a nice boy, and he was laughing. She herself no longer suffered from nausea and dizziness. Her healthy appetite stirred. Marduch had gone out in a hurry on an important mission—he would come back to her safe and sound. In her house there was a creative poet, an attractive, intelligent male sitting behind a closed door, feeling the pain of his people. And she was a good-looking woman. She had seen proof of this even in the way the police sergeant had looked at her. One small detail only marred this wonderful picture she was painting—the radio. It kept broadcasting depressing songs and confusing announcements. She went and turned the dial, dreamy-eyed, searching for some tune that would complement the fresh breeze purifying the kitchen, the sun shining outside. The happy tune came to her over a distance of thousands of miles, perhaps from Europe, perhaps from South America, it came especially to her on the wings of the wind and penetrated to the depths of her soul. The slices of potato sizzling in the bubbling oil seemed like flowers, and her whole body was given over to the breeze and the tune. Her lips opened wide and she danced over the floor.

"What station is that?"

Turning in surprise, she saw the poet standing in the doorway, smiling. She couldn't—or perhaps didn't want to—conceal her feelings. With gleaming eyes and soft voice, she asked coquettishly, like a young girl, "You like it?"

Just then the poet was feeling less poetic than his hostess. He was hungry, and the cooking odors had drawn him to the kitchen. Nevertheless, he had seen not a few women in this mood in his lifetime, and he closed his eyes and nodded, murmuring, "Wonderful, wonderful!"

Shula, delighted that he understood how she felt, looked at him and whispered softly, "Lunch will be ready soon."

"I'll help you set the table."

Shula laughed. "No. Go sit in the living room and I'll call you."

"Yes, sir!" He laughed, and vanished.

When Shula called "Come and eat," Naim galloped into the kitchen with Ido mounted on his back. He immediately understood the meaning of Shula's wink, and seated the child on a chair, saying, "Now we've finished playing. We're hungry and we're going to behave nice."

The child obeyed him. "Yes, Naim! *Ahalan*, Naim! We're hungry and we're going to behave nice."

"I put the beer in the freezer," Shula said to the poet. "Here's the opener." She was sitting at the table already, serving large portions to the boy and the poet.

The poet's knee accidentally touched Shula's bare knee—she didn't flinch. He placed the bottle against his cheek and exclaimed, "Wonderful! It's like ice, really. Feel it." He held the bottle out toward her face, but she touched it with her fingertip. Withdrawing her knee, she smiled at him and said, "Enjoy your food."

The poet thrust his fork into the meat and immersed himself in thought. More than anything else, Jewish women reminded him that he was an Arab. Some made him feel desirable, but their very way of doing it showed him that he would always remain beyond the pale. A less sensitive man would have found comfort in this: for these women poured all their sweetness down on him, while demanding and expecting nothing in return. On the contrary—they were dismayed if they suspected that the poet might think anything was expected of him. They placed him on their beds of flowers, took his breath away with their charms, but did not ask him to take on the duties of a gardener. He was the eternal guest—an endearing guest, but nothing else. Several of these Jewish women had suffered no less than he. Two or three had wept real tears because he was an Arab, because they'd had the bad luck to fall in love with an Arab, of all people.

That was worse than anything.

The tears were genuine. The irony was that his soul was scalded by them. None of these women had ever noticed, much less considered, his suffering. Most of them came to terms with their fate, and when the time came they would lock the garden gate in the poet's face and hasten to open it to the first Jew who looked like he might make a husband. The poet would smile, sometimes. If the traditional, nationalistic Jews had any idea how many solid families were fashioned by his magic touch, they would have been grateful to him. After each such affair the poet's wounded heart would bleed in a few poems. He would resolve to stop getting burned in this fire. He had sworn it again today, after his telephone conversation with Daphna.

But a poet is always a poet, his oath a poet's oath. Feminine beauty would always captivate him. His knee touched Shula's once more. The delicate, warm limb slipped away, but he didn't give up hope. Smiling brightly, he turned and poured another glass of beer for himself. "Excellent!" he said in a husky voice, making himself a bit more comfortable. The knee under the table was still there, and its touch so attractive that he had difficulty swallowing. Shula turned away to cut Ido's portion for him, and the poet longed to gaze into her gray eyes. It seemed to him that a rosy color was spreading over her neck and into her averted face, and that her fingers were none too steady. But now that he had pressed his knee against hers, she pulled it away and kept it away. As he set down his glass, she turned back to him. He gazed into her eyes for a long time; she did not bow her head and finally he was unnerved. His eyes grew heavy. She was so close to him and yet so distant. And he could not tell if she was moving away because she wanted him to follow, or in order to hide in some secret, empty place.

We lay on the roof, a torrent of light streaming down between our beds. Everyone had climbed down off the roof and only we were left. Until then I had never touched a girl's face. I would get tongue-tied in the presence of girls—I was so shy, and I had this insane desire to scare them with my brilliance. She was lying there, her body outlined under the blanket, and it seemed as if she didn't expect me even to open my mouth. Her smile streamed down on me like light. A pain I had never known before, burgeoned in my heart. I realized that I was about to be robbed of my youth. All at once I leapt out of childhood, into the dark gravity of adulthood. It's only when we look back that we lie to ourselves, painting the past over with romantic colors. Actually, we were as serious as any druggist among his flasks of poison.

The girl's smile restored my youth for a little while. The sun grew stronger and I was boiling under the blanket, but I was afraid to show myself to her undressed. All of a sudden I wanted to hear her speak. She was smiling and gazing at me in astonishment. At last I could not control myself any longer. I said, "I'm hot."

"Take the blanket off."

I was so startled that I didn't pay attention to her voice. I had forgotten that in these sections of the city, the men walked around at home wearing only underwear, even in front of women they didn't know. I wrapped myself even more tightly in the blanket and she laughed. "I heard that you don't fast on Yom Kippur," she said.

I was irritated. I knew that her brothers observed the religious codes, and it seemed to me now that she was deliberately raising a barrier between us. "Actually, on Yom Kippur I eat mice," I said.

"Actually, you're rather sensitive," she said.

Silently I thanked God for my dark complexion. She had made the remark as if she were stating a simple fact, as if she were saying that the sun was already high in the sky. But I felt foolish. I made a face and rolled my eyes, and she burst out laughing.

"Why are you laughing?" I asked.

"Because you're not like they said you were."

"What did they say?"

"That you fight with the police. I heard you've even been shot at, and you spend a lot of time with Muslims."

"So what?"

"I thought you'd look like a thief at least."

Her mother called from downstairs. "Nedira, come down. We've got to buy some bread."

I stared at her unashamedly. I wanted to see her come bursting out from under the blanket. But in one nimble, mischievous movement, she threw the blanket over my head and scampered from the roof.

I didn't see her for three hours. Closed up in a stifling room, I longed to read a book or see her face. Her mother implored me to go out into the interior courtyard and breathe a little air, and when I refused Nedira said, "Nana, let him be. His lordship doesn't feel comfortable in our company."

Another hour passed, and then I saw Nedira's bare arm extending a plate through the doorway. On the plate were *pitta* and chicken livers and a baked tomato. My nostrils opened wide, but I didn't want to play games. Finally I said, "I'm not a dog."

As she came in, unsmiling, she stumbled, and the tomato flew off the plate. I caught it in the air, sank to my knees and looked at it, squashed between my hands. I thought she was going to laugh, but she didn't. She put the plate on a chair and came over to me and wiped my hands in her little hands, and when she saw that both our hands were red with sticky juice she unhesitatingly tucked up her skirts and cleaned my hands with them.

"No!" I cried, trying to retreat.

"What's the matter? I'll wash the dress." Her hair fell down over her shoulders and I knew that her thighs were bare, but I was standing over her and I only saw the back of her delicate neck. No, Shula, I didn't kiss her. I wanted to touch the nape of her neck. You're the first woman I ever kissed. I said to her, "After you wash the dress, change your hairdo. Put your hair up."

And so she did. I was in their house for two weeks and until the moment we parted I yearned to touch the nape of her neck, which she bared for me. The house would swoon in the burning sun, then cool slightly as blessed night fell. The stink of vegetables and rotting fruit wafted in from the nearby marketplace. People came and went. Brothers, sisters, visitors. Debates flared and there were several vociferous quarrels. But we could not have cared less. Nedira took me by the hand and led me back to my lost youth.

Two weeks passed, and I yearned to get out of the house for a while. That morning Nedira cooked something special to distract me, but I was resolved. "It's dangerous," she said. "They're liable to catch you. They're looking for you."

"I'll have to go someday. I'm not going to hide here forever."

It seemed she had not considered this. "Where are you going?" she asked. "Where will you go if you leave us?"

"I don't know. Another town, maybe."

"We don't have relatives in any other town."

I laughed. "There are loyal comrades anywhere I might go." That's how much faith I had in the world.

"And you'll go for good?"

"I don't know. I may have to leave the country."

"And I'll never see you again?"

The conversation had begun to be depressing. I shrugged. "In the meantime I just want to go for a walk."

"No!" shouted her mother, who had been eavesdropping. "I won't let you so much as stick your heretic's mug out the door of this house. What do you think you came here for? So I could hand you over to the police?"

I insisted. That evening the family convened. There was a stormy discussion. The epithets "mule" and "donkey" were heard over and over. Finally Nedira's father lost control of himself and shouted at me, "Go!"

The next day they lent me a long robe that reached down to my ankles, leather sandals, and a strange head cloth. At ten o'clock, telling Nedira's mother that I'd be back at nightfall, I left the house. All that morning Nedira had avoided me. I crossed the crowded marketplace and came out into the main street. I skipped two bus stations, stopping to wait only at the third, so that if I was caught they would not know where I had come from. I wanted to visit Karim. When I got on the bus I noticed Nedira getting on too. Angrily I kept my distance from her, sitting by myself. I ignored her when I got off and walked along the street toward Karim's house without turning to look back. I met a gardener sitting on the curb and asked him where he worked. He pointed at the house opposite and said, "Are you looking for work?"

"Yes. But why are you sitting here if you work over there?"

"I'm resting, cousin. I'm dizzy from this heat."

My suspicions were aroused. The house opposite was surrounded by shade trees and he was resting in the blazing sun. I pointed at Karim's house and asked, "Do you work for those Jews, too?"

"No."

"If you don't mind, I'll go ask them. Maybe they'll hire me."

"God be with you, cousin. Ask them, and the Prophet Mohammed be with you."

I hesitated a moment. "Are you sure they're home?"

"They're all at home—all of them."

My suspicions grew. There was something odd about his certainty, his encouraging smile. I hesitated. In the underground, you sometimes find yourself in a situation that resembles driving a car. If you're about to overtake another car, and for some reason you hesitate, then you have to give it up at once. It's nothing to be ashamed of. I thought to myself, I'll get rid of this gardener with a joke, and skip Karim's house and return to my safe haven. But Nedira was following me, and I thought that she would laugh at me for such a fruitless trip. Everybody talked of the exploits of the underground—I was afraid of disappointing her. If not for Nedira, I would have gone back to her house immediately. Instead I rang the doorbell on the courtyard gate. It was as if I had knocked at the gates of hell. Immediately I heard whistles and shouts and orders from every direction. Men appeared among the trees. Rifles came poking out from between branches. The gardener I had spoken with had a gun in his hand and was blocking the street off, together with two or three other men. There were uniformed police at either end of the street. I was on the verge of doing the unexpected—I was about to rush into Karim's house and make my escape from there by way of the neighbors'. I climbed over the wall, then jumped down into the shadows beneath the trees. Men were waiting for me there. I stood up straight, bracing myself for the final struggle, but I remembered that the robe I was wearing was made of fine cloth. They would have torn it off and exposed me naked to Nedira. Yes, that's what I thought of at that crazy moment. I could not avoid the blows. They led me out, kicking and hitting me. Nedira stood there, her hair up, her eyes torn, her face gaping in a frozen scream. I didn't hear her voice.

"Mommy, the meat's no good."

Shula felt the poet and Naim staring at her with astonishment. The poet put his hand on her shoulder and said in his soothing voice, "You're very tired. You almost fell asleep."

Shula, who was quick to blush, tried not to, but the blood rushed to her face. "Don't you want some more?" she said to Ido.

"Yech!" He twisted in his chair.

She picked up the dish and was about to throw it into the sink behind her, but the shocked look on Naim's face made her hesitate. He could not believe that perfectly good meat could be thrown away. She gave him an inquiring look.

"Sure!" he said.

"Do you want mine too? I'm not hungry."

The poet's hand rested on her shoulder again. "You're anxious."

Shula looked at his green eyes, then at his long fingers on her shoulder. She said nothing.

"The Egyptian army has fucked the Israeli army but good," Naim said. "The I.D.F.'s been routed, shattered. So many prisoners. Have you heard the radio?" he asked them both. "Maybe Marduch's been taken prisoner too, so he's okay."

"Naim, is that any way to talk?" Shula protested weakly.

"It's the truth, Shula. The Israeli army's been broken. But there's no need to worry about Marduch. All he has to say is that he's a friend of the Arabs and he'll be treated like a king. We'll all vouch for him, I swear. We know Marduch . . ."

"What did you hear on the radio?" Shula interrupted him.

"The Egyptian flag's waving all along the eastern bank of the Canal; Egyptian tanks and troops are marching across the Canal like soldiers on parade. Their planes fly undisturbed. The Israeli armor's been burned out, the artillery's smashed. And the Israelis! Corpses and more corpses," the excited youngster cried, putting down his fork.

"That's enough!" cried the poet.

"Why?" the boy asked, puzzled. "It's a victory for the revolution. Didn't you see the Egyptian TV? The funniest thing is the prisoners. Barefoot, hair a mess, heads bent. Where's the arrogance—where's it gone to? But like I told you, Shula, you don't have to worry about Marduch. He's one of ours. In the new state he'll be a real big shot."

"Naim," she said, "is that why you threatened the old man?"

"No. Can I have another glass of juice? Thanks a lot. At our house everything's rationed, even the juice. My parents still haven't decided when we're allowed to drink it—on Mother's Sabbath or Father's Sunday. Where were you and Ido when the sirens went off today?"

"At my parents'. They don't have a shelter, so we stayed in the house."

"Who needs a shelter? I didn't want to scurry into any lousy hole. I wanted to see the Arab planes coming for the first time ever to do a real job on Haifa. I was near Memorial Park and a civil defense warden with a club told me to get down into the shelter. I told him to go to hell. It was funny—the club shook in his hand, he went completely pale, he insisted I go, he tried to push me into the shelter by force while I stood there arguing with him. All of a sudden I heard a shout in the park, and the old man you saw, the siren had caught him pissing in the flowers, and he started running like mad with his fly open and everything hanging out, so I went over to him and helped him and told him to button his pants. His fear vanished and he became a normal person again and buttoned his pants and then we went down into the shelter, and I waited there for the Arab planes—but nothing! Half an hour we sweated down there, and then the all-clear sounded and I wanted to run out of there, but the old guy wouldn't let me. He grabbed my hand and asked me to help him climb the stairs. What could I do? I led him like you lead a stupid blind man, you saw what a miserable old geezer he was, just about ready to fall apart, five minutes it took for every step. I was just about dead when we arrived up top. Then he put his hand on my head and blessed me and asked me what my name was. I don't know why, but I told him my name was Mahmoud—I just felt like it. You should've seen how his hand flew off my head—like he had dipped it in a toilet by mistake. He opened his filthy mouth and started screaming about dirty Arabs, about how all these disasters are our fault. I ask you, Shula, was that fair? He hates Arabs—okay. But what did I do to him?"

"And what did you do to him?" asked the poet.

Shula was exhausted. "He threatened to kill him and the old man went crazy. If it wasn't for the police sergeant who happened to come along, the crowd would have taught Naim an awful lesson."

"Shula," Naim said, polishing off his third helping, "You're great!"

"You ought to thank the cop, not me."

"I mean the phone call. You didn't say a word to Mother."

"Why should I?"

"You're terrific. Ido, let's go play in your room."

"No," Shula said. "Ido's going to sleep now. I'll give you a book and you can lie down and rest a while."

"I'm not tired. Shalom, and thanks again for everything."

"You're going already?"

"It's good you didn't tell my parents. Shalom."

Shula washed Ido's face and hands and put him to bed. Although it was rare for her to stay with him very long, this time she tarried. She finished telling him his story, she yawned into his hair. Her eyelids grew heavy, she leaned her head against him.

"Shula wants to sleep," said the child.

"Uh huh."

"Shula will sleep and I'll protect her."

She knew what this meant—she had had experience with it. The child would tug at her eyelids from time to time to check whether she had fallen asleep.

"Is Daddy coming?"

The question did not make her tremble. "No," she said in a drowsy voice. "Now will you go to sleep?"

"You're bothering me, sitting here."

"You're right, Ido." Nevertheless, she did not move. She was afraid to leave the room. The silence in the apartment frightened her. She hoped that the poet had gone to his room, but she knew he was sitting in the living room, waiting to ambush her. The word "ambush" made her tremble again. Once more she felt his knee groping for hers. She had been disturbed by the touch of his hand, so self-confident. It was only when she looked him in the eye that his confidence had crumbled, to be replaced by a kind of hesitant entreaty. She was angry at herself for fearing him.

The two men she loved were far away, in mortal danger,

perhaps already killed. Naim's vivid report had set her imagination to work. Both Marduch and Rami had absorbed the shock of the first wave, the initial brunt of the invasion. But still she was not really frightened, only beset by a vague anxiety, a foggy nightmarish feeling. She felt a dim sort of need to be held by someone. Again she was angry at herself for imagining things. The poet had meant only to make a simple gesture of sympathy, such as the situation demanded. And if he desired her—well, he was only a man, and she, as a woman, ought to be proud. He would not take her against her will. What happened further depended completely on her.

In this way she found the courage to bestir herself and leave the bedroom. The poet was, indeed, sitting in the living room, reading. She remembered that there was no armchair in his room. "Ambush?" She smiled at the idea and proceeded to her bedroom. Later she would admit that it had been a mistake to smile. The stillness of the apartment was heavy with expectation. She had stolen from Ido's room, closed the door furtively, and crossed the living room, making directly for her bedroom wearing a smile that might be interpreted in more than one way. What man would not have started wondering? Not to mention an Arab, jealous of his manhood. To make matters worse, she had stood in the doorway and favored him with a look of apology for leaving her guest to himself.

This was not how the poet understood her look, and later Shula had to confess that he was not the only one to blame. The poet—a refined and experienced male—rose carelessly from the armchair, threw the newspaper on the table, and whispered to her as he moved nearer, "Do you know that your neighbor's discovered everything?"

She would have done better to leave the bedroom, and at any rate she should not have whispered back but what he said frightened her. "That can't be," she said. "You're just imagining it. Tuvia's a nice old man."

"Maybe, maybe," he said, standing in the doorway beside

her, so that she could not close the door without hitting him. "But he's also a very sly old man."

She laughed nervously. "Don't tell me you're like my mother—do you think everybody outside the Party is an informer?"

"No. But this guy knows all the tricks of the secret police."

Her shoulders jerked. "Tuvia?"

The poet put his hand on her shoulder and the spasms ceased. "As soon as you left, he came down and started puffing through the keyhole."

Laughing good-naturedly, she ventured to shake his hand off her bare shoulder.

At that, the poet invaded her bedroom. He glanced at the green mountain ridge and the clear sky visible through the window. Shula's bed was unmade, the closet open; there was a house slipper lying on the rug. Shula felt as if the poet was seeing not these things, but rather her inner self. Again her shoulders jerked, but this time the poet was too far away to reach out his hand; he stood at the window, near the bed. "So what did you do?" she asked.

"I had to let him in. We had a good long wrestling match, and then he left. When the siren sounded he took his wife down to the shelter and then came up to ask me to join them, but I refused, because I didn't want to go on arguing with him in front of the people in the shelter." The poet was looking into Shula's eyes, approaching her. "I thought, I don't care if this building gets blown to bits, I'm not going down to the shelter." The spasms in her shoulders grew stronger, and Shula stammered irrelevantly, "Now Tuvia knows I'm hiding an Arab in my house."

The poet froze in his tracks. Shula, recovering, noticed that although his greenish eyes were resting on her, he didn't see her. He raised his hand, began to say something, changed his mind. Stepping past her, he said, "Excuse me, I'm going to my room to rest."

19

It was the second night of the war. The few children playing in the street had dispersed and vanished early. On the distant ridges of the Galilee the last light waned. The cars, their headlights painted over, groped their way through the sudden gloom. The night before there may have been some expectation in the air, but tonight there was none. Tuvia was sorely affronted. He went out onto his balcony and, when he saw Shula staring into the distance, tried to withdraw; she noticed him. "Good evening, Tuvia."

"They tricked us," Tuvia said. "They really fixed us."

"I dropped in to see Hannah."

"I know."

"Where were you? Hannah was worried."

"I had to get out of the house before I went crazy."

"Have you heard anything about your grandsons?"

"The same as you've heard about Marduch."

Shula fell silent, and looked down into the dark sea. The old man's tone was hostile, as if Shula herself had inflicted some wrong on him. And yet he had always treated her so warmly. She decided to ignore him.

Several minutes passed. Then Tuvia asked, "Where is he?"

She shook her head and kept silent.

"Has he gone?" the old man said expectantly.

Still she kept silent.

"So he's still with you."

I'm disgraced as far as he's concerned, she thought. He must be seventy years old, and still he sees everything as a man does. Another man of his tribe has gone to fight in a war of life or death, and here his female is consorting with the enemy.

"Tell me," he asked her, "aren't you being foolish?"

"Tuvia, let up on me, will you?"

He noticed the depression in her voice. "Where's Ido?" he asked, with surprising tenderness. She waved her hand as if to shake him off.

"Are you crying?" he said.

"Tuvia, really . . . "

"Listen, I want to come down and take him to stay with us."

"He went out with Shoshana."

"So late?"

"She took him to her place."

"You're angry with me."

"Yes."

"Maybe you're right to be. Why don't you come up and visit us again?"

"Thanks a lot."

He was not unaware that his talk irritated her, but he sensed that it also comforted her to have him on the balcony. It would have comforted her even more if he shut up, but silence was not among the pensioner's virtues. He was tempted to stretch his hand down to her. Suddenly he said, "I hear your mother's footsteps."

Shula stirred angrily. "What, is she coming?"

"She's already here." Tuvia and Shula's mother despised one another. "Good luck," he said, and disappeared.

Her mother pushed the doorbell. She was always a little

nervous coming to Shula's place. Shula, who would never intentionally insult anyone, who shunned conflict, could be surprisingly rough on her mother. Shula opened the door and said, "Why did you come?"

Tova wore a shapeless dress. She looked at her daughter and explained patiently, "I told you I had to drop in at the clubhouse, so I came by here too. How often do I have the chance?"

"Now of all times, in the blackout? You came on purpose."

"Child, at least close the door."

Shula closed the door behind her mother and went quickly to the balcony, forcing Tova to follow, although she would have preferred to sit in the kitchen over a cup of tea. "You know very well," Shula said, "that there aren't any more buses at this time of night."

"What?" Her mother took the opportunity to get her own back. "Has your Great Power gone kaput already? All these years they've been telling us how prepared they are to stand and fight on all fronts; now when war comes there isn't a bus to save your life."

"The buses are taking the soldiers to the front."

"They're taking them to their deaths."

"Mother!" Shula screamed. "If you've come to torture me, you can just go."

"Where to?" her mother asked—she still had not been invited to sit down.

"Home."

"I thought I'd spend the night here."

"Absolutely not."

"Child, I told you this wasn't for you. It's not as simple as you think. It's not easy to care for a strange man. Sometimes a woman can hardly stand to look at her own. If you want, I'll take him to our place."

"We've already talked about that. It's settled."

"Maybe you'd like something to drink?"

"Yes." Shula allowed herself a bit of pampering. "Tea."

Her mother's face lit up. "Right away. I'd like something too."

Shula raised her head. She could have sworn that the pensioner was playing hide-and-seek, peeking at her from time to time from his balcony, his ears pricked up. She scanned the street, but she knew that Shoshana would be bringing Ido back only at eight o'clock. The child would be tired. Shula's mother came out on the balcony carrying a tray. "I put a little lemon in yours."

Shula looked at the expression on her mother's face and said, "How did you know?"

"I'm a nurse," Tova said, with a trace of pride. "You think I'm just a stupid old woman, but I'm not blind."

"What should I do?"

"Are you sure?"

"I don't know."

"Well, so Marduch finally did his bit, and now he goes off to play war—now of all times."

"You're always complaining about him. Marduch hasn't played much in his life; this rotten world of yours has afforded him very little amusement. He's like you, Mother. His conscience bothers him whenever he's having a good time. I only wish he was playing war. Then he could worry about saving his own skin when he came under fire. But he went to fight, Mother."

"For those generals?"

"You're angrier at him than the Arab comrades in the Party are."

"That's what you think, child. They just don't dare tell you what they really think."

"What do you know about Marduch? Nothing."

"Well," her mother began, "if my little girl chose him from among all the men . . . " She stopped.

Shula smiled. "Admit it, Mother—you've always seen him as the lesser of two evils."

For quite a few seconds Tova could not reply. She had put a sugar cube in her mouth and was gagging on it. "I don't understand a word of what you're saying—all your insinuations."

"You understand perfectly well. When I was still in school you were terrified I'd bring you home an Arab son-in-law."

"Did I ever once say a word to you?"

"No, not directly, not honestly. But I'd see the expression on your face whenever I mentioned a dark-skinned guy."

"Yes, you did talk a lot about those fellows."

"Just to bother you."

"Naughty girl."

"Rami was the only one I loved."

"The son of that . . . " Her mother hesitated.

"That degenerate," Shula completed her sentence.

"But," her mother said, "you did finally choose a man who was practically black."

"Because he's Marduch, not because he's black or red or blue. And also because I was a silly coward and gave up Rami."

"You still haven't forgiven me."

"No."

The old woman fell silent. The sugar had dissolved on her tongue and now it seemed she could not summon the strength to pick up her glass and wash it down. "You'll never understand a person like Marduch," Shula told her.

"Maybe," she answered wearily, her voice distant. A moment later she recovered, gulped the rest of the tea, lit a cigarette, and said, "It's hard to understand a political-minded man like him running off to a war that's not his own."

"Marduch's different from the other comrades."

"He's one of a kind."

"That's not what I meant. He didn't come to Israel as a tourist, not even as an immigrant. He didn't want to come here at all. He had sacrificed so much back there—he couldn't just get up and go. But they didn't want him. They dumped him as if he were a leper. He almost forgot, in the desert, that he was a Jew. He begged them to let him stay, and they laughed and said that merchandise like him wasn't wanted there or in any other country. The world's full of unwanted revolutionaries. He didn't have a penny, he didn't have a profession. They told him that only Israel would take him, and he was sure that they were making fun of him; he was afraid it might be another scheme to destroy him. He was certain that as soon as he stepped onto Israeli soil, he'd be arrested and led off to a new jail, where they would settle accounts with him. When he stepped off the plane he got a shock. He glanced all around surreptitiously, but no one had come to handcuff him. Here he found a home, work, even the freedom to go on cursing anything he wanted . . ."

"And also a beautiful girl who he never dreamed he'd be worthy of."

"Israel gave him refuge. He feels deep in his heart that he owes a great debt to this country. He sees the faults, all right, but he'll never forget that this was the only state to give him a home."

"He should be happy."

Only now did Shula notice that her mother was not fighting back as usual. Instead, she lit a fresh cigarette with the butt of the one before, and kept silent.

"What's happened, Mother?"

"Nothing."

It hit her with the force of a blow to the solar plexus. "Mother, why didn't you call Goldschmidt a degenerate?"

"What a question."

"Mother!" Shula screamed.

"Yes, child."

"Rami!"

"Just rumors, child."

Her mother's hand touched Shula's hair, her neck, then took firm hold of her shoulder. She got up and took Shula's head in both her hands and pressed it to her bosom. "Child, it may be nothing but a rumor. His brother arrived this morning from up on the Golan and said something."

"What?"

"I don't know very much about these things. It seems there's some new weapon, something that's deadly against tanks. And you know that Rami spends too much time with tanks." There was disapproval in her voice, as if Rami were a hashish smuggler who ought to be prepared to bear the consequences.

Shula was trembling. "If it wasn't for his tanks, Mother, you'd have been sitting in a refugee camp long ago."

"Let's not go into that now." Tova humored her. "But if that's what you think, then why do you insist on putting Fatkhi up in your home?"

"Mother," Shula said, staring ahead vacantly, "when Ido comes back, put him to bed."

"Where are you going?"

"To Kiryat Haim."

"Are you crazy? You're going to drive in the blackout?"

"Tuvia!" Shula cried.

The pensioner, as if waiting for Shula to call, stuck his head over the railing. "What is it?"

"Tuvia, do you have some blue paint for the headlights? I have to go to Kiryat Haim right away."

"I'll go down to the car right now."

"I'm telling you, this is completely unnecessary," her mother said.

Shula went to the bedroom and put on a white flowered dress. For a moment she was uncertain whether she ought to turn up in such a dress. But then she said, "To hell with it," and snatched the car keys.

"Drive carefully, child," her mother said at the door.

Tuvia stood beside the car, his task accomplished. "Who is he?" he asked.

"A lieutenant colonel in the armored corps." I said that to impress him, she thought, disturbed by the numbness that had taken hold of her.

"I guessed as much. His poor parents."

"He's the one who's been killed!" she cried. Easily moved to tears, she tried to weep now, but couldn't. She tried to put it into her mind that she was going to see his parents, not him. Since leaving his garden when they were both hardly more than children, she had never set foot in Rami's parents' house.

Three or four cars were already parked beside the garden gate. Shula looked at the house. Blankets covered the windows, but shafts of light filtered out onto the lawn. She got out of the car and stood hesitating at the gate, afraid of the dogs. Rami and his dogs. He had grown up among dogs. All the dogs in the neighborhood seemed to gravitate to him. On occasion one would accompany him to school and intrude into the morning drill, to the great amusement of the students. "Rami Goldschmidt!" the principal would shout into the microphone. "Fall out and take your friend home. He may very well be more clever and industrious than you, but you'll have to explain to him that this isn't the place for him."

Rami would leave the ranks, the strange dog following him. He would never tell the principal—preening himself on his sarcasm—that the dog wasn't his. He would gaze at the animal affectionately, as if to make up for the insult it had suffered in front of the hilarious crowd.

Once Shula told him, "Your dogs resemble you."

It was a fact. He always chose large dogs, solid and muscular, that aggressively demanded his love. And they were jealous of Shula. She was pleased when Rami held her hand in school, where their classmates could see, but not at home—the dogs would growl at the sight. She sent him an invitation to her wedding. Courtesy demanded it, and she was sure he wouldn't come. The hall was full of Party members, Jews and Arabs. And he came in uniform. The insignia on his shoulder caused some excitment—a high-ranking officer at a Communist wedding. The other guests thought it took courage: Rami was endangering his reputation. When he approached to shake Marduch's hand, Shula saw that her old boyfriend was bewildered. But then he turned to her and his confusion vanished. "You're beautiful," he said, unsmiling, terribly serious.

She knew she was blushing. She heard herself blurt out, "Now you'll have only the dogs to take care of." When embarrassed she was liable to say foolish things.

He was used to her talk, but now it was obvious that he couldn't find a suitable reply. He took off his cap and recovered some composure. He said to Marduch with a smile, "So? The dogs are nice too." Then he turned away. He wandered around the hall until he found a couple of relatives sitting all by themselves, and dropped down beside them. Shula approached him and shouted through the deafening racket of the orchestra: "Aren't you going to ask me to dance?" He shook his head and smiled, stubbornly refusing. She felt foolish standing in front of him, holding her bouquet. Blushing again, she ruffled his hair with the flowers and went to look for Marduch.

Yes, she had always been afraid at the gate to Rami's garden. The animals terrified her with their growling. Rami would laugh, he would pry their teeth open with his fingers and stick his hand into their jaws to show her there was nothing to it. But she continued to be frightened of the dogs, and they continued to be jealous of her. She would swing the gate open and call out to him. Once she told him, "It's either me or those dogs. The way I stand here shouting, the neighbors must think I'm stuck on you."

"I don't care if the whole world knows I'm stuck on you. From now on, I'm going to call for you so loud that all the neighbors will hear. Anyway, I'm more afraid of your mother than you are of my dogs."

A few days later, her mother came into Shula's room. "Has that degenerate's son gone out of his mind? It's not enough that those dogs of his keep the whole neighborhood in an uproar—now he's barking, too, all day long. Why can't he use the doorbell?"

One summer night they went out to the moonlit beach. Shula removed her sandals and walked barefoot in the moist sand, the surf foaming around her ankles. Suddenly a large wave broke, and she leapt away from it with a joyful shriek, straight into Rami's arms. She extricated herself and returned to the water. The next time a wave made her jump, Rami kissed her. They were both wearing shorts, and they went into the water up to their knees. A great wave broke over them, inundating them. Shula shook with cold. "Come on, let's run," Rami said. Hand in hand they raced over the driftwood and crates and bottles that the sea had thrown onto the shore; then they sat, breathing hard, on a mound of sand. She said, "Look how dirty my feet got from that tar."

Kneeling in front of her and fishing out a handkerchief, Rami briskly rubbed the soles of her feet. It was a pleasurable feeling. Shula leaned on her elbows, threw her head back, and closed her eyes. When she opened them, the sea was shining in the moonlight over Rami's head, and her lips had opened wide, of their own accord. She hoped he would stop. For a moment she thought he'd been swallowed in the silvery sea, and she wanted him to come. Her hands thrust into the sand, her breasts rose toward the moon. His shadow crept over her, covering her body. Bringing her knees together, she caught his head between them. Pierced through with painful delight, she let go of him. Then a dog's ferocious barking shattered everything. A great black shape came bounding over the sand, leapt onto Rami's back, and threw him to the ground. Rami, startled, wrestled with the beast. Then they noticed two figures tramping through the sand in their direction.

Shula's mother screamed, "What are you doing to the girl?"

"I'm drying her feet," Rami said simply.

"At one in the morning?"

Rami was astonished. "Is it that late?"

His father burst out laughing.

Tova exploded. "Degenerate!" she cried.

His father ignored her. "We were worried about you two, we didn't know where you'd disappeared to. Then your mother got the idea of letting the dog loose, and he led us here."

"Look at you, you're all wet," Shula's mother screamed at her.

Shula got up and ran barefoot over the sand, Rami and the dog following her. In the distance she could hear her mother grumbling and Goldschmidt laughing.

Shula now put her hand out to the gate but immediately pulled it back in fright. The dog was howling angrily at her, and she almost called Rami to come and restrain it. Then she remembered, and pushed open the gate that had been gnawed on by bared teeth. Someone opened the door to the house. Rami's younger brother came out and called, "Who's there?"

"Me," she whispered.

Rami's brother didn't recognize her voice. His father's head appeared behind him. "Shula," he said.

The howling of the dog grew even more intense than before. They didn't know that she dreaded the animal and was just barely managing to control herself. Pale and trembling, she reached the door—she had nearly turned to run away. Rami's father took her hand and led her inside like a child. People were sitting in bright light. "Rami's girlfriend," he said.

Coming into the strong light after so long in the dark, she was dazzled. The many unfamiliar faces seemed to add to the brilliance. She stood helplessly in the middle of the room, sensing that they expected something of her, that they had been waiting for her to arrive in order to begin something. Goldschmidt still held her hand, caressing it with his left hand and smiling like a drunk. "Rami's girlfriend," he repeated. "Ever since she was a child, we've called her Rami's bride."

A red-faced woman in a kerchief burst into tears. Shula, turning to Goldschmidt, saw that his face was wracked and his eyes blinking behind his glasses. Suddenly she understood why they had all looked at her that way. They expected her to give them a clear answer, a definite verdict. There was still doubt, there was a glimmer of hope. Now they were waiting for her to break down or shed a few tears. But she could not oblige them. Her gray eyes hardly flickered. She freed her hand from Goldschmidt's and approached Rami's mother. The woman was trembling, her features distorted by panic. Seeming frightened of Shula, she turned this way and that in her chair, as if on the point of fleeing from this young woman who had come to confirm the terrible news. Shula bent down and stretched out her hand, but the woman did not seem to notice. Suddenly, however, she got up on her thick legs and, swaying, threw her arms over Shula. "Rami!" she screamed.

Goldschmidt and the younger son tried to calm her down. With one arm she held them off, with the other she pulled Shula toward her, forcing her to sit beside her. She buried her head in Shula's bosom, as if she might find some evidence of her son in the body of the girl he had grown up with, in whose company he had blossomed. "You loved him, didn't you? Didn't you? Shula, my Shula. He came back from the wedding and told us everything and laughed and laughed, but we knew he wasn't really laughing—he was crying like a child. It was terribly cold that night and he went outside in the garden and sat in the dark next to the doghouse. The dog barked, but Rami was silent. He was so alone, Shula. He's alone now too. They haven't found him. They say the burning tank went rolling over the lines to the Syrians. It went rolling over in flames. There was no one to go running after him. He's alone there now, in those mountains. . . ."

"Yes, yes," Shula whispered.

Rami's mother held her at arm's length, taking her by the shoulders, gazing into her face, and lovingly, gently scolded her, as she had when Shula and Rami ran wild as children. "Why did you abandon him, why did you leave him alone?"

Shula felt that the tears must start to flow in just another moment—but they refused to come.

"Mother, let her be," Rami's brother cried.

His father gestured to him to let his mother alone. The youth was still in his muddy uniform. He had the gait of a sleepwalker, his face was gray, and his eyes gleamed strangely with the feverishness of slaughter.

"Ron," Shula said, "were you there, too?"

He ran his tongue over his burnt lip. "Yes, the whole time."

His father dropped down beside him, but the boy moved away, huddling by himself as if fearful of any human contact. He was a stranger here; he was still back there, on the battlefield. His father, not realizing, turned to Shula and said, "You remember our Ron from when he was a baby. You and Rami would fight all the time over who was going to push his carriage."

Although she knew that she should show consideration and delicacy toward Ron, she could not help questioning him, for the questions burned inside her. "Did you see him? Did you meet him?"

"No!" Ron said, waving his arm. He fled to the window and stood mumbling into the blanket: "Yesterday afternoon his voice came on the radio. You all don't know him, you don't know anything about him. Right at the very beginning, in the first hour, he was wounded. There were lots of casualties in the first bombardment. A stranger hearing him on the radio would have thought, how cool that guy is! But I know him.

There was despair in his voice. Not the despair of a man who's been broken, but the despair of a father who sees his sons being slaughtered. He knew that they were all going to die. I grasped that when he asked about me over the radio, twice. That's not like Rami—to ask about his brother over the radio." The youth turned to them in distress. "Father, I was embarrassed to speak with him. The radio operator told me to come over and I was afraid they'd say I was the colonel's spoiled kid brother. I told the radio operator to say that I was okay. Rami didn't believe him. The battalion was finished, it was dying. At first we thought we'd screw them good, but when their first wave was broken others came to take their place. Tanks and artillery and planes. Many of the boys realized that this was the end and you felt that they wanted Rami to lie to them, at least, to tell them that rescue was on the way. But he refused to lie. I don't know why. Maybe he wanted them to feel that they were the only ones left guarding Israel. Actually, that's what I meant when I said there was despair in his voice. He demanded more than mere sacrifice from the boys. I saw his tank get hit. Rami ran to another tank. That was hit, too. He jumped on a third tank that already had smoke coming out of it. . . . "

The youth fell silent; the faraway look came back into his eyes. His father approached him, but Ron pushed him away roughly and fled the room.

20

Shula had no idea how long she had been sitting in the car, parked on the crest of Mount Carmel, her chin resting in her hand, gazing out at the darkened Jezreel Valley. In the distance the eternal red flame of the refinery flared from time to time, as if it had collected its strength to leap upward and disperse the darkness weighing down upon it, only to exhaust itself and retreat humbly under the pressure of the darkness. Rami's dead, she repeated to herself. It was the second night of the war. For Marduch, too, it was the second night of the war. She tried to experience her own fear but couldn't—neither her fear nor her grief over Rami's death.

What's happening to me, she wondered, dismayed by the equanimity that had descended upon her.

She started the car and drove home. The first nip of autumn was already in the air, but Tuvia was standing on his balcony in his undershirt.

"Shula, you forgot to lock the car."

She shrugged and continued on her way to the entrance.

"Shula! Don't leave the car like that."

She had to retrace her steps and lock the door.

"You've got guests," he told her as she entered the stairwell.

Yes, Shula had guests, and her mother was running to and

fro among them, serving them, her face beaming. Entering the apartment, Shula saw Fuad, Shoshana, and the poet, and also Emile; without Amalia, thank God. Ido was already sleeping. She glanced at her watch—past ten already. As she entered, the visitors fell silent, as if she were returning from a funeral.

Rami was dead.

And still she did not feel the pain she was expecting, hoping for. "I'll go wash; I'll join you right away," she said with a smile, with something close to gaiety. As she closed the bathroom door behind her she heard them whispering; her mother said to Shoshana, "You don't know her."

Looking in the mirror, she saw an abundance of black hair and a fine forehead and gray eyes and soft lips and a smooth neck, and she was disappointed. Rami and Marduch hadn't left any traces on her body. She undressed and examined her breasts and thighs, and there too she found no signs. She ran her hand over her shoulders and stomach. Her flesh was pure and virginal. She turned the faucet and threw a handful of fragrant powder into the tub. Immersing herself in the water, she was seized by revulsion. At last the tears came.

When she came out, she found her mother blocking the way. "Child, I made you something to eat."

"Leave me alone now."

"I know you're upset, but you have to eat something. . . . "

"Stop nagging."

"Were you at your father's?"

"I forgot."

"Nu, it doesn't matter. He can take care of himself. But I was so worried about you, in this blackout. I thought that as long as you were in Kiryat Haim you'd go over to your father and phone me here, give me some word. How are his poor parents?"

"Do you mean the degenerate, or his wife?"

Her mother disappeared into the kitchen. Shula tried to

turn her attention to her guests. She vowed silently not to divulge anything, but Shoshana already knew. She had known Rami many years before. In the beginning, when she had first come from Yesud Hama'alah, Shoshana's rough ways repelled Shula, but this changed as she got to know Shoshana better. Unlike the other comrades, Shoshana had found no fault in Shula's being with Rami. "A great guy," she said.

Shula was afraid that she would be offered words of condolence, but her fears were groundless. The three Arabs were in a state of great agitation. A certain madness had come over them; they found it difficult to sit still. They shared something that put a great distance between them and the Jewish women, even Shoshana, who spoke Arabic well. Shula sat down beside her and was asked, "How did it happen?"

Shula hesitated. She was always conscious of her Jewishness in the presence of Arabs. Marduch, too, was conscious of his Jewishness, yet had no difficulty establishing connections with the Arabs. He considered them his equals. She did not. Every time she dealt with them, she felt she had to descend to their level. When Marduch chided her, calling her a racist, Shula was unable to defend herself, save with a smile. As time passed he had grown used to this smile, which at first angered him. Once he said, "At least you're not a hypocrite, like your mother."

Still Shula hesitated. Shoshana had asked because it was the natural thing to do, and now the Arabs were staring at her curiously. Fuad's bulging eyes provoked her. She was too tired to choose her words—they just escaped her. "He was a battalion commander," she said with unconcealed pride. "One of the youngest commanders in the armored corps. I spoke with his brother, but I didn't understand very much of what he told me. The tanks exploded one after the other as if something mysterious was killing them. It was certain death for all the crews."

"Rockets!" the poet cried.

"What?" asked Shula.

"Anti-tank rockets," the poet explained willingly, ignoring Shoshana's reproachful look. Excited, he lit another cigarette. "It's a wonderful weapon—it's operated by infantrymen. Shula, you must have read about the heroic Soviet soldiers who stood up to Hitler's tanks. A single soldier with a Molotov cocktail would confront a tank and destroy it. Today the same thing's happening right here, in our own part of the world—another heroic chapter is being written."

Shula could not understand. "You're happy, Fatkhi. You're happy," she said.

"Not about the death of your personal friend. For more than fifty years they've been making fun of the Arabs. Once I saw a Jewish carpenter fly into a rage and curse his apprentice for not gluing the Formica on right: 'That's Arab work!' he shouted. Shula, did you know that influenza is an Arab term? *Enf-al-anza,* meaning, the goat's nose. The constellations Vega and Rejel—they're Arabic names. When I heard that Jewish carpenter talking about Arab work, I remembered the Arab doctors and astronomers who served as beacons at a time when Europe was sunk in the darkness of the Middle Ages. Today the Arab soldier is wielding this modern weapon with dexterity and devastating effect; and he's right on target."

"They're shooting at Marduch, too," Shula murmured.

The poet smiled calmly, almost childishly. "Marduch isn't shooting toy darts either. He's shooting to kill. That's what the game is all about, Shula. Up until now, Israel's wars were like sporting events—the Israeli soldiers were like British gentlemen in the heyday of the empire, going into the jungle and wiping out defenseless elephants and lions with the most modern guns. But today Israel is at war with an opponent who's equipped with the same weapons. I'd like to hear what that carpenter has to say now."

"It's all a game to you."

Emile, unruffled, noticed Shula's pallor. "Don't take him so seriously," he advised her. "He's a poet. That's what poets do—they exaggerate, they tremble all over."

"It's not just his imagination," Fuad said. "It's the Arab-Muslim truth."

The poet stubbed out his cigarette. "What are you talking about, Fuad?"

Fuad turned on him angrily. "You know what the Cairo newspapers are calling this war? They've already got a name for it. The War of Honor they're calling it."

"The War of Honor it is."

"Honor my ass!" Fuad burst out. "If a soldier goes to war merely for the sake of his honor, he'll accomplish something symbolic, win some token victory, and then stop in his tracks. God Himself won't be able to move him another step."

"And you'd like that next step to be all the way to Tel Aviv, eh?" Shoshana said.

"For now I'd be satisfied with Beersheba," Fuad said. "But there's no chance of that."

"The Christian gentleman doesn't have much faith," the poet spat.

"Listen, mister," Fuad said contemptuously, "it sounds like you hung around too long at your Jewish carpenter's. Go to the refugee camps. They don't give a damn for your games or Cairo's prattle about honor. What they want are the stone houses of Haifa, the fisherman's quay in Jaffa, the gardens in Zipori . . ."

The poet was shaking. This is no way for an Arab to talk or think, he told himself. Something has undermined Fuad's Arab soul. Honor. The poets who roamed the Arabian peninsula even before the advent of the Prophet Mohammed had set honor as the highest virtue, the essence of life; and this determined the Arabs' code of behavior to this very day, even in the most up-to-date laboratories, the universities of Beirut and Alexandria.

The poet said in a whisper, "Honor is the essence of an

Arab's life, Fuad. Honor demands that an Arab pay for his friend's drink in a teahouse—that he kill rather than see someone else pay."

"But he's not ready to be killed, Fatkhi—Arab women enjoy that privilege. Think of all the Arab women who've been butchered in the name of masculine Arab honor. No other people has sacrificed so many women on the altar of honor. The Arab warrior who came out of the desert perfected the sword and brought down mighty empires with it, but he never used his sword in a duel. The Arab will kill for honor, but how many are prepared to die for it? We don't sacrifice our lives for the sake of honor. That's a European-Christian game that's not designed for the Muslim Arab."

Shula's mother entered bearing apples, pears, and grapes. She set a plate and knife on the table before each guest and seated herself on a low stool, her eyes wide open and her ears pricked. She was thrilled to be sitting in the company of these Party leaders. But if she hoped to hear pearls of wisdom, she was disappointed. The debaters suppressed their ardent feelings. Fuad shifted in his chair and calmed down. Emile lit his pipe and smiled cordially at her. The poet helped himself to a bunch of grapes.

"How are you?" Fuad said, turning to Shula's mother with exaggerated warmth.

Unaccustomed to oriental etiquette, Tova replied, "Oh, well—so-so." There was nothing wrong with her health; in her own way she was almost content. But she thought that it would be out of accord with Party principles for her to say that she was happy. She had never, even for politeness's sake, told anyone that she was well. Strangers supposed she was afraid of the evil eye. But no—it was simply inconceivable that under an exploitive, unjust regime, anyone should feel entirely well. If he wasn't suffering from his own distress, there was always the distress of others. She sighed, pursed her lips, and said, "That's how it is!"

There was a knock at the door. Everyone turned to Shula. Before she could say anything, the pensioner called out, "Shula, it's me."

Her mother groaned. "Why?" she asked the others. "What do we need that pervert for?"

Shula got up and opened the door. Tuvia's wrinkled woolen shirt exuded an odor of mothballs. The poet began to get up and leave the room, but Tuvia motioned to him and said, "Don't be afraid, I haven't come to browbeat you, my friend."

"I'm not afraid of you," the poet muttered.

The pensioner, looking weak, dropped into a chair.

"What do you want?" Shula's mother demanded.

"Nothing. You're a nurse by profession. You might at least ask how my wife is feeling."

"By the way you're strolling around at night, her condition can't be critical."

"She's better, thank God. Got to be careful, though—her heart, you know. The flu could be dangerous for her."

"So go upstairs and sit with her."

"Mother!" Shula cried.

"Never mind," the pensioner murmured. He had long since become used to her mother's way of talking. "I sit beside her for hours at a time. Sometimes she drives me away, and I'm happy she does. It's getting hard for me to hide the truth from her."

The poet's suspicions were aroused. "What truth?"

The pensioner tried to smile. "I wasn't referring to your secret. She still hasn't grasped how serious this war is. She's got grandsons in the Sinai and on the Golan, too . . . How are things in Kiryat Haim?"

"They still haven't grasped what's happened."

"Poor people."

"Do you want a cup of tea?"

"Yes, please."

"Sit down," Shula's mother said to her. "You're tired. I'll get it."

The pensioner said to the poet, "Please forgive me for bullying you this morning—something came over me."

"I don't give a damn," the poet growled.

"That's your privilege," the pensioner said humbly.

"If you only knew what happened to Naim today," Shoshana said to Shula. "They nearly murdered him. He takes too much after his father."

"Woman, you're talking nonsense."

"It's your doing, Fuad. He's only a child and you talk a lot of nonsense when he's around. Naim threatened some poor old man, and the crowd wanted to tear him to pieces. Luckily a police sergeant and some woman in a car happened on the scene."

"Fascists!" Shula's mother gnashed her teeth. "For a few words they'd murder a child." She was holding the tray.

"It was Shula," the poet said.

Shula silently shrugged it off.

Her mother turned pale. She leaned toward Shula and said, "You must have been with Ido. And you went mixing in with some wild rabble, in your condition?"

Shoshana gaped. "What condition?"

Shula blushed, and her mother hastened to say, "Two days already she hasn't been feeling well. Maybe it's on account of the germs that her good neighbor breathes on her all day."

"Snake," the pensioner whispered to himself. Suddenly they heard a terrible screech of brakes and held their breath in fearful expectation of a crash. Car doors banged, followed by a tumult of voices. Emile went onto the balcony and leaned over the railing. When he returned, the pipe was trembling in his hand. "It's a police squad car."

Fuad crossed one leg over the other and lit a cigarette. "Fatkhi, go into your room and close the door."

"I'm staying here. I won't be cornered like a rat."

"You're a real man," Fuad said.

Tuvia hurried to the balcony, and Shula's mother shrieked, "Stop him! That bastard's going to call the cops up here."

"Good evening," Tuvia said on the balcony.

Someone down below replied, "Good evening, sir."

"I told you," Shula's mother whispered to her. "Your Marduch was too trusting with this viper!"

"Are you the one?" the policeman down below asked.

"Yes."

"Aren't you ashamed, a man of your age?"

"I'm sorry, Officer. Maybe there is some light showing, but my wife's sick, and that civil defense guard came up and banged on the door like a madman. I had such a hard time calming my wife that I got upset myself. I'm sorry I got angry and talked back."

"Sir," said the officer, "you know you're supposed to respect the blackout, and be careful about it. It's for your own safety, after all."

"Yes, Officer."

"So I hope that settles it. Best wishes to your wife—I hope she has a speedy recovery. Goodnight."

"Goodnight. Thanks."

The pensioner returned to the living room. Shula's mother knew that he had heard her cry, but she had already recovered from her embarrassment—revolutionary vigilance demanded it. He gave her a challenging look, but she leveled a righteous look right back at him. The pensioner dropped into his chair, took a sip from his cup, and said, "Your tea is really refreshing."

"Mother," Shula said, "I'll drive you home."

"What, in this darkness? It's out of the question, child. I was worried enough until you came back from your crazy trip. You've got a guest and Ido has to be taken care of and you're not feeling well.

"You're going, Mother."

"I won't leave you like this."

"I'll keep an eye on things here," the pensioner offered.

Shula's mother turned to him but said nothing. The look that passed between her and the old man depressed Shula. Suddenly there was a queer, obscure understanding between these sworn enemies, and it related to what Shoshana had said lightly in the kitchen: "Shula, sweetheart, that crazy poet of ours is setting his sights on you." Her mother and the pensioner were mobilizing to protect her chastity against the Arab in her home. "Mother," she said in a determined voice, "I'm taking you home right now. You can't leave Father by himself."

"I'd rather walk. I won't let you drive again in this darkness."

"I'll call a taxi for you," Shula suggested.

"No need," Emile said. "I'll drive her."

Again her mother and the pensioner exchanged glances. He sipped from his tea, taking pleasure from it. With Emile standing behind her in the doorway, Tova glanced wordlessly at the old man once more. This time the pensioner nodded his head.

"You really had us worried, sir," Fuad said to him.

The pensioner turned to Shula. "Were you suspicious, too?"

"I was alarmed," she admitted. "It's hard to believe that you would do such a thing, but you had me worried anyway."

"That's not nice of you, Shula."

"I was taught not to trust anyone."

"That's awful."

"I know."

"What a code. You grew up in a lonely world. Not to have confidence in anyone. . . ."

Shula nodded her agreement, angering Fuad. "Comrade Shula, what do you mean, a lonely world!"

"I know I didn't suffer like your refugees or like Marduch, but that's not what we're talking about. We're talking about the essence of loneliness, Fuad. We believe in the masses, but we're scared to death of the individual. The masses, class, nation—those are all abstractions, words. Words are all we believe in. We don't believe in people, we don't trust them. So what's left?"

"Why didn't you turn him over to the police?" Fuad asked the pensioner.

"I would have done it without thinking twice if I had any reason to suspect he had committed a security offense, or was planning to."

"But he's wanted."

"So you say."

"You're a cunning old man," Fuad said.

"And you're a bunch of hypocrites," the pensioner replied. "You know what the difference is between me and all of you? I don't hate Arabs and I don't love them, just like I don't hate or love the Japanese. You all hate Jews."

"A thief doesn't hate his victim. The one who's been robbed, on the other hand, has nothing left but his hatred. But that's irrelevant."

"So you don't deny it. I knew it. You can call this story 'Islam and the Hard Nut.' You yourself figure in the story only indirectly. You're a Christian, and maybe that's why you shout so loud. But Islam is the religion of most of the Middle East, and Islam has a certain attribute, a kind of secret power of absorbing and assimilating any foreign body that penetrates it. Look what happened to the pagan Mongols—they came to destroy the Muslim empire, they won all the battles, wiped out the cities, killed the caliph, and adopted the Muslim faith. And look at the atheistic Turks—they conquered the Arab world and a short time later became fanatic Muslims. The power of Islam is to very efficiently destroy any foreign body that refuses to be assimilated. The Egyptian Copts and the Sudanese blacks have almost disappeared. And then, all of a sudden, a new breed comes on the scene and builds itself a state in the heart of the Muslim world. It's a hard nut with a tough shell acquired over generations of persecution, and you can't devour it without first cracking it. That's what the Nazi Mufti understood, back in his time. The Muslims today understand it, too. Of course they call themselves revolutionaries because that's in fashion, like it's the fashion to talk about a democratic secular state. But make no mistake—they mean to shatter this nut, to annihilate it completely. So how can you expect people who came here from the ghettoes, survivors of the Holocaust, to believe you? Why should they believe you when you say you're prepared to live in peace, like the Germans and the French in Switzerland?"

"Switzerland," Fuad smiled. "Would you people accept us like the French accept the Germans there?"

"I would."

"Then you're my friend," Fuad declared solemnly, stretching out his hand in a dramatic gesture. "But how many people are there in Israel who share your view?"

"Very few," the pensioner said. "But what bothers me is that in your camp there aren't any."

"I still say you're a cunning old man. So you think we're a bunch of hypocrites?"

"And how! You bamboozle the world with your hypocrisy and fool yourselves as well. You speak two languages, one to foreigners and another among yourselves. You're so mixed up with your own hypocrisy you're afraid to reveal what you really think, even to an old woman who's devoted her life to you, like Shula's mother."

"Yes, that is a bad quality," Fuad admitted.

"Tell me the truth, Fuad. Do you feel that you're oppressed, you personally? Why, you have more freedom here than you would in any Arab country."

"Freedom? Don't be naïve. You step on my feet, then tell me I ought to be happy because I have the right to scream with pain."

"Be honest, Fuad. Are you in pain?"

"Terrible pain. Worse than our poet. Don't forget, before

you people laid hands on this country, I tasted a different life. The poet grew up suffocating. For years I needed a special permit to leave my village for Haifa. If I ride on a bus today, I'm considered suspicious. I'm a stranger in my ancestral land, a hostile element, an unnecessary, unwanted person—how could I stop speaking in two languages, even if I wanted to? Allah, sometimes I'd like to put all of you into the palm of my hand and squeeze and squeeze. . . . Why don't you say something, Tuvia?"

"Because I haven't got an answer."

"Then go to your people," Fuad shouted, "and tell them."

"They'd spit on me, just like your revolutionary friends across the border would put a bullet in your head if they found out you'd offered your hand to a Zionist like me. How did we come to this, Fuad? This isn't what we hoped and dreamed for. I weep for Shula's officer, and the poet doesn't even try for her sake to conceal his joy. How did we come to this?"

"Ask your people, not me," Fuad mumbled.

"I'm asking you. We're guilty, both of us. Young men are slaughtering each other in the desert—and we're to blame, we parents are guilty. Me and you, both. There's a terrible abyss dividing us."

"We'll cross it," Fuad vowed to him.

"I hope I don't live to see the day. And you, a father and a husband—aren't you afraid?"

"Sometimes. But when they check my identity card and ask me to come to the police station, I forget my fears. If they beat me senseless for acting as a revolutionary—all right. But even when I'm just sitting peacefully in the hills of Galilee, my Galilee, I'm a dangerous Arab. You understand?"

"Yes. No need to shout."

21

Standing at the kitchen window, Shula gazed at the city spread out below. It seemed as if the seething asphalt had overflowed the streets and flooded the city—in the pitch-black silence nothing could be heard except the military vehicles speeding on their way. A jet came roaring out from among the stars, rattling windows with its thunder, inscribing a mysterious message in the sky. Then it disappeared. The flashing lights of medical evacuation helicopters skimmed down to the city from the dim hill country to the east. These aircraft on their way to Rambam Hospital seemed to etch a trail of agony on the sky.

Maybe Rami's in that one, Shula thought, fixing her gaze on a helicopter whose chopping sound was as yet inaudible. She saw him in her mind's eye, stretched out, unscathed, eyes shut, brow smooth and relaxed, uniform immaculate. Then she heard the din of the helicopter and trembled, as if it were flying straight at her. She shook off the hallucination. It's probably carrying casualties that need immediate evacuation. There's no room yet for the dead. And Rami isn't a corpse. He stormed through the Syrian lines in a burning tank, and nothing is left of him, not his eyes nor the smell of his sweat nor his solemn smile, not even—it wrung her heart to think of it—his gold chain. She had married another man, he another woman, yet he always wore it around his neck. All these years he had worn it in the tanks. When he congratulated her on her wedding night, she had seen the fine links of the chain hanging from his neck down into the hairy carpet of his chest.

She had promised to buy him a chain and he asked for one with a Star of David. They were sitting in a bus on the way to Haifa, quarreling over trifles, as they often did in those days before he was drafted. Rami refused to have anything to do with the Party—he wouldn't budge. She had introduced him to some of the Party's intellectual luminaries and they had despaired of him. Although deep in her heart she admired his steadfast resistance, on the surface she was furious at him. He had everyone against him. Her mother and the cell leaders, the people who visited her house, her few friends, and especially her two permanent suitors. They were worst of all, really villainous. Haim the student and Mahmoud the teacher. They were at odds with one another, constantly competing, always trying to trip one another up with nasty tricks, but when it came to their common enemy they formed a pact and poisoned Shula's soul with their lies. Rami was in the employ of the secret police, sniffing around the Party. Rami had underworld connections. Haim and Mahmoud were prepared to swear on their revolutionary honor that they had seen Rami necking with a girl on the beach. And he was just a lad. Shula could not cope with the pressure. She made his last few weeks before the army hellish. She berated him for no reason, until he lost his composure and answered her back, giving as good as he got. It was only on the seashore or in Kiryat Haim at twilight, walking barefoot at the water's edge, that they found some peace. But these moments were dishearteningly brief.

She had said, "What bad taste you've got. A Star of David yet."

"It's not my taste that bothers you, it's the Star of David."

"Right."

She was wearing shorts and a light blouse, and the sea breeze whistling through the window of the bus toyed with her hair. Rami felt resigned that morning. "I'll take whatever you feel like giving me," he said to her.

In the jewelry store, she overturned the display trays, making the old owner angry. She inspected the various pendants and medallions, then glanced at Rami's chest and whispered, "You've got a real forest on your chest. Anything I get for you will disappear in there and no one will see it."

Rami grinned. "Except a Star of David."

Shula closed her eyes and pointed at the tray. "That one!" she cried to the shopkeeper.

That had been on a Friday. The next day, her parents took part in the annual Party picnic dedicated to the Red Army, in a grove in the hills around Jerusalem. Every year Shula joined them, but this time she refused. It was the last Sabbath before Rami's call-up. He lay on his belly on the carpet in her room, flipping contemptuously through the Party magazine.

"Turn over," she said, and he did so.

"Where's the present I bought you?" she cried.

"Here," he answered, startled.

"I don't see it. You must have lost it in the shower."

He ran his fingers hastily through the hair on his chest and drew out a tiny object in the form of a beetle, or perhaps an anchor. Shula gazed at it in dismay. "That?"

"You chose it yourself," he said to her with a comforting smile.

She was close to tears. "I didn't see, I had my eyes closed when I picked."

Rami laughed. "The high priests of the Party have ruined you. What's beautiful is forbidden; only what's ugly is allowed."

That Shabbat ended disastrously. She threw him out and locked herself up in her room. In the evening her mother found her staring blankly, her eyes red. "Child, why didn't you tell me you were sick? I wouldn't have gone and left you alone."

During the two or three days before Rami and Shula said good-bye, she got used to her gift. She would stick her hand under his shirt and grope around until she found the tiny object, and they would laugh.

Marduch knew all about Rami. She had told him bit by bit, choosing precisely their most tender, joyful moments together. In the beginning she had led him, dazzled and confused, to her orifice. Full of enthusiasm, inexperienced, he would venture alongside her to the mountain peaks that her body was striving to reach. They would stretch out limply and he would lose himself in the happiness streaming from her body to his. As he floated peacefully between her tender shadows, she would tell him about Rami. Sometimes as she talked her hand wandered over his body, caressing him. It did not occur to her that she was hurting him. Once he asked, "So why did you two separate?"

His husky voice surprised her. She got up on her elbow and looked at him and saw the strange expression on his face, the same one that emerged whenever he talked about his youth. She said to him, "Because. We were children, both of us. I didn't have the courage to tell everyone to go to hell; and he was proud."

When she heard of Rami's divorce, she said to Marduch, "I want to call him up."

"No," her husband said.

His jealousy both pleased and provoked her. "I'll go and visit him," she threatened, her smile concealing surprising desires.

He gazed at her in silence. "Disgusting," he said, finally.

"Why?" she flared. "Are you jealous?"

At this Marduch went to Ido's room. For three days there was a prevailing chill in their bed. The fourth day, alone in the apartment, she had gone to the telephone and, her hand trembling, dialed Rami's number. Her face was burning. When she heard the ringing at the other end of the line, her knees started to shake, and she replaced the receiver. Everything she planned to say had escaped her, and she feared that when she heard that voice from her childhood, she would begin to stammer.

Now Rami's lost and gone, she thought. The golden chain is melted, it's melted and Rami's arms and legs along with it, they're as black as the basalt rock of the Golan. And yet her heart was still unmoved by the sorrow, the pain, that she expected. There was a horror growing in her womb. She put her hands over her belly and murmured, That's all I need now. . . . But then she glanced around at once, afraid that the poet might see her this way. The living room was dark; no one was there. Stricken with shame, she leaned her arms on the windowsill.

Remembering Marduch made her choke. She visualized him trapped in one of the bunkers on the canal, buried under the earth with tanks roaring overhead, artillery shells shattering the concrete, Arab troops charging toward him screaming, "Allah is great!" They saw him as a representative of the arrogant state that regarded them as cowards and wretches. They wanted Marduch so they could smash that myth of Israeli superiority and erect another in its place. They yearned more to humiliate him than to kill him. For decades they had nursed their wounded pride and waited for the moment when they would see surrender in the eyes of the Israeli fighting man.

That Marduch, of all people, should have to pay this price.

Frightened, she glanced up toward the pensioner's balcony, but no one was there. The trees were covered with dew. It was chilly. She shuddered and murmured, hugging herself: "You're going crazy. What's this nonsense about bunkers, the canal? Marduch's not there, he's far from there. He's still on the road."

Instantly she had another terrifying vision. A great wave has swept Marduch away, into the desert sands. Marduch is wandering in the desert, his lips cracked from thirst, his eyes blinded by the sun. Victorious enemy columns pass him by, rushing toward his home, his wife and son. They're in a hurry, they have no time to stop and take him prisoner. Their cannons belch forth fire; their laughter is proud.

He stumbles in the sand. Marduch, defeated.

But now, angry with herself, she rallied. Even in her imagination she could not see Marduch defeated. How many times in his life had he fallen, only to rise again, his spirit tempered by the ordeal? A lion did not grovel before a mouse. Then Shula sneered at herself. Marduch wasn't a lion and the Arabs weren't mice. One of them was in her house at that very moment.

Remembering the poet, she turned away from the window and went into the darkened living room. He was sitting silently on the armchair, the transistor radio in his hand emitting indistinct, rasping noises. Believing him to be asleep, she walked by on tiptoe.

"It's cold outside," he said.

"Are you hungry?"

"Yes."

He followed her into the kitchen. She opened a bottle of grapefruit juice and pared some cheese. Seeing her struggling with a can of sardines, the poet took the opener from her. Sitting at the table, her hands emitting a strong smell of fish, she began to sob.

"I'll make tea for you," he said.

She wiped her tears with the back of her hand and looked at the poet. He was a very charming man, but not one to share your troubles with. At least, not so far as she was concerned.

"Do you have any lemon?" he asked. "Sardines without lemmon are worthless."

"I forgot to buy some."

"*Maileh*. So be it."

Shula smiled. "You use typical Hebrew expressions."

He brought the food to the table and said, "The equivalent Egyptian expression is *malesh*. There's a whole philosophy of life contained in that word. It expresses their capacity to adapt and resign themselves to every situation. We Palestinians say, *Walah Yahmah*. Our expression is an exhortation, a declaration that we shall overcome. I like your Jewish *maileh* because it sits right in the middle, in between the fatalistic resignation of *malesh* and the obstinacy of *Walah Yahmah*."

Shula was not absorbing any of this. Her eyes were on the poet's shapely, knowledgeable hands, which were resting on the table. "Aren't you tired?" she asked.

"Very. But I'm afraid to go to sleep."

Shula, too, was afraid to sleep, lest she wake up to find the world in ruins. "Try," she said. "maybe you'll be able to."

He wanted to say that he was on edge, that he needed a woman. Their eyes met, and Shula blushed. She got up immediately. "I'm going to wash. I'm dying to sleep," she lied. "Good night."

"You haven't touched your tea."

"I don't feel like any," she said, trying to make her voice as frigid as possible.

She turned the key in the bathroom twice, and still did not feel safe. She took a hot shower and dressed hastily, hoping that she would not find him at the bathroom door. He wasn't there. She hurried to her room, blurting as she passed the kitchen, "Leave the dishes. I'll do them in the morning."

There was no answer.

She closed the door to her room and stood beside it, her heart pounding. Then she sat on the edge of the bed and listened, against her will, to the sounds on the other side of the door. The poet, in the kitchen, slid back his chair and stood up. She heard his footsteps echoing in the empty apartment, until they were obscured by the din of a helicopter. She heard water running in the bathroom. Now her fear of him was adulterated with her fear of herself. This was the first time she had experienced such complicated feelings toward an Arab. Perhaps it was due to Rami's death and her concern for Marduch, perhaps to her nausea and helplessness and terror. A monster was taking root in her womb. She so much needed sympathetic support. She couldn't turn to her mother. Rami would have understood. Marduch could have understood.

She heard Fatkhi walking into the living room, then suddenly stop. Shula leapt to her feet and retreated toward the window. She thought the poet was approaching her on tiptoe. And then she heard the radio, first in the living room, then from the poet's room.

She should not lock the door. Ido might need her. She took off her dress, put on a nightgown, made her bed and lay down, knowing that she would not be able to sleep. She got up, went to the window, and raised the shutters. As she did, as if waiting for a signal from her, the pensioner above her raised his shutters, and so did the poet in the next room. She was certain that the pensioner's massive head was poking from his window. She shivered again in the chilly night air and returned to bed. Down below, on the wide stone staircase leading to the street, she heard the heavy footsteps of two men. One's bald and the other one's got glasses, little Shula said to herself. Her parents had often gone out to meetings when she was a child. In that house among the trees in Kiryat Haim, her nights were imbued with fear and terror of unknown voices to which, in order to protect herself, she would attribute imaginary faces and shapes. Now one of the voices belonged to a bald man and the other, she decided, to a man in glasses.

The bald man said, "I'd cut their balls off, all of them. Who needs them!"

The man in glasses said, "But they're like trash—there's no end to them."

"No end to them? Kill them, I say. Kill them all."

"Did I say no? But how, damn it, how?"

"I'd go up in a plane and screw them good. They've gotten arrogant; they think they can do anything."

"The thing is, it's our fault. We've played around with them, given them democracy. What do they understand about such nonsense? The whip is what they need. Before we got here, everyone thrashed them, and things were nice and quiet in the world."

"And today the whole world licks their boots because they've got that stinking oil."

"That's not the only reason. I'm telling you, the world's delighted that the Arabs are about to wipe out the Jews."

His companion muttered something in reply. As they climbed higher, their voices faded. Probably neither of them had ever slaughtered so much as a chicken. Shula, the poet, and the pensioner, each in his own room, were embarrassed by the realization that the other two had heard. Shula felt guilty—for the first time in her life she understood her mother. She felt an urge to apologize to the poet, as if she herself had given vent to that poison. But it was very late. Had the poet been a woman, Shula would not have hesitated. What would he say if she knocked at his door? A woman who knocked on a man's door at night had only one way to apologize. Nonsense, you coward, she scoffed at herself. She got up, put a robe over her nightgown, and turned on the light. But now she remembered there was a war on and she turned off the light, went out to the living room, sat in the armchair, turned on the small lamp beside the television, and called, "Fatkhi, I want to talk with you."

The poet came out of his room, expressionless, a cigarette in his hand. He sat on the couch a good distance from her, his handsome face averted. "What do you want from me?" he said.

She forgot all that she was going to say. Again it occurred

to her that at such a time of night, when a man and a woman were together like this, there was only one way to apologize. But she could not do that, because Rami was dead, because Marduch might be, too, because the panic in her womb was distracting her.

The poet looked at her and said, as if he had read her thoughts, "I'm an Arab."

"No!" she cried.

"This afternoon when I was in your room you cried when you realized that the neighbor knew you were sheltering an Arab."

"That was stupid of me."

The poet nodded.

"And I hurt you."

"Very much."

She nodded in turn, saying nothing. No. She was not prepared to meet his conditions. Maybe in another place, at another time, she would have made an extraordinary gesture for his sake. Persuaded that mere words could not erase the impression created by other words, she said, with a shade of hostility, "What do you want?"

"Fuad says that it's hard to be a Jew, but that being an Arab in Israel is a million times harder."

"A million times?" She was struck by the magnitude of the exaggeration. "Do you believe that?"

"I'm not so good at arithmetic. But I could kill those two," he said, getting to his feet. Shula, misunderstanding his sudden movement, drew away, but he didn't notice. "I can't argue with you," he told her.

"Why?"

"Because you're a beautiful woman and we're both . . ."

So he is thinking of compensation, she thought, growing angry. Her gray eyes flashed. "That's nonsense."

"You can't understand. You're a woman."

"Thanks! Nice of you to notice."

"When the war broke out I was visiting in Jenin with some old friends. By chance, three Palestinian freedom fighters happened to come to their house, and I saw them. A short time later one of them died. Since then I've been thinking: That young man's death left a gap in the ranks; why don't I, Fatkhi the Arab, whom everybody despises, whose name is scorned in Israel—why don't I go and take his place?"

"Are you prepared to throw grenades at women and children?"

"I'd throw a grenade at those two who were talking under the window."

"Fatkhi, isn't there another way?"

"I used to believe there was. Fuad still enjoys searching for it. I'll be honest with you, Shula. I don't see any other way."

"It's either us or you?"

The poet fell silent. Then he returned to his room and shut himself up. Shula turned off the lamp and sat in the dark, horror blossoming in her womb. She was frightened. From earliest childhood the Party motto had been drummed into her. Lift up your head, face the future with a smile—it belongs to you. Now she sat utterly alone in the darkness, her eyes closed and her limbs frozen as she tried to peer ahead into the future.

I'm glad you woke me, Shula. Yes, I know, I'll get up and change my pajamas. I'm soaking wet. Did I cry, too, in my sleep? I don't remember crying. I was . . . I was . . . am I still shaking? It was horrible, Shula. I saw the end of everything.

I'm in a kind of Israel of the future, an ultra-modern, brand-new home in a wonderful complex of lovely apartments with wide corridors and interior courtyards full of light, where an enormous community lives in comfort and tranquility, tanned children and robust men and smiling women, everyone happy, and they congregate in the building's giant auditorium and listen to a man in civilian clothes who everybody knows is from the army, and he's smiling and they're laughing, and in spite of that there's a certain feeling of danger in the air, because somehow it's clear that what he's saying is fateful, but it's as if the audience doesn't grasp the extent of the catastrophe, and their faces are calm while the officer quietly tells them what remains to be done, and I'm standing to one side and I realize that disaster is at hand, and I know that every time a war breaks out I'm called up, even though they don't always want me, and the officer notices me and invites me to join in, waving me over with a kind of careless gesture that makes it obvious that it's all the same to him, now that the tanks and the cannons and the planes and the sons and fathers who went out to repulse the danger have all been destroyed and nothing's left, and he's saying what he has to in a cool tone of voice, like an experienced skipper, and what he's saying isn't explicit, yet every individual understands that from now on it's up to him to save his skin as best he can, and the auditorium's already emptying, the building's residents, middle-aged men and women, are running about in the thousands in the hallways, and someone at the end of a corridor announces excitedly that he's gotten hold of some Hajji and whoever wants to should go in and see him in some room or other, and dozens of men go streaming in that direction, and I get up on my toes and see a Muslim religious functionary surrounded by Jews, and he's hurriedly converting them to Islam, furtive as a con man, he's getting frightened himself already, and I start to flee and in the corridor I meet Tuvia, who's standing straight and tense, wearing World War I army boots and carrying an ancient rifle on his shoulder, and he's going to use it against the enemy, he's waiting for the first enemy soldier to appear in the hallway, and immediately I take up a firing position behind a railing, because although I don't have any firearm, I want to go down fighting, but when the first enemy soldier appears, he's surrounded by hysterical women pleading and begging him for something and he's helpless against them, his uniform is in shreds and his submachine gun slips from his hands and he begs the women to let him alone, but in vain.

And I run off to a large room full of silent, disconsolate women, with glazed eyes, and through the window I see a wide patch of lawn where a great crowd of men roasting in the heat of the sun is being hustled into the chilly shade of the building to ensure that they will suffer as soon as possible from the icy night that is approaching, and they're moving along quietly and submissively, and I go downstairs to join them because I'm one of them and I ought to be with them, and as I walk across the grass an enemy soldier puts his hand on my shoulder and gives me a slip of paper on which is written an office address, and he indicates that I should go there, and I go out to look for it but I can't find the office because the street names have been changed and there's no one to ask directions; the streets are familiar but the signs are strange, and suddenly I find the office on a corner and I go in and they're waiting for me, and an examiner, a woman in uniform, approaches me and starts examining me, poking a stiff finger into sensitive places, looking to see how I'll react and hoping I'll cry out and I can't, I turn this way and that but her finger always finds the most vulnerable places, and when she lets me go she can't decide but sends me to another place for further examination.

I go out into the street again, this time accompanied by a soldier, and behind a green wooden fence stand row upon row of chubby, well-dressed kindergarten children, all silent and stunned, watching me and my escort pass by them like chicks in a cage, and they're nice and healthy and I know that they'll keep standing there until they wilt like abandoned flowers, and further along boys and girls sit pressed one against the other on benches in the street, and several young women with bare, sagging breasts clutch infants, and on the corner young men silently form groups and plan dirty things, and the soldier winks at me and says with a laugh, "They're waiting for the dark. . . . Are they going to give it to those girls!" And when we get to the next place, an officer with a club in his hand receives me, and Israeli women soldiers are stretched out on the concrete courtyard, lying on their backs with their legs spread apart, and the little children and the girls on the benches are silent, and the women soldiers writhe and groan and scream, and a woman in uniform walks about among the women on their backs, seizing an infant from time to time and throwing it into a dark room, and this uniformed woman smiles and says that everything is so well ventilated that the smell cannot reach the Israeli women soldiers, who therefore cannot imagine the fate of their tiny babies, and someone shoves me so that I'm right next to a woman soldier twisting on the concrete, and she lifts her sweaty head, gapes, and breaks into insane laughter. "Do you want some, too, darling?" And several mothers come stealing in among the women soldiers, trying to feed them bread smeared with chocolate, and the officer pulls me toward a burning stove, and the woman in uniform throws cubes of meat onto a skillet and someone else throws in crumbs and it sizzles louder and the officer points with his club at the skillet and tells me, "Eat!" I recoil in shock, and he threatens me with his club, and I feel I am about to vomit, my face twists, and he shouts, "Don't you dare, vomiting is forbidden!" And my face is about to split from the effort, but the crumbs on the skillet are too much, too much, I can't, and the officer yells, "It is forbidden to vomit!" and I keep retreating, I can't any more. . . . It's good you woke me, Shula. So good, oh God.

What's that you're asking? It's not important now. It was only a dream. I know that I'm still shaking. A dream can make you do that. It's natural.

What does it matter to you what the crumbs were that they threw on the skillet? They were . . . they were . . .

22

Upon seeing Shula's face in the morning, the poet reflected that even beautiful women were sometimes repulsive.

He had risen early, gladdened by the news reports that had been broadcast by the Arab radio stations all through the night. He entered the kitchen barefoot, made himself coffee, and stood drinking it as he looked out at the harbor. From where he stood he could not make out the feverish activity on the wharves, but he did see the cranes and the ships lying on the gray water, and he smiled. Who would manage this from now on? He had never believed much in that nightmare of the Jews. The threats broadcast from the other side of the border were, in his opinion, nothing but bluster. There would be no massacre here in Israel. Instead, there would be a thoroughgoing changeover. The director of Haifa Port would be an Arab, and his second-in-command would be a Jew. This is the way it looked to the poet. No one would be thrown into the sea. Many Jews would elect of their own free will to leave the country, those for whom romantic dreams and the desire to govern were their only ties. As soon as those dreams were shattered and the tables turned, they would scurry to the airline and shipping offices and take themselves off to live with their relatives abroad. Didn't droves leave anyway, every time a little economic crisis hit them where it hurt? In spite of repression, eviction, and contempt, the Arabs had held onto their land since '48. The Jews were a passing phenomenon.

But . . . and here the poet lit a cigarette. But the murderers would not escape unscathed. They would be brought to justice. And the expert technocrats would be obliged to remain here, against their will, to pay with their expertise for the injustice meted out to the Arabs. They would continue to pilot ships in and out of the harbors, to oversee the conveying of water in the national pipeline to the Negev, and to operate the nuclear reactors of Nahal Soreg and Dimona, until the Arabs learned to take over these tasks. They would be paid generously; later, they would be free to leave.

Standing on tiptoe, he tried to make out his birthplace in the western Galilee, the village of Mazrayah, through the early morning mist. The village was covered with dew now, its fragrant autumn fields expectantly awaiting the blessed rains. What a shame that the poet's father had not lived a few more years to see this day. He had died an ugly death, denying all that he had lived for. It was as if he knew his end was near. Everyone else, even the doctor in Nazareth, had believed he was just having another attack of hemorrhoids. He would writhe in pain, sitting on the toilet in terrible agony. He had already stopped going out to the fields and finally he could not summon the strength to go down to the mosque. Fatkhi returned from Bulgaria, and his father took the cartons of cigarettes he had brought for him and fell back on his bed. The very act of sitting was a torment for him.

"If you don't pray, you won't get any mercy from Allah," Fatkhi's mother, a devout woman, murmured. His father, furious at her, heaved the Koran with its red binding and gold tooling to the top of the clothes closet. The holy book flew through the air like an affronted bird, its pages fluttering like wings.

"Shut up, woman!" Fatkhi's father growled, his narrowed eyes full of hatred.

The woman stood her ground, "If you'd kept the faith and prayed and washed and purified yourself five times a day as the Prophet commanded, Allah would have cured you of your curse. Throwing the Koran! In the name of Allah the merciful and compassionate! Do you think it is stone from the river bed? There's no fear of God in this house any more."

"My son," Fatkhi's father said to him, "I want to see the village."

It was raining. The wind was howling. Fatkhi smiled. "We'll take a drive there when you feel better. But what's left there for you to see? They destroyed everything you had, Father."

The old man's troubled eyes gazed at him sorrowfully. "The land is still there. No one can destroy that. Is it all lying fallow?"

"No. They've sown and planted it."

"And the hill is where it was."

"Exactly where it was." Fatkhi wanted to end this depressing conversation.

"And you can still see the sea from on top. They haven't dried up the sea yet, have they, my son?"

Fatkhi felt that he was being mocked, not only by his father, but by generations and generations that had come before him. "It's still there," he cried, "the sea is still there."

"Then we'll go tomorrow."

"In this storm?" Fatkhi bridled. He was tired after his trip from Bulgaria. All this happened before they paved the road to Kfar Mandah; the heavy rain would have turned the track into a boggy mush. On several occasions the poet, along with other passengers from Nazareth, had had to get out of the car in the heavy rain and push, arriving home in the evening wet and muddy. "The road is closed," he said to his father. "There isn't a driver who'd dare leave the village."

"We'll make it out to the Shafram highway on a tractor."

Fatkhi's mother held her head in her hands. "He's gone crazy. He can't even sit on his behind, and he wants to go bouncing on a tractor like a youngster. Fatkhi, my son, climb up on the chair and take the Koran down. Maybe the book will put a little sense back in his head."

"Tomorrow," his father said.

"All right," Fatkhi said. He was certain that overnight his father would forget his insane idea.

Before opening his eyes at dawn, Fatkhi heard the angry wind and rain beating furiously against the windows. He felt a firm grip on his shoulder. "Get up, my son."

His father was standing over him, his hair grizzled, grayish face cleanshaven, mustache trimmed. He held himself as erect as the cancer spreading through his body would allow him.

"Haven't you dropped that idea of yours yet?" Fatkhi said angrily.

"I spoke with Mansur, and he's willing to take us in his taxi."

"We'll need a boat, Father, not a taxi."

"Get up, my son, get up."

When he saw Mansur's old taxi, Fatkhi said, "It'll break down before we see the highway."

Mansur defended his vehicle's honor. "It's not all shiny and fancy like Wasfy's little whore of a car, but it's powerful enough, all right."

They were standing on the balcony, sheltered beneath a concrete slab, and the rain, driven by the wind, was coming down in great savage sheets. "Look at the road," Fatkhi shouted. "It's as slippery as soap. The tractors have ploughed deep ruts into it."

"We'll make it," Mansur insisted—he did not want to lose the fare that Fatkhi's father had promised him.

"Let's go!" Fatkhi cried angrily.

His father looked up at the dark sky and was fleetingly moved by the fear of God. "Allah's blessings on Mohammed and his people," he murmured, staggering into the taxi.

They pulled out of the village square and headed toward the mud track that was lost in rain and gray fog. With exhausting effort, Mansur navigated the taxi; its tires skidded in the mire, spraying a fine sheet of mud. Sweating in spite of the bitter cold, Mansur did his best to hold the taxi—which was sliding diagonally—on a straight course, but its back wheels seemed to be trying to get ahead of the front, and once, as if in despair, the car turned completely around, facing back to the village. With all the rolling and swaying, Fatkhi's father, in agony, no longer looked so obstinate. His face had turned as gray as the fog. Unable to sit any longer on his open, bleeding wound, he took hold of the front seat with both hands and knelt in prayer.

Fatkhi exploded. "You're exempt from the Ramadan fast if you're ill, and from the pilgrimage to Mecca too. What's gotten into you, Father?"

"You're hard-hearted, Fatkhi."

The car skidded completely around. His father lost his grip, and Fatkhi heard his father's teeth knock as his head struck the door. He turned to help him to his feet, but his father cried out in pain. "We're going home," Fatkhi said.

"No. We're going on."

Fatkhi froze. He was sure now that his father's mind was failing him. The old man stared fixedly ahead into the fog. He had forgotten his agonies. All his strength was directed out into the rain. "Another day," Fatkhi promised his father, speaking as if to a child. "On a clear sunny day I'll take you there like a king. We'll go to the ruins and from there you'll look out over the sea."

"Today. Now."

"Why the hurry?"

"Because tomorrow I won't be able to get out of bed."

The taxi skidded again, and this time two wheels settled in the deep ruts made by the tractors. Mansur fell against Fatkhi, and Fatkhi's father fell on the floor. Fatkhi thrust the driver away and said, "All right, that's it."

His father, on the floor, said, "No. We'll go on by foot."

He would have, too, judging by the look on his face. Rescue came in the form of a jeep with front wheel drive, driven by the capable Wasfy. "The blessing of Allah be upon you," Mansur groaned at him. "Get us out of here."

"I'll get you out, but not the taxi."

Mansur protested, "Stop joking. Do you expect me to leave it here in the rain?"

"It's not an onion. Nothing will happen to it, besides getting clean."

"Wasfy, have mercy."

"If I try to pull your old taxi out, I'll get stuck myself."

"We'll move to his car," Fatkhi's father said.

Fatkhi sighed with relief. Wasfy was headed home. The fat mechanic got out of the jeep, tramped through the mud, opened the taxi's rear door, and lifted Fatkhi's father in his arms. "Where were you all going? To the doctor?"

Fatkhi's father said, "No, to my childhood village, my boy."

To Fatkhi's stupefaction, Wasfy showed no surprise. He sat the old man beside him and waited until Fatkhi and Mansur got in. If Mansur was an expert at driving in the mud, Wasfy was an acrobat. Turning the jeep around, he pivoted in his seat for a look at Mansur's fallen expression. As they reached the shining black highway, he put his hand on Mansur's knee. "Leave the dough to the baker, boy, and get back behind the plow. We made it, Abu Fatkhi, we made it." Then he touched Fatkhi on the shoulder, saying, "Your father's fainted."

Instead of driving to the village, they went to the hospital in Nazareth. When he opened his eyes and saw the strange bed he was in, Fatkhi's father started cursing nonstop in a toneless, maddening voice, and he continued blaspheming heaven and earth, abusing the Jews and the Arabs, the sun and the rain, his sons and his wife, until he gave up the ghost.

Fatkhi heard someone stirring behind him and turned away from the window. At that instant he was all forgiveness. He smiled at Shula and said good morning, and she answered, though without smiling. It was the third morning of the war. Marduch's probably the one keeping this wall between us, the poet thought. "I'll make you some coffee," he offered benevolently.

"I'll have tea." She looked away from him. Standing at the stove, she put the kettle on the large burner. She was like fickle weather, he decided. Now she was beautiful again, an attractive woman from the back as well as the front. The poet gazed excitedly at the black hair cascading over her shoulders, the proud body in the scanty gown, the shapely legs. Had she not been standing so straight, so stubborn and proud, he would have approached her and put his hand gently on her shoulder. A few moments passed, before he realized that she was crying. At that he approached her and took her forcefully by the shoulders. She turned to face him. "Marduch's dead," she sobbed, "and I'm pregnant."

He thought that she was going to rest her head on his chest, but she withdrew and sat on a chair until the kettle started whistling. Fatkhi turned off the gas and said, "I'm sorry, I'm really sorry."

The certainty in his voice frightened her. "He ran off," she murmured. "He ran off as if nothing could have been done or organized without him."

"I heard the phone ring twice during the night," the poet said. "I hadn't imagined that they would inform you like that."

"Inform me? Of what?" Her gray eyes were frozen.

The poet hesitated. "What you said just now . . . Marduch."

"His aunt called from Tel Aviv and his sister from London."

"Then why did you say he's been killed?"

She had trouble explaining to him that it was a premonition. "It's been three days, and I haven't heard anything from him." Then, remembering that Fatkhi was an Arab, she stopped.

The poet was angry. What a cheap trick, he thought. She kills Marduch and throws his corpse between us. The poet felt like shouting that he didn't give a damn about her, didn't feel the slightest desire for her. Or just get up and take her, he said to himself, enraged. With her retarded child asleep and the neighbor locked in his apartment upstairs, she had come to him in a skimpy, transparent nightgown and dissolved in tears—why these tricks?

But now she had stopped crying, and he sensed that he had missed his opportunity to sweep her into his arms. She said soberly, as if reading his thoughts, "Fatkhi, you can't understand everything."

"No," he answered in a dull, almost hostile voice.

"You people don't understand our fears and anxieties at all."

"Who are we and you people?"

"The Jews and the Arabs," she said, lowering her eyes.

"You poor people. Now we lambs, the victimized ones, are supposed to go to your wolves and calm them down. What do you want us to tell them—that they have nothing to fear, that we're still miserable, cowardly lambs, that you people will go on for years ripping at our flesh?"

"That's not what I meant," she said defensively.

"It's what I understood, Shula."

"It's not just our fault or yours. It's a fear that's run through many generations."

"And we Arabs have to pay."

"I'll make breakfast for you," she said in a pacifying tone.

She seemed even more beautiful now. Yet she was a Jew, one of those people, a drop of the wave that had inundated his people. It was more comfortable to see her that way. If there was to be hatred—let it be pure. Sex only confused true feelings. If she wanted to sleep with him, he'd oblige her as just another desirable female. And if she was unwilling, he would not beg. "I've run out of cigarettes," he said.

"I'll go buy you some right after breakfast," she said, like a good housewife.

"That'll take time. . . ," he grumbled.

"Have you smoked them all already? I brought you three packs yesterday."

"They're all gone."

"You'll kill yourself."

Her concern pleased him. "I don't smoke like this all the time. It's just that I'm not sleeping at night now, because of the war."

"Neither am I," she said.

The poet refrained from smiling at her. He had come to understand that his smile, ordinarily his most effective weapon, caused her to recoil. When she saw it, she immediately closed up and withdrew into herself. She confused him. "You haven't drunk anything," he said. "Not coffee, not tea."

She waved indifferently, revealing the dark patch in her armpit. I've got to be careful, he told himself. Her graceful movements excited him. "Let me brew some coffee for you as only villagers can," he said, not looking at her.

Her laugh rang clear. "You're a good actor."

The poet, his back to her, seemed to be concentrating on his work at the stove. "Do you know," he said, "why the Negroes are natural actors, why they seem to have acting in their blood, why they're so convincing on the stage? Because from the time they're little children, they're obliged to play two roles—the role of the Negro in white company, and the role of the black among their own. . . . I've got this friend in the village, Wasfy's his name, and not even I can tell when he's acting and when he's being sincere. You people say the Arabs are liars, that they talk out of both sides of their mouths, that there's no trusting them, that they do not speak their hearts. Not one of you understands that it's an act, a game. The Israeli Arab, like the American Negro, learns to act at a very tender age."

"We're back to the same old argument again. Well, what role are you playing now?"

"The Arab waiter serving the Jewish lady her coffee in the absence of her husband. You see, I'm even barefoot."

"I don't want any," she said, firmly refusing the cup.

"You don't want the coffee, or you don't want the waiter?"

"Neither."

"Too bad—it's good coffee."

"Too bad for you."

"Hell," he exploded. "That's all you people have ever wanted me to be, ever since I left the village—a stupid waiter, grateful for every nickel that's thrown his way. You're insulting my coffee."

"It's poison, not coffee."

"Madam, in a play you don't use real poison. At the most, if a person's particularly disgusting, you spit in his cup."

"And did you spit into this coffee?"

"Almost," he admitted.

"You hate me."

"Not much." he said.

"You're not acting now?"

"No."

"Why do you hate me?"

"Because you despise Arabs."

She reddened, and it moved him to see the color spread over her pale skin. Again he had an urge to touch her. He was relieved to have no doubts about her; he knew she wasn't trying to seduce him.

"Do you people act with Marduch, too?" she asked.

"Just a little bit. But he understands what's going on right away, and that ends it. Him you can't lead by the nose. You know why? Marduch's a professional actor, too. He lived as a Jew back there, and here he lives as a black. One actor can always see through another."

"You mean Marduch pretends? That can't be."

"Oh, it can indeed! He pretends, all right, but he doesn't lie. What do you really know about Marduch?"

"Only what he lets me know in his weaker moments," she admitted.

"And you love him."

She blushed, but answered bravely, "I think so."

The poet was surprised. "Doesn't the pretense bother you?"

"No. On the contrary. Sometimes I like it. It makes him seem stronger than he is, a man who doesn't groan when he's in pain."

"That's selfish of you," he cried. "You know he's in pain, but you'd rather have him pretend and smile."

"Maybe I am selfish, but there's nothing more repulsive than a man who's always trying to arouse your pity."

"And we Arabs are not such fine actors."

"No. To breed an actor like Marduch takes generations of oppression. I hope that you never come to that. The coffee really is good."

"Thanks. I'll go get dressed." He was not afraid to smile at her now. From his room he heard her speaking on the telephone with Shoshana. Then she approached his door and said hesitantly, "I'm going to get some cigarettes for you. If Ido wakes up, tell him I'm coming right back."

"Shula," Ido screamed. "Where are you going?"

Shula was already gone, so the poet had to attend to the child. As Fatkhi entered Ido's room, the boy watched him with extreme suspicion. The poet sat cautiously on a chair near the bed and smiled his magic smile, but to no avail. "Who are you?" Ido said.

"I'm Fatkhi, your father's friend."

"Why?"

The poet was confused—his smile evaporated. Now the

child felt threatened. Fatkhi was moved to anger. "What do you mean, why?" he spoke roughly, in spite of himself.

"I want Daddy!"

"*Uskat wa-halazneh* [Shut up and that's that]!" the poet blurted resentfully. "Your father's gone away."

"Who are you?"

"Ido, you know me. I was here with you all last night."

The child drew the blanket over himself, leaving only his suspicious eyes exposed. "Call Daddy, I want Daddy."

The poet heard someone knocking softly on the door to the apartment. He got up with relief and made his escape from Ido's room. He knew it was not Shula, but it didn't matter—he would have opened the door to anyone just then, even the police. There seemed to be something contagious about contact with a disturbed child, a moron. Fatkhi was accustomed to a measure of quiet reasonableness in conversation with other people, but talking with the child was like conversing with a dark, empty hole, and for a moment he had not known who was disturbed and who was sane.

Tuvia was standing at the door. When he heard Ido screaming, he sidestepped the poet and hurried to the child's room. The poet dropped into the armchair. Now that lousy old man thinks I'm a child-eater, too . . . staying with Shula is no picnic. What a fool he had been to let Amalia and that idiot Emile bring him to this madhouse. A retarded child, a disturbed woman, and a husband who's split right down the middle and whose presence in the house is palpable, despite the fact that's he's somewhere far away, fighting for his life or slaughtering Arabs. A man like Marduch was a disaster for a woman like this. Was she blind? What did she see in him? Shula, like Abla in Jenin, amazed the poet. Women who loved their husbands were an enigma to him. How could they desire a strange man and love their husbands at the same time? His fiancée, Hiam, was not so complicated. Or was she? Who knows? What was happening to him here? There had been moments during these last few days when he hoped the police would come. If they arrested him, it would be no tragedy. A week or two of discomfort, and then out you come into the sunshine, brilliant and respected and admired more than ever before, your loyalty and steadfastness confirmed. People have more regard for you, they listen attentively, as if you'd acquired additional wisdom and knowledge behind bars. What was wrong with that? If the Arab armies reached Haifa, it would be a tremendous advantage to be found in a Zionist prison. What would you say if they found you hiding like a mouse in an Israeli soldier's apartment? Why, they'd laugh at anything you said. What were you doing while we were spilling rivers of blood, struggling to vanquish the monster? You were lying in the lap of a Jewish woman! Pui! A bullet between the eyes! Go shove your poems, poet. You call yourself a man—you'd be better off wearing a dress, you eunuch, dancing at weddings for the women, you filth. Look at him—the great Palestinian. Didn't I tell you all it wasn't worth lifting a finger for them? How many of our comrades fell fighting for this scum? In '48 our fathers' corpses made mountains while these scum abandoned their homes and refused to fight the Jews. And now, you cross the desert, you lose your best friends left and right, you rush to liberate your brothers who are rotting under the Zionist yoke, who you suppose to be fighting also for their freedom, risking their lives, and what do you find? They're hiding in the homes of Jewish criminals. Are they worth all this? Great Allah—the Jews were right. They deserve nothing; they were born slaves and they'll die slaves.

The poet searched for a cigarette but could not find one.

And Shula—what would her fate be? The Arab soldiers, unlike other victorious troops, would not unload their fear into the body of a woman following the slaughter. The Jews, during decades of enmity, had insulted and mocked the Arab fighting man. Now the Arab soldier was purging the insult with his blood, and to make his victory complete, he had to prove himself the equal of the Jew whom he had defeated. The Jewish woman would pay the price.

Downstairs in the street, the poet heard shouting, the thud of army boots, and a tumult on the staircase. They were coming after Shula, they wanted her body. Shula—Marduch's wife, who had given him refuge, albeit halfheartedly. He was a man, wasn't he? How could he stand aside and watch? When an army was occupying a town, no one would arrest soldiers fresh from the hell of combat. If he wanted to rescue her, he would have to fight them.

Kill an Arab soldier to protect a Jewish woman?

He trembled. Better to close his eyes, shut out the sight of Shula stretching out her arms to him, crying. But as long as he lived he would carry the degradation within him. Until the day he died, he would be hounded by the feeling that it was he, not Shula, who had been raped.

Then and there he made his decision. He had to call Wasfy and get out of here today. He would not stay another minute. This was a trap. He got up to go to the phone, but now Tuvia came out of Ido's room, carrying the child in his arms.

"He's calmed down a bit," Tuvia said.

But the poet felt as though he were already far away. He smiled distantly at Tuvia.

"Where did Shula go? Why did she leave the child this way?"

"She went out to buy cigarettes."

"For you?"

"Yes, for me. I ran out." Even the decrepit old man didn't bother him any more.

"I see that you're not happy here any more. But you really shouldn't go. When your troops come, you'll already be in occupation of the building."

"That's what you people did in '48. We'd hardly abandoned

our houses and you were already swarming over them like a cloud of locusts."

"You were a kid then. You just remember what you've been told."

"I didn't have to be told. I remember very well how we were forced to flee our house in the middle of the night."

"Where to?"

"Many went to Lebanon. My family went to Kfar Mandah."

"That's where the difference lies. Marduch and Shula and I haven't any place to flee. We're stuck here. We can retreat to a certain point, but after that there's just complete annihilation. Have you heard of Kibbutz Yad Mordecai? During the War of Liberation it was just a dot in the desert, but it halted the Egyptian army."

"Now things have changed. You people will need more than rifles to stop a torrent of Arab tanks. You're living in the past, my friend."

"It's not the past, Fatkhi. It's a matter of responsibility, a responsibility that even our children bear. If what we've built here is destroyed, all traces of the Jewish people will disappear—nothing will remain, here or anywhere else in the world. You don't understand what it is to be a Jew."

"I don't care to understand, not so long as I'm treated like a worthless primitive in my own country. You people, your time has come and gone."

Shula found them quarreling. She threw the things she had bought on the kitchen table and took Ido from Tuvia. "Tuvia, this house is drowning in politics already. Don't make it worse, please."

"We were just having a discussion like two civilized people. Isn't that right, Fatkhi?"

The poet, shrugging off the question, said nothing. As Shula, Ido, and the pensioner left the apartment, he sighed with relief. He went immediately to the telephone and called

Wasfy's garage. Then he made himself coffee and waited, smoking.

An hour later the Buick came to a halt in front of the building. Catching sight of the poet's face, Wasfy shouted, "*Ya Salaam! Ya Salaam!* Aren't the Jews treating you right, man? Tell me, where do you belong? Back in the village you skulk around like a cock that's had its tail plucked off, in Jenin your face gets smeared with pitch, and here you look like a virgin on her wedding night. . . ."

"Shut up!" the poet interrupted. "What's happening outside?"

"Happening? Well, I'm happy."

"You're always happy."

"What can I do? I wasn't born to weep. You know what the distance is between the womb and the grave. You're wasting your life, man."

"What's happening at home?" the poet demanded.

"At home? Well, they came to arrest you and didn't find you. For the first time in their lives the villagers told the truth—they said they didn't know where you were. It was like the earth had swallowed you up. I was an idiot to agree to the engagement. Hiam's going to spend her life waiting at the prison gates."

"This won't last much longer."

"Why, are you leaving the Party?"

"No! Their state is on its way out."

"*Tuz!*" Wasfy cried contemptuously.

"You're blind."

"Fatkhi, I work and live among them; I see them, and you tell me I'm blind."

"What do you see?"

"They were caught in bed and now they're on their feet already. Convoys, I tell you. The garage is close to the main highway, and the earth is shaking, Fatkhi. Convoys. They're rushing up to the mountains, day and night. There's a restaurant next to the garage, and some son of a bitch set up a table full of sandwiches and drinks on the sidewalk. He stands there waving like a madman. Everything's free, step up and have a drink. Does anyone stop? They smile at him, wave, and rumble past. Tell me, is that the way defeated people behave?"

"The Syrians are slicing down to the Sea of Galilee, Wasfy."

"In '48 they surrounded half the Sea of Galilee; what came of that? And you don't see the ships cruising at sea. I don't have to tell you about the planes. . . . The only ones you see are theirs. So who's blind?"

"You don't see the whole picture, Wasfy."

"No, I'm not educated like you, Fatkhi. But I know my Jewish partners."

"Is the road to Jenin open?" the poet asked.

"You're crazy. You want to take another excursion there?"

"Not an excursion. I want to go there. Are you willing?"

"Like I said, you're crazy."

"Are you willing?"

"Fatkhi, wake up; your're dreaming. If the Jews haven't dismantled their state by themselves, no way will you do it for them."

"You're a slave and you'll always be one."

"Is there any coffee in this house? Who lives here, anyway? I don't see anyone, I don't hear anything."

"The husband went to war."

"And the wife?" Wasfy's eyes glittered. "Man, oh man! You're alone with the woman. How is she?"

"That's enough."

"Don't put on an act, man. Is she worth fucking?" Wasfy was already wandering through the apartment. He opened the bedroom door and peeked in; and the delicate scent, the flimsy gown thrown over the chair, inflamed his imagination. "Fatkhi," he cried, "stay here and forget Jenin."

"Go."

"Is she coming back now? I'll get in the car and have a look."

"Get out."

"You're jealous. We're family, don't forget."

"Get out."

"Man, I've never known anyone as selfish as you."

23

They sat down for lunch in gloomy silence. Ido felt the tension; it spoiled his appetite. "Shula, I want to go to sleep."

"Excuse me," she said to the poet, getting up. She washed the child and put him to bed and returned to the soup, which in the meantime had turned cold.

The poet did not touch the main course. He sat and smoked, his fingers drumming on the table. "I'm leaving," he announced.

Their eyes met, but she did not blush, just shrugged slightly. "What will Marduch say?" she said.

Again he wanted to touch her. "What business is it of his?"

"I didn't treat you very nicely."

"It's not your fault. The circumstances . . . "

"I'm awful!" She was close to weeping with guilt and relief that he was leaving. His hand began to stroke hers, and she did not pull away until the telephone rang. She got up, an appeasing look in her eyes.

Still it was not Marduch on the line. "I was just over at your place. What do you want, Mother?" Shula burst out.

"I wanted to know if you'd arrived safely, that's all."

"And why shouldn't I?"

"I thought . . . you were so . . . my child, why don't you come over and stay with us?"

"Have you gone crazy?"

"How is he?"

"He's fine." Her mother meant the poet, not Marduch, and this angered Shula greatly. "He's leaving today."

"Don't let him," her mother yelled. "He mustn't."

"Who said?"

"The higher-ups, of course."

"You and the higher-ups can worry about it."

"Child, you're a comrade too."

"I'm sorry I belong to the Party."

"You're depressed today, child. One doesn't talk about such matters so thoughtlessly. Wait until Marduch gets back and then we'll talk calmly."

Shula's temper flared. Only now had her mother remembered Marduch. "Marduch's left the Party," she lied.

"When?" Tova shrieked.

"When he put on his uniform and waited for them to come and take him."

"I knew it, I knew it," her mother wailed.

"Shalom."

"Wait," Tova cried desperately. "Are you sure? He didn't actually say anything, did he? Your husband couldn't be such a snake. And you would chase after him, without the slightest idea of what you're doing."

"Shalom," Shula said, and set down the receiver. "That was my mother," she said, returning.

"You don't treat her very nicely," said the poet, who had taken in only the general tone of the conversation.

"She gets on my nerves."

"Who doesn't?" he mused. But now he was astonished to see her eating with gusto, her eyes sparkling. "You're happy," he said to her.

She nodded, and her hair bounced on her shoulders.

"It's good to see you like this," he said with admiration. Her happiness captivated him, as if her true nature had just now been revealed to him. So she can be warmhearted, joyful. His appetite stirred, and he too began to dig into the main course.

"I've finally decided," she said cheerfully.

Her high spirits lent him confidence. "Does it have to do with me?"

His voice was so obviously expectant that she burst out laughing. "No! No! I'm leaving the Party."

"Are you joking?"

"Do I sound like I am, Fatkhi?"

"No." It saddened him.

"Ever since I was a girl I've known it wasn't for me. All these years I've been a slave to foreign ideas. Now all of a sudden I'm liberated, free—I feel like I've won my physical freedom. You don't understand. I was like a person in a wheelchair who doesn't know he can walk and run and jump. I can go anywhere I like. No one's going to guide me. No one's going to choose my path for me. From now on every step is going to be an adventure. It's wonderful, isn't it?"

"It's a betrayal."

"Of what?"

"Of your principles, Shula."

"That's the whole thing, Fatkhi. I never had any principles. They were forced on me against my will."

"This is too bad, it really is."

"It's not a great loss to them. I never was one of those comrades who could be depended on when the going got rough."

"You underrate yourself."

"Fatkhi!" she cried angrily. "The first compliment you ever gave me, and when is it?—just at the moment that I'm leaving the Party."

"And Marduch?"

"Let him worry about it. That's what I told my mother, too.

I won't stand in his way. If he wants to continue in the Party, I won't bother him. I'm free."

"You really are happy."

"Yes."

Her bosom rose and her face absorbed the light streaming through the window. She looked at him, her eyes steady, as if waiting. He was confused, yet he knew this was a precious opportunity. "You look like you'd like to celebrate," he told her.

"That's absolutely right." Her gray eyes were fixed on his face.

"There's someone ringing at the door," he said.

Shula opened the door and cried happily, "Daphna!"

The poet froze. It can't be, he thought, it's not possible. Then a strange joy took hold of him, as if some difficulty had been cleared up. Yet, as he left the kitchen, something troubled his mood, some reflections deep in his consciousness. If this student, Daphna, who had been called up by the army, could find the time to come from Tel Aviv to make love to him—for he had no doubt but that this was why she had come—it meant that the Israelis' situation was not as desperate as was depicted in the announcements from Cairo and Damascus. At the same time, he felt uncomfortable—was this because he was in Shula's house, or because he was near her?

Such thoughts did not occur to Shula, who was unaffectedly delighted. Her voice changed, her body grew animated, her eyes rejoiced, her teeth flashed. She caressed Daphna with her hands, with her eyes, until the visitor became embarrassed, and the poet too, puzzled as to the meaning of her excitement.

"How are things in Tel Aviv?" Shula prattled like a young girl.

"All right, okay," Daphna said, stealing a glance at the poet.

"Shalom, Daphna," he said.

"Shalom, Fatkhi."

"Are you tired, Daphna?" Shula cried.

"I came from Safed. I got special leave to see my brother. He's wounded."

"How serious?"

"Light burns. Can I call home? My mother's going crazy and my father's sick. . . . "

"Of course, what a question! Please go ahead," Shula said, pulling the poet into the kitchen. "Help me," she said to him. "Quick we've got to make her something to eat. She must be starving."

During his stay at her place the poet had observed Shula closely, but now it seemed to him that he had never actually seen her. He doubted whether she would have welcomed Marduch himself with such joy. "Are you friends, you and Daphna?" he asked.

"Me and Daphna? I know her from Party meetings."

"Is that all?"

Her eyes flashed. "What's wrong with you? You heard her say that her brother's been wounded, he's in the hospital. Do you know what she's been through since this morning? Come on, don't stand there like a robot. You make some salad for her and I'll fry some meat. Did I light the boiler? Yes, good, she needs a shower. Poor girl . . . "

The girl stood in the doorway to the kitchen, looking quite well, tanned and strong, her nostrils dilated at the pleasurable fragance of the food, her eyes resting on the poet's body.

"Are you hungry?" Shula asked her.

"And how."

"In a minute everything will be ready."

"Can I have a sandwich in the meantime?"

"Sure! What kind?"

"Whatever you've got. Actually, I'll make one for myself."

She took great, youthful bites. Standing there in her short skirt, she leaned over Shula's shoulder to check what was sizzling in the skillet. Her breasts under her knitted blouse were brown—she must sunbathe naked at the seashore, Shula thought to herself.

The poet's stupefaction grew. All of Shula's self-restraint fell away. She wrapped her arms around the girl's bare shoulders, led her to the table, and stood beside her, serving her graciously, her voice ringing brightly. "How did you know that Fatkhi was here?"

"He called me at home."

The poet bit his lower lip, and Shula shook a finger at him and laughed. "Isn't that in violation of Party orders?"

Maybe she's crazy and I haven't realized it till now, the poet thought. That retarded child didn't fall off a tree. But why does Daphna, of all people, bring out this side of Shula?

"I'll get the bathroom ready for you," Shula said to her. "I'll change the sheets in Fatkhi's room and then I've got to rest a while. I'm dead tired."

The poet was surprised, but not Daphna—she found nothing extraordinary in what Shula was doing. "Thanks," she said, with her mouth full. Shula called from the bathroom, "There's a clean towel in here for you, Daphna, the red one."

"Thanks," Daphna shouted, a fork in her left hand, her right hand on the poet's apathetic knee. "What's the matter?" she asked.

"When I talked to you on the telephone, you sounded like you were sitting on the Eiffel Tower."

"I felt like I was at the bottom of a hole."

"And I was throwing stones inside."

"Fatkhi, you know very well how I feel about you. You see I am here."

"Thanks."

"What's got into you?"

"I guess it was naïve of me to think that I'd always be good for you, even when things got rough."

"And who said you weren't?"

"You did, on the telephone."

"You're too sensitive, sweetheart. And anyway, I didn't know you cared."

"You're mistaken."

She laughed cheerfully. "You're well known; people hear things about you, sweetheart."

"What if I said I am willing to marry you?"

She looked at him in surprise. "You don't have to make promises to . . . " And she laughed.

"You're awful."

"It's natural. I'm normal and so are you, in spite of the songbirds in your head. I could give you a warm letter of recommendation."

"Don't be crude."

"You're blushing, sweetheart."

"I was speaking in all sincerity."

"What about the virgin from Kfar Mandah?"

"I'm prepared to give her up, if you consent to marry an Arab."

"You're fantastic!" she replied, admiringly. "Now we're even. I'm going to take a shower. By the way, your hostess is super."

Shula had shut herself up in her room. She didn't want to listen in, didn't want to hear, but she heard them speaking in spite of herself. She heard Daphna's chair being pushed back in the kitchen, and then her footsteps. Daphna closed the bathroom door softly but did not lock it. She belonged to a new generation, one that had cast off many restraints. Shula was not comforted by this thought, however. She stood next to the window, her back trembling, afraid that the poet was going to burst in on her and pour out his anger—I am not a German officer and Daphna isn't some whore out of Guy de Maupassant.

Shula knew that she herself was no paragon of virtue. She had done things she had regretted, over the years. But this time, she felt right in the midst of doing it that what she was doing was contemptible. She felt besmirched. For a moment she wanted to go into the bathroom, help the girl get dressed, and drive her to the bus station.

I'm a procuress, she cried silently.

Nonsense. The girl had come of her own free will, hungry for food and for the poet. Perhaps she had not figured that Shula would lavish so much affection and encouragement on her. Twice she had winked at Shula, grateful for her understanding. She considered Shula a progressive, liberated woman.

Here too Shula found no comfort. She was willfully exploiting the girl in order to get herself out of a perplexing situation, presenting her in all her robust sensuality on a silver platter to the poet. Not that the girl minded; on the contrary, she was content, whereas the poet was shocked, but not angry.

And why should he be? True, he wanted her, Shula. But there had been poor communication between them. The poet repeatedly misinterpreted her behavior. When she sought human support, he saw desire. She might have granted his wish. There were moments when she had been close to doing the deal that women did—sex for affection. Standing in dark confusion by the window, seeing in her imagination Rami's body bearing down on her from among the stars, Marduch's crushed body stretched out on the sand, she might have taken any hand extended to her, even one held out in lust.

But the Arab poet asked too much. He wanted to add a small clause to the deal to which she could not consent under any circumstances. He wanted to sleep with her as an Arab man with a Jewish woman. He demanded that she indemnify him for the injustice done to him and his people. But she did not believe she owed him anything. She was a child of four when he and his brothers and parents chose to flee their village in the middle of the night. Before that, they had said, we want it all. Certainly he had suffered since childhood, but that was not her fault, and she would not say it was by bestowing her body on him.

In spite of everything, she was a woman of experience. She knew there were times when it was permissible, even right, to use sex for ulterior purposes. She had done so more than once with Marduch, without feeling that it diminished her as a person or a woman. When he was trapped in a nightmare, caught by his secret terrors, shaking, covered with sweat and screaming, she would embrace him, in full consciousness of what she was doing; calm and unaroused, she stared upward at the dark ceiling, stroking his head, smiling the smile of a nursing mother. The poet, however, had not wanted her for shelter, but, rather, as the representative of a guilty people. This she could not be; for the Party, in spite of its best efforts, had failed to implant feelings of guilt in her.

Shula lay on the bed and listened. Daphna came out of the bathroom and pranced to the kitchen. Her voice was fresh, provocative, full of sunshine. "What's the matter with you?"

"You must be tired." he said gloomily.

"Not that tired."

"I am."

"So come to bed."

"Don't shout! Aren't you ashamed?"

"Of what?" she said, astonished, as if he were saying she ought to be ashamed of having legs.

"This isn't a hotel."

"Of course it isn't a hotel. It's a lovely apartment."

He whispered, "Shula's liable to hear."

"So what? She's cool."

The poet's chair scraped on the floor, as if Daphna were pulling him by the hand. Fingers struggled with a key. Shula remembered that never since moving into the apartment a few years before had they locked the door. The key squeaked in the lock. For the first time there was a hint of impatience and nervousness in Daphna's voice. "Sweetheart, what's happened to you?"

"Shut your mouth!"

"Don't be rude."

"I'm sorry."

"That's better. Never mind that shitty key."

"A lot you know."

"Is she likely to come bursting in?"

"Don't be an idiot."

"So what are you afraid of?"

"Are you cold?" Rami had asked.

"Freezing. Where are you going?"

"To gather some driftwood for a fire."

"No! I don't want to be here alone."

"But you're shivering all over."

"I'll dry off. It's nothing, I'll be dry soon."

They sat beside the splintered hulk of a boat that was sunk in the sand. The hull, which had turned white in the sun and the salty breeze, protruded a little from the sand and gave a deceptive, homey feeling. Rami stood and bowed to Shula. "Please come in." The wind tore the words from his mouth and scattered them in the night.

She got up, laughing. "You're crazy!" She was young; his antics enchanted her.

He linked his arm in hers and they walked around the sandy boat. Inside, Shula stood laughing, embarrassed. They were too old to play in this sandbox, but his playfulness excited her. "This is the boat you found? I thought it was a yacht at least. . . ."

They had walked over a mile along the beach to reach his discovery. "Don't you like it?" Rami asked her.

"I'm freezing to death."

"Take my towel."

"It's wet, too, and it stinks of you and your dogs."

He was hurt. He was a boy; every insult penetrated his soul. "Come," he said, "let's go home."

"I'm cold."

"What can I do about it?"

"You brought me here."

The boy was at a loss. "What do you want?" he said submissively.

She pulled him by the shoulders, her teeth gleaming in the darkness. Her bathing suit was wet from the sea, and she was trembling.

In the distance they heard a dog bark. "Sit down," Rami told her. Barking dogs always bolstered his self-confidence.

She sat obediently on the rough gunwale, while he energetically rubbed her goose-fleshed thighs with his cold hands. The blood began circulating under his touch, and she stretched out her legs and wrapped them around his muscular, hairy body, sighing with the nearby sea. He stood and moved behind her. "Now your arms and shoulders."

"And my back. It's cold."

"Your bathing suit's covering it. I'll take it off."

"Don't you dare."

"You'll catch pneumonia—your mother'll kill me."

"She's the only one you're scared of."

"Isn't this better?"

"Ahh." Off came the cold, wet fabric, and in its place came his warm touch, exploring in amazement, shrinking back, holding fast, retreating and attacking.

"Forget the key!"

Fatkhi was not a man to suffer even small defeats in the presence of women, especially in the arena of love. For love was indeed an arena, and every untoward incident, even trivial, depressed him. He struggled feverishly with the stubborn lock and finally won out, but when he turned the key it seemed to him that the squeak could be heard all over the house. Suddenly he felt tremendously fatigued. For two nights running he had had almost no sleep. The war, his descent from hope to doubt to despondency, his secret struggle with Shula—all these had weakened him. Now he regretted having bothered with the key. She must have heard. In her house, this is swinish, dirty behavior. She had not the least bit of cunning about her, and yet she knew how to mislead him, how to slip agilely out of his grasp.

Well done! What, actually, did she owe him? She deserved respect for her courage and delicacy. She had given him refuge in wartime, provided for all his needs, and tried to make his stay as pleasant as possible, in spite of her anxiety for her husband.

Don't be led astray. Don't let her pretty face deceive you. Deep in her Jewish heart, she despises you. She pities you as she would a dog on the run from her countrymen.

Maybe it's her pregnancy that's making hr crazy? But she played hide and seek, clearly she did. With her right hand she beckoned, with her left she pushed away!

I'm not right for her. A disgusting little Arab.

"Have you finished counting?" Daphna asked from the bed.

"Counting?"

"Yes, the ships in the harbor. You've been staring out the window as if you'd lost something."

His weariness grew. But a man like him could not admit weakness to a girl stretched out on a bed, not to save his life. "I forgot the cigarettes," he said.

Daphna yawned loudly. "You know what? Go play with the fucking lock and I'll go to sleep. I'm dead tired."

"The lady is offended."

"Offended? By you?"

"You didn't come all this way to fight, Daphna."

"You know very well why I came. Don't be smart."

"Don't shout."

"I'm not shouting. If you've decided to be faithful to that village virgin of yours, you might have said so."

"You're talking nonsense."

"Oh, leave me alone."

"Is this your room?" she had asked Marduch.

"Yes."

Shula hated the look that came into his eyes whenever he thought he was being scrutinized. When he moved from that prison in the desert to Israel, a country enjoying its first prosperity, he had felt as if thousands of severe eyes were scrutinizing his movements, his stammer in Hebrew, his old ways of life. Shula could not make him understand that he was among equals here; she almost gave up trying. But her heart was wrenched by the yearning look in his black eyes and by his desire to flee. For him, even the terrible past was preferable to this alien present. And she knew tht she was not the woman to help him, should he fail, for he feared her scorn more than that of anyone else.

He sat on the other armchair, tense and expectant.

"I thought you'd have a bachelor apartment—everything upside-down," she said. "Are you always so well organized?"

He nodded. At that time he spoke little of his life in prison. He was ashamed to tell her where he had acquired his orderly habits.

Though she saw that he was wracking his brains for something to say, she felt comfortable in the silence of the room and the dark night outside. She took off her shoes and folded her legs under her. He smiled apologetically, like an uncertain boy, and she realized that he had never been with a woman. She held back a laugh, afraid of hurting him. In those days he misjudged many things.

He stirred in his armchair. His brain was like a well gone dry and caused him agonies. "I'll take you to the bus," he said.

"Too late—I've missed the last one."

He was looking at her legs doubled up beneath her, and for a moment Shula thought that he must suspect her of meaning to strike roots in his room. At the same time she knew that he thought her too beautiful for him. She unfolded her long legs, and he turned his head away from the revelation of her thighs. Her feet groped for the shoes on the floor. "You're throwing me out," she teased him.

"No, no!" he cried.

She smiled. Silly boy, she thought.

"Do you have a boyfriend?" he asked gravely.

"People say you are."

"Me?" he cried, shocked.

She smiled easily and bent toward him. "Yes, you, you."

He blushed. "And what do you say?"

Enough, she said to herself. Don't make it too easy. Let him learn to be a man. "Never mind," she said. "What about you?"

"I . . . I love you. I hope I don't offend you."

"You don't."

He looked at her with astonishment. "Doesn't it matter to you at all?"

"Where did you grow up?" she scolded him.

To her relief, he was not frightened. He simply waved his arm behind his shoulder. "There, you know, back there."

"Back there," she mimicked him. "Did the men back there squeeze confessions out of the girls before they dared to do anything?"

"I know you're laughing at me." Suddenly he wearied of the effort, got to his feet, and stretched. "I'll take you home in a taxi."

"You'll go broke if you take all the girls back home by taxi."

"I never did it before," he said heatedly.

She burst out laughing. "You're missing a lot." She tucked her legs beneath her again and did not budge.

"You're staying?" he asked.

She nodded, gray eyes gleaming.

He was alarmed. "I've only got one bed." And then, as if he had said something coarse, he added hastily, "I can sleep sitting up."

Her gray eyes kept gleaming.

"You can go to sleep," the poet said to her in a conciliatory spirit.

"Thanks a lot."

"This is the first time I've ever seen you angry."

"Because you got on my nerves."

"I'm sorry." He moved closer to her. She was streched out on the bed, her body like a carved pomegranate, hundreds of bright delights winking at him with a ruddy light.

"You can be a man when you want to."

He had never slept with an Arab woman. Sitting on the edge of the bed, he wondered how Hiam would respond when the time came. A female is a female, he said to himself. He did not have to touch Daphna's clothes, which seemed to fall away in the heat of her passion. Proud of her body, she reveled in her nakedness, urging him on with her moans.

But this time; he was not aroused. Today he wanted to do the conquering, in his own way and his own good time. The girl writhed as if in torment, her mouth twisted. His hands moved over her body slowly but surely, and she heaved and trembled, and his teeth jabbed into her firm, bronzed skin, and she sobbed and her moans excited him and accelerated his stroke, and he smiled at the sweat on her forehead, and by now the aroma of soap had receded and her body gave off his own smell. Suddenly she looked ugly to him, and then he took her.

24

It was the third night of the war, and in the city by the sea anxiety reigned. Where was the army, where were the muscles of the state? Why were they dawdling? Almost every home had sent its strength to the fiery front. Very few people knew that at this very moment these men were girding themselves for a desperate struggle. Shula knew it, because Rami had already fallen and Marduch had not called. Nevertheless, she felt as if she had escaped from a vicious circle of suspense and tension. Today she had patiently answered Ido's questions, gone up and visited Tuvia's convalescing wife, and baked a cake, whose total failure did not make her cry. Three times today she had jumped to the ringing telephone. Her mother had asked how she was; Amalia had wanted to know whether the poet was still taking refuge in her apartment; and an aunt, worried, had telephoned from Amsterdam.

The poet saw that she was no longer afraid of talking with Marduch. She had said nothing about Daphna's visit, not a word, not the slightest allusion; and he studied her as if he were being led into a game whose rules were still unclear to him. Women are all crazy, he told himself finally, but still could not calm down. Shula was not just another female meant for sex and nothing else, no more than was Abla in Jenin. Both women had caused him to feel like a passing shadow, eye-catching but not worthy of deeper consideration. Since Daphna's departure, he had indeed been acting like a shadow, walking about on tiptoe, speaking little, shut up in his room as much as possible. He even lowered the volume of his ever-present transistor radio. He had shrunk to the size of a midget in his own eyes.

Tuvia's visit today was also irritating. The crazy old man had decided that, if the Arabs were able to knock the Jews around a bit, as seemed inevitable, then some good might come of it. "Now that your people have salvaged their honor, maybe they'll finally agree to sit down at the negotiating table. Because we both know very well how it will end. The war will end as usual."

The poet flared. "That's where you're wrong, sweetheart. For the first time, you people are going to be handed an outcome that you won't like."

"You'll have to slaughter us all first."

"That old story again! We can humble you without slaughtering you, just like you did to us in '48."

"You fled; but we have no place to go."

"Neither do we. No one wants us!" the poet shouted. "We're Palestinians—not Jordanians, Syrians, or Egyptians. As long as a single Palestinian survives, he will stand up and claim that which has been stolen from him."

It seemed that the old man had not wasted his time that afternoon. "I was lying down and thinking. There is a solution. I am now in favor of establishing a Palestinian state for you people. You have a right to it."

"Thanks a lot. Tell your leaders."

"I don't care what they think," the pensioner said. "I do my own thinking. It's only right. I've even been thinking about the Israeli Arabs. Why should they be second-class citizens? I don't want any down-trodden citizens in my state."

"So all the Arabs should be wrapped up in a bundle and thrown over the border," the poet shouted.

"Absolutely not," said the pensioner. "When the Palestinian state comes into being, all the Israeli Arabs will receive Palestinian nationality. You people will continue living here and your state will safeguard your rights. You'll be able to identify proudly with your own nation, free from double loyalty."

"And thus the Israeli Arabs become foreign nationals in their own homeland!" the poet shouted.

"That's no good either?" Tuvia lost his temper. "So what are you doing here?" he screamed. "You won't be satisfied with anything short of total destruction! So why do you have to hide with a Jewish woman whose husband has gone to sacrifice himself?"

"Sir, no dramatics, please."

"I shit on your good manners. . . ."

Shula burst into the room, her face pale. "Tuvia, Fatkhi, the whole street can hear you shouting."

Tuvia leapt up, pointing at the poet with a trembling arm. "Shula, you're harboring an enemy in your home."

"Tuvia!"

"If you go on keeping him here it will be treason."

"Get out of here," the poet told him.

"Did you hear that?" the pensioner said to Shula.

"You're insulting him."

"He's an enemy," the pensioner yelled.

Shula wrapped her arm around his shoulder and tried to pull him from the room. The pensioner gave her a look and shook her off. "Get rid of him, I tell you."

"Come, come outside," she said, trying to calm him.

Later, as night was falling, Shula thought resentfully that the night, with its fears and terrors, does not spring up from within but, rather, comes on the wings of twilight, like these stars. While Marduch showed no sign of life, the life budding in her womb gripped her by the throat. Without Marduch, she would not be able to bear the burden of another creature like Ido. The destruction of Marduch would mean the end of Ido too. In her mind's eye she saw Ido in an institution, shaking with fear, injured. He would pursue her like a ghost—tears came to her eyes as she washed him tenderly, rested his forehead on her shoulder, and blew softly on his long eyelashes.

"Shula," the child said, "you're making your dress wet."

"Do you love Mommy?"

He looked at her as if mulling over her question; then she saw that he was drawn to a couple of gleaming buttons on her blouse. "Shula," he said.

"I know," she said, hugging him. "You love Shula?"

He nodded yes, but it was obvious that he had his doubts. Shula accepted this. It had been a whole day since he had mentioned Marduch to her. For better or worse, the child was beginning to adjust to the new situation. She went out with him, his small body in her arms.

The child waved over her shoulder at the poet. "*Ahalan*, Fatkhi!"

"*Ahalan*, Ido," the poet answered without expression. It's all an act, he said to himself. Now that Daphna's gone, she's grabbed the moron as a shield. It never occurred to him that she was no longer troubled by him, or that she feared neither him nor herself. So little troubled was she that during supper, she treated him with frank affection, and later she took a shower without bothering to lock the door. He was tempted to open it and ask, "Do you want a towel?" just to scare her. When she came out in a flowered gown, fragrant, fresh, and smiling, her legs flashed with a wicked gleam and her coquettish voice fluted close to him. He could feel the heat of her body. "Do you want something before I go to sleep?" she said.

He inspected her body, staring long and hard, but this time it was he, not she, who blushed. "No," he answered dryly.

"Good night," she said, taking her leave with her eyes and her mouth and her shoulders—which had stopped jerking. He was astounded when she did not even bother to close her bedroom door. From where he sat, he had only to throw his head back in order to see her through the doorway, stretched out on her bed in the dark, beneath the open windows.

Down in the street someone whistled and then an adolescent boy yelled, "Turn off that light!"

A few seconds went by before the poet realized that the light from the living room was passing through the open doorway, over Shula's body, and out the window. He leapt to the switch and turned off the light.

"If you want to read, you can close my door and turn on the lamp again," Shula said.

"Good night," he said, and went to his room.

Shula was disappointed. Now that she no longer feared him, she wanted him close, not to be alone in the darkness. But he was shut up in his room, she in hers with the stars in the black window, while Tuvia hawked up phlegm above her, he too in darkness, and someone wrapped up in a black shroud like a crow points at an open hole. He's alive, but no one believes it. They trundle him along on a long, narrow cart, refusing to pay any attention to her, and she cries out, "Mother, he's alive! He's moving, trying to tear the shroud away so he can breathe. Mother, if they don't let him breathe he really will die!" And the soldiers stand all in a row and a band plays, out of sight behind a wall of gravestones, and her mother stands there with tears of pity in her eyes, her broken arm slung in a triangle of red cloth, her voice as dry and strident as Amalia's. "Let the poor man alone." And Shula screams at her, "That's what you've wanted all these years. Now you're happy, aren't you?" And a crafty smile emerges from behind the tears, and suddenly she realizes that it's all a fraud. The black crow is cursing, not mourning, and the soldiers carry wooden rifles to strike him over the head and force him back into the hole should he get free, and there's a cord attached to the conductor's baton, shining in the sun, stretching back behind the gravestones, and it isn't a band he's leading, but gigantic loudspeakers that drown out the cries of the man who is about to be buried alive, and she screams, "You're burying him!" And her mother smiles openly now, her arm perfectly sound in its red bandage. "They've got to, child, he can't be left this way. Don't be selfish, think how the poor man's suffered." And she is furious that first they robbed him of his youth and now they won't let him die in peace, and she screams, "You thieves, at least kill him first with your bayonets!" And all at once she realizes that she has as much right to lie as these scoundrels do, and she screams, "This isn't Marduch! Marduch is home, protecting Ido, teaching him to play chess."

At once the loudspeakers fall silent. Suddenly everyone rushes to the hole. Crouching on their knees, they scratch at the earth, sending pieces of white cloth flying in the air, and Shula's mother stretches out on her belly with her head in the hole, then stands up and brushes off the dust and says, "Come and see."

Shula hesitates. Quaking, she leans down and peers inside. In the hole lies Rami on his back, his lips bare and dirty, a gold chain glimmering on his hairy chest.

"I knew it," Shula whispers.

"Liar!" her mother cries.

"They killed Rami."

"It's Marduch," her mother whispers, with hatred.

She woke beneath the black window inlaid with stars. For a long time she could not overcome her trembling. She was terrified by the hatred pervading her mother's voice. Her mouth was dry and she wanted Marduch to bring her a glass of water and put his arms around her.

"I can't," Tuvia said in his window. "Go to sleep, Hannah, go to sleep."

At the sound of the pensioner's grumbling voice Shula grew

calmer. She groped for her slippers, went to the kitchen, and opened the refrigerator, taking heart from its greenish light. She poured a glass of water, held it against her temple, then drank. The ball of fire inside her went out, to be replaced by despair. Bent over, she went back to bed. There was no comfort in the band of light showing under the poet's door. She could not tell him about her dream, much as she wanted to tell someone. If Ido were an ordinary child she would have laid down on the bed beside him.

She had experienced this kind of fear in her childhood, especially when she could not make sense of the sounds in the night, when she could not dress them up and give them faces. But these voices came from within her, they were silent, they didn't really exist. Her womb had no voice, the future didn't whisper, Rami's body was as dumb as a stone. She knelt like a little girl on her bed and nearly called to Tuvia through the window, but Tuvia would not hear. She had insulted him, thrown him out, and now he would let the whole street know what was happening in her home and to her body. And suddenly Shula lost her fear. Filled with great happiness, she lay with her hand touching Marduch's body, which was stretched out on the bed beside her; his black eyes gazed at her in the darkness and his body's hairy warmth was delicate and muscular; and she felt joyful and her womb was pure and smiling, and she groped at his chiseled muscles, rigid and tender. "How did you get in?" she asked. "I'm sure I locked the door."

His voice was the sound of the wind gusting through the trees, caressing her naked body, whispering into its curves. "A locked door is not a chastity belt."

She burst out laughing. Finally she was free to laugh; all the dams had cracked, and laughter imprisoned for years broke through like the autumn rain.

"You ruffian!" she cried.

"You waited for me," he said solemnly.

"I knew you'd come. The book said that you'd been killed."

Fearful misgiving stole into her heart. She stretched out her arm and felt around in the darkness. She was alone in a dreary, wide expanse of starched bedsheets. The white emptiness horrified her. All of a sudden she realized that she was not alone in the room. A real figure stood between her and the open door, silhouetted against the thick darkness of the living room.

"Who is it?" she screamed.

"I didn't mean to frighten you," the poet said, his voice purposeful.

"You scared me to death!" She was still shaking.

"Turn on the light for a second."

"There's a blackout."

"Just for a second."

She flicked the switch on and then off immediately. His suitcase was in the doorway. "You're dressed," she said, startled. "Are you leaving?"

"No," he said gravely. "I came to you because you are my friend's wife. Now please get up quietly and put on your clothes and get Ido ready for a trip. Are you completely awake?"

"Are you sure *you're* awake? What's going on with you?"

"The Israeli armored corps has been completely destroyed at the canal, Shula. Your army has finally been routed. At this moment there's no real Israeli force between the Egyptian armor and the heart of Israel."

"You're talking nonsense."

"I know what I'm saying. You just don't want to believe."

"Just a minute." she said, getting up and putting a robe over her nightgown. The poet followed her out, closing the bedroom door. She sat on the sofa in the living room, he on the armchair facing her. "Do you understand what I said?" he asked. "Just now they announced that the Israeli tanks made a desperate effort to dislodge the Egyptian bridgeheads east of the canal—they attacked, and a tremendous battle broke out. The Israeli tanks were wiped out, down to the very last one. They're burning all over the battlefield. High-ranking officers have surrendered or been captured. The Egyptian army is on the offensive and no force can stop it."

"Where did you hear all this?"

"From Radio Cairo."

"Ah ha."

"It's true, Shula. It's the truth. If the war continues this way it will inevitably end with the defeat of the Israeli army. You have no idea what huge masses are gathered on both fronts. What the French imperial army succumbed to was far less devastating than this blow. . . . Listen. You and Ido are to dress, take only what you need, and go down to the car."

"Where to, may I ask?"

He felt her anger. She still would not believe. "I've got a friend, a dentist, in Jenin. He and his wife are wonderful people. I was their guest on Friday and Saturday before the war broke out. I won't say that they'll be overjoyed, but they will take you without hesitation, Shula."

"Thank you."

He heard no mockery but distrusted her calm. "If you're afraid to drive yourself," he said, "I'll call my brother-in-law Wasfy. He's got a car; he'll drive us to Jenin."

"No, Fatkhi."

"Why?"

"Do you know why Marduch ran off to the desert?"

"In truth I don't. I admit that it puzzles me. I can't understand him."

"I'm guessing, just guessing, Fatkhi. Maybe he had reasons of his own. Maybe I didn't understand them on Yom Kippur . . . "

"What does it matter now?" the poet cried.

It was as if Shula had not heard, as if she were having a vision. "The Israel Defense Forces are not the French armies, or the Red Army either. We were taught that the Red Army is the army of the people. The I.D.F. is the people itself. Even my mother knows it. Don't believe her if she tells you she wants the I.D.F. defeated."

He wanted to get up, take her shoulders, and shake her, to rouse her from the fantasy into which she had retreated. She was in danger. At that moment Fatkhi realized that he loved her as he had never loved a woman before. An urge came over him, a childish urge to take her hand in his and walk off with her. All this he put into a whispered word: "Shula."

She heard him clearly and, as he had intended, she was moved. She leaned forward and touched his knee with her fingertips. "There will be no columns of refugees here, Fatkhi."

He was struck by the way she pronounced his name. He felt close to her. Her fingers rested on his knee once more. "Go, go by yourself," she said.

"That's nonsense. . . . Why?"

"Even if everything you say is true, I would not abandon Marduch's house at such a time."

"Is it love?"

"Right now, I'm just worried about him."

"Then . . . "

"No, Fatkhi. I'm staying here." And she stood and turned off the light and opened the door to the balcony. Her face was a pale patch in the darkness. The dark, heavy sea stretched out before her. She seemed to him a delicate tendril liable to be uprooted by the storm. He almost said, "I love you."

"I'll call Tuvia," she said. "He'll watch Ido while I drive you over to Amalia and Emile."

"Yes," he said with quiet rage.

"You hate me," she said.

"Does that matter now?"

She said nothing. He rose, and his dry lips searched for hers in the darkness. She recoiled; he felt a chill, as if a wall, cold as death, had arisen between them. At that moment they ceased being a man and a woman. He was an Arab. She was a Jew.

www.ingramcontent.com/pod-product-compliance
Lightning Source LLC
Chambersburg PA
CBHW030810310726
48980CB00006B/446/J